MW01242860

Also by Calvin Barry Schwartz

Vichy Water

THERE'S A
TORTOISE
IN MY HAIR

A JOURNEY TO SPIRIT
A NOVEL

CALVIN BARRY SCHWARTZ

This is a work of fiction. Names, characters, dialogue, and incidents either are the product of the author's imagination or are used fictitiously and any resemblance to actual persons, living or dead, entities, events or locales is entirely coincidental.

Copyright © 2021 by Calvin Barry Schwartz
Published by Earthood Media, LLC
Front cover art and design by Ricardo Fonseca
Back cover art by Calvin Barry Schwartz
Interior design by Indie Pub Solutions

ISBN: 979-8-218-29574-5
Library of Congress Control Number: 2023910078

All rights reserved. Printed in the United States of America. This book, or parts thereof, may not be reproduced in any form without written permission except in the case of brief quotations embodied in critical articles or reviews. The scanning, uploading and distribution of this book via the Internet or via any other means without permission of the author is illegal and punishable by law. Please purchase only authorized electronic editions and do not participate in or encourage electronic piracy of copyrighted materials. Your support of the author's rights is appreciated.

Publisher's Cataloging-in-Publication (Provided by Cassidy Cataloguing Services, Inc.)

Names: Schwartz, Calvin Barry, author.
Title: There's a tortoise in my hair : a journey to spirit : a novel / Calvin Barry Schwartz.
Description: [Newark, New Jersey] : [Earthood Media], [2023]
Identifiers: ISBN: 979-8-218-29574-5 (paperback) | LCCN: 2023910078
Subjects: LCSH: Life change events--Fiction. | Families--Fiction. | Marriage--Fiction. | Aging--Fiction. | Spirituality--Fiction. | Vietnam--Fiction. | LCGFT: Bildungsromans.
Classification: LCC : PS3619.C48565 T44 2023 | DDC: 813/.6--dc23

To Fran; you have always supported, instilled, guided, and loved. No way all of this happens without you.

To Neil; ditto, with love, support, energy, and spirit.

To Delilah; again ditto, for being there with love, support, social media acumen, and spirit.

To Riley and Logan; you're new to this game but the energy of love transference is invaluable.

To Mom and Dad; your smiling countenance looks down on me every day.

Family is a blessing and enduring gift. You all are such a gift.

Contents

Chapter 1: Lah-Di-Dah   1

Chapter 2: How the Tortoise Got in My Hair:
It's Never Too Late for a Happy Childhood   5

Chapter 3: Growing Pains   13

Chapter 4: An Ohio College Sweatshirt   19

Chapter 5: Rutgers in the Sixties   29

Chapter 6: Goodbye, South Orange   41

Chapter 7: Great Scott   51

Chapter 8: Growing into Me   59

Chapter 9: Hell No   69

Chapter 10: Winding Down   81

Chapter 11: A Very Good Year, Eventually: 1976   91

Chapter 12: Getting Our Feet Wet   113

Chapter 13: Jersey New Eye Life   121

Chapter 14: Italian Enchantment   129

Chapter 15: The Dream Realized   133

Chapter 16: A Freshly Paved Road   143

Chapter 17: *Something*   149
Chapter 18: On the Road to Revelation   157
Chapter 19: More On the Road Stories   163
Chapter 20: Winds of Change   169
Chapter 21: And Now, Ladies and Gentlemen: The Change   181
Chapter 22: A Decent Descent   187
Chapter 23: Hitting Bottom Takes Years   197
Chapter 24: The Spirit Arrival   203
Chapter 25: Casablanca Water   213
Chapter 26: The Business of 2004   221
Chapter 27: Saint Anthony   231
Chapter 28: A Marble Rolls Up a Hill   237
Chapter 29: Published   245
Chapter 30: A Spirit Gang   251
Chapter 31: Evolution Revolution Resolution   255
Chapter 32: And Along Came October   269
Chapter 33: Who Am I?   277
Chapter 34: Stories about Stories   285
Chapter 35: A Thickening Plot   295
Chapter 36: A Time for Alma Mater   303
Chapter 37: An Old-Fashioned "The End"   309
About Calvin Barry Schwartz   327

Acknowledgements

This is a novel about spirit. For the second official time in my writing life, I need to thank my grandfather Colman, who died in 1937. I never knew him, but was named after him. From my first day on Earth, he's been hanging around, guiding, and moving me. So much of me is him. My gratitude is everlasting. When I watch *Fiddler on the Roof*, I imagine Colman and my grandmother Rachel coming to America in 1900. Spirit is powerful stuff—the energy that propelled me to write this story.

Never enough words and love for Fran, Neil, and Delilah, living and loving throughout this whole project. I brought it to dinner many nights. Their patience and contributions are beyond (my highest praise word).

Constant sources of support emanated from Dr. Michael Kerner; a sixty-year friendship.

LinkedIn, as I thrive on social media (102,000 pairs of eyes in my networks) was a perfect vehicle for connectivity, networking, and bringing people into my literary sphere. One-stop shopping. With a completed manuscript, I found Janice Deaner there; a content editor who guided me to change some direction.

Then a webinar on Pipeline Symposium with Karen Richardson. I recruited Karen to guide me on every path to being published. Her vast knowledge and experience were that jolt (a favorite word) to bring this story home. She was that matrix to tie it all together (a daunting task) including her recommendation of publishing industry veteran and extraordinary literary editor Alyssa Bluhm.

I sent Alyssa a few chapters to see if there was interest. She signed on for this multi-month project. Never in my days have I experienced editing, perfection, command, thoroughness, and brilliance as Alyssa delivered. Interestingly, her persona, notes, and editing changed my whole interpretation of this project. My words made her laugh and cry. She did the same to me. Alyssa Bluhm; what a gift.

And to my alma mater, Rutgers University. You continue to teach the children and me well. A life source close to home.

And to Mother Earth. May you stay below a 1.5-degree rise in temperature next decade.

—Calvin Barry Schwartz
April 9, 2023

Chapter 1

LAH-DI-DAH

Life is for the living, so maybe it's a good time to die. You pass someone on crutches or in a wheelchair at a mall and never really notice them. The invisibility of disability. I never want to be invisible. "Bury me deep beneath the sea, where people are free." This was the first line of a poem I wrote in high school. I never finished the poem. Actually, I never finished anything in life—until a few years ago. I'm a stream-of-consciousness writer, which means if I began seventeen times, I would tell that many different stories.

I need to tell my story and how I wound up at this strange day in my life. On one hand, I'm just middle of the road and class. On the other, I've been gifted. I've journeyed through a life of haunting spirituality and ridiculous happenings you can't make up. There have been many pieces in my life, scattered like a jigsaw puzzle on a game board in my mother's Newark kitchen. In her home, there was never a room that belonged to my father.

My agenda today begins with a bag of sand in the basement. It's not beige beach sand, but gritty, steel-gray granules. I cut open the bag, fill an empty nonfat milk container, and stare around the unfinished basement at boxes of old vinyl records, apothecary bottles, *Life* magazines, and a nonworking sewing machine. Resonating with me are Sylvia Plath's words, "Dying is an art, like everything else."

Jersey Shore, here I come. Heading there in late spring, Route 18 is traffic free. Destination is Belmar, epicenter of the Jersey Shore, where I was conceived in the attic of a long-gone hotel. My mother told me that story six months before she passed. When I met Belmar's mayor at a party a few years ago, I told him why I liked his town.

At the drawbridge over the Shark River leading into Belmar, just off Ocean Avenue, is the jetty that may've been witness to ships sailing to the Second World War. When I was ten, I discovered its meditative appeal and spent carefree summer hours dreaming, wishing, and hoping, perched on craggy boulders that smelled like decaying fish. Not a year has gone by when I haven't spent time on the jetty, snow or tropical storms notwithstanding. In a brisk northwest wind, I stand at the jetty tip, ocean spraying me, and dispatch the milk carton sand to the wind. The need to watch the sand blow in the wind to my possible infinity keeps me there until the carton is empty. I could almost hear Donovan's "Catch the Wind."

I sit down on my favorite boulder. Ocean mist from waves crashing against boulders slaps my face—a good slap of inspiration. I stretch my right foot and take a perspective picture of a white vintage sneaker against the jetty, horizon, and sky. Who knew that picture would one day become this book cover? It is a good day so far; I am gifted to see things as they might be.

Facebook notifications and email were checked. Social media allows me to also keep a visual surveillance (lurking) on certain dormant relationships. I inhale deeply, squint at the sun overhead, and see a seagull scoring something to eat. I'm not alone anymore; a fisherman and a woman carrying a pail plant themselves too close. Always afraid of a fish hook catching me in the eye, I walk into the sand and sit on a tree stump polished smooth from time, surf, and wind. Another deep inhalation before my phone call.

"Hi. You'll never guess—unless . . . But then again, you probably will."

"Wow, it is you. When I woke up this morning, you were the furthest thing from my mind. Why and how? It's been a few years."

I clear my throat; it was shutting down with nerves and parched oral epithelium. I need to be relaxed. "I know it's been a while. Shall I tell you that you've been on my mind? How are you, by the way? Where are you? Hopefully close to the ocean, because that's where I am."

"I don't care why you're calling. I think it's a good thing. If I remember, you said you'd be back one day. I moved to a small apartment in Ocean Grove. Are you near?"

I am so near; it is eighteen minutes to the front porch. I love when the door opens before a knock: a sign of desire, anticipation, and imagination. We hug, push away to take ourselves into visual digestion, and hug again, marveling at how well we both look. We reminisce back a few years, our last time together: a fast-food dinner. We didn't know each other long before that, first meeting at McLoone's in Asbury Park on a Tuesday music night.

With the day I've had and decisions I've made, I just want raw sex. I don't care about positions or protocols. Guilt is finally dead. I comment on the wine glasses and open bottle of merlot on the night table. It's funny—virtual strangers in the night, taking off clothes, staring at lumpy, sagging bodies a distance from their prime, and thinking nothing of it. It's all about pure, matter-of-fact sex. No sweet nothings, promises, or appointments for return engagements.

I have to go. It has been a good two hours. A little washcloth refresh in the bathroom. A kiss at the front door. I turn around, wave, and suddenly know where I have to go next.

The SurfWind is a Jersey Shore institution for hot dogs, cheese fries, and all the relish you want. I need everything on their menu now—or at least one side of the menu. It's been a long time, 1975, since I've masticated a hot dog: real beef with pastel-colored nitrites. It's been a lifetime since I last consumed a four-legged animal. Perhaps my hormonal pathways are activated by the craving for nitrites.

It is time for another phone call. Maybe dessert and more sex in Livingston.

Forty minutes north on the parkway, up Mount Pleasant Avenue (a perfect name for a street) to a Livingston diner, I purchase two large black and white cookies. My friend likes those cookies; I like the 1960s *Psychology Today* game, Blacks & Whites, better. Strangely, the condo door opens as I arrive. I throw the bagged cookies into waiting arms, then a hug. I explained my place in the universe on the drive up, so we just go to bed. Cookies and coincidentally more merlot are just fine for me afterwards. Why do so many remote souls in my social media connections know to fun me with merlot? Have I been that obvious?

I refresh with another washcloth, then say goodbye. You get to a point in life, like standing at the end of a jetty, when human communication and fornication become an emotional routine. Best now to quote Annie Hall, "Lah-di-dah."

How did I arrive at this day? It's a wonderful life—or was? Should I start this memoir on the day when I rolled over six times in a Volkswagen and should've been as crushed to death as the car, except a spirit took over the steering wheel? Or should I start with my father's facial expression after the birth of his firstborn—me?

Chapter 2

HOW THE TORTOISE GOT IN MY HAIR: IT'S NEVER TOO LATE FOR A HAPPY CHILDHOOD

It was August 1945. Two weeks earlier, President Truman had given the final okay to bomb Hiroshima and Nagasaki. My mother was extremely pregnant, and my parents were violently, excessively poor. So when my mother's water broke, she had no car to drive to the hospital—instead, she walked the two blocks from our house on Goodwin Avenue to the Beth Israel Hospital in Newark.

Eight hours of pushing and praying preceded my arrival. My father was not around for support. He was a remarkably consistent man, never around to support those close or far. Aunt Edith found him at a neighborhood bar he frequented a few blocks away, and she briskly escorted him back to the waiting room.

The doctor came out. My father jumped up, yelling in a barley-and-hops-pitched voice, "Doc, don't tell me anything. Just show me."

His reddened face pressed to the glass while the nurse held me up. Hands flailed wildly, drunkenly. His elbow rubbed the foggy glass to discern my gender. "My goodness, I see a penis."

He was a happy man, realizing his long dream to get that tough, impressionable son. But his blood alcohol level still indicated he was under the influence, so he named me Cameron Simmons. If I'd been able to speak when I was born, I would've implored right then, "What the fuck. Why the hell burden me with such an off-the-wall name? Like I'm getting called Cam throughout the decades. I'm going to need all the help I can get."

Why would I need help? My mother had pushed me out for eight hours. Things were tight down there, so I was born with a messed-up head pointed so dramatically, so embarrassingly, that my mother insisted I wear one of those dopey heigh-ho hats from *Snow White and the Seven Dwarfs* for the first year of my Newark life. I was perceived as a dummy, slow to fill out and develop a personality, and I'd have to wait years into elementary school before I could tie my own shoes. If there was an art to tucking the laces unobtrusively into my shoes, I had mastered it.

Jack Simmons, the father here, had been a New Jersey–honored athlete, a basketball player, an exceptional high school drunk, the funniest, tallest senior at Plainfield High School, and a legend in the number of girls (even some mothers) he bedded. Great expectations for his son to continue in his footsteps. At my first birthday, there was no prospect for my standing up, walking, or being remotely syllabic. Disappointed, Jack was convinced I was just a really slow kid, intellectually and physically.

"There must be a tortoise walking around his hair under the dopey hat." My father repeated this often.

I lived much of my life reminded about my nameless friend the tortoise. Lah-di-dah.

The street where I lived all those formative Wonder Bread years,

Goodwin Avenue, was nestled in the Weequahic section of Newark. If you've read the novelist Phillip Roth, who had a thirteen-year head start over me living there, then you're familiar with the demographics, plots, and complaints of most of the section's first-generation Americans with Eastern European backgrounds. If not, the maple tree–lined street had sixteen two-family houses, thirty-two families, of which one was Italian.

Leave it to me to have enraged the one Sicilian on a hot July night. I was twelve and embroiled in a tense game of Sneaky Joe, hiding in obscure places, trying not to get caught by the kid with the flashlight. None of my street urchin friends ever went near Joe Zullo's house. He was a big, mean, bald, heavily accented man who drove a milk truck. I reasoned he probably went to bed early to deliver milk by dawn's early light, so I hid in his dark basement, a perfect place to win the game. The basement had no pull-chain lights, so I tripped, sent things crashing, and Joe found me. You really do see stars when you're slapped hard. It's funny that today, "zullo" in the Urban Dictionary means "one who is chill as fuck." I never told my father, nor anyone else, about the slap and stars. Jack would've surely retaliated, being a boxer in the back of bars during the Depression. Dad was a tough, tall man who'd contributed DNA to a son who ostensibly always had a tortoise in his hair.

My mother, Amelia, was the youngest of three children, to Colman and Rachel Crast, Russian immigrants at the turn of the century. My father's family, Simmons, mostly came from Russia and Poland—to this day, no one is sure what their real name was, hiding out or camouflaging from the czar and his pogroms. In all the growing-up years I had with both my grandmothers (my grandfathers died before I was born), I never asked them what it was like to live in that kind of hell. I was too occupied by my love for the Brooklyn Dodgers, mostly because they broke the color barrier. For me, Russia was just a reason to hide under school desks during the Cuban Missile Crisis.

Jack was an old-fashioned shoe salesman, climbing up ladders to find stock and shoving samples onto the feet of mostly women customers. He did those Cinderella mechanics every day and often found time to slip into an alley in Elizabeth, New Jersey, to place a horse bet. Synchronicity (spirit) first came into my life during the summer of my fifth birthday. I talk about it now, but it would be six decades before I'd start to comprehend what it's all about and when it began for me that summer day.

Sure, I walked and talked later than most of my contemporaries, but I did make up for the lost time, flirting with hyperactivity and verbosity. When it was time for my mother to clean the house, she tied me to the garage with a rope. Loving freedom, then and now, I broke away from captivity and walked around the corner to the bus stop. Six women waited, each thinking I was the property of the other. Kids' fares were free. I sat at the front, loving the bus and playing pretend. The last stop was Penn Station in Newark. The police were looking for me now. Life can change in only a matter of seconds—a cop saw me about to board a train to New York City near a strange man. The policeman grabbed me, and soon I was headed home in the back seat of his squad car, happily chewing a Chiclet. Just seconds—synchronicity and spirit in a life.

Throughout this memoir, I refer to "a life," not "my life." As time goes by, and the world turns, I'm less sure it's my life, wrapped in déjà vu, and growing spirituality. Am I a conduit, messenger, entrusted or gifted? A reason to believe.

The first report on my progress as a student at Maple Avenue School was issued in November 1951. It was typewritten and signed by Senta Bormann, my first-grade teacher. I did good work, she noted, and I was more advanced academically than socially. How remarkably perceptive; social inadequacy would last into my second marriage. She goes on to describe the roots of my behavior and pathways, clearly defined, "He is quite restless in class: moves tables, talks, walks . . . At present he seems to be overly concerned with the 'me.'"

I was at a bar in New York City with my son a few years ago and finally explained the necessities of being "me." It was born when I was born and choked me every day of my life—until these last few years, when I let it lift and move me.

I never heard a word of support from my father that I was something, somebody. He was never proud or loving, and I can't remember if he ever put his arm around me. In those two decades before college, we spent one day together: father and son at Yankee Stadium. A hot day, we got there early and watched unorganized baseball in a lot across the street. At game time, we sat along third base near the Baltimore Orioles' dugout. Two innings in, dad fainted in the heat and I spent the rest of the game in the infirmary. Lah-di-dah.

I did love my childhood, but I never knew anything else—so maybe this isn't all love but reaching out, trying to fix and understand it, or shout from these pages, like James Cagney did in *White Heat*: "Made it, Ma! Top of the world!" Actually, maybe I *am* close to the top and there's nowhere else to go. I never knew who I was until recently. I'm just a traveler, negotiating curves with asthmatic-like insecurities; it takes my breath away.

Back at Maple Avenue School, in second grade, I was too shy and insecure to raise my hand to go to the bathroom. And when I did, it must've annoyed Mrs. Steinberg, so she'd tell me to sit still. Once, I left a puddle under my desk and discovered elementary school embarrassment. Later, I told my mother everything, including the fact that her friend Pearl was bombed. Eventually, she figured it out, with the tortoise in my hair—there was a poster commemorating Pearl Harbor on the blackboard.

The grandfather clock in Principal Irving Townley's office was fascinating to me. I watched its precise movements while I served out frequent detentions. Fidgeting never warranted that punishment; stabbing Billy Seaton with a pencil did.

The highlight of sixth grade was the love letter I got from Lynn Orange, the prettiest girl in school. It was the first and last love letter I'd get for thirty years, until my girlfriend, now wife, sent me one on an Air France charter to Martinique.

I hid that letter from Lynn under my mattress, thinking my parents could never understand what it meant to me. A girl liked me; no one had ever liked me. If I was allowed to act on the affection, who knows, it may've opened pathways of self-worth. I could've been that contender, sitting in the back of a car, thinking I had class and was somebody. Instead, my mother found that letter one day while efficiently making my bed and turned it over to my father. He should've been proud of me. Instead, they yelled and confiscated it, warning me to stay away from that girl, who would never amount to anything. I continued looking for that letter for years, carefully going through my parents' dressers and closets right up until I left for college.

My mother was a smart lady, but she was trapped in the expectations of first-generation Americans. This means she was always a good daughter to Rachel and had no realistic aspirations of getting a college education, leaving home, rising out of tenement living, or becoming someone. It also meant she'd unleash that energy of betterment on her children from time to time. Her devoted daughter status was severely tested when my grandmother had a leg amputated due to diabetes. It meant years of extra care, emptying the commode, and wrenching from sights and odors. Sometimes I'd hide just beyond the doorway and watch her cry. Our family was being tested; my parents slept in the dining room and I doubled up with my much younger sister, Carol, in a suffocating room with two small beds. These conditions did not necessarily make us close, but we were still young enough to get along.

How do I know my mother was so smart? In sixth grade, around the time I got that love letter from Lynn, my mother bought me *How to Win Friends and Influence People* by Dale Carnegie. I rebelled initially, as she forced me to stop reading a Jim Thorpe biography. The brilliance in her redirection is that I lived the next sixty years adhering to those basic tenets of life: If you don't have anything nice to say, don't. When I mentor college students, I still refer to Carnegie, continually marveling at this enduring wisdom.

Knowledge is good, my mother preached tirelessly. "People can take material things away from you, but no one can take away what you've learned," she'd say. She also drove the ethics of hard work into my constitution. "It's a privilege from God to be able to get up and go to work."

The winter of my sixth-grade discontent, my mother facilitated my employment at Kravitz's grocery store. Well below the age for working paper stipulations, I performed menial tasks like stamping prices on cans, washing the coleslaw pan, picking up huge brown bags of bagels from the bakery (and eating three on the way back—they never counted them), and delivering orders with my sled when it snowed.

One delivery was particularly memorable. A foot of snow, three boxes of groceries, a sled trip of six cold, windy blocks, three flights of stairs, and three trips up to an old lady with short, steel-gray hair secured by purple netting. Not even a thank-you and, of course, no tip; a quarter could've made my day and gotten me into the Park Theater. Most of my life, I've waited for karma with celestial interventions—but not on this day. I took a coin and called the fire department on the old lady, a false alarm. My guilt lasted a long time.

The summer before seventh grade, a few extra dollars in the family budget allowed me to go to Newark Y Camp on Chancellor Avenue. When they gave out awards at the end of camp, even though I hit the most softball home runs, I got a concocted recognition of second-best baseball player. There was no second-best in any award category, but camp counselor guilt prevailed.

Every day before camp began, we played Bombardment. I never tried to catch the ball; I was a dodger extraordinaire. But this prolonged the game. Finally, I was warned to attempt a catch, but I resisted. My punishment was to box the toughest, biggest kid in camp, Howard Jackson. I finally got recognition from my campmates: sympathy. Later, as everyone boarded a bus to go swimming, I hid in the dense foliage, then walked the few miles home, crying. Mother went to camp the following morning. The counselor was fired. Years later, at six foot five, I met that Howard Jackson fellow again; now I'm a foot and a hundred pounds superior. I let it be.

Just before Maple Avenue School graduation, June 1959, marching into the auditorium to "Pomp and Circumstance," I tried so hard to fill up my autograph book, getting to all the popular kids, pretty girls, tough guys, and the teachers who made me write the Declaration of Independence on the blackboard. Lynn, my love letter friend, even signed—but with no reference of her affection for me.

The prospect of high school in September filled me with fearful anticipation. How would I ever compete academically, athletically, and socially? The summer of '59 clarified my career direction when I got a job at Crast Pharmacy under the bipolar eye of the brilliant druggist, businessman, and streetwise urban philosopher, my Uncle Harry Crast, a Rutgers pharmacy school graduate. My mother put me on a bus that first day with a 1940s football helmet to protect my head when working in the low-ceilinged basement and a brown bag with two tuna sandwiches on white, crusts cut off. I'd later write for the *Rutgers Apothecary News*, the pharmacy magazine, about how grateful I was to have a basement to work up from. My mother pounded away for years on my becoming a pharmacist, stressing the security of having that profession to fall back on, never thinking I'd abysmally fall into it, with all the exquisite medicines at my disposal.

Chapter 3

GROWING PAINS

Two weeks before my freshman year at Weequahic High School, my Uncle Harry Crast died suddenly; the obituary mentioned "a short illness." My mother was devastated, crying hysterically for long periods. Harry was her older brother, a voice of reason and intellect, and a man of charity to his mother, community, and sister.

Waiting to go to the funeral, I looked out our living room window. The maple trees blew wispy in the wind; cumulus clouds bumped into one another. I hoped to find an answer out the window, an apparition, a sign that Harry was all right and there was no need to worry. It was almost there—something soothing, silent, and sad. Out there, beyond, was something. I keep using that word, "something." I've spent a lifetime trying to define "something," but the process began this funeral day.

For the three-month summer vacation, I worked in Uncle Harry's store, feeling his piercing stares whenever I did something wrong, as I often did. Supposedly, it's hard to be wrong when all you do is dust shelves and sweep sidewalks. When he finally trusted me to fill up the beer bottle ice box, I was rough in placing quarts of warm Ballantine beer inside, so two bottles exploded—and so did my uncle. When I was sent back outside to sweep, I realized I'd never seen my uncle smile, laugh, or approve of anything.

At Uncle Harry and Aunt Evelyn's house, Harry now resting in a Woodbridge cemetery, I watched people eating bagels, cakes, and odorous whole fishes, some with eyes still open. Much later, I pretended to be sleeping on the sofa. My mother raked her fingers through my hair gently. I didn't move—a trick I'd learned.

A woman next to my mother asked, "Do you know how he took his life?"

"Sleeping pills."

"But why? He had everything to live for. A thriving business. Two sons coming into the business."

My mother, always keen to say more with less, responded, "It just was his time."

It'd take thirty years for me to find out why, but I was uncomfortably aware my uncle and I shared a conglomerate of the same genes. Because of our gene pool, I was never thrilled about going to pharmacy school or marrying any woman named Evelyn. A few days before high school, I proposed studying history in college instead. My mother just stared—less is more. Future pharmacy study was inevitable for me. No way to reverse the course of a maternal-determined river.

Perhaps it's best now to eliminate any anticipation of conquests and achievements in my time at Weequahic. My four high school years never saw a date, a party, a dance, a spun bottle, or a spot on the bench of the varsity basketball team. There are songs written about being a loser, trapped in an image, living on the wrong side of the tracks, being bullied and alone. By today's definitions, I was victimized. If I could've only learned how to play a sax, piano, or guitar. Girls love guitar players. A contender sits in the back seat again. High schools are not places to draw out a reclusive soul, especially with cliques, social climbers, and an abundance of pretty people everywhere I didn't belong. At my school, I stood no chance of acceptance, but I did receive a hard-raining, bitter rejection that lasted a lifetime.

Thirty-five years later, at my high school reunion, the kids who sat together at lunch were still sitting together—this time at a banquet table. Perhaps it's refreshing that some things resist change. Would I be writing now if I looked like Hubbell Gardiner? When it came to Weequahic reunions, I stayed away for decades, wanting to forget those kids. But a funny thing happened when the invitation for the thirty-fifth reunion arrived. I looked in the mirror and saw the long hippie hair of Dorian—no Gray—a flat stomach, and a fifty-something guy who looked forty. For once, I was feeling highly self-confident.

Sipping merlot and gazing at my graying assembled peers, I wondered if I'd see Lynn Orange. Suddenly, her vision appeared. Carrying this Lynn thing around since sixth grade, I made the first motion towards her. How I wanted to remember Lynn just as she was at our June 1963 high school graduation—but time changes and mixes me up.

Somewhere in my matrix of malignant thoughts, I thought to charm Lynn, as I was perfectly capable these days, and get a consensual room upstairs. I could finally take out all my aged frustrations and sleep with my first high school classmate. But the notion passed as we mechanically hugged.

She clasped her hands together, beseeching Father Time. Big Daddy, where are you when I need you to help me deal with mendacity on a hot tin roof? I know you can't go home again. Lynn was home a long time ago in another galaxy. She looked wonderful. We exchanged pleasantries—I hate responding to those. How are you, where are you living, do you have children—who really gives a shit? Finally, she said, "I'll see you later." No, she wouldn't. I'd never see her again. That's the reality that slapped my face.

At midnight, the lights flickered and my classmates disappeared into the New Brunswick night or to rooms an elevator away. I couldn't help but wonder if any of them were jumping into bed together; that's the romantic in me.

Basketball played a central role in my developmental years. My father, Big Jack, excelled on the hardwood. Bequeathed to me was an old cigar box stuffed with articles on his prowess from the long-gone *Courier News*, which showed he was the high-scoring star. Once, when he was injured, Plainfield lost and the headlines lamented Jack Simmons's sprained ankle.

Subconsciously, I needed to get close to my father and win his approval. Was I that sophisticated to recognize the means to get to Jack's heart? Well, when I was twelve, I was obsessed with playing back-yard basketball. My friend down the street, Simon Prince, had helped me nail a backboard to my garage. At the same time, I was beginning an enduring growth spurt that would leave me last in line and in the back row for a lifetime. It wouldn't stop until I was six-foot-five.

According to a study done on tortoises in the hair, obsessive-compulsive tendencies are concomitant. I was shooting hoops as close to 24/7 as possible. In ninth grade, I made a lamp in wood shop. By the light of a 75-watt bulb strung up by two extension cords, I shot baskets in the backyard on many cold winter nights, kept warm by several layers of Bamberger's wool sweaters. When I got sick of my backyard, Maple Avenue School had a net and a metal basket rim. Once, after a six-inch snowfall, I climbed the fence on a weekend and shoveled half the playground so I could shoot around.

Problem extant was my severe absence of self-confidence and that freaking tortoise in my hair. My freshman year at Weequahic, I made the junior varsity team—barely. What doomed my career was not being able to run the weave, figuring it out, running behind the player you throw the ball to. I was hindered by the tortoise, but at least I could tie my sneakers now. I resigned myself to playing streetball and joining the team at the Newark Y, where I'd win a state championship and an MVP award. For all time and perpetuity, Jack never once saw me play organized ball. Fuck, I'd done it all for his approval.

Years later, at a celebration of Weequahic's storied basketball accomplishments and state championships, I talked to Chris, an All-State, All-American, and one of my everlasting idols. He asked why I never played for Weequahic and in college. He said I was one of the best players and jumpers he ever knew.

"Why couldn't you have told me that back then?" I told him.

Early the next morning, smiling and reminiscing, I stared out the window, waiting for an avian arrival to finally harbinger the departure of the tortoise.

Chapter 4

AN OHIO COLLEGE SWEATSHIRT

There was no Rutgers pharmacy school in my immediate future; the tortoise saw to that. Like my father, I was consistent in a few things, like being a solid average-C student, a purveyor of unimpressive college boards, and a good invisible basketball player—no colleges ever saw me play. Rutgers and Cincinnati rejected me. Howard University was a stretch. But the University of Toledo's admissions program was seeking to expand their horizons by bringing in an influx of Easterners from New York and New Jersey—so I had a new home.

My parent's brand-new Pontiac Catalina carried us out to Toledo in September 1963. Jack did all the driving, mostly silently, contributing very few words or pep talks as we navigated the Pennsylvania Turnpike. We stopped briefly for a dichotomy of urinals and gas. On the drive, we were passing through the inauspicious Kittatinny Mountain Tunnel when I had an epiphany about how to handle myself in college. Epiphanies are simple gifts, mysterious where they come from, but life changing. In Toledo, no one knew me—no stereotypes, no visible tortoise—so I could role-play, pretending I was everything I dreamed of being in high school: cool, athletic, and intelligent. Halls of ivy could finally level the playing field. This plan was brilliantly conceived for an eighteen-year-old, crew-cut, emaciated virginal kid from Newark.

Maternal desperation interrupted my cool thinking as my mother delivered a sermonette about dormitory behavior and routinization. This meant studying hard to get a scholarship, which would save money so my sister Carol could go to college. My brilliant mother—her instillation of guilt had a resounding effect. And yes, she said, I still needed to lay my clothes out the night before.

Jack drove all night so I could arrive at the dorm by 10:00 and claim the lower bunk bed, in case I had issues of height and homesickness. But my roommate, Ted "Tank" Stone, had already secured the lower bunk before departing to nearby Lansing, Michigan, for pre-orientation sex. Amelia lined the drawers, arranged my socks and underwear, and taught me a crash course in how to do laundry with soap tablets while Jack fidgeted, wanting to go home. After a pricey brunch at the Colony Restaurant, we hugged outside Dowd Hall and said our goodbyes, which we'd never done before. Mother cried and I held it all in. As they drove around the quad, I saw my mother twisting, turning for a last look. My father said nothing at the last scene.

Abject loneliness propelled me to the ivy-covered, picturesque University Hall, where I finally lost it and cried. I'd never really been away from my parents before.

The stark reality that I wasn't in Jersey anymore hit me again later that night in my dorm room with Tank, who was from Tenafly, New Jersey, and our next-door neighbors from West Virginia. Darryl, an appropriate representative of Appalachia, kept walking around me, staring at the area above my shoulder, looking for my horns. He'd been taught that back home in God's almost-heaven mountain country.

I'll never forget Darryl's Southern drawl inquisition, "You a Jew? But you're so tall. Can you dunk a ball?" Damn, Amelia hadn't prepped me for how to handle this situation.

During freshmen orientation week, I drifted over to the gym for full-court basketball pickup games. I never told Darryl I could dunk, but it was easy for me; wearing ankle weights for four years helped. During one game, I was being guarded by George, a giant—he was close to seven feet tall. Accelerating into a layup and going airborne, I dunked right over him, a former NBA player with close ties to the Toledo coach. I had no reality check on my skill levels; no one ever enlightened me. A few weeks later, George came to my dorm and offered a chance to play for the school team. Excited and in disbelief, I said I'd get back to him with parental permission.

When I called home, Dad answered. "Guess what?" I said. "I was offered a chance to try out for Toledo basketball. They want me. I'm so excited."

"Wait, Son, let me get your mother."

Mother shot me down with at least a hundred years of guilt and immigration stories. College was strictly a time for me to become a pharmacist. Multitasking was not my strong point. Our argument ended at the phone booth right outside of Ace Drugs. For the rest of my life, I'd perseverate on being a contender, sitting in the back of a black car with rear window shades, wondering what I could've accomplished on the hardwood.

Still, word of my basketball abilities spread across campus, and soon two fraternities had set their sights on me. I settled on Pi Epsilon Epsilon, mostly because they had good exam and study files and were active on campus, which meant they teamed up with a Protestant fraternity and sorority to stuff the ballot boxes every year. They controlled undergraduate life.

One Wednesday night close to midterms, during rush season, PiEp was having a rush party: coeds, high school seniors, beer, and punch. Mark, the head of rush, came to my dorm room in his ROTC uniform to sell me on why I had to be there. "If you want to be in the frat and don't want to be blackballed, you've got to be there tonight," he said. "We'll drive you back and forth."

I told him I couldn't go. "I've got an exam tomorrow. I have to study and sleep."

"I'm not supposed to do this. Come with me now. Party with us. We'll bring you back at 2:00 a.m. and you'll take this little pill and you'll be able to study all night. I promise you'll ace your exam."

Carefully, he unwrapped a folded napkin and showed me an orange, triangular pill. He explained it was Dexedrine—truck drivers took it to stay awake and go cross country; housewives took it to lose weight.

Life would change for me at 2:00 a.m. that night, and it would stay that way for many years. In the meantime, I did ace that exam. I climbed the cinder block dorm walls all night, shoving every random factoid I could into my overzealous brain. It was my first high, and it was nice.

For the first time in my life, I felt a real sense of belonging, that I was part of something, now elected vice president of the freshmen pharmacy class. I never mattered back in high school, marveling at the same kids getting elected to class office every year. When I heard my name in the pharmacy assembly being nominated, rare goosebumps arrived.

To celebrate my rise to relevance, I scraped together loose change— Mother's inflexible budget was $22 weekly for food, dentists, books, and miscellany—to purchase a blue Toledo sweatshirt. I wore it incessantly. Recently, someone from my Toledo days sent a picture of me on campus wearing a Rutgers sweatshirt I don't remember owning. I had no reason at the time to wear anything from Rutgers, who'd rejected my application. How prophetic.

GIRL LIFE

In the first two months on campus, I intersected with the opposite sex more than I ever had in my first seventeen earthly years. Intersecting was nothing more than a dance, a movie, a walk in a cemetery, or a frat party. Freshmen were relegated to the dating pools of senior high school girls. Looking back, desperately trying to expunge memory pixels, I even once went to a high school dance with a girl named Evelyn Smith. I'd rationalized that I'd never been to one back in Newark, so it worked.

Evelyn was tall, dark, and shy, and we were so much alike. She was Cathy and I was Heathcliff, except there was no love and kissing on the moors. Out of public view, we held hands. First base was a long way away, with no instructional picture book to look at under the covers, and no help from my roommate, Tank, who was still running up to Lansing on weekends to get laid. I figured we'd put a man on the moon before I'd ever get laid. I turned out to be right.

I was just role-playing a cool guy in my mind. Conceptually, intimacy was one of the hardest things for me to visualize: getting there, going inside. What bothered me most about anticipating the actual ascension, as I called it, was the freaking tortoise in my hair. That son-of-a-bitch, land-dwelling reptile in the order Testudines (not *testicle*, but close) residing in my hair would make it impossible to find the place of entry without a plethora of embarrassing pokes. It was a constant source of worry. Remember, this was 1963; marijuana was reserved only for the cool non-virgins on campus, which meant sexual dynamics were plainly different.

Evelyn was an overachiever, trying so hard to please. One Friday night, she invited Tank and me to her mother's for a home-cooked meal and announced she was knitting sweaters for both of us. The ambiguity in her allegiance and affection caught me off guard. Tank liked the idea; I didn't. I had issues with loyalty, so I never saw Evelyn again. She mailed the sweater to my house in Newark. A few years later, she died in a head-on car accident.

When you're feeling down and pessimistic, a good chance to bust out is an PiEp Roaring Twenties Party, according to my big brother, Henry. He'd resupplied me with Dexedrine and fixed me up with pretty blonde Karen Foster, a local dentist's daughter. I was totally enamored with Karen—after the party, I called her five times for a movie date. All five times, Karen's mother answered. Karen was always studying. This hard rejection would last a long time; I feel it even now as I write. I learned to reevaluate rejection. In the future, I'd attempt two phone calls and be done. My ego must be maintained at all costs.

Rebounds work in basketball and in dating, so after Evelyn and Karen, I found myself at another frat party infiltrated by high school and sorority girls, where a girl kept staring and smiling at me. I inhaled deeply before I went over to ask her for a dance. She told me her name was Jill Mann, another high school senior. Eventually, she'd sign on for the next three semesters as my legitimate girlfriend. The next morning, the Beatles released "All My Loving," a song I came to associate with Jill.

Here are the news highlights at eleven: After three semesters—Jill spent her freshman year at Miami University, Ohio—I'd mention a late-night party at my frat brother Harvey's apartment. Johnny Mathis's "Twelfth of Never" played softly while Jill and I sat in a corner chair, romantically kissing. My hand quickly swept her breast, buried deep beneath an itchy mohair sweater. I was petrified over prospects of rejection, which never came. It was just a few seconds in my life, but that memory of achievement lasted a long time.

The state of my virginity was an ongoing challenge for my older brothers. They often yelled, "Let's get Cameron laid!" The solution was at the Clock Restaurant, somewhere over a rainbow in northwestern Ohio, an old-fashioned whorehouse. Apparently, all my frat brothers had relinquished their virginities similarly. The following year, living in the frat house meant road trips of substance, usually six of us sitting evenly spaced out in the front and back of the vehicle. A full moon and a warm Midwestern breeze accompanied us while we got lost for hours on back roads. Time approached wee hours when a flat tire deflated my night of ascension. The man on the moon for virginal disposition continued to loom.

A month later, back in the same car, the gang went to see this new movie *Mary Poppins*. One of my frat brothers suggested being high to see it. Six Dexedrine tablets appeared in the car right as the sky hauntingly darkened and a powerful wind effortlessly scattered solid cement stanchions—the coming of a tornado told. Everyone ran into the theater while meteorological curiosity kept me outside—until a violent wind threw me through the theater doors. Seconds in a life, a thousand feet closer, the tornado touchdown could've sent me to the Land of Oz.

COMMON SENSE ACADEMICS

I was a long way from Newark, miles and grades. I found comfort in the library and laboratories of Toledo pharmacy school. I quickly learned that early grades could follow you for years; get that positive reputation because professors looked for the easy way out, and what was past was prologue. The blue book on Cameron said he was a fastidious student, but the tortoise was still very much around. Soon, I became a provisional member in a biological honor society. A few blinks later, and I was in a variety of campus organizations. Amelia was proud. Jack didn't give.

Next came an achievement that signaled my first meaningful distancing from my reptilian nemesis. Something intelligent was seeded deep within my molecular structure, something that needed nurturing, excavation, and an ego boost. During my spring semester in 1965, I signed up for a tedious, consumptive lab experiment to make raw, nascent aspirin by the end of school year.

Preceding the first week of the aspirin lab, the assistant dean had delivered his infamous canned speech: "Don't buy aspirin from the local drug store, crush it up on the last day of lab, and cut lab for all sixteen weeks. We assay your samples and know your purity and Bayer's. If you hand in crushed Bayer aspirin, you'll be expelled. Every year, there's always one student who ends up on the unemployment line or in the army. Don't do it. Good luck."

Every week brought a new product yield, a mysterious powder.

One week, I added a liquid that irritated my nostrils, then I stirred it, heated the beaker with a Bunsen burner, and sprinkled it with magical bibbidi-bobbidi blue crystals. A pink powder (pre-cursor to aspirin) smiled back at me. During the long hours, I feigned interest in my lab mates' progress, prancing around and saying, "How you doing, Nate?" The allure of summer vacation hangs over spring semester, beckoning toward freedom, bare feet, and carefree living. If you fail lab and don't produce enough aspirin to quell a headache, then it's Toledo, Ohio, summer school for you—a depressing prospect.

One week before the semester ended, it was all coming together. Shaking, rattling, and rolling a beaker. Adding acid, pouring off, and heating gently—but I didn't see "gently" in the recipe. At the end of the day, my beaker was empty—I'd failed. Too much heat wiped out sixteen weeks of work. I panicked. I asked my lab mates for help, thinking if everyone contributed a negligible amount, I'd be able to spend summer at home in the city of Newark. But out of the twenty-five students in my section, not one (not even my fraternity brothers) would part with a minute amount of their lab product.

On the last day of lab, our aspirin samples were due, and we needed to clean our glass and laboratory ware. My lab station had a container of Ajax cleanser on the shelf above the sink. As I poured the flocculent cleansing powder into my beaker, I observed the similar physical properties to aspirin powder. Amidst my disappointment I reasoned, with a newfound common-sense approach to life, that handing in Ajax— by *mistake*—was not a reason for expulsion. The assistant dean never mentioned handing in Ajax. I filled my sample jar to the top, and I got an A in the lab.

I'd officially finished my first two years of college. I had a girlfriend, had been elected fraternity house manager and secretary, and was involved in campus life. What I'd conceived driving through Pennsylvania with my parents, to role-play into acceptance, had worked perfectly. I was a happy guy, content to live with my virginity as long as others perceived I was getting it. Image was everything. Teachers gave me better grades, even if I didn't deserve it—and despite the tortoise, I flirted with the dean's list that spring semester, thanks to Ajax cleanser. Was it all becoming too easy?

I was at a good place in life. A few weeks before heading back to Newark for the summer, I rented a duplex apartment a block from the frat house with my brothers Nate and Harlan. We celebrated with near beer (weak, shitty beer), Peter, Paul and Mary's new single, "The First Time Ever I Saw Your Face," and Harlan on guitar. It was a perfect memory and place to come back to in September. Yet there was *something* (that word again)—something restless, disturbing—that screwed around with me, like incisor teeth gnawing at my cage. The view from the frat house windows were depressingly squalid, so I had nowhere to meditate. But, fuck it, I was free. I loved Toledo. The possibilities were sweet. September would be sweeter.

Chapter 5

RUTGERS IN THE SIXTIES

As Newark evolved with the times, my parents loaded up their Pontiac Catalina and moved to suburban Maplewood, another changing place. Maplewood: a white-bread-and-mayonnaise place to live. Historically, no Jews, Blacks, or Italians were welcomed in their country club or town hall. At the bottom of a dead-end court, my parents rented a duplex, where I'd be sleeping on a foldaway couch in the living room for the next two years.

The summer of 1965, a time of turmoil and the jungle war in Vietnam, deposited me at Crast Pharmacy to work closely with my cousins, Mark and David. No more washing shelves in the basement or wearing a protective football helmet. This time, I was awarded my own register key to take care of customers—a huge ascension.

But there was something I couldn't explain; a feeling of longing, uneasiness, queasiness, and destiny out there beyond my parents' living room windows. This strange aura battled euphoria with my perfect life in Toledo. Out of the clear restless blue that first morning home from Toledo, something made me decide to apply for a summer course at Rutgers University–Newark. My theory was that taking this required political science course now would free up some mornings for sleeping late come autumn in Toledo. Rutgers accepted me for summer school, even though it had rejected me for full-time studies.

A few seconds in the life, and I had made a decision that would change where I was headed; a pathway to the infinite universe. Although we can feel the sun's warmth on our face, we can't understand why things happen—no matter how high, introspective, or ridiculous we are.

My well-known poli-sci professor came from Rutgers–New Brunswick, very much an epicenter of East Coast intellect, protest, and free speech and thought. The class demographics included Harvard, Columbia, Michigan, Duke, Rutgers—and me, a graduate of Maple Avenue School in Newark.

The back of the class, away from all those hands raised for questions and professorial challenges, was my comfort zone. I could never compete with Ivy League brains. My ego was wonderfully practical; it knew its place, where to sit, and whom to talk to. Then I got an A in the course, planting a subliminal seed. I realized I could hold my own with anyone. I hoped the tortoise was rocked a bit from my hair—which was getting longer into the sixties, thanks to the Beatles. (Thanks to Amelia's conservatism, I was still nowhere near a hippie.)

Summer at Crast Pharmacy was uneventful until my cousin Mark showed me how to count pills in a tray with a spatula. I was on my way to being a pharmacist. One day, Mrs. Vetrone, a good customer, came in with her niece Angela, who was visiting from Italy. I was hit with the same thunderbolt that hit Michael Corleone when he saw Apollonia for the first time. Angela came into the store almost daily, and I'd ring up her Juicy Fruit gum. Her English and her face were perfect. We became so comfortable with each other that I even walked her home one day, taking deep breaths for three blocks, trying to oxygenate my nerve to ask her out. I deliriously did; never been higher or more smitten.

Back at the pharmacy, Aunt Evelyn had surmised the reason for my disappearance and reminded me of the extremely large crucifix around Angela's neck. For the next few days, Aunt Evelyn—uncannily resembling Margaret Hamilton's career performance as the Wicked Witch of the West in *The Wizard of Oz*—made me dust and wash all the cellar shelves, keeping me away from Angela. I rationalized that there were too many hurdles to pursue with Angela. We never shared a goodbye or even a kiss in our ill-fated, nonexistent relationship.

One midsummer night, I was sitting at dinner with Amelia, Jack, and Carol, mashed potatoes before us, when something hit me—another spiritual intervention it would take me decades to finally begin to understand.

My mother and father, as if choreographed, picked up their coffee cups in unison. "Mom, Dad," I told them, "I'm transferring to Rutgers pharmacy school in September."

Comically, as the timing was perfect, they spit out their coffee. "What do you mean?" Mother asked loudly.

"I mean, I'm leaving Toledo and coming home."

My father stayed silent late into the night. He added not a word to the conversation.

Dabbing at the new coffee stains on her blouse, Mother was getting emotional. "But you're so happy in Toledo. Close to a scholarship. A girlfriend. Good grades. Nothing makes sense. Why, Cameron?"

I had no clue. I couldn't start explaining what "something" was in my life, or how I'd look out windows into the universe or sit on a Belmar jetty and dream of tomorrows.

"I know how hard it's been for you and dad financially," I told them, hoping this simple fabrication would pacify my parentals. "Carol has to go to college too. Rutgers is a state school, so it's much cheaper. I'm doing it for my sister." In reality, I had no idea why, how, or who was behind all this. But it was an entity. I sensed that.

FIRST YEAR RUTGERS

Transferring from Toledo to Rutgers meant a loss of a year's credits with new courses to take. I didn't flinch losing a year. It kept me safe with a student draft deferment (2-S) as the war in Vietnam flared up, putting the fear of jungles, rice paddies, and snipers into my generation's consciousness.

The Rutgers pre-med, pre-pharmacy program liked the German language because medical schools also liked the Aryan twist; it helped prepare the mind's pathways for general anatomy—so I was told. My German professor, Herr Beckmann, was a real Bund guy, a throwback to the pro-Nazi organizations in America during the 1930s and 1940s. He didn't like me. No matter what I turned in, I failed. Whenever I compared test results with the blonde, blue-eyed Fatherland students, we had the same answers, but they got A's.

At the final exam, I resigned to realizing a dream. Three minutes into the exam, I walked up to Beckmann, threw the blue book in his face, and shouted, "Fuck you" at a high decibel before storming out.

Of course, summer school in Jersey City awaited me after that. Another German professor, Dr. Mars, taught summer school. At the first class, I sat in the front row wearing a large crucifix I'd bought at a jewelry store, smiling, acting German. I got an A in the course, and an invitation to study in Germany the following year.

FRIENDS

If, at the end of a life, you count your lasting, long-haul friends, and there are five, you've done a credible job. The tortoise still governed aspects of my socialization, so I began that first year at Rutgers over-compensating. I tried too hard, probably obnoxiously so. I always knew my friend list would never be complete, but I'd have short-term contenders.

One morning in the pharmacy school lunch room, furnished by vending machines and an abused ping-pong table, Julian Tuller mentioned meeting me in Toledo. My memory couldn't retrieve him, so I stared blankly. I was very good at that.

I'd noticed Julian prancing around Rutgers, though. He was confident, well connected, and I was positive he wasn't a virgin like me. He had classic movie-star qualities: blonde wavy hair, piercing blue eyes.

"We met at a frat rush party," he told me, "But I don't need fraternities, so I never got involved. I do very well on my own, if you get my drift. Call me Tuffy. Everybody does. I'm not tough, just smart."

Julian had also transferred out of Toledo pharmacy school. There was a subliminal chemistry between us. He was the rich, experienced, worldly traveler who knew how to navigate life well beyond his years, and I was wide-eyed and naïve in every sense. Our friendship blossomed quickly. In short order, we studied and cheated together, forming an iron-clad pact to fix up the other if either one of us was dating. Never fully understanding Julian's willingness to agree to that seemingly one-sided pact, I thought the future was bright.

During Christmas vacation, while studying for finals at Julian's Victorian summer house in Allenhurst for the solitude and quiet of the Jersey Shore, I began to appreciate my new friend's magnetism. The doorbell rang and two girls came in, Florence and Nancy, friends of Julian. It was a surprise setup for me. I wasn't ready, soulfully, physically, or spiritually, so I sat on the sofa with blonde, heavily made-up Florence, talking contrived world history while Julian and Nancy went upstairs for a few hours—a scene right out of *Summer of '42*, me embodying Hermie's purity.

Back at Crast Pharmacy, working Christmas Eve, I met Bill Tyler, a newly hired clerk and a student at Montclair State. I was impressed with Bill's family tree: his older brother was a priest at Sacred Heart, and his younger brother idolized my basketball background. A year later, our friendship brought us together at midnight mass at St. Leo's. The experience raised my consciousness and ecumenical awareness for the rest of my life. In the pew, I followed the lead on when to stand and kneel. Bill's father took care of the plate when it passed. I already knew the words to most Christmas songs. "Adeste Fideles" would always be spiritually haunting to me—I imagined singing it on Christmas Eve, in the middle of the Italian Dolomites, in a medieval castle with family and friends gathered around a fireplace.

My friendship with Bill Tyler grew out of the dust and floor-to-ceiling shelves at Crast Pharmacy. Bill and I were solely responsible for keeping those shelves clean with rotated stock. When we were both off on a Friday night, we'd go to a movie or a musical production at his church. A thespian and multitalented performer, I'd get to see Bill in a few musical leads. He would go on to see the world, climb Mount Everest with the son of the Sherpa guide who'd taken Sir Edmund Hillary to the summit, visit the Taj Mahal, and one day spiritually change the course of my earthly existence—but not for several more years.

Diametrically opposed to my German language failure was my world history success. Professor Honcharuk illuminated his Rutgers classroom. All his students wanted to absorb everything in his class and feed it back to him, hoping to impress so he knew us by name after a few weeks. The day he called me Mr. Simmons in class, I felt high and mighty.

Honcharuk's class was open seating—mathematically, no students would sit next to each other more than once, if they practiced his spirit of intent. He preferred a different view from his stage every day. But somehow, each class, I sat next to Carla Brown, a pretty girl whose eyes twinkled when she spoke. Half the time, I subliminally sought proximity to her; the rest of the time, she took charge. We were usually the first students to arrive, so we'd have ample time to chat about the assignment, Vietnam, and Dr. Martin Luther King Jr. The electromagnetism between us was strong enough to form cellular bonds, and we were on the way to compounding.

Midterms in world history had both of us cruising near an A. In a moment of spontaneous combustion, I asked Carla to lunch to celebrate our impending excellence. I thought it would be fun to take her to the Weequahic Diner, whose clientele still counted souls from my high school. She said yes, but a diner serving health salad and pickles pre-meal was not necessarily her kind of place. I repeatedly asked if it was all right—my tortoise insecurities were alive and well.

The lunch rush was over, so a sprinkling of wandering eyes noticed a Black girl and White boy sitting together. This was a big deal in 1965. Our conversation turned to race and our species, and I apologized for being heavy on our first date. I told her about my journey to realizing the depths of racism despite being a young boy on a bus in downtown Newark.

She smiled, eyes twinkling, and said, "Is this what this is, a date?"

I stuttered and inhaled deeply, sucking courage into my lungs. "Our time here is a compound combination of things. A celebration of great midterm grades, our commonality of being minorities, and to find out why we always sit together. I like the official date idea."

"I love the way you talk and watching you squirm to get out of a situation," she said with a laugh, "but you know this can't be an official date. It could start a race war, so let's pretend we're doing a class assignment. How does that sound?"

Fantasy contained me for weeks. I imagined bringing Carla home to my parents and sister for dinner, or holding hands at a Weequahic High basketball game. Nothing sexual, just simply getting along. Our species builds so many walls to discourage human contact, making us forget big pictures and our nothingness place in the vast universe. Later in January, over winter break, we saw *Thunderball* together. After the movie, we met at a coffee shop in Montclair and talked for a few hours. The waitress shot us annoyed stares, wanting her table back. I left the largest tip of my life, then walked Carla to her car, where I asked for a kiss. It approached perfection, but I never saw her again. I knew why.

SECOND YEAR

My second year of Rutgers pharmacy school was exclusively located in the turn-of-the-century building just a mile from downtown Newark, which would serve its role in New Jersey history, as I'd be in the last graduating class in 1969 from Newark. The following year, the school moved to Piscataway on the main Rutgers campus.

Julian and I got closer, relying on each other to negotiate a horrifically boring curriculum. That meant cheating, cutting classes, and taking Dexedrine the night before any exam.

Our study group soon grew to include Arvin Leonard, a sophomore transfer student from Newark College of Engineering. He was a classic geek. He came to us with crew-cut hair, a slide rule in his shirt pocket, John Lennon specs on his large, pronounced nose, and a soft-spoken manner. Girls were an abstract concept to him, and his mother served him orange juice with a straw. His world was mathematical, logical, and celibate. Our study group needed his brain.

I've always sought out enigmas purposely—refreshingly real, quirky, accomplished personalities that sometimes battle rejection and misperception. As Arvin transformed before us that year—both in terms of appearance and personality—he became an enigma to us too.

Within a year, Arvin became a werewolf of downtown Newark. His hair grew everywhere, over his face and down to his waist. He was a full-blown hippie, influenced by periodic doses of LSD and amphetamines. He started getting laid with remarkable frequency. There was no going back. Where I had once been welcomed into his parents' West Orange apartment because they thought I was a steadying influence, they eventually slammed the door in my face, blaming my nonexistent influence with Jekyll, their son.

I yelled through the door, "I have short hair. Arvin's change is cultural, beyond all of us at Rutgers."

Our roles later reversed when I turned to Arvin to fix me up with his girlfriend's sister, Margaret. Margaret's family spoke German in their home. When I picked her up for our first date, I greeted her father in German. He was drunk and unaware I was even taking out his daughter. I turned out to be equally unaware that his daughter was sixteen.

We went out to the movies a few times and one pizza dinner. I'd kiss her goodnight just outside the apartment door, shouts of German coming from on the other side. A few months into this Lolita situation, my father's single brother James, a chemist, went to Europe and entrusted me with the keys to his bachelor apartment in lower Manhattan.

It was a perfect spring night when Margaret and I crossed New York State lines and the apartment threshold. I was aware of our age difference by then, but I thought this was a divine intervention deal. The eighth-floor view was worth the trip alone, but I could think of only one thing: the ascension, becoming a man. Music on Uncle James's Blaupunkt radio filled our senses. I removed her blouse. Her bra was next. It was all dreamy. We shared the passion—she wanted this as much as I did.

Then a hard reality set in. This was all wrong. Back outside her apartment door, with German curses on the other side of midnight, I kissed Margaret goodnight and never saw her again. I'd remember this as a precipice night and thanked my celestial stars. But I was still hopelessly a virgin.

Fuck you, tortoise.

I'm sure the tortoise whispered back to fuck myself.

Spring semester, Butch joined our study group. What bullshit we fed ourselves! Our reason to believe, like the popular folk song, was to find ways to cheat, get good grades, have fun, and become registered pharmacists.

An upcoming midterm exam in microbiology loomed—a brutal multiple-choice exam. I needed a good grade to keep my scholarship. Our gang of four decided to be proactive, so we hoisted skinny, hairy Arvin over the professor's cubicle wall and acquired the test and answers.

That night, we put our hands together in a pact, agreeing to get 80s across the board. Anything higher would've alerted the authorities.

Come exam time, I watched the other three get up and leave way too early. The following morning, we were all called into the dean's office. The threesome got 95s. No one had ever scored that high. I got an 80, which also raised eyebrows. There was no proof we had cheated—still, our grades defaulted to D-minuses. Our study group dissolved.

A pharmacy fraternity party was coming up. I needed a date, and my cousin David had someone he said would be perfect for me. I idolized Cousin David, a meticulous, predictable, perfunctory pharmacist. He was the family's quintessential bachelor, always a new girl and car in his life. He and his latest girlfriend, Caryn, fixed me up with her sister, Bonnie.

Customarily, before ringing the doorbell to pick up a date, I'd stand for a few seconds, inhaling deeply and saying personal prayers that the blindness in the date would be visually rewarding.

When Bonnie answered the door, for only the second time in my life, I was hit with a thunderbolt. Bonnie was violently beautiful, taking my breath away with her dark hair and deep, sultry voice. Just being with her was a jolt for my embryonic ego; people at the party stared at her beauty while I held her hand.

In the back seat coming home from the party, we kissed like old friends. She put her arm around me and returned all my advances. At her front door, I asked her out again, and she instantly accepted. It had to be a beginning love. The world was perfect.

The next three weeks became routine: movies followed by late Saturday-night snacks at the iconic Claremont Diner. Old-world values made me open the car door for her and pay for everything. We did our talking and kissing in my car, parked in front of her house, away from her mother's watchful eyes. I was finally a fan of cul-de-sacs with their finite traffic flow. We'd kiss for a while, then talk about Vietnam, her boss, a local pediatrician, and Mary Martin, her favorite celebrity. The car wasn't private enough to venture beyond kissing to breast palpation. Funny thing, there'd never be the right place or time for that.

On our fifth date, still sitting in the car at 4:00 a.m., talking mostly, Bonnie informed me we could never be anything more than good friends.

"What do you mean?" I asked.

"Cameron, you're such a nice guy. I like you. But I've been having an affair with a stomach doctor. We love each other. I don't know what will ever happen. It's not fair to you to go on like this."

I was completely clueless what to do or say. What ran through my mind in between freaking inhalations was finding a way to preserve something with Bonnie. My ego needed her for selfish reasons—even if I wouldn't be losing my virginity to her, I had to keep hanging on.

"Bonnie, what we have between us is special," I said, once I finally went verbal again. "I wouldn't want to lose you. So, let's stay friends. Nothing has changed. Are you all right with this?"

"Are you sure?" she asked.

"One more thing. I will always respect you and never ask any questions—unless you need my broad shoulders."

She leaned over, kissed me, and went home. I never told anyone what a schmuck I was, continuing to hold doors and pay for everything.

Six months later, my old nemesis, jealousy, weighed heavily on my unused broad shoulders. I devised a plan. I knew Bonnie met her doctor lover on Wednesdays for lunch at the Claremont Diner. With the powers of gentle persuasion gifted to me, I went to a pharmacy fraternity pledge named Lou, grabbed him by the collar, and told him what he had to do to get into the frat.

Dressed as old men with beards and trench coats, we camped in the diner parking lot one Wednesday and waited, camera at the ready. Two hours passed; Lou was not a happy guy. Finally, just Bonnie came out—no stomach doctor in sight. My plan hadn't worked.

Instead, I had to finally accept the way we were. My platonic relationship with Bonnie endured for a few more months, but not with the same frequency as before. One fine day, she and I had a Saturday date to see Bill Tyler in a church production of *My Fair Lady*. Bonnie called to cancel an hour before—it was obvious she had an appointment for sex with the stomach doctor instead. Beyond disappointed, I said, "I'll talk to you tomorrow."

But our tomorrow never came. Bonnie had finally crossed the line in the sand. I purged her and recovered my sense of self.

Chapter 6

GOODBYE, SOUTH ORANGE

Julian and I did a road trip to Philadelphia and Washington, DC after my Bonnie drama. Julian was perceptive enough to know I needed something. On the southbound Jersey Turnpike, we discovered our chasm on Vietnam, military service, and political thought. Enough energy for the car to accelerate to a hundred.

In Philadelphia, we stayed at Julian's friend's house. After hamburgers, the doorbell. Two girls. Julian disappeared upstairs with Ellen for the night. Maggie stayed with me, but informed that she doesn't put out on a first date. "It's too bad, Cameron, that you're geographically undesirable. I really like you." Such is a life; the only thing I could think.

A few weeks after our road trip, Julian started dating a college freshman, Arlene, who was passed along to him by his father. Julian's and Arlene's fathers did business together, therefore Julian had to behave himself with her. Anytime a girl was not conquerable, Julian lost interest quickly. But before Arlene's chord was cut, in keeping with the provisions of our pact, Julian fixed me up with her cousin Wendy, a junior at Buffalo University.

I delayed calling up Wendy, hesitant to get blindly fixed up again. Julian reminded me Wendy was the daughter of a prominent dermatologist who lived on an exclusive street in trendy South Orange. Plus, their family was Semitic—all desirable traits to my mother, Amelia. On that night, I listened to the news about one of my life's heroes, Dr. Martin Luther King Jr. He had just delivered his "I've Been to the Mountaintop" speech to a rally of striking sanitation workers.

A strange feeling hung over me as I tried to decipher Dr. King's words: "It really doesn't matter with me now, because I've been to the mountaintop, and I don't mind." The next day, he was assassinated.

When I called Wendy, we talked for a comfortable hour. She was studying to be an accountant, was an accomplished violinist, and her voice soothed and captivated. We decided to see *2001: A Space Odyssey.* The movie trailer lent itself to getting high in a theater. When I walked up to her front door, I was amphetamine-elevated, feeling good all over, especially as she lived in a house approaching mansion status.

Dramatically, the front door opened to reveal her tall, skinny, pretty persona. I sensed instant like. Crossing into the foyer, I thought, "Thank you, God," but the fear of date failure was always there.

Wendy's family had gathered together in the library for introductions. Effervescently, I greeted Dr. Paul, Mrs. Paul, and her younger siblings, Samuel and Melody. Out of left field, Dr. Paul asked about my father. I sought to vocationally elevate Big Jack. "My dad manages the largest shoe store in Elizabeth," I told him. To my knowledge, Elizabeth had only one shoe emporium.

At the movie, we talked throughout, held hands on and off, and I sensed a certain feeling of like. At Don's Drive-In afterward, we absorbed each other's faces, smiles, laughs, and frowns—we shared a sadness over the passing of Dr. King. We kissed for a long time in my car when I took her back to her house, but she said I wouldn't be able to see her for another month until she was back for summer vacation.

The beginning of summer vacation was intensely Wendy. I'd see her most nights after work at Crast Pharmacy. After a few weeks, I had dinner with her family. Her mother cooked and two servants attended. For me, a skinny kid from Newark, South Orange was the big time of dating.

My mother basked in the stories of Wendy's family's lifestyle. "My son with a doctor's daughter," she'd marvel. "And they have a Cadillac *and* a Lincoln."

Despite my social inadequacies, I had an innate ability to jump quickly into most relationships, which means I could get serious even faster than Julian. By the end of June, Wendy and I were a real deal. Somewhere in our time together, I uttered those difficult words for the first time: "I'm falling in love with you." I didn't necessarily know if that was how I really felt, but I was running out of sweet nothings; I needed an infusion of imagination.

With my mother in one dugout, ecstatic over prospects of serious things, and Wendy's mother in the other, pushing us together, the field of dreams was golden matrimonial. I'd later find out Wendy had a strange boyfriend in Buffalo whom Dr. and Mrs. Paul had been trying to get her to break up with for the past year. To Wendy's parents and siblings, he paled in comparison to almost-perfect Cameron.

One early summer night, the sky pink with wispy sunset cirrus clouds, the Atlantic Ocean a block away, I took Wendy to Deal Lake. I put my arm around Wendy and asked her to wear my fraternity pin. In 1968, this was significant; an engagement to be engaged someday. I wished Julian were there to yell in my ears, "What the fuck you doing, Cameron?" I was still definitely, wholesomely a virgin, and now I was almost engaged. My rationalization was that I had a dozen fraternity pins. It wasn't as if this was the precipice of decisions, a once-in-a-lifetime commitment. In theory, I had a dozen more contemporary girls to pin.

Bonding with Wendy's siblings was next in the process of solidi-fying our relationship. With Samuel and Melody, three and five years younger, we picnicked at South Mountain Reservation. Ten years earlier, I'd climbed a gentle mountain there as part of a Newark Y camp excursion. When I'd reached the top, I sat down, looked toward Newark Airport, and dreamed of being someone's father. What would it feel like to guide and advise a young life? I was mildly obsessed with parenthood, and I wasn't even a teenager yet.

At our picnic, I role-modeled for Wendy's young brother and sister. Coincidentally, the radio played the 5th Dimension's "Stoned Soul Picnic" and the notion of divine intervention blew in the wind.

I was relatively happy with Wendy and her family. My mother made tuna salad every other day, trying for my good side, as I was achieving beyond expectations: a doctor's daughter. I was sealed in the book of life. I was still a virgin, safely, without peer pressures or parental inquisitions.

Back in January, I'd dated Carol Green, a one-way-street relation-ship. She was obsessed with me, while I was mildly repulsed by her caked-on makeup, insecticide-like cologne, and overbearing person-ality. But I was a nice guy, never really sure how to say no or goodbye. Carol had invited me down to her house in suburban Hillside on one cold, ominous night. Her parents were away for the weekend. When it started to snow, Amelia called every fifteen minutes, reminding me of the dangers of being alone with a girl, the inconveniences of unwanted pregnancies, and the spiraling cost of auto insurance if I got into a snowy accident. I might've ascended that night, but Amelia prevailed.

There was a gentler theme when I hung at Wendy's house with Mother Paul floating nearby. I liked calling her mother's name. Wendy's mother would show me around the house to look at their furnishings, gardens, and pool. "Cameron, everything you see around here—this new $50,000 necklace, the house, Wendy's Italian violin—well, it's all from Dr. Paul's medical practice," she said. "There is only one way to acquire things in life and be able to enjoy them. Be a doctor. And the necklace is because Dr. Paul loves my brisket."

One night, my parents and sister were down the shore at Belmar. The house was all mine. Wendy was coming over. I got high too fast and my heart started to pound through my chest. Terrified, I closed my eyes to pray and recollect to the best of my powers, when suddenly I was levitating in my bed, at least a foot in the air. I yelled, "Please stop. Help me!" The world went dark.

An hour later, Wendy was lying in bed next to me. Of course, nothing happened, except a few hugs and kisses. Her breasts, anatomically small, kept escaping me.

In July, the Paul family rented a RV and went to explore America. Wendy and I talked once a week, postcards filling in the gaps. The promise made on their return, besides showing me all their Kodak memories, was to get me a membership at their swim club. Imagine, Cameron Simmons with a swim club membership. I was moving on up.

One Sunday, temperature hovering around 90 degrees, Wendy and I went to the swim club with her cousin Arlene. I offered to get us hamburgers and wait in the long line at the grilling station. Just as I arrived back at the table, a girl was just about to say goodbye after talking to Wendy.

"Cameron, this is Valerie Scott," Wendy introduced us. "We went to Columbia High School together."

We shook hands and made some small talk, and she eventually disappeared. But something internally persisted—her blonde hair, smile, elemental sexual attraction . . . something. In that moment, I'd been clueless about what Valerie would come to mean to me. Our story would pick up much later.

Meanwhile, the Wendy story plot continued to thicken. Mother Paul was making her special brisket dinner for me. A few hours before, she called. "Cameron, dear, please do Dr. Paul and me a favor and bring your college transcripts with you. We'd like to look at them."

"Huh? My transcripts? I don't understand."

"We'll explain. You'll like where we're going. See you at seven."

The brisket was stringy and tasteless. I thought Dr. Paul was a certifiable schmuck for spending $50,000 on it. Fortunately, I was mature enough to avoid inundating meat with wrist-shakes of ketchup. After dinner, Mother Paul asked me to join her and the doctor in the library. She dismissed Wendy and the kids to the den. Her subterfuge annoyed me.

"Cameron, I think you must know Wendy can only marry a doctor," she said softly. "This lifestyle is what she's used to. A pharmacist is not acceptable to our family, so Dr. Paul and I will check out your transcripts and see what has to be done to get you into medical school. Fortunately, pharmacy courses are transferrable."

"I appreciate your effort," I said, "but I just want to be a pharmacist. It's in my genes. It's my destiny."

Her face contorted in discomfort. "We'll decide what's best."

Dr. and Mrs. Paul went on to rip my academics apart. They yelled whenever they saw Cs and Ds. Wendy and her siblings walked in during their parents' severe fit after they saw my German failure; they left crying.

"We'll continue this again soon. In the meantime, Dr. Paul will make some inquiries," Mrs. Paul said.

And that's how it all went down. Traumatized, insecure, but resolute in my own career choice, the winds of war were now blowing around me and over the luxurious hills of South Orange. Something had to give.

As summer wound down, autumn started its olfactory resonance in the late-night air, heralding exams, Halloween, and the holidays. Wendy was leaving for Buffalo to begin an externship in a large accounting office via her father's lengthy tentacles. In a kinder way, her parents continued their campaign to change my career. Two nights before Wendy departed, we drove to an everlastingly deserted spot in Livingston, where one day they'd build a mall. An obscure road led nowhere, with tall trees, a grassy knoll, and a lineup of boulders.

Holding hands, sprawled out on a smooth boulder, we stared at stars and verbalized our shared dreams. I think this was real love. Of course, I loved the opulence all around this girl—that's what bothered me. I knew all about my inexperience in love and my parents' struggles with money. Was it messing with my sensibilities? Somewhere in the endless pathways between my two ears, bouncing around like a pinball machine, were my mother's words, "It's just as easy to fall in love with a rich girl as a poor girl."

Kissing on a boulder was fun. We both liked raw nature. Wendy, apparently hotter now, said, "Cam, let's go into the car."

This was a revolutionary moment, and the beginning of the rest of my life. We kissed intensely. We stopped to suck air. I removed her blouse and beseeched a higher authority to help with the bra. I was about to become relevant, to experience naked breasts for the first time at twenty-three. For a second, shimmering in the moonlight, I touched one of her small, naked breasts.

As if life was a comedic script, a car approached quickly, its bright lights instilling us with fear. It was the local police.

While they checked my license, we dropped Wendy's father's name and explained it was our last night before college. They laughed and gave us 30 minutes to finish talking but said to keep her blouse on.

Once the cops drove away, I laughed at how fortunate the night was in that they had never asked me to get out of the car. "It would've been embarrassing," I admitted. "I've never been like this before. You did it to me."

"We have to do something about that," Wendy said, recognizing the need to elevate our relationship and become real adults.

We hammered out a pact. The last week in August, I'd sneak up to Buffalo. We'd both do it for the first time. None of our parents would know anything. This would strictly be a weekend in a motel in Niagara Falls. The best-kept secret in the world.

Anticipation of a perfect weekend energized me. When the last week of August arrived, I told Amelia and Jack I was heading down to Villanova, Pennsylvania, for the weekend to hang out with friends. An hour before my getaway, Mother Paul called.

"Cameron, I understand you're leaving soon to see Wendy in Buffalo. She told me it's getting cold at night, so please stop by the house before you go and pick up a few sweaters," she said. "Oh, and I instructed Wendy to get you a room in a bed-and-breakfast. We'll pay. There will be no motel."

This was devastating, a knife through my heart. What is sacred in this world? Once again, my issues with loyalty had flared up—Wendy had destroyed my dreams and my trust in her. Ten hours of driving for a bed-and-breakfast. I asked Wendy why she'd told her mother.

"She sensed it in my voice. I was so excited to see you. So, I told her everything," she explained. "But I have a plan. Tonight, you sleep in the bed-and-breakfast. My parents paid. Tomorrow, we go to a motel."

Niagara Falls was a great precursor to getting laid. Romanticism was as pervasive as the mist all around. Hot and moist, filled with years of inexperienced desire, we kissed for an hour in bed. Rainbow colors corralled my groin, blue and purple. At the exact moment of my readying to climb on top, Wendy jumped out of bed and ran into the bathroom and disappeared for twenty minutes—an eternity. Suddenly, she shrieked from beyond the door.

"Cam, I got my period. Do you know how to use a Tampax?"

I was totally clueless. "What about your mother?" I suggested.

Ten minutes later, she came out wearing six pairs of underpants. She offered to help me cum, but I told her no. Imagine, a doctor's daughter doing these things. Besides, I was flat-out flaccid, well beyond thoughts about sexual ascension or help from her. Aiding and abetting my weakened penile condition were thoughts of failing at Tampax insertion. With our backs to one another for most of the night and with no reason to make out, we slept well. The loss of trust can suck out the last molecule of oxygen from a burgeoning relationship.

Morning finally came. I dropped her off with an obligatory kiss and a promise to call when I got home safe. That would never happen.

I wanted to be in my car heading to Jersey. Somewhere around Albany, I heard the Beatles' "Hey Jude" for the first time on the radio, and suddenly I knew the world was all good.

When I got back to safe, secure Maplewood, it was time to get high and write an appropriate, expressive "Dear Wendy" letter I titled "Goodbye, South Orange." I let Amelia read it, with one request: "No comments, please."

"Goodbye, South Orange," 8/25/68

It seems I could only look back on past yet recent memories. How ecstatic and carefree I feel now. It's strange, but now I see little children laughing and dancing gaily around a Maypole, but so slowly they danced, as if in slow motion. The sun was so very bright that I had to squint. Oh, but they are gone now.

Then I saw a great vast body of water—an ocean with its towering waves thrashing the sandy, desolate beaches. The water was such a clear, dark blue—its perfect union with the sky at the distant horizon was only upset when little ships sailed on by. But suddenly the sun vanished behind a great surge of dark gray, ominous clouds; a storm came, but then it passed.

Finally, I saw a little girl with bright green eyes. She was running, dancing, and singing. She was so happy. Far away from the little girl, I also saw a little boy with searching brown eyes. He was running, jumping, climbing, and he was so happy too. Then the two children were ushered home, where they ate a nourishing and carefully planned meal. They had such a good time again after being dismissed from lunch. Later they prepared for sleep and dreamt of promising, pleasant things.

The children are running now and time is running so fast, as if to overtake them. One day they bumped into one another while they were still running. The boy picked the girl up, looked deeply, apprehensively, then affectionately into the pools of her green eyes, and held her hand tightly for only a brief moment. She ran off again, and so did he. This time they were running away from one another, on a straight, rigid, freshly paved road. Their backs were turned and they didn't see each other crying. As long as the road remains straight, they won't hurt each other again, for they can't bump into one another.

Maybe they will stop crying. Maybe they will get tired of running.

Oh, but it is foggy now. It might snow, or did they buy popcorn or a box of candy? They will both be late for lunch; that would be terrible.

Cameron

Chapter 7

GREAT SCOTT

A week slipped by after the motel room with Wendy and the ill-fated Tampax adventure. Surprisingly, I was well on the way to moving on with life and Rutgers pharmacy school.

My cousin Mark suggested getting right back in the saddle. Did I need any help? he asked.

In my back pocket was a little brown book, frayed, flattened, but filled with girls' numbers and a system of code for their corresponding appearance ratings. The code wasn't sophisticated, just an arrow up, down, or horizontal. The night after I met Valerie Scott at the swim club, I found her Maplewood number—something made me look for her. She landed an arrow up in my book.

It takes solid energy vibes before launching into something new or making a first phone call. Just outside Crast Pharmacy: a phone booth, folding doors, and Superman dreams. Arthur Ashe had just become the first Black person to win the US Open, so I was in a hopeful mood.

I thought about Valerie and dialed her number. "Hi, Valerie. I'm Cameron Simmons. We met at the swim club. Wendy Paul introduced us. Well, we just broke up and you're on my mind."

It was the best line I had, but it worked. We set a date for the next Friday at a New York City movie. It was déjà vu, to an extent: another doctor's daughter who lived in a comfortable suburban home (this time in Maplewood). Valerie was studying occupational therapy at Seton Hall University. Her brother was at Harvard, and her father, Dr. Alan Scott, had earned a dental degree after the war from Michigan— indications of a good gene pool. Her parents weren't around when I picked her up, so I didn't have to embellish my father's shoe-selling career.

First dates and movies should be cerebral events, spurring conversation with determinations of intellect. At an East Side theater, we saw *The Heart Is a Lonely Hunter*, a penetratingly sad character study. Halfway through, I said, "Shoot, didn't mean this to be so down on a first date."

Valerie squeezed my hand, whispering, "I like it—don't worry. I also like you."

Early on, we discovered our shared dislike of racism and concern for feminism. We discussed our support for Tommie Smith and John Carlos, who'd just done the Black Power salute at the 1968 Mexico City Olympics. On my feminist side, I told Valerie some of my life's heroes were women. Valerie was into my thoughts, capturing my every word. It was a dream that this girl and I felt the same way about important parts of life.

Back in Jersey, we went to Gary's in Maplewood. Relationship acceleration was my forte. Before we finished the fries, I had my arm around her, which morphed into us kissing in a crowded restaurant. Later that night, my cousin Mark's wife, Linda, got a phone call from her good friend apologetically telling her she saw Mark kissing a much younger blonde girl at Gary's. In the scheme of shared genetic material, Mark and I were more like twins than cousins; similar height, weight, haircut, and general gyrations. We moved our bodies the same way. Linda and Mark just laughed; he'd never left the apartment.

Valerie and I were in bonding mode. I met her parents; quiet people. Every time I was there, they disappeared upstairs and left the den for us. Of course, I was still virginal, but the intense chemistry between us suggested inevitability.

With Valerie, a semantical quandary existed—should I call it love-making or getting laid? Whatever it was, Mark signed up to help. After a month, he gave me keys to a vacant apartment in his building owned by Aunt Evelyn. His instruction was to avail myself an abandoned mattress. Valerie was aboard.

After an hour on the mattress, we were topless, grinding away at each other. I almost said I loved her, but that's like a nuclear discharge, with no going back. It's hard not to say the "love" word when most of your clothes are scattered. Ascension was so close.

Suddenly, the apartment door opened. We scrambled. A comedy script again: Aunt Evelyn had come by to drop off a vacuum cleaner for the morning. I expressed laments while Evelyn escorted us out. A right time would come when it was all meant to be—sex, and finally telling Valerie I was in love.

Meanwhile, panic consumed me on the Rutgers front; my grades were in a free fall, precariously close to getting me thrown out of school after five years. I was supposed to be graduating in June. Amphetamines fueled my studying all-nighters, but I was scared of side effects, like forgetting everything I'd studied an hour after the test. Naturally, I progressed to experimenting with strong sleeping pills after being high. It was a vicious circle of despair and reliance.

One of my favorite holidays was coming: Halloween. Dressing

up in costume was not my thing; knocking on doors and threatening neighbors for failure to produce excessive chocolate—*that* was my thing. Most folks knew I came in peace.

This Halloween would be important. I'd finally return favors to Julian, fixing him up with Valerie's best friend, Alice Yaney. I don't mind jumping the gun and letting you know: seven months later, Alice and Julian were married. I did good.

Alice and Julian's chemistry was an instant heat reaction. After indulging in burgers yet another time, our foursome went back to Valerie's house for the night to watch *The Tonight Show Starring Johnny Carson*. Her parents had escaped Jersey Halloween machinations for a weekend in Las Vegas. To discourage trick-or-treaters, we kept all the lights off. When Johnny Carson brought out his first guest, Monique Wilson, we looked at each other blankly—who the hell was she?

When Julian and Alice went to bed, his wink found me. Six hours of knowing each other, and they were sleeping together. Valerie and I shared what little space there was on her single bed. It was also her time of the month. We kissed intensely but unsatisfactorily; my poor, tired, colorful groin.

Our first episode of discontent came when she got up for a cigarette at four in the morning. Each time her lighter cast a flame, it hurt me to see her body cells die, taking eventual time away from us. This night I confronted her. Her promise to cut down didn't assuage me. I was resolute.

Morning brought a strange feeling of domesticity. We got up together, brushed our teeth, and yelled down the hall for Alice and Julian to come to breakfast. Valerie made eggs while I stood behind, massaging her neck and shoulders, wanting to say I loved her. It just wasn't the right time. Portable radio news accentuated bad timing— President Johnson was announcing a halt to all US bombing of North Vietnam, hoping for fruitful peace negotiations.

I waved my hands in the air. "Can this be true—peace talks? An end to this living hell of a war?"

Imagine being on a frontline, rice paddies all around, with orders to kill a human being. The war consumed my daily life, knowing one day I'd have to deal with who I am, what I believe is right, and perhaps meet my final destiny too soon.

Julian nudged me again to join the National Guard with him. I didn't respond.

DECEMBER DREAMLAND

One morning in early December 1968, I stood in the upstairs bathroom of my parents' house. My sister Carol was at school. Amelia was at an insurance agency in Millburn, where she worked as a bookkeeper. Big Jack was working on Route 22, still selling shoes.

I stared into the mirror for a long time. "Mirror, mirror on the wall, you see a tall, skinny Rutgers senior, flexing his bicep, smiling that he's in love and will probably graduate in June."

Not waiting for a response, I went to the living room window to reflect. There was never anybody outside, walking an invisible dog or pushing a baby carriage. No babies were born on this side of Maplewood. No bus carrying the Graduate, Benjamin Braddock and Elaine Robinson, ever passed my street. Where was everybody? Sometimes I thought my whole generation was sucked into the war—fighting, dying, maimed, dodging, hiding, praying, or burning draft cards. Richard Nixon had beat Hubert Humphrey—a pharmacist, of all things—and made Henry Kissinger his security advisor. We needed advice; the death toll was approaching 30,000 and our troop level was at 550,000. I was so consumed with war and peace. I was a pacifist, despite what Julian thought, just because I elbowed a kid's head on a basketball court.

When Valerie and I weren't talking about school or Vietnam, we were scheming up ways to spend a weekend together. We'd have to sneak away so our parents were confident we were not shacking up. It was such a repressive world in 1968. Julian, a great resource, like a forerunner of

Airbnb, came up with keys to his uncle's Jersey Shore summer home in Allenhurst. Julian had told his uncle he needed a quiet place to study for finals. The house on Allen Street, an eight-bedroom Victorian with a picturesque porch, was a block from the ocean. It would be perfect for a few days.

Julian's last words, as he surreptitiously handed me the keys and a Fourex rubber, were, "Cam, you've got two days, almost alone in a town that has less than fifty winter residents, to come back to me a complete man. Don't let me and yourself down."

On a bitterly cold and windy Friday night, I told Amelia I was off to Villanova, Pennsylvania, my fictional place of weekend college escapes. If Amelia ever asked who I went to see, I'd stutter through outright lies. No one existed for me there; Villanova just sounded impressive. Instead, I met Valerie at her friend's house in Old Bridge. She'd concocted a similar story for her parents.

Then we were off to Allenhurst for our special weekend. It was like a honeymoon of sorts—except that Julian had told us to bring our own sheets.

Our kiss in the car before putting it into drive was historic—filled with more passion, tongue, and excitement than I'd ever felt. On an obscure street in Asbury Park, near the boardwalk, the Yellow Pages guided us to a small Italian restaurant that served the best veal down the Shore. I never ate veal; it's white but is supposed to be red—the bleaching side effects of tetracycline antibiotics.

At the restaurant, we shared wine and entangled our feet under the table. It was our most romantic dinner because we knew how it would end. A late start had us closing the restaurant near 11:00 p.m. In that certain feeling, despite the cold, we walked the boardwalk, briefly stopping by Convention Hall. Julian had told me about a secret music spot on the third floor of a building downtown called the Upstage Club, which could be the final impressive moment of the night.

Julian's words bounced around in my head: "An hour there with some of the best live music anywhere, and Valerie will be all yours for the taking."

Two floors above a shoe store, the Upstage Club's ambiance was mildly psychedelic. The walls of its steep stairs were all painted brightly. The club didn't serve alcohol, so the musicians basically jammed all night. For an hour, Valerie and I held hands, shared an occasional kiss, and explored each other's eyes over a cup of tea and amazing rock music. The band was Steel Mill, fronted by a long-haired Bruce Springsteen.

We got back to Julian's uncle's house on Allen Street near 1:00 a.m. Before getting out of the car, we stared at the bifurcated white house—somehow this Victorian appealed to our impending ascension to adulthood.

Next was a scene from a movie. I suggested *Gone with the Wind* as we walked down the second-floor hallway, filled with multiple bedrooms for all the O'Hara children.

"Where do we go, Cam?" Valerie asked.

"Let's take the smallest room, far away from the master bedroom."

I wish the rooms had been numbered so I could fixate on this night's magical number. We attended to the housekeeping, then hugged briefly. We were silent as we turned our backs to each other to undress, shy at our first time being partially nude together. We went under the covers in just our underwear. What followed was unsophisticated foreplay, my hands mostly around her, meaning to be gentle with her breasts. Then we were naked and I was on top, hoping for easy access.

Just at that moment, she asked, "Cam, what about a rubber?"

I reached for Julian's gift. My hands were nervously shaky and sweaty. There would be no way to open it in a timely fashion—but Valerie was so smart. For a brief moment, it seemed she knew too much, but she rescued our moment. "Don't worry about it. Come back to me," she said.

We were good for each other; she knew me well and hand-guided

me inside. It was everything I'd hoped for over the last years of unfulfilled dreams. Timing was perfect, mature, and romantic.

Finally, I told Valerie how much I loved her, gasped to God, and
then began a lifetime of rolling off and saying, "Wow." She agreed. A
few hours later, round two, then three . . .

Everything about the night was worth the wait. When I got up
for the bathroom, sitting at the bed edge, I realized I just gotten
laid for the first time. Gazing at Valerie sleeping, I also knew I'd just
made love to the girl I was going to marry. Cameron Simmons now
had to figure out how to ask the question. Appropriately, I visualized
Scarlett O'Hara saying, "After all, tomorrow is another day."

Chapter 8

GROWING INTO ME

Christmas is a time full of special memories: *A Christmas Carol* with Alastair Sim, midnight mass, hiding a Christmas tree in the basement when I was nine—and now, getting engaged. The formal process began with dinner in Bergen County at a restaurant on the top floor of a hotel, with whiskey sours and prime rib. Valerie had no idea what was going down, just that I needed some private time with her. Back at her house, her parents slept while we were alone in the den. After a quick session of love-making—which meant staining her den sofa, despite most of our clothes staying on—I had something to get off my mind.

I took her hand and asked if she'd like to take a journey with me, a long walk, always together, always in love.

"What do you mean, Cameron? A long walk where?" she asked.

"Everywhere. Nowhere. Somewhere. As long as we're together."

"What are you asking me?" she pressed.

Surprisingly, the real words were hard to get out. I was being obtuse for a reason. Just in case she'd turn me down, I'd turn around and say, "I really just wanted to walk." I always had to maintain my ego.

"Valerie, will you marry me?"

She kissed me, and we were officially engaged. All the mechanics of planning a wedding were set in motion.

In January 1969, Julian, Butch, Arvin, and I were studying for finals in the Newark Rutgers Law Library (incidentally, Ruth Bader Ginsburg was teaching at the law school at the time), one of the quietest places in Essex County. I shared my good news with the gang.

"When do you take the plunge, Cam?" Julian came over and hugged me. Our first hug of friendship since the beginning. Arvin and Butch started laughing as if I'd done the impossible dream. Always hard to shake stereotypes.

"November, the night before Thanksgiving. Our parents met over her mother's meatloaf dinner to discuss details."

Later, in a small law school conference room, Julian and I talked marriage, war, and our futures. "Are you having trouble concentrating?" he asked, offering me a blue pill. "Come fly with me."

"What is it?"

"Ritalin, ten milligrams—a kinder, gentler high. It'll make you concentrate and climb walls only halfway." I took the pill, keen to try this new source of getting high.

Next, Julian confided that Alice was late and that they were worried, and certainly not ready for a shotgun wedding. My mind raced with horrific scenarios of pregnancy, societal challenges, financial entrapments—the general fucking-up of lives. Since the first time Valerie and I had sex, I'd been lazy, never using protection. Worry consumed me for weeks, until Valerie confirmed she was safe. In turn, I became a forced supporter of prophylactics and inner peace.

A month later, Alice was officially pregnant. Julian, with all his connections (underworld and above), found a third-year medical student who'd do an illegal abortion. Confidence was high they were making the right decision. Two days after, Alice went into septic shock—she was feverish, hallucinating, and approaching death. She couldn't go to a hospital and mention her illegal abortion, so Julian took her to a friend's apartment, where another doctor friend administered the necessities. We all prayed. A week later, Alice slowly came back to us.

During Alice's episode, I had a subtle revelation in my relationship with Valerie. We began to disagree. I'd say black and she said gray. I'd say Claremont Diner for supper, she wanted Gary's. Valerie came from a house where her father, Dr. Scott, dominated everything. A man ruled her world. Just the opposite for me; Amelia ruled mine.

Our relationship was the first meaningful, substantive one each of us had ever had. Our experience was nonexistent, so we became two contumacious souls in the night, rigid and unforgiving. It was all there, exposed, shining brightly, a preamble to our relationship constitution, and it escalated over time; it would never go away. We didn't know why this was happening. Our love-making was good—and we were confident it *was* love. But soon arose a conflict that would pull our young souls apart.

Two weeks after Alice was back to the living world, Valerie came over my house. Sitting on my bed, the mood turned somber. She got up and paced back and forth; something was wrong.

"Cam, I'm late. No period. I'm never late."

I marvel at how fast the human body releases the chemicals that cause fear and panic. It was devastating. Almost humorously, my immediate thought was about telling Amelia; I feared her reaction. Jack would probably be proud of me for finally knocking up a girl and ridding myself of the tortoise—the one *he'd* brought to life.

"What do we do? Actually, we'll get married sooner. Shit, so many problems. Are you sure?" I said, my head spinning.

"I'm not sure. I'm just late."

Two weeks later—the worst two weeks of my life—she was still late. One morning, over Raisin Bran and an imagined stimulant, a bright bulb illuminated to save the day. There in my pharmacology textbook, underlined and highlighted in yellow, was a section on pregnancy tests. Cousin Mark gave me a package of four pills for Valerie. If she wasn't pregnant, her period would come. And my life was restored in two days. I thanked God for getting my life back.

Pharmacology continued swirling around my sensibilities. One of my classes was discussing metastasis, lung cancer, and the perils of smoking. A gory film showed a smoker's lung black with cancer and imminent death. I thought about the woman I was going to marry who still smoked, her every inhalation killing a few more cells—sickening.

A few hours after that horrific film, Valerie and I were finishing making love in her bed. I dressed. She watched with her hands folded behind her head, comfortable and satisfied.

I told her about the film we'd watched in class. There I was, like Abe Lincoln, delivering my Maplewood nicotine address. "I can't live anymore with you smoking," I said. "So painful, watching you a die a little. We may've just made love for the last time. I'm prepared to walk out now and never see you again. Either you give me your cigarettes now and go cold turkey forever, or one last kiss goodbye. I mean it."

A carton of Marlboros walked out of the bedroom with me; our union preserved—for now. Years later, after our divorce, I bumped into Valerie at a South Orange street fair. She was smoking again, a perfect, enduring, "Fuck you, Cameron."

POST-VALENTINE SECONDS IN A LIFE

In fifth grade at Maple Avenue School, exchanging Valentine's Day cards was an insipid bourgeoisie rite of passage. Pretty and popular kids walked off into the winter sunset with a preponderance of cards. I got a few and then the pipeline shut down for years—until Valerie hallmarked me with a beautiful love-filled card.

Back at her house for the night, her parents in Florida, we made love like the best of times. Afterward, heralding variety, with Julian's constant coaching, I brought up oral sex.

Valerie dismissed the idea. "Not now," she said. "It's a very ugly part of the body."

I dropped the subject cold, blaming the tortoise.

The almost humorous aspect of my oral proposal was my complete cluelessness about it. My closest visualization to oral sex came not from porn films, but from a pharmacy fraternity stag party the year before. Two women had been hired to perform. One of my Eastern European fraternity brothers, who didn't know any better—or did he?—jumped onstage and orally submerged himself. He sent shockwaves reverberating through the staid conservative world of pharmacists in training. Our fraternity was kicked off campus for the rest of the year and a permanent image was implanted in my malleable mind.

At the end of February, Valerie and I drove down to my reopened pharmacy fraternity house, which was nothing more than a refurbished storefront across the street from a high school. Our brother numbers had dwindled since the stag party and I knew no one would be around. A pool table, small empty refrigerator, and a few posters (not of the Caribbean or New York Knicks, but of Selsun dandruff shampoo) completed the ambiance. I wanted Valerie. She wanted me too. We were in a good place that day, which made being inside each other a special event. But the place was eerie. Ten seconds in, I stopped, overcome with that *something* feeling.

"Let's go," I said. "I can't finish this. Something is telling me to leave."

Just a few seconds in a life. A few minutes later, the frat house and next-door cleaners were firebombed at virtually the same time that men and women from the Black Organization of Students took over Conklin Hall at Rutgers University in Newark. They were protesting the scarcity of Black students, Black faculty, and minority-based academic programs on campus.

The rumor was that a local gang prank had reduced our frat house.

I love saying that Rutgers University is one of the most diverse public universities in America today, its student body 52 percent minorities. A joy how times change. As Bob Dylan sings, "Yes, how many times must a man look up before he can see the sky?"

SPRINGTIME FOR CAMERON IN MAPLEWOOD

All roads were leading to my successful graduation in June. Acing first-semester pharmacology (I loved my drug studies) helped me to get the hell out. Pharmacology was life-changing. When we studied aging—a few paragraphs on supplements. From those paragraphs onward, I began daily ingestion of up to sixty a day. I'll swear it made a difference. Here I am a septuagenarian, and writing coherently.

Six years had been enough education, but I would've matriculated three more years if it meant safely staying in New Jersey and not facing induction into the army.

Graduation was held at the football stadium in New Brunswick. Jack, Amelia, Carol, and Valerie accompanied me. In the midst of the processional, Julian and I stopped for a moment during "Pomp and Circumstance" and hugged.

"We look like jerk-offs in this cap and gown. If I had the balls, I'd be wearing nothing underneath," he laughed. "Hey, we made it. All-night studying, cheating, and fun. Friends forever."

During the ceremony, as we listened to the valedictorian talk about war, racism, and nuclear proliferation, I stared up at a cumulous cloud in the sky. I got a warm feeling, wondering what it would be like to be here with a child of my own. Little did I know that in just twenty-seven years, I'd be back.

A few days after graduation, Julian and I met for coleslaw, potato salad, and corned beef at a South Orange deli. Julian was in a pharmacy internship just down the road, hating every moment of it and looking for any opportunity to escape.

"Cameron, you've got mustard on your shirt, lip, and probably crotch," he laughed to ease into a change of topic. "I'm signing up for the National Guard next week. Six weeks of summer camp soon. Seriously, come with me. No more obsessing about the draft. Sure, it's a commitment. But it's better than jungles and guns and death."

Julian was one of the great orators, salesmen, and motivators in my life. Through twists, turns, and detours, I'd always think back to him, pondering what he'd do in a particular situation. I still needed him. Inside my soul, I was pulled in opposing directions, searching for anything, something. A few days prior, Nixon had met with South Vietnam president Nguyễn Văn Thiệu to drastically reduce our troop levels.

"I have to believe Nixon is doing the right thing," I told Julian. "Cutting troop levels means less draftees. I'm hanging on here. Maybe the war ends before we're done interning. I can't commit to the Guard, and maybe not even to Valerie. Relationships suck. Why'd you ever give me the keys to your uncle's summer house?"

INTERNSHIP

A few weeks after graduation, I began an internship, internment, or whatever defined the next year of my life, at Ring Drugs in Millburn. I never understood why Julian didn't grab this opportunity to work for his relatives around opulence, upper-middle-class, and wealthy Short Hills. Julian nudged his uncle Don Ring for a month to get me the internship there. A pure friend. An internship was an integral part of my total pharmacy education—a year to learn the practical aspects of dispensing, compounding, and merchandising.

Don Ring was my official preceptor—an old-school pharmacist and Rutgers grad who knew my uncle Harry Crast. Don was a brilliant master at human deception. His philosophy was to lowball prices because people loved the illusion of accommodation discounts. When he first opened the pharmacy, he started numbering prescriptions filled at 200,001 to subliminally suggest he was already busy and successful. People loved to be around success. "They're like moths to a lightbulb," he often said smugly.

Don was consistent; not only did he discount drugs, but he also paid my internship salary at $150 per week for fifty hours. So be it. After a few weeks, satisfied I knew what I was doing, Don made me a make-believe pharmacist. He gave me too much responsibility, filling prescriptions with little oversight. The upside was that if I made a customer's urine turn blue, it would permanently hyper-state me into being obsessively diligent and careful. I was determined to be a damn good pharmacist . . . who still loved to get high from the meds on the shelves.

Don never gave me any feedback, not even a smile or compliment. It didn't take long for my respect to turn into contempt. But the customers kept me hanging on. I loved the lady, a majority stockholder in a big company, who fixated on laxatives and toilet paper, and sent a car service down every few days for her evacuating order. Or the owner of a local deli who suffered interminably with a nail fungus, with origins ostensibly in the pickle barrel.

Introspectively, I was bothered and disenchanted with this scene. I didn't like being stuck in the back, counting pills in my hand, typing, pouring, and answering the phone a hundred times a day. Don was so cheap; he used the back of blank bank deposit slips to take phone orders. Deep inside, there was *something* battling in me, trying to get out, to be free, to feel worthwhile. Pharmacy stuff was unfulfilling, so I began resorting to amphetamines more during the day, which meant sleeping pills at night to get me down. I'd like to say it wasn't a real addiction, but rather an affliction that wouldn't be solved until I was long gone from the smell of an apothecary and the roar of Don Ring. There was a creative side to me, repressed and buried and trying to get out—and it would bring me to the edges of earthly existence and finally spiritual revelation until finally free.

The next logical step in my pharmacy career, though, was the state board exam. After interning for a year, I would be done, thrown out, useless, until I took the state board exams to get my permanent license to make more money and be alone in the back with all those magical medicines. That bastard of an exam encompassed everything I'd learned, forgotten, or didn't give a shit about, like making soft, slimy suppositories destined for anal absorption. Not once had I ever been called upon to make one. I'm not sure I could've ever kept a straight face dispensing a suppository. "Oh, yes, sir, have a nice day. Don't forget to remove the tin foil before you insert it into that prodigious asshole."

Four state boards were notoriously difficult: Florida, New Jersey, New York, and California—virtually all blue states. There was no reciprocity, which meant I had to retake the exam if I was heading to those states. Two practicalities would occupy my consciousness for the next year: the draft, and studying for the boards. Valerie floated somewhere in between like a particle of dust, making my allergic eyes tear.

On and off for the first few months at Ring Drugs, I tried to study for my boards. Every question I'd ask Don, he'd say, "Not now, Cameron. Go clean the backroom shelves." I cleaned those freaking shelves weekly. The wood stayed dank and odorous until the next week. I hate that smell—after that internship, I'd never clean wood again.

Halfway into 1970, some boards of pharmacy announced an experiment with a national board exam. Everyone would take the same test, opening the doors to freely reciprocating your license to any state. This was revolutionary. Some might say professional boards were made up of a gaggle of old, tired, seersucker-wearing administrators.

There was no way this over-the-hill gang, only a few months before the boards, would start making up a whole new exam. I concluded that somewhere out there in the vastness of America, one state had a review book that would be used verbatim for the test. I bet everything on this premise. Instead of studying, I wrote away requesting a pharmacy board review book from every state that had one. As they arrived, I studied each one. From a Midwestern state, with its endless cornfields bordered by straight, narrow highways, a review book arrived—this had to be the one. I memorized its questions and answers.

The best orgasm of my life up to now was taking the Board of Pharmacy exam and knowing most of the answers. Still, in keeping with my low profile, I was the last to leave the exam.

ONE GIANT STEP

Our wedding now a few months away, Valerie and I scored an affordable duplex three blocks away from both sets of parents in Maplewood. We were in the same complex as Julian and Alice. The rules of engagement were to begin furnishing, but we couldn't live together until we married on November 26. The bed came first, so at least we could stop ruining the sofa in Valerie's den and steal away to our place for sex. Next, a television in the bedroom. In a giant step, I'd finally convinced Valerie it was time to explore our bodies with a variety of sex. Unwrapping a picture guide book, we went under the covers to hide from ourselves.

Another harbinger of disturbing relationship things to come was Woodstock Music and Art Fair. I was still basically uncool, tortoise persistent, but I decided to go with several frat brothers to experience it all. Valerie forbade me to go. Buried deep within her was a controlling personality. I was clay being innocently molded. Our battles a week prior led to us going days without talking. When the guys honked to pick me up for the music festival, Valerie and I were barely civil to each other. Once again, seconds in a life. I had my hand on the rear door handle when Valerie ran out with a stark warning. If I went, she'd be gone forever. Shades of her giving up cigarettes, a sweet revenge. To this day, I regret not going to Woodstock.

Six days before our wedding, Nixon signed the amendment for the Military Selective Service Act of 1967. On our honeymoon, they drew my number, 115, guaranteeing my chance to see Southeast Asia.

On the beach in Puerto Rico, we fought about everything—dinner, what tours to take—so I walked away. I didn't see her for two days. A fucking baby I was. She was too.

Chapter 9

HELL NO

Hell no, I won't go to Vietnam—a battle cry for my generation.

Why was I opposed? I never contemplated growing a beard, crossing the Delaware River, getting a farm in Amish country, and reading the Bible every day. But, soulfully, I was a pacifist. The British could have never won the Revolutionary War; they were too far from home—as were we in Vietnam. I sensed we were still there to save face and not be humiliated by losing a war. When the Pentagon Papers revealed Secretary of Defense Robert McNamara knew we couldn't win, that was confirmed. Once the Vietnam War ended, I knew American companies (hamburgers and soda) would rush to do business there, forgetting the precious lives lost.

Whereas the Vietnam War became about saving face, World War II was about saving humanity. For World War II, I would have enlisted on December 8, 1941. I would've driven an ambulance, parachuted into France, or run a saloon in Casablanca in order to smuggle out members of the resistance, like Victor Laszlo.

The year 1970 would be my time to look in the mirror and see if I knew who the reflection was. Valerie and I began a new life together, full of marital bliss and conflict. We settled into married life, bought several months of prophylactics, did laundry together at her mother's every Saturday, and explored recipe variations for tuna noodle casserole. And we talked about my deferment ending in May, after my internship—no more safety net. Life as we knew it would change. Paranoid, selfish, and delusional thoughts were all there.

A curious thing happened one night after we made love in the missionary position. For an hour, Valerie and I talked in bed. To her credit, she said she'd support whatever I decided to do about enlisting in the war. I choked up. I had no clue about anything, but all I could say was, "I love you."

One night, the news reported that Donald Sloat was killed in action by using his body to cover a hand grenade, saving three fellow soldiers. I walked outside into the snow flurries, looked up at a dark, starless sky, and asked why. Then I knew how to begin my journey.

The next day, I called Dr. Smith, Amelia's family physician of twenty years. During my checkup, I marveled at Dr. Smith's knowledge, swagger, and warmth. I was still searching for career choices, so I decided to become a general practitioner just like him, right down to his heavy wheezing. I wanted it all for three weeks—until I realized the journey there would include gross anatomy studies. At a Rutgers bio lab a few years back, we'd experimented with electrical stimulation and contraction on a frog's leg muscle. It began with pithing the frog: a needle through its brain. No way could I ever do that. In the lunchroom, I found Lou, the same fraternity pledge who'd helped me spy on Bonnie, and made him do the experiment for me. Soul searching, I knew I could never pith a frog or mess around with a cadaver in anatomy lab. That was the end of my medical career.

My checkup with Dr. Smith was meant to look for hidden maladies that might keep me out of Vietnam. Did I have flat feet, poor hearing, intestinal irregularities, failing eyesight, or a heart murmur? A good guy, Dr. Smith offered to write a letter about my heart and stomach problems, which existed if the writing was creative enough. He wrote that letter which I still have. I had a dozen manufactured ailments; heart down to feet.

My first year at Rutgers, I was sucked into a pharmacy fraternity mostly because of my basketball ability and six-foot-five height. I stood out in a white lab coat, which fell short to my knees. Our frat basketball team had players with hoop history, which translates to kicking the shit out of the other three frats in our makeshift pharmacy league. Our arch rival, Kappa, lost to us 79–12. No holding back, I scored 49 points in that game, dunking the ball often.

News travels fast to downtown Newark. The following October, in 1966, I received an interdepartmental communication from the Rutgers-Newark basketball coach, asking to meet. Too many long labs and an unyielding Amelia kept me chained to Bunsen burners and beakers; I had no time for basketball. But the coach arranged for me to play on a scrimmage team, occasionally working out with the varsity. Scrimmaging was fun and helped restore traces of my wavering sanity, amidst organic medicinals, physical pharmacy, and nonspecific bullshit in the school building.

The results of our scrimmage games were usually lost and buried, especially when us old-timers ran the varsity team into the urinals. After one phantom victory, a teammate and I talked about his great jump-shot accuracy and gray hair. "Are you prematurely gray or just way older than me?" I asked.

He had an almost uncontrollable, high-pitched, cartoonlike laugh. "Way older," he said. "I graduated Rutgers Law, now in private practice. Informally, I'm Andrew Vowel." We bonded with a firm handshake.

"Huh. Vowel—a real last name?"

"Let's leave it at that. By the way, for what it's worth, I see clients trying to avoid the draft."

I told him about my 2S deferment until 1970. "But the war could end by then," I said.

"No, it won't," he laughed with a sardonic smile that stuck for a week in my cerebral viewer. Synchronicity in the universe had brought Andrew Vowel to play on my scrimmage team. Counselor Vowel maintained a legal office in Upper Montclair, a hip, trendy, area. I met with Andrew there, fascinated that I had a lawyer now. We agreed that my route to proceed was conscientious objector status. I'm a pacifist; I pleaded my case. Andrew reminded me that this particular road was not easy and probably not winnable. Muhammad Ali was pleading the same thing—he eventually landed in the Supreme Court, though with better results.

The issue of money arrived. "Cameron, I know you're a struggling student intern, so I'm not charging you," Andrew said. "But I will ask something in return. You're on the road to being a licensed pharmacist. How about someday I ask you to do a service for me?" I agreed, always one to remember loyalties and good deeds. Somehow, his last name, Vowel, started to have meaning.

But soon after, Andrew called to withdraw from my case. There was nothing he could do. Three years later, when I was a registered pharmacist, Vowel called me to do a service: become the pharmacist-in-charge of a health center in an inner city. My father's brother, Ira, was an attorney in Plainfield, New Jersey. His specialty was paranoia and divorce—he advised me to avoid any dealings.

Without Andrew's legal counsel, anxiety consumed me. My existence here on Earth was up for grabs. I looked in a mirror, trying to see beyond my reflection to glimpse mortality. Was this a face of a future obituary? What would the *Star-Ledger* say about me? How many people would show up to my funeral? Where could I go now? I needed obscurity. Could I live in a small tent underneath the Turnpike bridge at the Holland Tunnel exit? No one would ever find me there.

From where the next impetus came from, I'm not sure. It wasn't spiritual. There isn't a spirit or presiding angel who would ever guide me into what I did next. In an unscientific and reckless way, I began the process of gaining one hundred pounds to become overweight: a health risk, and physical rejection for military service. My loose goal was to eclipse the 300-pound mark via a never-ending ingestion of crumb cake, seven-layer cake, ice cream, sub sandwiches, and french fries.

In the middle of all this madness was Valerie, always mystifyingly supportive. Valerie was five-foot-three, alluring, and skinny. Her paltry 100-pound frame would eventually have to support a 300-pound husband during sex, during which I was usually on top. A good woman, despite often being confrontational, she never complained.

When you set your mind to things, you accomplish. After looking in a mirror at my fat fucking face, where I'd attempted to sprout a moustache to divert attention, I weighed myself. I lamented the 311 pounds facing up at me.

The tortoise still had to be crawling around up there somewhere. By May, someone with authority informed me that being overweight was not a permanent exit out of military service. They'd give you six months to lose weight, and no matter what, you'd still be inducted. It had all been an embarrassing waste and a health affront; diabetes was rampant in my family. A schmuck I was. Back to the issues at hand: getting out and losing weight.

APRIL SHOWERS

The end of my long, winding educational career was in sight. The Beatles had just released "The Long and Winding Road." Soon my internship would end, I'd take the pharmacy boards, and become free as a butterfly.

September was setting up to be a powerful month. I knew I'd passed the boards because I had all the answers, but I was forced to wait until September to be notified I was now a registered pharmacist. It would also take until September for my local draft board to get wind that I was now available since my 2S deferment and internship ended. A greetings letter for a physical and induction was down the nearby road. Miracles were not an option in my life.

As a registered pharmacist, I could finally make a good living and support my wife, who was becoming even harder to live with. Valerie was a hoverer, endlessly all over me. Amelia was the same way, and the deep-layered conflict that was insidiously pulling me and Valerie apart was my difficulty distinguishing wife and mother. Months into our marriage, our frequency of sex was demonstrably less. Something was there, growing, rearing, pulling, distancing us away from each other. We were too young to grasp the dynamics at play, the subtle inevitability residing in our cute apartment.

One night in bed, while we watched the Academy Awards, I felt amorous, needy, wanting to hold her. Randomly, not knowing what the hell possessed me, I blurted out, "Should we be thinking about a baby?" I immediately apologized—I was smarter than that, but also curious how she'd react.

She stared at the ceiling then me. Not a word, frown or smile. It was almost scary. Finally, "Not yet, Cameron. Some day. Over the rainbow." I stared back with a faint smile, leaving the rainbow remark alone.

The award for Best Picture was next. *Midnight Cowboy* won, so I gloated, reminding Valerie how she had refused to see it with me. We didn't make love for days afterward. Gloating should never be mixed or stirred in bed.

A week after April 22, 1970—the first Earth Day—Nixon went on TV to announce he was sending American troops into Cambodia to win the just peace we desired. Right before he went on, Valerie had been on top of me, taking charge, her least favorite position—and my favorite, demonstrative of my political leanings, but also the weight thing. I was still a big boy, despite losing twenty pounds after peaking over three hundred.

Nixon wiped out all our good post-orgasmic feelings. "More lives are going to be lost to save stubborn face," I said, my voice cracking with tears. With my day of reckoning coming in September, I didn't know what to do.

"Cam, I'm always going to be here for you, no matter what you decide," Valerie said. Despite our inane stupidity, she had this sensitive side that made me want to just stay inside her, absorb her, and love her.

We talked about what had been on my mind and deep within, wherever my soul was. A hard rain was going to fall, landing explosively on Valerie.

"As I see it, I have two options," I told her. "It's also optional for you. I'd understand until the end of time, whatever you decide. First, I'm prepared to fulfill my obligation—"

"You'll go in the army?" she stopped me abruptly, hope distinct in her shaky voice. I think she really wanted that. It was easy; the least disruptive for all of us.

"No, I mean I'll go to prison and serve my time. It won't be fun, but it may be the right thing. Or I'll go to Canada, be a pharmacist, and eventually die of old age."

There: two drastic paths. We'd have a long, hot summer to develop these ideas into some form of practicality. We'd hope, pray, dream, and read about life in prison for the war resistor and about Canada's best places to live. I still have a pamphlet on life in prison for the war resistor. Valerie ended our bedtime talk by saying she'd wait, no matter how long prison was, or go to Canada with me. Then she ran downstairs to bring me a cold plate of tuna noodle casserole.

RECKONINGS

In early May, a peaceful noon rally at Kent State turned into a thirteen-second volley of gunfire, killing four students. Valerie and I had quarreled the night before. But now, watching the news in horror, we hugged and squeezed our bodies into each other for support. Hardly ever remembering what we argued about, we proclaimed our love for each other. Whenever the story comes up in a documentary, Kent State triggers contempt and frustration in me. Soldiers killing students, with no culpability. How could I ever be a soldier?

My internship ended that summer with an expected thump. Preceptor Don Ring had always promised to keep me on as an extern, which meant I was nothing—not an intern, nor a registered pharmacist—until I got notice in September that I'd passed the board. But without warning, Don fired me and hired a new intern—another life lesson about loyalty.

Scrambling to find work and support my sense of self and my wife, I interviewed with a food market chain, Shopping Cart, which was looking to add pharmacy departments. The deal was to stay on as licensed pharmacist in September.

But the celebration of my new professional ascension to registered pharmacist was quickly and severely tempered. On September 23, a letter arrived telling me I was now listed as IA, reclassified for military service. I fucking hate September 23. With the letter in my hands, my knees wobbled and my hands shook. I felt sick to my stomach, paralyzed with fear of dying. I had nowhere to run for help—no one in my world was connected enough to get me out of the war.

A week later, I got a letter that I was to report for a physical and subsequent army induction. The drums in a metaphysical dirge banged slowly. *How will I die in Vietnam?* I thought. *Sniper, bomb, jeep accident? Will they at least find my body to send back to New Jersey?*

Valerie hugged me. "Cam, we'll get through this together. What do we do now?"

With fourteen days until my induction, Valerie and I spent our time hammering out prison viability. We finally chose to go to Canada instead, to a small town near Toronto. The wheels were now in motion for me to become a real war resistor and disappear into a strange new world, far from the comforts of Maplewood, California burgers, amphetamines, and Fourex rubbers.

Times were desperate—then a light bulb. Julian, still in the National

Guard, promised to smuggle the military medical manual that listed all the conditions preventing induction. It was a large book. Maybe somewhere in those hundreds of pages was something (my favorite word) to keep me out of the army.

At nearly midnight, thirteen days before induction, the doorbell rang. I opened it to reveal a brown bag containing the manual. With a reassuring voice, Julian, the deliverer warned me, "Never tell a soul where this book came from." The best hug of my life lasted a few impatient seconds.

4:44 SUNDAY MORNING

For the next week, my companion was the military medical manual. I was in emergency panic mode, pulling my second all-nighter to pore over it. My physical was on Wednesday. Valerie stayed away, no hovering or nagging. I had to find a medical reason to get out of the army.

Of course, my personality was all fucked up, given that I was taking high doses of amphetamines to keep me awake through the all-nighters. Paranoia, erratic movements, perseverations, bulging eyeballs, and shaky hands—all symptoms. Twice I heard a phantom knock at the front door and opened it while holding a serrated meat knife.

One day during this time, I walked into the bedroom while Valerie was cutting her toenails in the nude, looking hugely sexy, sitting spread open on the floor. Freaking drug side effects left me feeling unaffected and sexless.

How strange that Valerie never knew I took drugs (just white-collar ones; amphetamines were still normal prescription drugs at the time, not yet class II substances). Two years later into our marriage, when I was finding it hard to sleep and come down from the occasional amphetamine, I'd recklessly take Seconal or Nembutal—strong barbiturates. Like the candy that melts in your mouth, not your hand, I'd pop a bunch of those red or yellow submarine-looking capsules. One night, still high and angry, I popped perhaps ten, enough to take out an elephant at the circus. Something (someone) was with me, watching over, blessing and protecting me. When the pills kicked in, I collapsed in the kitchen, crashing into the table with an open chocolate syrup can. That's how Valerie found me in the morning: brown, sticky, and comatose. All the textbooks on drug overdoses indicate I should've died.

Back to my second all-nighter—it would be the last night of my attack on the medical manual. I'd read it twice over the past week. Anger consumed me. The uppers were wearing off, so I was barely able to stay awake. Pushing myself, I skimmed the pages, knowing the sun would rise soon. My Jules Jurgensen watch, a gift from the Scotts after I proposed to their daughter, showed 4:44 a.m. when something in the manual caught my eye. I rubbed my eyes and read the sentence again. Buried in the middle of the book, halfway down a page, was a solitary obscure sentence: "Orthodontic appliances cause a one-year exemption."

I went to bed and awoke Sunday afternoon, delirious with the prospects of having found a real reason to fail my physical and perhaps avoid the draft permanently. I was twenty-five, and a year exemption for braces on my teeth would take me to twenty-six, out of draft age. The best part: Valerie's dad was a dentist. Problem extant, he was a member of the Ethical Culture Society, a WWII proud veteran, and would never be deceitful as a health professional.

Sunday night, Valerie and I went for dinner at the Scotts'. I followed her father into the basement, where he liked to smoke, stare at the wall, and listen to Johann Strauss. Valerie came downstairs to tell us Janis Joplin had died of a heroin overdose. For a brief moment, I was frozen in shock. Then, with a look of encouragement, Valerie prompted me to talk to her father.

With a deep breath, I told him about our decision to move to Canada. "I don't know anything about how you'll see her again," I said, "but I just found out that if I have braces on my teeth, I'd get out of the army forever."

He coughed, not from excitement, but because of his cigarette lungs. "Are you sure about that?" he asked. I nodded.

On the spot, he called an orthodontist in Springfield to whom he referred patients. The next morning, I went to the orthodontist's office and sat there for most of the day with my mouth wide open. After an endless amount of time, I walked out with a full set of braces.

Wednesday morning, I went to my army physical on Broad Street in Newark. When they asked if there was anything that might affect my draft status, I opened my mouth, hoping my new oral appliances might reflect the overhead fluorescent lights into the examiner's eyes. I failed my physical—the best high ever after a long, winding road toward freedom.

As dentistry would dictate, I severely needed braces. I went on to wear them for three years—right until Valerie and I got divorced. The orthodontists never charged me because of the arrangement with my father-in-law. I could never afford to pay them after the divorce, so I just disappeared from their practice. Living again with Jack and Amelia, an inspiration arrived one morning. Prophylactically, I ingested a gram of Penicillin VK tablets, grabbed a rusty plier, and ripped out my braces one quadrant at a time over a four-week period—each time to the horror and cries from sister Carol, because my mouth filled up with blood before I spat it out all over our parents' new American Standard sink.

In the words of Janis Joplin, "Freedom is just another word for nothin' left to lose."

Chapter 10

WINDING DOWN

My relationship with Valerie never really had a shot to wind up, jump-start, and prosper. The doom and gloom officially began the night before our betrothal. We were fighting over how to word the thank-you card for her Aunt Flo and Uncle Moe's engagement gift. I wanted serious, proper verbiage; Valerie wanted gushy mushy. In my opinion, they didn't deserve it, but that escalated to her thinking I was putting down her whole family. It's just a few meaningless words, I explained. For me, this was all the beginning of a life lesson; you either get it or you don't. No power, oratorical skill, or charm can change blue to red, or vice versa. Valerie was red and I was gray, although she voted for McGovern.

I'd eluded Vietnam, but I was still possessed. Often at dinners, seemingly in conjunction with tuna noodle casseroles, Valerie and I talked about the war; a circumspect topic where we found agreement.

When Radio Hanoi broadcasted Jimi Hendrix's "Star-Spangled Banner," we both didn't like it. We liked the *New York Times* publishing the Pentagon Papers. On some things, we were a perfect match. Well into the next century, Valerie long gone, I'd always know she had much to do with my soul and existence by having a dentist for a father.

In the summer of 1971, without knowing who Lenny Bruce was, we got tickets to the Broadway play *Lenny*, starring Cliff Gorman. Of course, we argued for an hour on the train: should we eat at a deli (me) or Asian restaurant (her), so we did Italian as a compromise. Babies we were.

As the curtain went down, a bright light bulb clicked on, and what followed was a lifelong fascination admiration for Lenny Bruce. He was a free-speech fighter, a comedic pioneer, and an American hero who used dirty language. Part of Lenny's draw was his use of speed and my use of amphetamines—the same drug. I memorized his bits, subscribed to his social activism, and bought all his vinyl records. Voraciously, I read everything on his life, saw biographical films about him, and wondered what happened to his daughter, Kitty Bruce, after he died. The full circle of life, years later, had me hug Kitty backstage at a comedy festival.

Always conscious of extricating the tortoise from my hair and establishing my independent presence in the 1970s, Valerie and I waited for the right time to experiment with marijuana. Two joints rested in a white sweat sock in my underwear drawer. In July, when the State of Washington became the first to ban sex discrimination, we lit up, inhaled, and passed it back and forth, waiting to feel good. That never came. Blank stares and frustration over our inability to be elevated led us to bed for love-making and promises never to indulge or attempt it again, a promise I'd keep until 2012.

LABOR ACTIVISM AND OPPORTUNITY

On the work front, there was peace in my time; I enjoyed the responsibilities of dispensing medicines to make people feel better.

Shopping Cart was a progressive regional food supermarket chain, quickly vertically integrating with pharmacy departments, bakeries, and twenty-four-hour operations. A few internal conflicts gently surfaced in the first few months I worked there. I resented when customers asked me where the marinara sauce or plastic straws were—I was a freaking health professional. The chain management were grocery life thinkers, so they had no clue how to manage pharmacies. A deepening chasm between me and the management began to foment, swirling around like the drain in a bathtub, sucking things in, like me, soon enough, with labor issues.

Something else to add to my persona, solidified in 1971, that would haunt my life: I am always late. There is no explanation or triggering event. My wives have considered my lateness as a general disrespect for myself and them. While I was self-loathing and self-destructive with the uppers and downers, often flirting with my funeral arrangements, I loved and respected people, needed them to like me and the cold cereal I was eating. Punching time clocks at Shopping Cart was painful because I was always consistently late. I couldn't change. Eventually, it got so bad that I'd tell people genetic testing had revealed my lateness was due to missing a remote telomere, the tip of an obscure chromosome. Most people believed me, until I let slip a Cheshire smile.

Handwriting was all over the wall as communication difficulties deepened between Shopping Cart's grocery bosses and pharmacists. Management was clueless on how to approach their professional pharmacists, so something (that word again) triggered within me. I never understood that people looked up to me, besides the obvious height thing. Maybe it was an intrinsic expectation people had of me, but all the years of failing to realize that and respond by opening up turned people off and away. I could've been well down the road to acquiring more friends if only I'd known people expected me to make the first move. Unaware of that element, sometimes I made the first move by talking to key outspoken pharmacists in the company. I began to put into motion feelers for forming a pharmacist union at Shopping Cart.

The National Labor Relations Board listened, and after taking a vote, Amalgamated Pharmacists formed. The union committee and I wrote the contract in my apartment while Valerie served tuna noodle casserole. A distinct probability to my union organizing efforts was vendetta; management would never forget me.

Working life at Shopping Cart became uncomfortable, always feeling eyes and ears on me, watching, listening. Throw in a dash of paranoia, some manufactured by amphetamine side effects, and I began to think the store produce manager was one of them. When Valerie's cousin, pharmacist Sam Port, called to talk about a business proposition, I jumped. Sam wanted to partner with me in a pharmacy franchise based in Chicago, securing Union County and opening twelve small prescription-only pharmacies over a five-year period. *Why me?* I wondered. Well, my father-in-law, a wealthy dentist, could supply funding for growth. Sam took 51 percent and I got the balance. After taking a year to develop, we finally opened our first store, Just Prescriptions. Amelia preached about never burning bridges, so I resigned from Shopping Cart with dignity.

The concept of Just Prescriptions was a few vitamins, aspirin, and, of course, prescriptions—no space for shampoo, shaving cream, or sanitary napkins. Low overhead was the game. I'd be tied up as a one-man operation for a long time, so Valerie and I decided to take a few weeks off before the grand opening. Who knew it would be our last meaningful vacation together? The idea of doing all three East Coast capes—Cod, Hatteras, and May—appealed to me.

Each in our own methodology, we both sensed an end to us. These past few years of fighting, distancing, failing to understand the other. I remembered back to Valerie's sardonic smile when I brought up having children. How strange that I could never tell Valerie, only now in this memoir, that I never envisioned children for us. And I desperately needed to be a father.

By the time we got to Cape Cod, John Dean, a hero of mine, with his amazing power of recall, was testifying at the Watergate hearings.

Pills did me in. It had been raining all week and I felt sick, so I stayed in bed all day, watching him testify while Valerie nagged at me until she finally disappeared. We had dinners together, but it was all unnatural. We were coming undone.

When I met John Dean at Rutgers a few years ago, I told him he cost me a marriage because I obsessively watched his testimony for a week.

"Did you remarry?" he asked.

"Of course," I said.

"Then I don't feel guilty," he said, flashing a rare smile I recognized from his testimony.

Back home, Just Prescriptions opened to a surprising amount of interest. Not having the head for business, I did wrong things despite having the franchise watch over me. Personality wins out; people were drawn to my honesty and caring. Now established in the community, six months into the venture, a man wearing a Humphrey Bogart hat walked into the store, trench coat collar popped, adding to his mystique. He turned out to be the bespectacled, balding Larry Reed, who would become my mentor. As a retired man with power and money, his newly carved place in the world was to give back. In months to come, I was elected to the board of directors of the area Chamber of Commerce, and nominated for and inducted into Outstanding Young Men of America—all Larry's orchestration. When a letter from Nixon arrived in the mail extending his congratulations, I threw it away.

As a favor, I went to speak to the county chapter of epileptics at a local library. I went improv, offering to fill their prescription medicines just above cost, before insurance as we know it. Spirituality guided me inexplicably. A few weeks later, a national organization in Washington called to ask me to develop a mail-order prescription program for their millions of members, the forefront of a new industry with a captive audience. If handled correctly, I'd be on my way to unimaginable wealth. Money would've gone to my head and up my nose, whisking me to Tahiti, shacking up with natives, and obviating my future meeting with a higher angelic authority. Money was not healthy for me. Something (that word) made me turn this opportunity down—it was a surreal feeling, and a strong, persuasive, and sensual one. A destiny was out there for me, and it wasn't in the store or pharmacy profession. If all that money was in a mattress, I wouldn't be writing this memoir.

LAST DANCE

Ignoring our parents' advice on both sides that it was time to live apart or maybe start all over again, Valerie and I agreed to try saving our marriage one more time. We planned to redo our first date, go into the city, see the new Streisand and Redford movie, *The Way We Were*, have dinner, and maybe try avant-garde sex later, inspired by a porn movie we saw together. The movie was a portent of things to come—the end of the onscreen relationship was too much like us, the way we were. Something I said while Valerie and I stood on Broadway afterward turned into us yelling, turning a few tourists' heads.

"Are you coming with me now? I want to go home. Forget dinner." Valerie's voice eased into a sob.

"No, I'm going to eat." I walked away, leaving her alone in the city.

Valerie took a bus home alone. While I was still in the city, her father picked her up and moved her essentials back home. A couple years later, my Uncle Ira, the paranoid attorney, helped me sign divorce papers. I kept our apartment.

INEXPLICABLE

Some people are put on this good Earth to live in a small outpost on the northern coast of Antarctica. Experimentally alone, surviving, waiting six months for supplies and company with the opposite sex. And some people, like me, need a few thousand neighbors, a mother close by, and someone to live with. I don't do alone well. Valerie was long gone, missed and not missed. Pills were frequent again. Unhappiness, unfulfillment, always close by in good times, messed me up even worse now in bad times. The train track was headed to a one-way-in, no-way-out tunnel of darkness and depression. Like a black hole at the end of the galaxy.

I was intelligent enough to know I could try slapping my own face into sensibility. I went cold turkey from the pills as a last-chance gasp. It was a bad scene trying that without clinical professional help. I was slip-sliding away. I heard voices all over the apartment. If it was windy, I heard a banshee shrieking through the spaces in the doors and windows. Everything was bleak, faded. My eyes hurt. When thoughts of doing bad things to myself surfaced, I got the strangest sensation in my stomach. I felt pain all around, but it felt good, seductive. I wanted more of it. There was a correlation between thinking bad things and the pain intensifying; it felt like being in an opiate state; anesthetized.

Holy shit, I was seducing myself into ending life as I knew it. *Just do it*, I said to myself. *I hate this life. I'm nowhere and alone.* I grabbed a bottle of wine, chugged it, took a Seconal, filled the bathtub with hot water, stripped, grabbed a box cutter, and got ready.

Earlier, something had made me turn on the TV in the background. One of the channels was playing a movie. In the bathroom, the tub water was too hot. Then I heard Claude Rains's voice. I always thought he could've been my grandfather Colman, whom I never knew. I loved Claude as Louis in *Casablanca*, so I ran out to see him as Mr. Jordan, an angel in *Here Comes Mr. Jordan*. I stood nude and watched for a few minutes before collapsing on the bed.

In the morning, I researched antidepressants and came up with my own cocktail to get through this nasty time. Some say amphetamine withdrawal is worse than heroin. It was bad, but methylphenidate and imipramine eased me into sanity, restored my soul, and saved me. And I did it all by myself.

MORE INEXPLICABLE

Richard Nixon resigned from his presidency on August 9, 1974. Twenty-one days prior, I moved back home with Big Jack, Amelia, and Carol. I got my old room back, but it was now pink and girly. Just Prescriptions was on shaky ground, as Sam was no longer my relative through marriage, and future funding through Dr. Scott was gone with the wind.

A few days into Gerald Ford's presidency, after closing the store at 7:00 p.m., I loaded up accounting books (for Amelia to work on) into my shiny red Volkswagen and drove home toward Maplewood via Meisel Avenue in Springfield. I always took the same nightly route; a perfect creature of habit. I was wearing my white lab coat, its pockets a good repository for chocolate chip cookies, eight in a cellophane package. Stopped at a red light, the car to my left revved its engine, as if provoking a drag race. A middle finger preceded the driver peeling out. Accepting his challenge, because I was still angry with the world, I chased him with gritted teeth, accelerating to fifty miles an hour in a twenty-five zone. I was almost up to his rear bumper, then I was even. All of a sudden, the road broke sharply to the left. Neither of us saw that coming. It was dusk, with limited sight. Everything happened so fast. The other car hit me as the road curved, so I swerved away; a natural reaction, but the jerk of the wheel was too much for a light Volkswagen. My car tumbled, rolling over. I held on tightly and closed my eyes—I had no time for fear, but I knew I was finally going to die.

I prayed through pursed lips, "Dear God, please take me without pain. Please don't rip an arm or leg off my body. Take me now. I'm sorry."

Suddenly, the car stopped with a thud. I was upside down; the car door was over my head. Eyes now open, I was dazed, confused, and disorientated. I was not in heaven or hell, but in the middle of a lawn in Springfield. I touched all my limbs, appendages, and body parts to see if they were still intact. Those were the days before seat belts, so I'd moved around during the impact. Everything on my body was still as I'd left it, but my compact Volkswagen was compacted, basically crushed. Smoke was everywhere. My senses were heightened to get the fuck out of the car before it went up in flames. I grabbed my store's books in the back seat, climbed out the top, and sat down on the front porch steps of the house I'd landed in front of. By this time, several witnesses ran over, looked inside the car for a dead body, and when none was found, they came over and asked who had been in the car.

"It's me. I was in that car," I told them.

There wasn't a scratch on me; no blood anywhere. I reached into my lab coat pocket; the chocolate chip cookies in cellophane hadn't even crumbled. Police and ambulances arrived. I sent the ambulances back to Overlook Hospital.

When a cop asked what happened, dishonesty overcame me. "A car hit me on the curve and I swerved to avoid more impact," I explained.

The cop walked me over to a huge tree, perhaps planted during the Revolutionary War, next to a large telephone pole. "Your car went between this tree and pole," he said. "If your car had impacted either one, you'd have been crushed to death. It would appear your car is wider than the distance between, which means we have no clue how you got through there."

Years later, I came to realize what happened to me that day is beyond earthly explanation. Whenever I'm in Springfield, I still drive to the site of the accident and thank my spirit connections. But this spiritual moment was just the beginning for me.

Chapter 11

A VERY GOOD YEAR, EVENTUALLY: 1976

The thought crossed my mind that I don't like the month of April and didn't much care for this new year of 1975. I was still hurting from my divorce from Valerie. On a warm spring morning, with the aroma of blossoms in the air, I arrived an hour late at Just Prescriptions to open the store, but it was padlocked by Sam Port. A sign on the door said it was closed, and all prescriptions would now be filled at Port Drugs. Because we were no longer relatives by marriage, with no money to open more stores, he'd exercised his 51-percent ownership and there was nothing I could do. Shopping Cart hired me back as a pharmacist. My sixth sense said my return was much too easy, because I was a union organizer who'd pissed them off. They'd get even one day, but they needed me for now.

Somewhere, I read things—good or bad—happen in threes. When seeds of change are planted like that, I do my share to water the notion.

In 1976, the musician and activist Paul Robeson died in Philadelphia. Robeson sang a version of "Ol' Man River": "I'm tired of livin' and I'm afraid of dyin'." A few months after, Phil Ochs, a great folk singer whose anti-Vietnam sentiment I strongly identified with, committed suicide. Phil's passing bothered me. I hate saying that I identify with it; that shuttles me to places I don't like to be. I'll grind my teeth and clench my fists, thinking if only I was close by to stop him and reason that he had so much to live for. Beneath the water's surface, I hoped someone would be close to me when my time came. Between these two deaths, I figured the third lousy thing that was going to happen was probably waiting backstage.

It was just another Friday in May when I punched the time clock at Shopping Cart and walked past the checkout registers and a small display of fresh white bread toward the pharmacy department. I was ready to greet Tom, the other pharmacist, when six company executives suddenly walked out from behind the rear shelving and surrounded me, much like Custer was probably confronted. The scene didn't bode well.

Andy Morris, my immediate supervisor, spoke. "Cameron, you're being terminated for tardiness. According to the union contract that you wrote and we approved, lateness three times in a row is a terminable offence. Please gather your things. We'll escort you out."

I knew it was my time, but I had to leave my brand on their carcass. "Gentlemen, I'm a union man, which means I'll take it further," I said.

"Don't bother," Andy said. "Your lateness is well beyond the three days. You've been back here a year. Our records show you've punched in late every day. That's hundreds of times in a row."

A huge smiled consumed my face. It was time to have fun with a long shot. "When you interviewed me upstairs, years ago, you repeated yourselves that the most important quality of an associate of this company is consistency. I was late that first day, so I decided to be consistent."

"Get him the fuck out of here," one of the executives whispered under his breath.

Two weeks later, I was back in the saddle, working for a large independent pharmacy that was involved with hospitals, doctors, lawyers, stewardesses, and local politicians. The owner-pharmacist had his palms into everything, everyone. It was a good place to learn for the future. In my first month there, I'd observed the store manager, a woman with no college education, was riding one of the longtime clerks, Dina, hard in a disparaging way. Dina was a young, pretty White girl who needed the job to save as much money as possible to marry her Black boyfriend. Violet, the manager, was an outright racist who disliked Dina's boyfriend and their mixed-race relationship. As Dina had become my friend, I took her cause to the owner, decrying all vestiges of racism in North Jersey. A week later, I was fired.

Going home to Amelia and my bedroom (still painted pink), I felt downtrodden and disillusioned. Of course, pharmacists were in demand, and I'd be working again in a week. But being a good guy and getting fired because of defending human rights was depressing. I wasn't in the mood to be depressed. Pushing myself hard, I had to get out of the house.

Way back, I discovered the Turtlebrook Inn, an upbeat bar and music venue that attracted an older, more professional, single crowd. Singles bars, walls with psychedelic flowers, and expressive dancing were never my strong suit.

On a Wednesday night, I headed to West Orange to the inn of my anticipated happiness. I downed an American beer from the Midwest, then another, looking for an edge and something to occupy my hands. A woman—I can't say a girl, as she appeared way older than me—walked over and started talking.

"I like tall men. I think you're the tallest one here," she said.

She was strikingly pretty, with black hair and stark eyebrows, which moved in concert with her flailing expressive hands. She was a well-oiled, animated lady.

"I am usually the tallest," I said. "Been wearing that title since my junior year in high school, when I grew freakishly fast. Was even tested for radiation poisoning because the growth was eerie."

"Really?"

"Nope. Just teasing. I'm Cameron."

She laughed and told me her name was Bev. We danced fast and slow, then shared a few beers. Soon, I was following her back to a Maplewood house with a nervous stomach that this was way too easy. Once inside, she politely offered me a hit on a joint, which I refused. Coolly, I intimated that no THC was necessary to take her all in.

Then came the line, "Excuse me while I freshen up and tinkle."

No one tinkles in 1975. A red flag poked me in the eye. Did I have the testicular appendages to disappear out the front door, which had a sheet of aluminum foil over the small window?

When she returned several long minutes later, I did a double-take and softly whispered, "What the fuck?" She was standing in black bra and underpants, stilettos, swinging a pair of handcuffs wildly, seductively. A whiff of insecticide perfume hit my nostrils.

"Oh, wow," I told her, "Did you ever dial the wrong number back at the bar. I might as well be from Kansas or Nebraska with my earthy values. Not my scene, but you made my night and swelled my ego, which needed this."

"Nothing here turns you on? If you've never tried it, don't knock it."

When I got home that night, I asked Amelia to cease and desist from worrying about my socialization. "What happened?" she asked.

"Goodnight, Mom," was all I said.

SPIRIT INEXPLICABLE

Damn, I was down enough to head back to the Turtlebrook Inn with hopes I'd meet that sadistic woman Bev, and this time she could do whatever to me. Handcuff me to the bedpost, make me crawl on the floor like a Saint Bernard, fuck me for three days—I didn't care. I always dreamed of marathonic sexual adventures.

Singles Friday night was crowded. I don't thrive in crowds, so I downed a beer quickly, ready to leave for Jimmy Buff's hot dog restaurant. I'd drown myself in two hot dogs, brown mustard, potatoes, onions, and peppers stuffed into a pita, all the ingredients swimming in luxurious cooking oil. I was poised for the getaway when a girl tapped me on the shoulder. "Would you like to dance?" she asked. She was blonde, bland, and tall, but something made me say yes.

During our slow dance, I could feel her rubbing close, which was a turnoff. When we finished, I decided to stay and forego hot dogs for another beer. I reached for my wallet in my sport coat breast pocket, but it was gone. I'd been pickpocketed for the first time in a life—by the bland girl who'd rubbed my crotch too close. Frustrations that had been building since I divorced Valerie, that had kicked the shit out of me, exploded. I lunged for her. I yelled that I wanted to kill her. The bouncer restrained me, but I managed to deliver one final verbal assault: "I just want my wallet back. Keep the money. I will haunt you the rest of your life because I am crazy."

What the fuck was happening to me? Yelling at a girl, threatening violence—and I'm a pacifist. I felt out of my own body; the sounds of the noisy bar were muted, silenced. The bouncer brought me a beer and apologized. I sat on a stool, numb, disgusted, and progressively angrier with my maker. An hour later, I was still stewing on the bar stool when the bouncer handed me my wallet. He'd found on it the floor, minus the cash, as I'd suggested.

After recovering emergency cash under the seat in my car, I thought to drive toward nowhere and never stop, maybe crash into a brick wall, find the top of any mountain with a view, or take a nap at my grandparents' resting place. Distraught, senseless thinking. A headache started pummeling me like a tornado, swirling around in my cerebral process. Everything was wrong with my fucking life: a divorce; firings in every job; a padlocked store; sleeping in a pink room; lonely, tired, disgusted, depressed—and, finally, pickpocketed. I didn't know what to do, where to go, whose shoulder to rely on. There was no one out there in the Twilight Zone for me.

All this down-thinking sitting in the car. What if I let the car run and closed the window? A wonderful way to die. Silent, peaceful, painless. Indeed, my new disturbed world. I thought of driving into New York City. I'd park, walk around Times Square, mumble a few curse words to a dude leaning on a window, and get stabbed.

New York, here I come. It was near 1:00 a.m., so getting stabbed on a lonely street was gaining probability. I started the car and headed toward Route 23, talking suddenly to God. When I reach for the stars and heavens, I talk out loud in the car. "Dear God, I'm tired of living and losing. I don't know what life is all about. Will I get in trouble if I just stop living?" I asked.

Route 23 would lead me to Route 46 and on toward New York, but I didn't give a shit. I'd never hit life's nadir before, but I was at my lowest place in the universe. "Dear God, I don't know what life is about!" I cried.

I was tailgating the four cars in front of me. The speed limit was 50, and we must've been doing 70. Weather conditions that night were clear, dark, moonlit. I noticed garbage or something on the road, then some of the cars suddenly swerved. The front car, then the rest of us, slammed the brakes. The lead driver, way up ahead, jumped out of the car and started running back, and the others followed; so did I. Just ahead, people formed a circle around something.

When I got closer, I saw it was an old lady—or what was left of her. She had been hit at tremendous speed. Body parts lay on road, ripped from her body. There was nothing for us to do. A bolt hit me. God had just shown me what death looked like, and it was horrible. Spirit brought me here at this precise time. What happened to this woman would've happened with or without me. This night of spirit would haunt a lifetime. I went home to my pink room.

NOTHING WITH FOUR LEGS

Some people don't get life's exigencies and lose touch with reality, forgetting where they came from and who helped get them there. They see a homeless person sleeping in a cardboard box on a Manhattan street and look away, unable able to see that person's face or the hopelessness in their eyes. Sights of despair are social aberrations, annoyances on their way to two-hundred-dollar dinners before a Broadway show. And still, we all pass naked through the birth canal.

I'd been down in the dumps, often staying long weekends in my pink room, listening endlessly to "Scarborough Fair." If only I could get there, beyond the window, ocean, or jetty. I dreamed that if a girl rang the doorbell, selling encyclopedias and wearing a nametag that said Rosemary, I'd find a way to marry her—but only if she had long, wispy hair that reached her ankles. I imagined meeting Rosemary at Woodstock, finding a clump of bushes, making love not war, and burying my face in her femininity.

One day, a cousin knocked on my bedroom door to give me the number of an exceptionally pretty, rich, tall girl from Short Hills named Lidia Taylor. He forcefully insisted I call her and teased that Lidia's mother owned Bonwit-Taylor (not Teller), and her father owned Sex Fifth Avenue, a Midwestern sex shop chain. I endured for a week, then finally called Lidia, securing a Friday night date. It'd been a few years since I'd dated substantively, so I researched what it was all about in 1975. Ladies and psychology magazines provided plentiful and relatable descriptors. The clear message: one needs to find commonality right from the starting gate.

The view from Lidia's street showed a mansion high on a hill, a weeping willow in the middle of the ascent. My ritual dictated a prayer before depressing the doorbell. I heard the chimes of St. Mary's, so I thought. The castle door opened to reveal everything described in Lidia's pre-packaging: tall, beautiful, blue eyes, smiling—all worthy of a whispered thank-you to God. I had no idea yet that this night would impact the rest of my life, that must have been a spiritual attachment, a reason for being there and meeting her.

No parents, siblings, or servants were present as we entered the library. Who has a library with a ladder? Not in my world. We chatted, exchanging backgrounds. Lidia studied fashion in New York.

I wasn't sure if I liked her next remark. "Oh, you're a pharmacist," she said. "What's your plan for tonight?"

I cleared my throat for insecurity and suggested going into the city to take in a movie and dinner.

"Movie is good," she said, "but there's only one real restaurant in the city where I like to eat."

"Excuse?" I said.

"Oh, I'm a vegan, so I only eat at this one vegan restaurant."

A magazine's first paragraph in big, bold print, flashed in my mind: FIND COMMONALITY.

"Oh, wow, so am I!" I lied.

Her face lit up with a broad smile, the best of the night. "This is wonderful. I've never gone out with another vegan before. How long have you been?"

Pridefully, I've always tried to live my life with as much veracity as possible. Sometimes, honesty brings conflict. Confidence let me say, "Not too long."

The schematic of the date: Lidia was way too tall and rich. I don't do rich girls well. The movie entertained. At dinner, I raved obnoxiously about my cooked vegetable platter. Back in Short Hills, I walked around the car, politely opened door, escorted Lidia to her front door, exchanged a verbal goodnight, and never saw her again.

The spiritual deal: Something clicked—I liked this vegan shtick. But my vegan world officially lasted six months. Almost every day was a battle with Amelia, who couldn't deal with separate food preparation. Compromise came when I declared I'd never eat anything with four legs again, but only two legs (fins and gills).

Evolution of thought would suggest I made this change to save animals, the planet, my soul, and my arterial system. The thing is, through all these early times of my dietary change, I still loved meat. Corned beef, pastrami, steaks, Italian hot dogs, hamburgers with chemically enhanced sauce dripping out of the bun—all helped me gain those hundred pounds for draft evasion. The day the Earth stood still,

I proclaimed being a vegan and relatively stayed that way forever; no more four-legged, red-blooded animals to eat. Where did this conviction come from? Something had moved and satisfied me.

Now, in current times, with red meat long gone from my diet, I have no desire for it. I care for animals, demonstrably so. Later in life, it paid off when I found out I have zero coronary artery plaque after seven Earth decades. That alone helped my cerebral blood vessels swish blood around to keep me sharp. Some sixth sense told me I'd never have to worry about dementia. They make movies about that kind of sixth sense.

TIPPERARY AND CHICAGO

When the news of the date failure with Lidia Taylor reached my concerned cousin, he decided I needed some serious relaxation, as I was still listening to "Scarborough Fair" in my room for days on end. On a summer Saturday morning, he escorted me to Jack Dunne, a sophisticated, experienced travel agent. An hour later, I'd booked a week at a trendy singles resort in the Caribbean, Club Med at Guadeloupe. I knew nothing about the place, other than Jack Dunne's admonition to bring plenty of condoms. Amelia packed two suitcases—including sweaters, just in case—which would turn out to be overdone. Who knew I'd be hanging out on nude beaches?

The scene at my arrival was wondrous: natives and club employees, all scantily clad, gyrated and danced suggestively. My roommate, (Club Med insisted on roommates) Ari, almost looked like Robert Redford, with a French accent. Ari was a physician doing a residency in New York. My small mountain of suitcases caught his glance. Sensibilities dictated not to unpack, but to follow him straight to the nude beach.

The bars were crowded with hundreds of people, including professional hockey players from the Montreal Canadiens. Curiously, a dozen eligible men seemed to have gathered around one particular woman—rightfully so; she was probably a centerfold somewhere stateside. Dinners were heralded by "Symphonies and Fanfares for a King's

Supper" (Masterpiece Theater). The club hosts played matchmakers, doing the seating. Ari and I worked together to score and discussed protocols of late-night room usage. The disco was always uncomfortably crowded, so I would stay outside, walking solo on the romantic beach. The moonlit scene of small waves kissing up against palm trees went to waste.

Breakfast was fun, surrounded by endless chocolate croissants. Seating was wherever. The girl who'd been surrounded by the dozen men at the bar sat down next to me one morning. I didn't know what to do or say; I just worked on my croissants to keep from talking. Patiently, she introduced herself as Jane Gardner from Chicago. I clamped up. Sensing our conversation was over, she wished me a nice day.

Ari went scuba diving for two days while I played basketball. On the third night, at dinner, he confessed perplexity as to why two good-looking, eligible guys (us) had not yet been laid when everyone else had. I didn't need to hear that, although it was self-evident. At the disco, I hung solo outside most of the night, refreshing my beer, beginning my self-pity, moving the bottle up and down from my lips. At 3:00 a.m., tired and poised to quit for the night, Jane from Chicago suddenly appeared, leaning on the brick wall next to me. Disco saffron light and moon spotlighted this intense beauty. No more clamping up—she was mine.

"Can I get you a drink?" I asked.

"No, thanks, I've passed my limit. It's been a wet night. A lot of drinks, guys buying them for me."

"I wonder why?" We both laughed. I felt loose, confident. Strange how quickly you can feel things, electricity; something was there in just a few moments. "You know, a hundred feet away is one of the most beautiful beaches in the hemisphere, away from the maddening sounds of the disco. Would you like . . . ?" I didn't finish, but she knew.

"That's exactly what I want to do, Cameron," she said.

Contour lounge chairs lined the deserted beach; it was 4:00 a.m.

Thirty minutes into lounging under the stars and talking, we kissed, held hands, and splashed warm water at each other. Everything was happening so fast. My mind raced, trying for practicality, subtracting romantic scenic ambiance, searching for reality. But it was real enough. Jane was a fashion journalist in Chicago. She revealed that she also disliked disco. We kept finding endearing commonality as a hint of pink sunrise lifted out of the water. Sunrise official, I walked back to her room for a good-morning kiss. Her exercise class was in an hour, and we were both busy the rest of the day.

The following midnight, we met back up at the beach. Deficiencies in my socializations abounded, but I excelled in bonding rapidly—I remembered how fast I'd almost become engaged to Wendy Paul from South Orange.

Intensity was all over us by 2:00 a.m. Jane told me her roommate had moved in with one of the GOs (folks who work for Club Med, sort of like camp counselors). "Why don't you move in with me?" she asked.

I quickly agreed. My two prodigious suitcases remained with Ari. Now into the mood of the club, I just needed a T-shirt, sneakers, bathing suit, and toothbrush.

3:00 a.m. Fourth morning. A little night music and déjà vu: Jane's period was winding down. In a blink of an eye, I was back with Wendy Paul at Niagara Falls. Jane was an eternity of difference: a woman who had been on all the continents, with people who mattered, changed small parts of the world, and sat in penthouse offices. The next night, we consummated ourselves in a marathonic way. In a few moments of downtime, my arms still wrapped around her, I wondered about what was meant to be, why she'd sat down next to me at breakfast. Could this be the reason to believe? Suddenly, I wished we were getting a slice of pizza in Manhattan, walking into the Port Authority Bus Terminal, sitting next to Ratso Rizzo and Joe Buck, sharing a stick of gum—a real world away from palm trees, nudity, and perfumed air.

We had sex often and passionately, as if we'd been together nine years, not three days. After one long sex session, she confessed that this had been her first orgasm in years. A previous boyfriend, who'd owned a private jet, just never did it for her. That blew me away—I needed a comeback.

"Private jet. Shoot, I've got my own private Chevy waiting for me in Maplewood," I said.

During the day, we each did our own thing. I played basketball while once, unbeknownst to me, she watched from behind a palm tree. At eleven o'clock on the beach, she had a yoga session. Meanwhile, I roamed dreamily, in a pinching state that this was all happening with Jane, thanking spirits for orchestrating it.

One day, I saw two club employees arguing with an American. It was a French resort, so nationalism separated the parties. The two Frenchmen started swinging a hot hamburger spatula at this short, defenseless American. All purchases at the resort—liquor, late-night food—required colored pop-it beads, not money, but the American only had cash. Things quickly escalated into a real fight. I needed to act, still cognizant of my pacifism. I'd been weightlifting, so I was a ripped, tall guy, rather intimidating to these under-six-foot Frenchmen.

From my intestinal linings, past my strong larynx, I brought up a deep, ethnic sound. "Leave da kid alone." I said it twice, menacingly clenching my fists, causing them to back off, put a hamburger on a bun, and hand it over to the American. He introduced himself to me as Ricky, and I had a new friend.

Ricky and I shared a smoke on the beach. I couldn't let on that nothing happens to me when I smoke and it was all a waste of lung capacity. The next day, we played tennis together. At the end of the week, we exchanged phone numbers, promising to stay in touch, until Ari told me my new friend was Ricky Carson from California. Way out of my league for those days, I never followed through.

On our last night, Jane and I went to the beach and had sex in the water. Inspiration hit when she screamed through an orgasm that I needed to be with her.

"You're right," I said. "I'm coming to Chicago with you tomorrow. It's a long way to Tipperary."

"What does that mean?"

"It was a battle song from World War I. How far was it to achieve peace? Finding you has been such a lofty but distant dream; I'm still processing how wonderful you are. So, it is a long way, even to Chicago."

Sister Carol and her fiancé—dispatched by Amelia—met me at Kennedy Airport (changing planes) to win back my sensibilities. One look at Jane, glistening in airport fluorescence, and they knew why I had to go to Chicago. My time in Chicago was magical. I explored the city by day and Jane by night. Her high-rise apartment near Lincoln Park and Lake Michigan afforded spectacular views for my first meaningful time in the city. Jane and I would stand nude at the window, locked in arms, like a scene from a movie.

Beneath the surface, I was almost put off by how sexually explicit and creative Jane was. With her, it wasn't possible for me to role-play that I was cool—she *was*. Jane had been around many blocks, but always with elite, game-changers, and a man who owned his own plane. Not in my world have I experienced what she taught me. At times, she was sexually clinical and matter-of-fact, which I wasn't used to, having taken eight months to go oral with Valerie. Jane's oral was a brave, imaginative new world. If I were hanging out with the guys in a bar, I'd tell them about things she could do with her mouth that I'd never seen in all the porn movies, in all the porn shops in all the towns all over New Jersey. But Jane's best lessons, for posterity, taught me how to please her.

One Wednesday, when Jane went into the office, I went to the Illinois Board of Pharmacy to inquire about transferring my license. That night, we had a cute date at Lawrence of Oregano, a fun, obviously Italian place.

Back home, we were drunk on cabernet sauvignon. "You're a pharmacist, a man of science," she said. "Can you weigh my breasts, so for once I'll know my fighting weight?"

Jane's breasts, institutionally speaking, were enormous, but I always felt it politically correct, even in 1976, to downplay. I knew how to proceed. On her bathroom scale, I supported each one with my hands, found the tare weight, and did the subtractions: just over nine pounds. Our little secret.

Eventually, we determined a game plan that I'd work back in Jersey for seven ten-hour days in a row, then take off a week to explore Chicago and jump back into bed with Jane. We'd go barefoot in Lincoln Park, ride a tandem bike, picnic with French cheese—every adventure topped off in her bed, which was never made.

When the raid at Entebbe filled the news, she took off from work and we stayed in bed for two days, no clothes or even underwear for the whole day. My second week there, Jane made me a White Russian and it became my new favorite drink, which would help to change the course of a life later on. Three White Russians followed by sweaty, heated fornication, and I'd be approaching nirvana. This was my Bicentennial Summer.

In August, as we got accustomed to each other, I mentioned perhaps transferring my pharmacy license to Illinois and moving to Chicago. I never assumed I'd move in with her; she'd help me find a place.

The seeds of a relationship were perhaps there with Jane. But in the world of Cameron Simmons, experience told me they were not. Something—*something*—strong, disconcerting was always around. I was thirty-one, and deep inside my tall body, buried within my cellular constitution, I knew I had to become a father and teach a child about the world. There wasn't a vision of Jane in my life in any kind of domestic scene. She probably had the same vision about me, or was it just the lamplight? Lamplight gives off such a warm glow.

Labor Day weekend, I flew out from New Jersey to Chicago. Those were the days when the plane was so empty, the flight attendants told me to just sit in first class. When Jane picked me up, we skipped dinner and went right to her apartment—just sex, a White Russian, and another round of both. Monday, we spent most of the day in the bedroom. A feeling of sadness surrounded us; one of those feelings you can't finger. I napped a long time—escapism from what I knew not. In the background, I heard the muffled sounds of Jane on the phone with her mother in Miami. The things you think you hear.

When it was time for my flight back to Jersey, Jane and I said goodbye at the airport gate. In the middle of a nice tongue kiss, I gently pushed back and said, "I just need to look at you. Take all of you in—soulfully, you know."

"What a nice thing to say, Cam."

I knew that was the last time I'd ever talk to her. Perhaps it was in her eyes too. A few years ago, I saw on Facebook that she had gotten married a few months after our Labor Day weekend. We both knew we just weren't meant to be.

THE BUCK FINALLY STOPS

Breaking up is hard to do. For a few days after Labor Day, I hung out in my pink room, listening to *Parsley, Sage, Rosemary & Thyme* obsessively. One day, to snap out of whatever was drowning me, I slapped myself in the face and went to the Turtlebrook Inn feeling strong and confident that I could play in any field because of how I'd scored with Jane. With elements of her now converted to particulates of my ego, I could talk to anyone, even my former Weequahic High School classmates.

At the bar, my bottle of beer traveled from my waist to lips, like the timed movements of a toy clock, when a girl resembling Marlo Thomas stood next to me. I initiated conversation. Connie, a nurse at Clara Maass Hospital, agreed to go out for coffee with me. At the Claremont Diner, we talked for two hours, using our commonality of a medical background, love of basketball, tuna salad, and ocean jetties to sweep us away to her garden apartment in Bloomfield. The moment we crossed the threshold, we partially ripped off our clothes and had sex standing up, leaning against her kitchen sink. As a side effect of my time with Jane, I found myself with lots of new knowledge to put into practice.

In the middle of the night, I asked to use Connie's phone. Embarrassingly, I called Amelia to say everything was all right, and at least I wasn't listening to *Parsley, Sage* anymore.

Intellectually speaking, Connie sealed my departure out of her life when she said, "Wow, you're the first guy I know who ever called his mother in the middle of the night from this bed."

"We'll always have Paris," I replied, before I got dressed, kissed her goodbye, and left—forgetting one sock behind.

A few weeks later, out of the blue sky, something came to me. The whole singles scene—characters like Jane and Connie—and the simmering stew of uncertainty and disappointment, weighed me down. At the kitchen table, bacon aroma wafting unperturbed around my flexitarian nostrils, I informed Amelia it was time for me to go to Europe, backpack around, and eventually try farming on a kibbutz in Israel. A socialist life beckoned. Devastated, Amelia began a lengthy campaign to dissuade me.

Undeterred, I traveled to embassies in New York City to discuss the usefulness of my pharmacy license in England, France, Belgium, and Israel. It was mid-October; by January, I'd be leaving America, maybe for a long time. With so much of my life governed by inexplicable events, I felt this was a destiny, almost as if there was no forethought or afterthought—just recklessly running toward *something*. But something also made me do it. Was this the same spirit who protected me from an overdose of sleeping pills or helped me survive the rollover accident in my Volkswagen?

I went back to Jack Dunne, the travel agent, to arrange my last fling—this time to Club Med in Martinique, coordinated with the New Jersey teachers' convention in November. Single teachers love the Caribbean and Club Med. I could be a busy eligible man. Amelia loved the trip idea, hoping I'd meet a teacher, stay in my pink room until I got married again, and settle around the corner, like I'd done with Valerie.

On a Saturday night, my cousin was getting married in South Orange. We weren't close, but my whole family was invited, which meant they were recruiting seat-fillers. During the cocktail hour, I chatted with another filler, my cousin Tess, who mentioned she was looking for company to a singles dance in the city on Sunday. The place, Wednesday's, was a veritable city street underground bar. When Tess walked away, Amelia swooped in with her sixth sense of hearing, and exhorted that I go with Tess to the dance.

"How'd you hear about that dance?" I asked her.

"I'm always looking out for you," she defended.

"No, Mom. You were eavesdropping. You want me sleeping in the pink room and not going to Europe. I'm still your little boy with the tortoise in his hair."

That Sunday was a cold, rainy fall day. The last thing on my mind was going to meet Tess in the city at a dance. Besides, I was leaving America in a few months; why bother? Still, every hour, Amelia knocked on my bedroom door to persuade me to go to the dance.

"Do this for your mother," she said. "I don't ask for a lot. Make me happy. I have a good feeling about this dance." Reluctantly, I gave in.

Rain intensified as I exited the Lincoln Tunnel. If the rain had been this bad when I'd departed Maplewood, I'd never have gone. The fucking *pièce de résistance* was that Tess never showed up—no call, nothing. The bar scene was crowded and noisy, filled with ostensibly only New Yorkers, so there wasn't a friendly, familiar face anywhere. I hate being alone in strange environs. But I didn't need this scene; I was Europe-bound soon.

Pissed, I snaked my way to an open space at the bar and ordered a White Russian, unaware my life was going to change forever. It takes just one magnificent second in the universal scheme to change a life. The bartender liked how fast I downed the creamy, caloric drink. By my third one, I skipped the straw, threw a $20 bill on the bar, and called my bartending friend over.

"Listen, I'm from Texas," I lied. "My father has a bunch of oil wells, so this tip is for you—"

My speech was interrupted by two girls who had just walked over to the bar. The one closest to me said to her friend, "This guy thinks he's really cool, and he's *not* from Texas."

I finished my soliloquy, then turned to the girl next to me, mildly pissed at her remark. The whole universe—my life and everyone impacted by it—was all based around this girl walking over and hearing me speak. If she'd walked over a few seconds later, I would've already said my piece to the bartender, she wouldn't have reacted to it, and I never would have asked to talk to her in a quiet corner.

When I looked at her, I saw her animated brown eyes and dark, short hair. I could tell she was intelligent, incisive and honest, all from her "This guy thinks he's really cool" remark.

"Can we talk about my coolness?" I said. "There's a couple seats over there in the corner. Would you like a drink?"

She smiled and held up a White Russian. "Sure, we can talk."

We talked for hours, stuck on a couple of seats in an obscure corner, as the music became increasingly more distant and irrelevant. Her name was Marjorie Field. After an hour, we were so comfortable with each other that she reached down my T-shirt and pulled up my neck chain with an accepting smile. When she mentioned being divorced, I confessed I was too and how I'd always hoped to meet a divorced woman. Theory being, there'd be less stumbling around, training, and adjusting.

There was obvious chemistry between us, so I offered to drive her home to Brooklyn, a place I'd never been. "Thanks for the offer, but there's a rule," Marjorie said. "If I came with my friends, I go home with them. If you'd like to see me again, call me for an official date and we'll go from there."

Later that night, she'd reveal to me one day, Marjorie called her sister and said, "I met the man I'm going to marry."

Somehow, Amelia was in the kitchen, doing ostensibly nothing, when I got home. "How was the dance?" she asked.

"Actually, I'm glad I went. And I met a nice Brooklyn girl. But, Mom, I'm still leaving in January."

Time was of the essence, so Monday night, less than twenty-four hours after meeting Marjorie, I called her for that official date. Marjorie also seemed to agree time was of the essence—we agreed to do dinner the next night, Tuesday. We went to Hisae's near Cooper Union—Ari from Club Med had once suggested the hip Asian restaurant, guaranteed to impress most women on a first date.

Hisae's was as underground as they come, with no sign outside, a descending staircase to get inside, and an indigent cat walking around for ambiance's sake. We sat at a quiet little table near a fireplace. The food was exquisite; we toasted our night with White Russians. As we talked, we stared into each other's eyes intensely, poetically. Marjorie was an elementary teacher in Brooklyn, with a master's degree. Our chemistry was powerful, perhaps too much so, because soon I attempted to apply verbal brakes by mentioning my impending trip to Europe. Nothing was allowed to deter my destiny, which was overseas—so I believed.

That didn't stop Marjorie from asking if I'd like to come up for coffee when I dropped her off back in Brooklyn, however. Once I made it inside, I stayed the rest of the week until Friday. My sixth senses had me leave a small packed suitcase in my car trunk, just in case coffee invitations led to stay-overs like this.

Those few days and nights with Marjorie were dreamy, right out of a romance novel. After she was done teaching for the day, we'd drive to the beach and walk barefoot, stopping for a kiss every few sinking steps in the sand. The next night, we had a fish dinner near Sheepshead Bay and walked around the harbor, looking at boats and pretending we knew the people on the decks.

During this time, a strange, inexplicable thing happened. I bought a pack of Gauloises, French cigarettes. Me, so anti-smoking, and in possession of one the largest vital lung capacities in Rutgers pharmacy school history, started smoking for the next ten years. It's one of life's great mysteries why I started, and even more haunting how I stopped.

On Friday morning, while Marjorie dressed for work, I told her my plans to spend the day at a museum or two in Manhattan, stop at Bloomingdale's to try this new chocolate chip cookie called Famous Amos, then meet her back in Brooklyn for dinner.

I set out on the subway to find some Famous Amos. I brought six bags back to Brooklyn, put them in my car—and then drove back to Jersey. Powerful bonding was going on between me and Marjorie—the ingredients of lasting relationships and marital licenses from city hall. But I couldn't deal with all the seriousness, spinning webs leading to love and permanency. Was I like Schrodinger's cat, dead and alive in the box at the same time? I couldn't commit to any relationship with Marjorie; Europe was too embedded cerebrally.

I didn't know what to do or say to Marjorie, so in the end I said nothing at all. I guiltily imagined Marjorie getting home and realizing I was gone from her, with no chance for her to call or contact me. I was leaving for Club Med Martinique near the end of November, and I knew there was no way she could ever find me if I disappeared from her life, so I could go to Europe free as a butterfly. I thought I'd succeeded in disappearing without a trace.

A week later, I was doing some last-minute packing for Club Med; my "last fling before Europe in January." This time, all I was packing was a gym bag, a few T-shirts, bathing suits, and new jock straps.

The phone rang; Amelia yelled that it was for me.

"Remember me?" said a familiar voice when I answered.

Incredulity slapped me around. "Marjorie!" I stuttered in disbelief.

She had found me by pressuring a friend of a friend, who ran the dance where we'd met—I remembered being annoyed that they had asked for too much of my personal information when I signed in.

Marjorie was taking the high road, not dwelling on my being a shit. She insisted I spend the weekend with her in Brooklyn before I left for Club Med. Stammering, I explained it was too complicated, and I'd call her when I got back from Club Med.

"No, you won't, but that's okay. Have a nice time."

"I will talk to you," I insisted before we hung up.

But she was right on all counts. I didn't intend to call her again, but I was impressed with her resourcefulness. As far as spending the weekend with her, I had a blind date on Saturday night. Back at the girl's house, we sat on a sofa in the basement and watched her mother sweep the linoleum floor; the broom washed over my shoes every time I got close to the daughter.

The Club Med Air France charter to Martinique left Kennedy on time. I sat in the back with my Gauloises, coolly laying my Lenny Bruce bits on a new audience with those around me. After a stop-over in Guadeloupe, the engines were revving up and everyone was belted in their seats when the flight attendant announced over the speaker, "Monsieur Cameron Simmons, we need to see you up front before takeoff."

No one gets paged on an airplane—I ignored it in total disbelief. A minute later, they repeated the announcement. I became frozen with fear—was I about to get busted and thrown into a Guadeloupe prison, like a modern-day Steve McQueen in *Papillon*? Except I was clean; I had no drugs in my sweat socks. What the fuck, the flight attendant paged me again, saying we couldn't take off until I came up front. All my new friends turned coat and pushed me.

As I walked up the aisle, passengers pointed and whispered, "He's Monsieur Cameron Simmons."

Finally up front, the flight attendant asked, "Are you Cameron Simmons?"

Beyond annoyed, I said yes. "What could you possibly want from me?"

"Regulations insist we deliver alcohol before takeoff, and not on

American soil," she said, handing me a bottle. It was Moët & Chandon champagne, with a card that read, "Have a wonderful time. Thinking of you. Love, Marjorie."

Overwhelmed with what Marjorie had done for me—besides making me a celebrity all week at Club Med (everyone knew me from the paging on the plane)—I called her within two hours of landing at Kennedy. At the end of July, we got married in her parents' Brooklyn backyard. Planes to and from Kennedy flew low overhead as we exchanged vows.

Love is a splendid thing. From that first sit-down with Marjorie at Wednesday's, I knew she was special. I'd tried to deny love at first sight, but as with so much of my life, after all the analysis, suppositions, and rejections, something entered my soul, and I knew it was destiny. Like the movie *Here Comes Mr. Jordan*, when Mr. Jordan says to Joe Pendleton, "This is your road, Joe," Marjorie was my road.

Marjorie would fill my senses with love, kindness, and devotion beyond anything I'd ever known. I didn't make it easy for her; I still tried to get to Europe. But you can't fight destiny by running away to another continent. My journey was beginning, but also complete. I was ready for the rest of my life when I said "I do."

Chapter 12

GETTING OUR FEET WET

Marjorie and I settled into marriage, learning, loving, and getting used to each other. Together, we would go to the beach, even if snow covered the oil-stained sand. We'd still kick off our shoes and let Brooklyn's ocean waves moisten our cold feet—our ritual of togetherness. Our early marriage times were textbook: our loving lasted for hours, and in between we spread a large pink Cannon towel on the bed for unmovable feasts of grapes, cheese, crackers, and red wine.

And still, we'd both have to get up for work in the morning. Marjorie taught a few miles away, while I worked as a pharmacist in Princeton—way over two hours from the Cannon towel. The Gateway Pharmacy, near the main gate at Princeton University, was a great intellectual gig for me. I could've stayed there forever, conditions permitting. The customers titillated: billionaires, publishing magnates, presidents of corporations, and those brainy students who loved our shampoos from around the world. But the boss man was paranoid and fixated on Fats Domino, which meant he played cassettes all day, every day.

After our wedding on July 31, we honeymooned for two weeks. We spent the first week hanging around Brooklyn. We caught a new movie, *Star Wars*; bumped into Ed Koch, who was running for mayor; and walked by the nude beach at Riis Park. I'm still convinced all nude beaches are inhabited by people who shouldn't be there. Of course, we dined at Hisae's again, the scene of our first date. The second week, sentimentality brought us to Club Med in Guadeloupe, a particle of our eventual meeting. We made love in the ocean day and night, with all the salty lubrication in the world to keep it pleasurable. One night, after three o'clock, we did it on the beach lounge chairs. There was no moon, but we wished upon many stars in a cloudless sky.

All the while, Marjorie and I sipped our White Russians dry. One day, the same day the Son of Sam killer was arrested, our conversation segued to children. "Marjorie, we've never talked about kids. I guess we assumed the obvious. Right?" I asked.

"Obviously, we assumed, but we do want them. The only thing now is how many."

"I don't care how many we have," I said, "just no more than six."

She laughed, "Let's be practical. No more than three." I agreed.

When we walked hand-in-hand to the tiny waves soporifically breaking on the beach, I pontificated what children meant to me. "When I was ten," I told her, "I discovered the jetty at Shark River in Belmar and spent that summer at the Jersey Shore, sitting on boulders, smelling dead fish, and dreaming of things, like playing baseball for the Dodgers and becoming someone's father. Maybe I should've gone to a shrink. How many kids dream away on becoming a father? I didn't even think of being an astronaut. They weren't invented back then."

I went on to explain that the older I got, the more I thought about children—raising them, teaching them, seeing the world through their eyes. I had to do it. It was part of what, who, why I am. "Not only do I need to be a father, but I have to be so involved in their lives. Imagine seeing the face of a child that first time sitting on Santa's lap in the mall, a few days before Christmas. Could their eyes be open any wider? And the love thing. I'd need to tell them ten times a day, minimum, how much I loved them. Loving a child completes me as a human being."

"Because your father never said it once to you," she said. Marjorie was so sharp. Every day, she gave me another reason why I loved her.

BROOKLYN APARTMENT LIVING

Some people are cut out for apartment living in a big city; I wasn't. Alternate side of the street parking put me in a bellicose state, devising vengeful alternatives. I got parking tickets often. One night around one o'clock, smoking in the living room and feeling particularly ornery, I went to the window. Our fifth-floor apartment butted up right against Bay View Hospital, a small community make-believe hospital, with pretend patients and television physicians like Ben Casey, Marcus Welby, and Dr. Kildare making rounds. I opened our window, took off my pajama top, exposing a Stanley Kowalski T-shirt underneath, and yelled loudly, "Stella! Stella!" right into the hospital window.

My excuse for this behavior was fatigue and an inner malcontent, driving four hours a day back and forth to Princeton. I'd gone back to taking uppers and downers—escaping, dancing around a maypole on crutches, searching, scratching, smoking, and eating obsessively. Was there ever a demon inside, camped out in my intestinal linings, fucking me up! I was one unhappy guy; uppers were just a temporary fix. Why was I so unhappy? A magma of molten volcanic creativity was stuck inside me, percolating with nowhere to go. It was a long way to Tipperary—the relief, the freedom of unleashing my inner self. Wouldn't it have been lovely if I had sought professional help a long time ago? But when I'm lost, I never ask for directions.

My obsession with food particularly clobbered me. One night, Marjorie called me at work in Princeton. Carol and her husband were coming over; I should bring donuts. I purchased three dozen at four o'clock on a Saturday night. The car trip home was fraught with Murphy's Law—every possible reason for traffic delay beat me up. Stuck in time and getting hungry, I ripped into the first dozen. By the time I got to Brooklyn, four hours later, I had rifled down thirty donuts, leaving just six for company. The state of my discontent became evident: I'd gained fifty pounds in six months.

One of those melancholy days, shrouded in fog and drizzle that never made it to rain, I stayed in bed all day. Marjorie came home from teaching feeling ebullient and upbeat, with student achievement stories to share. My sixth sense told me these student stories would go on for decades, until she and I were sitting in rocking chairs on a front porch somewhere, drinking prune juice on the rocks. I needed to get used to these stories for the long haul.

The sight of my despondence bothered her. "Cameron, what's the matter?" she asked. "I left you this morning exactly like this. Have you moved at all?"

"Yes—my bowels; the refrigerator door, to get orange juice. I'm sorry. My head is filled."

"Why? What about?"

So, I told her. A while back, President Carter had pardoned almost all the Vietnam draft evaders as long as they hadn't been involved in violent acts. My aged nemesis—guilt that I never served my country and evaded the draft—continued to bother me. I used to be proud of my ingenuity, but not anymore. Who was my friend, and who wanted to spit at me?

When Marjorie walked into the bedroom, for the first time in our marriage, I did not think about sex. Unhappiness and guilt took my breath away. So did uppers and downers. And I felt even guiltier. What the fuck was I doing to sweet, innocent, loving Marjorie?

Brooklyn was a colorful place to live: the best bagels and pizza anywhere; Fourth of July celebrations left significant depths of exploded firecracker paper on streets. Once, on Kings Highway, I saw a close John Travolta facsimile bopping around under the elevated subway. But being a city dweller was becoming increasingly tiring. I didn't like wandering around to find the Sunday newspaper, when in Jersey they throw it on your driveway. Commuting four hours a day to work was not for me. Hourglasses of sand can only be turned over so much, I told Marjorie.

In December 1978, Lufthansa at Kennedy Airport was robbed in an exciting $5 million heist—we lived only a few miles away. In the most convoluted way, I had a certain respect for the good fellows who committed that robbery. When I explained this to Marjorie, she got a glass of wine, sat in her underwear, and told me to go forth. Murders went hand in hand with organized crime, I told her, and society went crazy and jailed too many people. I liked criminals like Don Corleone, who was just taking care of his family. If you want to get murderers behind bars, go after corporate executives who knowingly sell products with faulty parts that put lives at risk. Leaving a bad product, with side effects that could kill, on the market an extra year can make more than enough profit to pay for lawsuits over a hundred deaths.

Marjorie was pissed at my thinking, so we went into the bedroom to make love, not war. Timing was perfect. A satisfied spouse, red wine, and the notion of compromise—physically moving somewhere that was equidistant to work for her and me. New Jersey would become a focus to change our lives, to move to a breath of fresh air and far away from the maddening world of fucking alternate side of the street parking. That particulate of caring and concern, a wondrous element of Marjorie's devotion to me, knew it was best to live in a better geography for both our work lives.

HOME STRETCH TO JERSEY

The year 1979 began with me getting a new job—what else is new? When I failed to acquiesce to my Princeton pharmacy boss's demand to submit false claims and overcharge rich customers, throwing away my Robin Hood tights, he fired me.

So, I rifled through pharmacy jobs all over Jersey. Marjorie was supportive of me finding a new gig—at least, she said, I wouldn't be attempting to bring home three dozen donuts from Princeton anymore.

Two weeks later, I landed a floating pharmacy job for Pharma-Assist, an East Coast chain. Every day, I would go to work at a different Jersey location. To celebrate, Marjorie and I decided to spend Saturday in bed, picnic on a Cannon towel, and get to know each other. When I insisted she assume the top position, which she didn't like, it spurred a revealing conversation.

"Cam, why do you always push me on top?" she asked.

"It's my feminist side," I said.

"Seriously?"

"Yes, seriously." I told her three of my role models were women: Althea Gibson, the elegant tennis player from the '50s who fought tennis opponents and racism; Mamie Till, mother of Emmett Till, who was murdered in Mississippi in August 1955; and Fannie Lou Hamer, civil rights activist, who'd said one of the most brilliant lines, "I'm sick and tired of being sick and tired." Marjorie was surprised that I'd never mentioned this before. That's the problem with fast romances: not enough time for probing and discovery.

When Kurt Waldheim, secretary general of the United Nations, declared 1979 was the International Year of the Child, Marjorie and I wordlessly looked at each other and decided we'd stop using protection and start looking for a home in Jersey.

It seemed a million miles away, beyond the sun and to the far reaches of the galaxy, when the Camp David Accords were signed at the White House, between Egypt's President Sadat and Israel's Prime Minister Begin. Marjorie and I thought maybe the world would be a better, more peaceful place to bring a child into. Our heads were in a good place. Our sex was plentiful and purposeful. How easy for mankind to sign treaties, seek peace, work to save the planet, and put the citizenry in such a good mood.

In pursuit of a new home, we devoted some of our weekends to trips across the Verrazzano-Narrows Bridge into Middlesex County, which was centrally located for us. In May, we looked in East Brunswick, off Route 18, the same road that opened this memoir. All systems were on for the launch. We found a house on Whitestone Road in the Lawrence Brook section. The following week, we brought Marjorie's parents along, as they'd be helping us with it financially. Everybody liked the house, with its large lawn, quiet street, experienced shade trees, and that certain feel. It was a place to call home.

Our need to feel like real Jerseyans brought us to an outdoor art festival in South Orange the following Sunday. Who knew it'd be a triple impossible day, bumping into everybody from a past life. First Wendy Paul walked by, my "Goodbye, South Orange" recipient. Out of the corner of her green eye, she noticed me, but kept walking. Good for her. Abstract art always magnetized me, and apparently also my ex, Valerie. Suddenly we were face to face. Embarrassment didn't even have time to set in, so I simply introduced my wife by saying, "This is Marjorie." A smart, savvy, streetwise Brooklyn woman, Marjorie just said hi and walked away. Valerie and I exchanged elementary nothings, not sweet or bitter, and said goodbye. Once more, I'd never see her again.

As we left, we ran into Julian and Alice. They'd moved to West Orange in my third year with Valerie and I hadn't seen or spoken to them since. We didn't speak at the festival either; we just kept walking, looking at art, pretending there was no sighting, familiarity, nothing.

Life is strange. Life is also resolution. I'd been to my last South Orange sidewalk art show. Lah-di-dah.

Chapter 13

JERSEY NEW EYE LIFE

We became East Brunswick residents in July of 1979. Marjorie commuted to Brooklyn to teach and I was still driving around the state as a relief pharmacist, which wore me out partly because there was no permanency or relationship building. Being cooped up in the same pharmacy for months was boring, as was being in a different place every day. I needed a happy medium. The profession of making people feel good made me feel lousy.

In my waning days at Pharma-Assist, I heard a code-red message on the loudspeaker. Richard Hoseman, a favorite customer of mine who was in his mid-eighties, had slipped and fallen. He always affectionately called me "Little Doc." When I got to him, he was sprawled in front of a motor oil display, not breathing. I administered artificial respiration and color slowly came back to his face. His eyes seemed ready to open when first aid arrived, but they broke the rhythm when they pulled me off him, so he died. I was devastated. I quit at the end of the week.

Marjorie endured my loss of work again, but I always rebound. By the following week, I was managing a pharmacy in Plainfield called West Side Drugs. Plainfield was a hard, inner-city place of despair and crime, but something made me feel comfortable, that I belonged—notwithstanding that my father had been born in this town.

At West Side I had yet another maniacal boss, who charged me ten cents just to call home. This coupled with his other assaults on my integrity would eventually catapult me away from this profession called pharmacy for good. I did not belong there.

Near the store was an eye physician who prescribed 1-percent cocaine eyedrop solution as a topical ocular anesthetic. Late on a Sunday, before closing, I was alone in the store and had to make a stock solution of cocaine drops. The pharmaceutically pure cocaine was stored in the safe. As I poured the powder onto a scale, my hand slipped, sending powder flying all over the counter. Not to waste the now-unsterile powder, with a medicinal plastic straw, I shot it up my nose. I felt nothing, thank goodness—I didn't need more abusive, reckless behavior in my life.

A few weeks later, my West Side boss also directed me to commit Medicaid fraud and submit false claims to the state for several claims per day. For a month, I refused to do anything illegal. Then my boss warned me, while standing so close that I could smell his putrid breath, to either do it every day, or I'd be fired. So, I was fired. The trip home to tell Marjorie was agonizing, precipitating several bursts of crying in the car over my failures as a husband, provider, dreamer, human. A block from home, my first concrete thought was what would happen to our pregnancy quest? Would that get put on hold, just like my life was again?

But through it all Marjorie supported and loved me. Something (that word again) gently aroused me on a Sunday morning in February of 1981. I rubbed my eyes, then I sat up in bed and looked at Marjorie sleeping, her back to me. "Honey, are you up?" I asked softly.

"I am now. What's so important?"

"Something just came to me. You know how I love and respect somethings," I said. "I've decided to quit being a pharmacist. No more. I don't ever want to walk into a pharmacy again."

"But what are you going to do? We just bought a house."

"I don't know. Something will come along," I said, trying to disguise my fear and guilt of letting down Marjorie.

Just then, I turned on the radio. WMGQ in New Brunswick interrupted its soft, mellow music with a commercial for the Edison Valley Playhouse. They were looking for actors for a play, *Frankenstein*, the same production that opened and closed on Broadway within a few days. Something made me think to audition. After all, I was six-foot-five and perfectly tall enough to be the creature, walking around the stage, crashing into things, pounding on people.

The script was interesting with the creature's viewpoints about how it felt to be put together from different body parts. Marjorie sat in the audience while I read for the part. Out of the corner of my eye, I watched her slowly sink below eye-view level—a clear case of embarrassment. Six weeks went by and never heard back about my audition, nor had I expected to, but I used this experience for years as an example of my determination and willingness to throw things at the wall, pursuing my dreams with quirky recklessness.

Four months later, I was sitting in the den chair, smoking, staining my T-shirt with mustard and ketchup, watching *General Hospital* and *The Rockford Files*, waiting for Marjorie to come home from teaching in Brooklyn. My unemployment was painfully hard and stressful on our stressed-out marriage. The good news was that I'd always hated the taste of alcohol, so at least I avoided slipping into alcoholic escapism.

In this new nadir of mine, a spiritual connection saw the depths to which I was sinking. An enduring life friendship was born on the streets of East Brunswick. At a welcoming barbecue for new neighbors on a cul-de-sac, Marjorie and I met Keith and Meryl Becker. Some friendships are instant, chemical, spiritual—so it was with Keith. He was a quintessential dilettante, ranging from music, history, electronics, sports, dirty comedians, so he knew endless assortments of people. And soon he began a job search for my salvation.

One day, Keith knocked on my front door, just as an episode of *The Rockford Files* was finishing.

"Cameron, I've got a friend who has a friend, who is an optician, who makes eyeglasses, and who has a friend who sells eyeglasses," he said. "The salesman could get you a job selling eyeglasses."

"Thanks, buddy, but what the fuck do I know about selling eyeglasses?" I said.

I didn't tell Marjorie about turning down the offer. Two weeks went by. Each night around midnight, I'd walk around the development, smoking, staring at the universe, looking for answers, something. Then, after seeing a shooting star, I realized that I had the balls to audition for a play, which I'd never done before—so I must have some leftover, low-hanging, resilient balls left to sell eyeglasses. I called Keith to proclaim my readiness, not knowing I'd comfortably reside in that profession for the next quarter century.

BROWN EYES

The interview for my first eyeglass job was with Michael Brown, CEO of Brown Eyes, a small optical company based out of Atlanta. Michael spoke about product lines from France, Italy, Finland, and China. My optical resume was nonexistent, so he set up a training session. Monday, August 3, became day one of the rest of my life.

Eyeglass sales was a commission-only, no-benefits, no-expenses, freewheeling enterprise. People liked buying from those they knew. I was so new; it was a hard beginning rain. Later in my career, I often said that if I had to start all over again, the learning curves and relationship building were so painstakingly slow that I would've given up and gone back to counting pills. But there was Marjorie, so loyal, loving, hopeful; no way could I ever disappoint her and go back to sitting in the den, sinking to lower depths of self-esteem.

My first day on the job was hard, cold, and fruitless. I felt like a small, red poisonous ant moving at the base of Mount Everest, about to begin my ascent to the top—a daunting, beyond-realistic vision. Each day, I walked into offices not knowing shit about my product or the customer's needs, stumbled over my pitches, and whipped my tail between my legs the instant I heard "no."

Five days later, I finally had my first sale: five frames. My commission was $15. I was off to see the wizard.

In all my years, I never let anyone into my head. It was my mother's wisdom, making me read Dale Carnegie, that made me a good salesman. I used to preach to my sales reps (when I became a manager) that there is only one time in a salesmen's life when they can really tell accounts to go fuck themselves: after you hit the lottery for at least $100 million.

Almost two years with Brown Eyes was a perfect launching pad for an extended selling career. My approach was to never give someone a reason to dislike me. I always went the extra mile, thinking of everything to enhance business and personal relationships. Selling was a science. I liked the business; there were no pills on the shelves to lift me up and crash me down. The highs after making a great sale were as good as anything off the medicine shelf.

Stability in my married life was a perfect side effect of finding myself as an optical salesman. Sex with Marjorie was often and for a purpose: getting pregnant. Basal thermometers, a few extra pillows, charts, and package inserts became bedroom fixtures. Marjorie was happy, so I was too. When you're having fun sex and becoming financially secure, time flies. One morning, in the bathroom together, me shaving and her doing her makeup, an epiphany slapped us. We'd been trying for a year, doing all the right moves—and nothing. For me, this quest was more obsessive, embedded in my soul, but we'd never openly discussed that, despite talking about everything else.

"We've been diligent for the past year. What happens now?" I asked her.

"I've been reading up on things. Maybe it's time for you to get checked out," she suggested.

"Shouldn't we flip a coin?"

"Not funny. The male plumbing is simpler. You're either shooting or you're not. With me, it's very involved. You go first."

In the blink of an eye, I was sitting in a New Brunswick urologist's office, my first time with the specialty. I thought urologists were for old men who couldn't piss anymore. Panic and disbelief accompanied me out of the office—I now needed a minor exploratory surgical procedure to find out why I might be shooting blanks. I had two weeks to mentally prepare myself for being put to sleep with anesthesia. Control freaks like myself do not like the prospect of being put to sleep on a slab table while a stranger explores their private parts. What if I was given too much anesthesia and I wound up sleeping with the fishes?

"I'm doing this dread for you," I said forcefully.

Marjorie countered, "No, for us."

The night before surgery, my wife, my pillar of support, suggested the new Paul Newman movie *The Verdict* to take my mind off my first surgical experience. The essence of the movie is that a patient goes in for surgery with anesthesia and comes out a life-long vegetable. I gyrated in my seat as the plot depicted the patient becoming that vegetable; a sleepless night for me. Medical worries came from my mother. The slightest headache? Cancer.

After the surgery, which went as well as possible, it was revealed that I needed a procedure called varicocelectomy. When the anesthesia had worn off, I asked the urologist why he didn't just do it while I was cut open and still sleeping.

"You never told us," he said.

"But I was sleeping." How I wanted to incorporate "fuck" into my response, but I realized he would be putting me to sleep again and messing around with my penis once more, so I pretended I loved everything he said.

A month later, with my plumbing now fixed, Marjorie and I went back to baby-making full time. New Year's Eve was poignant, hoping for a family in 1983. Marjorie and I shared a long kiss while the ball came down. "If our tongues didn't recognize each other," I said, "they do now."

Chapter 14

ITALIAN ENCHANTMENT

Back in December, a phone conversation had changed the course of my life. I'd gotten three messages through Brown Eyes to call someone named Jim Gordon. I never did, simply because I had no idea who he was. On occasional nights, I'd go outside near midnight to walk around the block, blow smoke rings to infinity, and ponder the universe's vastness. I'd say a few verbal prayers about becoming a father and how much my life needed a child to fulfill a notion of destiny. After praying and lighting another cigarette, I stared at a bright star as it winked down at me. Something was there, and I knew to call Jim Gordon.

   Right from the starting gate, Jim said my call was perfect timing— he had been close to writing me off altogether. He went on to tell me he was a regional manager for Incanto, an Italian eyewear manufacturer and distributor that had an office in Edison, New Jersey. *Incanto* meant *enchantment*. Every rep in the business dreamed of working for Incanto, and I told Jim I hoped I would too someday.

"Good. Stop hoping," Jim said. "Incanto is spinning off a new division, Vero—or *true* in Italian. You've built a solid reputation. You're liked across the board, unilaterally. The book on you is one of the best reps, who needs the best company behind him. Would you like to meet and talk?"

"You made my day," I said.

I had to contemplate the opportunity of my life at Incanto. All their reps were legendary money earners. Incanto fingered pulse and style. But loyalty was everything to me—how could I leave Brown Eyes when they had been so supportive? This decision was not easy, and time was running out before Jim would go elsewhere.

Marjorie wore money blinders. Keith, who was becoming a father in two months, urged me to go toward the money. Once again, I felt consumed by guilt. For a brief shining moment, in the maelstrom of oscillating back and forth on this decision, I thought about running away to Hudson's Bay, living in a small cabin near a frozen body of water, and writing poetry and eating fish every day. "Bury me deep beneath the sea," I'd written in my old poem from high school.

Finally, Amelia righted my ship of foolish thinking. "Cameron, there are no issues of loyalty in life when it comes to bettering yourself. If Brown Eyes is loyal, they'll realize Incanto is the best place for you," she said.

So, in mid-January, 1983, I joined Vero Eyewear and Incanto. I spent the first week at an orientation for the inaugural sales force at a hotel in Woodbridge, overlooking a Jewish cemetery and the busiest highway in New Jersey, Route 1. Among me were some of the country's leading optical reps. In meetings, I sat in the back, intimidated because I didn't belong. On the second night, I called Marjorie from a desolate phone in the dreary hotel basement, piles of used towels to my left. I was crying, losing it, embarrassed at my own inadequacies and inexperience. "I should've never accepted the position," I groaned.

"I'm not ready. All the reps here are so talented. I haven't said a word at meetings. I don't even know how to ask a question. Forgive me. I'll never make it here."

"Cam, I love you. Have faith in yourself," Marjorie said. "Remember the audition for *Frankenstein*? You can do anything. You will make it. I know it."

On the third day of orientation, we met the executives of Incanto and Vero, owned by Vincenzo Gallo and his son Antonio, a brilliant, incisive human. Antonio was the kind of guy who would break down and cry at year-end sales meetings, overwhelmed by sentimentality. Part of the brain team was Vice President Hayden Sommers, the most incredible mind, orator, and salesman I've ever met. It would take me twenty-five years to truly grasp what these three men were trying to accomplish together and how their vision shaped my life, soul, and mind.

Personal success as a sales rep is a self-fulfilling prophecy. The brain team at Incanto and Vero loved when their reps made piles of money because it meant the company was making even bigger piles. My manager was Stuart Westman, a seventy-something former auto parts salesman who once showed me his bonus check for $68,000. My goal was to become Vero's (this new division) first sales manager on the East Coast. Stuart told me, "Just keep being number one, a company man, and accept everything management has to say. Never stop working hard."

Stuart preached that I should never pull up to an eyeglass account in a fancier car than they had. Never suggest you're a super star earner, but always play the sympathy card. People want to feel good and help a poor rep out. There was a fine line between that and people buying from a successful rep; amiable personalities want to be liked and part of the in-crowd. There were many subtleties to the art of being a successful salesman.

And in time, I did make it at Vero. By the end of my first year, I was the number one sales rep. Life was falling into place. It felt like the wonderful ending of *Here Comes Mr. Jordan* when Mr. Jordan tells Joe, "This is your road." Of all the twists and turns in my life, once filled with science and pharmacology, who would've ever thought this eye stuff would be my road?

Chapter 15

THE DREAM REALIZED

With my income now stabilized, Marjorie and I banged away at becoming pregnant, which included interludes of romantic weekends. At Cape Cod in July, the air was filled with Kennedy mystique, the streets were lined with fish restaurants, and the nearby ocean was a constant display of picturesque waves. We had sex often. Life was good—except we still weren't getting pregnant. My plumbing was working now, so I asked Marjorie if she was ready to check her plumbing next.

It takes an enormous amount of energy to lift a rocket ship off the launchpad. Once it achieves speed and pulls far enough away from gravity, it requires less energy to move. Marjorie needed a lot of energy behind her to rocket herself over to a female doctor. One late night, as I pulled into the driveway, Marjorie was standing at the front door, her face pale and drawn, poised to deliver deflating news. Scar tissue from years of wearing an IUD was preventing pregnancy, the doctor had said. There was nothing much to be done, except trying to get into an in vitro program, which was still experimental at the time and not very successful.

At bedtime, we laid motionless with our hands behind heads, staring at the night-light near her dresser. We began one of the most serious, life-grasping conversations that would last for a year.

"This news sucks," Marjorie said, "but whatever happens or doesn't, I'm content to go through life just with you. I don't need anything else."

I thought it was way too early for us to talk about spending our lives just us together, no kids. "You know me—my dream, my soul, is to be a father. I don't care how it happens. I just need to be a father. Let's start researching in vitro. What about adoption?" I asked.

Marjorie got out of bed and started pacing back and forth. Then she turned on a table lamp and sat at the edge of the bed. "I don't think adoption is something I could ever do. The adoptions in my family were disasters with fucked-up kids. No, it's not for me. I mean, could I ever love a total stranger?"

So, we agreed to explore in vitro fertilization. Robert Wood Johnson Hospital in New Brunswick had a new in vitro program, but it had a strict acceptance procedure, perhaps based on odds of success. Our odds sucked, given our age—our eggs and sperm had been on the shelf too long. But desperation was all over me; I wore it like a new layer of pale white skin.

Eventually, we got a call saying we were accepted. Maybe they needed a lousy odds couple.

Marjorie and I hugged, then slow-danced in our minuscule East Brunswick kitchen. "Let the games begin," I whispered in her ear.

The "game" involved me regularly injecting her with Pergonal, a magical potion that upped our odds of conception. When all systems were in sync, I'd run into the bathroom, close my eyes, fixate on some turn-on image, and make a sperm deposit for implantation. On our first attempt, we prayed and paced, then frowned and cried when it didn't work.

Throughout all of this, life went on around us. Our friends were having children of their own. Of course, we wished them all good things, but deep inside us was an unspoken sadness in our barren world. The morning our friend and neighbor Meryl's water broke, her husband Keith called us from hours away, asking us to take her to the hospital.

"Do I have time to shower and have a bowl of cereal?" I asked. For years, we'd laugh about my insensitivity and failure to grasp time.

In vitro—not covered by medical insurance—set us back $10,000 a pop and would take decades to recover from financially. Our program allowed three pops, then you were out of the program. After our first failure, we took a few months to regenerate, then popped a second time. Again, a failure.

By the end of the year, we were down to our last attempt. Our hopes were fading into the cold reality that the extra bedroom in our house would stay white, empty, and sad. Every few weeks, I'd bring up the subject of adoption, which Marjorie continually rejected on the grounds that she could never love an unfamiliar child that way.

When I finished the year as the top salesman in the country, I was gifted the chance to pick any spot in North America for a ten-day trip on the company's dime. So, Marjorie and I were off to Hawaii between Christmas and New Year's. We were in paradise, but the only site I wanted to see was the beach from the scene with Deborah Kerr and Burt Lancaster in *From Here to Eternity*. It had looked so gigantic and iconic in the black-and-white movie, but in reality, it was just a few feet wide.

On our flight home, not quite halfway to Los Angeles, our plane lost an engine and turned back to Honolulu. Holding hands and lovingly looking at each other through the whole landing, Marjorie and I thought it was a good sign that we were alive and laughing, and so we rushed to do our last in vitro attempt in January.

A few days after implantation, Marjorie got a call that her hormone levels were up, which perhaps indicated pregnancy. All the money we spent, all the pain of failed implantations, were almost worth it for those three days we thought we were pregnant. If only I could've bottled that feeling and stuck it in the medicine cabinet. Then Bloody Sunday hit—Marjorie got her period. Devastated, we could hardly look at each other. Our words got lost trying to comfort each other.

A few weeks passed when my fatherhood issues festered again. "Marjorie, are you up?" I asked her late one night. Of course, I knew she was fast asleep.

She mustered a weak, muffled response. "I know you're about to nudge me about adoption. I've not changed my mind, so leave me alone. Talk to me in the summer when I don't have to get up early for school." Each time I brought it up, Marjorie was so resolute.

I wanted to scream. My biological clock was ticking too, spiritually, soulfully, and selfishly. Our disagreement felt like the end of our days. We were at an impasse, heading down a terrible road with a fork in it. The fork was our wonderful marriage, filled with so much endurance and love. But we were so different now in this arena that counted for so much.

Introspectively, I knew Marjorie could never change on this issue. I would never change either. Where did we go from here? I'd never bring up brinkmanship, glimpses of a sad ending in court. I didn't know what the fuck I was thinking, but it scared me. Could there be a world without Marjorie? My whole cognizant life since I was ten years old, sitting on that jetty in Belmar, dreaming of being someone's father, revolved around this.

The Ides of March arrived one late weekday night as I woke Marjorie up to talk about adoption once again.

"Cameron, no more of this," she snapped. "You can't do this to me when I have to get up in a few hours. Stop it."

I was on a Schwinn bike careening for a head-on collision with a Clinton Place Newark bus—a game of chicken, just like in *Rebel Without a Cause*. The only end was getting killed by the bus. In my heart, I knew our marriage was on the line. All the symptoms were there. But I had a last-gasp idea. Something had come into my thought process.

"This is the last time I'll ever bring this up," I said. "You've been saying for the past year how you could never love a stranger, an adopted child. It just occurred to me that when we met at that bar in New York, we were perfect strangers. We got married and we are *still* perfect strangers—who dearly love each other. We'll always be strangers. An adopted child is the same way—they'd become part of us, just like we are now."

Marjorie was silent in the darkness. I wasn't sure she was still awake. "That makes sense," she finally said, sounding fascinated by the idea. "Let's talk in the morning."

When morning came, neither of us said anything. We both played it cool, testing the waters. I sat in the den, smoking and eating a banana, wondering what would happen if I dried out the peel in the hot sun and smoked it. Would I get a potassium high?

That evening, Marjorie spoke first. "I thought about what you said all day. You are right. I think I'm open to adopting. So, what do we do now?"

"First we go upstairs and ceremoniously throw away that fucking basal thermometer," I said. "In everyone's circle of influence, there are people who've adopted. We just have to let them all know we're ready. Ask questions. Share our dreams. Throw it up on a wall."

Later Marjorie explained more about her decision. My constant campaign speeches—especially last night's, talking about our love, always being strangers, as a child would be—was a piece of positive energy. She had finally come to terms with her body's failure. The in vitro psychologist once asked if she wanted to be pregnant or be a mother. Coming home that day, she knew.

ADOPTIVE PROCESSES

The world soon knew of our new quest. It consumed me. Every conversation I had, I segued into questions of adoption, even my sales calls. In one breath, I'd be encouraging an account to buy a dozen designer sunglasses, and then I'd add, "A crazy question: Do you know anyone who ever adopted? I'm doing a little research."

On a two-day sales trip to South Jersey, I went significantly overboard. Deep in southwest Jersey, near Philadelphia, were small-town patches of farmland with elaborate gas stations, quick marts selling regular milk, five-and-dimes promoting sales on sewing thimbles. There were also adult boutiques with nude girls available for personal sessions in private booths. I'd never been in one. Late in the day, something pushed me through the windowless door.

Looking around, I knew these surroundings were as low as I could go. Dozens of private viewing booths lined the walls. In the center of the room was a rotating stage where a girl performed for the men in the booths. Inside one of them, I gasped for breath; it reeked of an unforgettable stench of human depravity. Onstage danced a young girl in her late twenties, obviously pregnant. Every minute, I fed the dollar meter, keeping the curtain on the booth raised. When she finished, she went to the back viewing booths for personal sessions. I watched where she went and followed her. Ten dollars gave me five minutes. This was totally not allowed, but I asked her out for dinner. Big Brother was listening on the phone, so I wrote my invitation out on an order sheet in my suit pocket. What the fuck was I doing?

At a diner just down the highway, we got a booth for two. She ordered a steak; smart girl, eating for two. It took about an hour to reach a comfort level, complicated by the fact that an hour earlier I'd seen every aperture of her nude body. To my credit, as a classy guy, I'd told her not to disrobe in our private booth. I just wanted conversation.

"This may sound crazy, but what are your plans for your baby?" I asked. "I'm on this quest to adopt a child." I can't believe that I'm writing this. Morbidly embarrassed. I think I would've wanted to adopt her baby.

Thanking me for being concerned, she complimented my powers of observation and said she was giving her child to Catholic Charities in Philadelphia. If I had met her two months earlier, the baby could've been mine. I thanked spirits for not meeting her two months ago. This was such desperation madness—there had to be a better way.

THE UNIVERSE PROACTIVE

In late April, my sister Carol was invited to a housewarming party in suburban Essex County. Most of the guests would be highbrow with an abundance of fixed noses, prominently elevated, as if starved of oxygen. She went back and forth whether to attend, disliking pretense, bullshit, and clothes from Saks Fifth Avenue. Sunday morning, at the last possible moment of decision, something made her shower, dress in a Macy's outfit, and go to the party. There, at the bar, Carol saw a young couple holding an infant. Someone asked when they'd gotten their baby.

"Last week, we flew down, went to court the same day, and here we are, a family," the woman explained. Eavesdropping her specialty, Carol jumped in to find out more. The woman ebulliently went on. "We used these two well-established women lawyers from Nanuet, New York, who only do adoptive law. They told us we'd be parents in four months. Four months was yesterday."

Marjorie and I spent the next month researching, inundating ourselves with everything adoption, still sitting with the piece of paper Carol had written out with the lawyers' names, London and Roldan. Finally, we got up the courage to call them and set an appointment for Wednesday, August 14, 1985. In the two weeks prior to the appointment, we perfunctorily went through the motions of work and play, but we were distant to one another, lost in thought. I cheated at work by splitting orders in half and submitting them over two weeks, so the week before our lawyer appointment, I could stay at home, sleep late, smoke cigarettes, and manage to stay far away from Marjorie, who was keeping busy in her own ways: reading, polishing silverware, and talking to her sister.

Nanuet was sixty-four minutes from East Brunswick. Marjorie was an early person, so we arrived to our appointment an hour early, fidgeting in the waiting room. Once, in pharmacy school, we'd taken a class trip to Lederle Labs in Pearl River, then had dinner at a nearby Nanuet restaurant. Something about the town of Nanuet had struck me. I could visualize living there, married with two children, working as the proprietor of a local pharmacy. I imagined a perfect *Twilight Zone* world, with summer band concerts at the town gazebo sponsored by my pharmacy. Nanuet was subliminal for years—and now I was there, ready to begin my quest for destiny.

The lawyers told us about their process. They'd direct clients to put personal ads in newspapers in adoption-friendly states, saying something along the lines of, "Professional loving couple seeks to fulfill their dream in life to become parents and share their love." If and when someone seriously reached out to us, we'd turn things over to them. It was uncomfortable listening to their technique, exposing ourselves to a great unknown burdened with things that could go wrong and break our hearts. Their last lawyerly words were, "You'll be parents within six months." Then the lawyers left us alone to discuss.

"We've come this far, Cameron. I have such a good feeling. Let's just do this," Marjorie said.

So, we signed on the dotted line, wrote them a check, and shook hands. We'd never see them again; just a few phone calls.

Next, a strange, dark, and occasionally hopeful world became our new reality. We got phone calls from several states, each one more emotionally draining than the next. Jimmy John had a stable of women he could implant and sell us the baby. Tammy Sue, a recovering drug addict, was three months pregnant. Her baby was ours if the price was right. Marjorie endured this for days, sometimes responding with tears, sometimes with laughter at the absurdity. Then Didi called, a pregnant seventeen-year-old. All systems were on. A few days later, Didi humanely backed out, deciding to give her baby to Christian charity.

A few quiet days passed and we were readying to renew our ads when Catherine called. Marjorie spoke to her for an hour. Catherine was nineteen, going to college in the fall, and was most concerned with giving her baby every opportunity at a good life—something she couldn't do. Whenever adoption talk seemed real, we put as much humanity on the line as we knew how, trying to determine how serious each candidate was, pleading with her to never change her mind. That disappointment, coupled with past in vitro failures, would be devastating. Thankfully, the situation soon became legal with attorneys on both sides. We talked with Catherine weekly, affirming her commitment to this agreement. How precious, thoughtful, and sensitive she was.

The second week in February, we got a call that she was in labor. On February 12, at 11:44 a.m., our son Noah was born. Marjorie tracked me down at work, and by evening we were flying south to become a family. Our long, arduous, emotional roller coaster of pain and joy had finally come to an end.

The next day in court, our attorney suggested we say nothing, just answer the judge's questions. Seven minutes later, the judge pronounced us a family.

When he got up and put his hand on chamber doors, I blurted out, "Excuse me, Your Honor. I need to say something."

"Go right ahead, Mr. Simmons."

"There isn't enough time for me to explain what you've done here by making us a family," I began. "This has been our dream for years. Our quest has been never-ending. But you should know we are two people filled with love, and you've given us a chance to share our love and experience the greatest joy and responsibility in life: to parent. Our gratitude is endless. Thank you."

"And thank you, Mr. Simmons," the judge nodded.

Two hours after the plane landed in Newark, we went to St. Peter's

Hospital in New Brunswick. Noah was having trouble breathing. It turned out we were just new parents who didn't know about nasal aspirators.

My dream beginning at the Belmar jetty when I was ten was finally realized.

Chapter 16

A FRESHLY PAVED ROAD

When we went to the hospital to pick Noah up before going to court, the nurse mentioned he was a very calm, special baby. A perfect early observation; Noah is still that way today. Once he was down in the crib on our first night together, I began a new daily tradition of giving him a goodnight kiss on the forehead and gently whispering, "Daddy loves you, Noah."

This nightly routine was born out of my relationship—or lack thereof—with my father, Jack. Not once do I remember him saying, "I love you, Cameron." So dramatic was this void in my life that when it was my time to be a father, I vowed things would be different. A dozen times a day, my son would hear his father loved him. In a convoluted way, Jack was a great father: He taught me by omission how to be a great father. Noah lucked out. Everything Jack wasn't, I had to be.

A few months before Noah's first birthday, toward the end of the year, Incanto and Vero had a joint national sales meeting on Route 1 in New Jersey. Designer eyewear was exploding, and the company was approaching exponential growth and profitability, so Vero was getting its own management team separate from Incanto. In the carpeted hallway outside the meeting room, Vice President Hayden Sommers offered me the Northeast manager position. This had been my dream for the past year. At the year-end company Christmas party, with Marjorie as witness, I downed in rapid succession twenty-six Bloody Marys to celebrate my promotion. The excitement of becoming a manager eliminated the deleterious effects of the alcohol. I'd be making more money as a manager, traveling and satisfying my need to teach, being creative, and giving of myself.

All the while, the tortoise was still hanging around, precipitating lapses in my development, confidence, and general sense of where the hell I was going in life. Something was inside me, shaking me up and making me unsure of tomorrow. It wasn't a conscious depression or unhappiness—just a feeling of being lost, looking for something out there in the dark of night. What was it? Everything was perfect in my life—my marriage, my son, and my job—but something unexplainable nagged at me, thus I was smoking more and eating with abandon.

The unknown was powerful; it could conjure up images and memories from a long-gone past. Absolutely out of nowhere, I was suddenly playing the pinball machine at Harry Becker's candy store, stealing warm bottles of Coca-Cola when he wasn't looking. I was with my mother in downtown Newark, shopping at Bamberger's and eating a sweetened egg salad sandwich at the luncheonette across the street. Or I was working at Jane Parker Bakeries in Newark on the night of the riots in 1967. I used to love sitting on the bakery roof at 3:00 a.m., getting the occasional whiff of hard rolls or jet fuel from the nearby airport, and dreaming about faraway places or the woman I'd marry and the child we'd have.

All random buried thoughts. When my mind would wander off to the most long-forgotten life episodes, I'd think, "Holy shit," amazed at these buried memories. Why were they coming? Was this part of the grand scheme for me?

Often in tandem with these mysterious regurgitated memories were feelings of déjà vu. No matter where I was—looking out the window of a moving car at a house, a barn, a clump of trees casting shadows—I knew I'd seen all this before. Or perhaps I'd be back someday, living in the house with a porch and a rocking chair. In the end, it left me feeling warm all over. This déjà vu business evolved soon after my first trip to Sedona, Arizona. Maybe it's a good thing I never sought help with it. Sometimes I feel as if I lived my whole life as a bespectacled individualist. Was I worried about someone throwing away the keys?

At Vero, my sales region consisted of New Jersey, Pennsylvania, Ohio, West Virginia, Delaware, Maryland, Virginia, Washington, DC, and Puerto Rico. Noah was still an infant, so the massive amount of travel wouldn't have an impact yet. Marjorie was glowing in motherhood, accepting my frequent absences and not missing teaching.

In the spring of 1987, all Vero managers went to Washington, DC, for a ten-day national convention of opticians and optometrists. Our job was to work the exhibit booths, socialize, and sell new styles to attendees from all over the country.

When a couple—an optician and optometrist—came to our booth from Great Falls, Montana, we had instant chemistry, and I sold them a pile of frames. Martha Olney, Vero's Montana sales manager, told me to take credit for the sale and keep the account, even though the couple lived a long way from New Jersey. Martha was a human dynamo, smooth and consummate achiever, with an effervescent personality. When I refused her offer, she insisted, and the company approved on the condition that I go to Montana once a year to service the account.

The next night, our company hosted a celebratory dinner over our successful sales at the convention. Two dozen reps ate and drank endless plates of Asian food, which hit the table every few minutes. Wine flowed, with some saki for ambiance. No meat for me. I reached for a shrimp dish with broccoli. One of the saucy shrimps evacuated the plate, landing in my lap and casting a nasty stain in an embarrassing place.

Martha, sitting next to me, knew what to do. "Trust me," she said. She dipped her napkin in a glass of club soda and started rubbing away at the stain. No one knew what was going on. I was shocked and embarrassed, but happy the stain dissolved. Suddenly, I understood why Martha had given me that account, and why she smiled so seductively at me.

On our last night in Washington, I had dinner with Martha at a quaint Italian restaurant. I orchestrated it mostly to thank her for giving me that account in Great Falls, which was totally out of the realm of company spirit. I was close to toasting the company, eyeglasses, and making piles of money, when Martha randomly brought up Baby M being given to William Stern, not Mary Beth Whitehead, in the famous surrogacy case. I explained that I was so conflicted because I'd recently adopted my son, and I would've done anything for him, including reaching out to any Mary Beth for help. Martha and I stared right through each other, so it was time to toast our night.

"Here's to you, Martha," I said. "I'll never understand why you are so magnanimous. No manager gives away territory. Funny thing, though, about Montana. I can't tell you how often I think of the state, its beauty and nature. And I've never been there. And now, just meeting you a few days ago, kind of like an angelic spirit, you're getting me there."

She leaned in close. "I don't know why I gave you the account. Something just made me do it. Hey, when you come out to Montana, take me out for a real home-grown steak dinner."

"It's a deal—as long as the restaurant has fish or chicken. Apologies to the meat industry in Montana, but I don't eat red meat. Not since 1975."

"I know a great restaurant. They fly in fish from California every day. I have a big ranch. You can stay with me," she said, smiling. "Montana hospitality."

That remark just slid away without me commenting or inferring. Back at the hotel, we hugged goodbye.

RUMBLINGS OF DISCONTENT

As Noah approached two years old, Marjorie, as if running for county freeholder, began campaigning for us to move from East Brunswick to a hot town called Marlboro that was exploding with growth and immigrants from Brooklyn and Staten Island. I'd have nothing to do with the notion of uprooting. I was comfortable where we were, close to our friends and in a convenient location for my work. And then there was the money to move, which we didn't have. In vitro had wiped us out. But Marjorie was relentless, using statistics to justify why Noah should grow up in a proper town.

How minds change is a curious phenomenon. A few weeks before Christmas, I was focused on driving around to drop off modest Christmas gifts to some of my better accounts. Marjorie had suggested a small gold box of six Godiva chocolates. A dozen wrapped boxes sat on the back seat. A snowstorm hit as I left Somerville, quickly accumulating and snarling traffic to a standstill. Hungry, and always frustrated when I shouldn't be, because life was good, I opened a box and downed the six chocolates. I was approaching 300 pounds at the time, but being tall, I hid it well under my 44-inch waist. In between cigarettes, I downed box after box as traffic stood still. When I was near home, a dozen empty Godiva boxes sat in the back seat. Turning off Route 18 and into our development, I pulled alongside a small lot and threw the empty boxes into the snow.

A week later, after the snow had melted, Marjorie noticed the Godiva hill on our way home from shopping with Noah. "Did you see that? Someone littered all those Godiva boxes. How disgusting," she said.

At that moment, I knew it was time to acquiesce to us moving, but I'd still have to slow things down. Over the years, I took courses at Vero and Incanto on how to deal with human change. Our species doesn't like change; we get into trouble dealing with it. Our house went up for sale in January. The development was still desirable, so we had potential buyers and real estate agents calling. I just couldn't deal with rapid change.

One cold, windy night, after a great day of selling, I came home late. Marjorie ran up to me for a hug. "A woman and broker came by this afternoon," she said excitedly. "They loved the house. It's almost a done deal. They're coming back with the husband in an hour. You're in charge. I'm going out with Meryl. Make sure you charm them."

A vision hit me. I didn't see myself being a Marlboro man yet. From the den, I watched Marjorie pull out in her car. My first job was to cover Noah with extra blankets. I turned down the thermostat, opened all the windows in the house, put on a heavy sweater, and waited a half hour. Then I closed the windows and raised the thermostat. The house was really cold. When the couple and realtor arrived, I charmed them. The wife and broker walked upstairs while the husband asked about the obvious chill.

"I'll be honest with you," I said. "We try so hard to heat the house, but the wind comes off the lake and it's brutally cold here all the time."

"I appreciate your honesty," the man said. "You're one unusual person."

Later, when Marjorie asked how it went, honesty prevailed. "I think well," I said.

The house stayed in our name until July, when we moved to Marlboro. Marjorie never knew how I bought us six more months in East Brunswick. On July 28, 1988, we began a new life in the last place on Earth we'd ever live.

Chapter 17

SOMETHING

Marjorie flourished in our home on Nance Road. She found her style, self-expressing with decorations. Nance Road was a fascinating street in that the twenty-two homes mostly had young children—a special sense of community. Noah had play dates and nursery school friends, some of whom endured into adulthood. Life was beautiful. Work was good. But something still nagged restlessly inside me. There were no more drugs in my life and alcohol had never done it for me, so for escapism I upped my cigarettes to more than a pack a day, and my eating habits were voracious, even without meat. My weight staggered past 300 pounds.

On a Friday sales call in Woodbridge, the buyer was busy, so I passed the time by chatting with another salesman for two hours. His name was Mike Hollings, an affable, short, and skinny rep from Phila-delphia. I liked him; we exchanged numbers.

The next morning, Stuart, my old manager, called. "Did you hear Mike had a heart attack last night? He passed away."

I was shocked. "I was with him for hours yesterday. Such a nice guy. How is that possible?"

"When it's your time, Cameron, there are no rules," Stuart said.

An hour later, I got terrible chest pains and couldn't breathe, so Marjorie rushed me to the hospital. It was the start of a new chapter in my life, running to emergency rooms often, swearing much like Fred Sanford that this was the big one.

I started rifling through cardiologists in rapid succession. Clinically, I had mitral valve prolapse, a common, non-life-threatening disorder. After six false trips to emergency rooms, Marjorie told me to drive myself on my next episode of severe chest pain. The cardiologist's isoenzyme test was definitive for a heart attack. An hour later, I was admitted into cardiac intensive care. Phoning Marjorie with the news and injecting her with guilt felt strangely good.

But by morning, I did not have a heart attack; they'd read the test wrong, not taking into account that any muscle movement, including cardiac muscles, gives off enzymes. A lesson for the rest of my life: You must be your own advocate and never depend on anyone except yourself. If you expect nothing from people, you'll never be disappointed.

Leading up to the end of July 1989, I was feeling strange, not myself. Sleep was fleeting for days. One night, July 20, just before midnight, I got on the scale to see I weighed 349 pounds. The last few days, like a mallet pounding reality on my head, I'd had a hard time walking upstairs, stopping every few steps to catch my breath. I was so fat, I couldn't even climb stairs. I was dying. That's the cerebral message that accompanied me to sleep that night.

Something (that word) got me up Monday morning way before the alarm. I felt almost as if I was being levitated, raised up in bed. Marjorie was sound asleep. My fists clenched as I felt something warm and comforting inside me. I had a clear vision of what had to be done. I jumped out of bed, walked into Noah's room, deposited my kiss, and went back to wake Marjorie. "Are you up?" I asked.

"I hate when you do that. What's so important?"

"I can't explain this. Something is inside me. Today I take care of all family business."

She laughed, knowing my routines. "Quoting *The Godfather* again. What do you mean?" Her patience was ebbing away.

"No more cigarettes. I'll throw them away. I'll drastically diet and exercise every day. I mean it."

"Cameron, just do one thing. Diet or stop smoking—no one can do both together."

"You don't understand. I'm possessed."

Possession is a perfect word. Something came into me, filling my senses with more determination than I'd ever experienced. I crushed my cigarettes satisfyingly in my hand. My diet consisted of 500 calories a day: a few pieces of pasta, chicken or fish, fruit, and salad—no dressing, no sugar. To keep my mind from cigarettes, music played in my ears 24/7. Simon and Garfunkel were companions, especially "Scarborough Fair," and Donovan's "Catch the Wind." Perhaps I listened to Donovan fifty times a day; it became my anthem.

Every night I'd walk a mile around the development. Two and a half months later, I'd lost a hundred pounds. The weight loss was so dramatic that on sales calls, if the account hadn't seen me in a few months, sometimes they didn't recognize me. Rumors abounded that I had AIDS. But my life was saved by something, I know that. My life was extended, given a purpose, a journey. In short time, I'd receive even more dramatic spiritual intervention.

Proudly, my exercise increased. I joined the YMCA, lifting weights and taking up tennis. Two summers later, temperature in the nineties, I played six and a half hours of tennis straight—singles, doubles, mixed doubles—and never once stopped to catch my breath. The power of healing the body, rebuilding it—I could've never done this alone. At the time, however, this spirit thing was not yet defined and solidified in my awareness. I only had an idea that something was out there.

Emerging around my dramatic weight loss, rising out of a deep-buried sense of self, was an element that would drive my life later on. It was a confidence that I could do anything, even talk to anyone on the planet. I was still growing, gaining momentum, nurturing myself, and something was there. I suspect the tortoise had helped keep those feelings buried. Like the Virginia Slims commercial, I'd come a long way.

In this period of discovery, I learned about my proclivities to being a groupie. Just being around the auras of celebrities was everything. Not ever would I ask for an autograph—unless they asked for mine first. I loved movies from the golden days of Hollywood, mystiques, World War II genres, back when the world was fighting for freedom and survival. Movies captured my imagination, energized my soul, and partially lit a fire within me to write a book. The rest of the fire came from angelic intervention.

In September, Vero and Incanto exhibited at Opti-Fair, a global eyewear exposition in New York City. After a long day of selling and bullshitting, the company took reps and managers to Gallaghers Steakhouse, which was famous for red meat, but I ordered fresh Hudson River fish. After dinner, twenty well-dressed eyeglass industry people hung out on the sidewalk on West Fifty-Second Street. I noticed local TV station vans and limousines lined up near the Neil Simon Theater for the opening night of *Orpheus Descending*, starring Vanessa Redgrave. "Anybody want to camp out at the stage door and catch the celebrities as they come out?" I asked the group.

I stood alone. Celebrities emerged, waved, got into limos, and disappeared into the night. Feeling good, imagining myself with Gene Kelly and Frank Sinatra, I threw my suit coat over my shoulder and headed back to the Marriott Marquis in Times Square, a very busy hotel at the crossroads of the world. There was usually a line to take the elevators up to the lobby on the eighth floor, but I was eerily alone tonight as the elevator door opened. I pressed eight and noticed a ticket on the floor. It was a ticket to the opening night cast party for *Orpheus Descending* in the ninth-floor grand ballroom. My hands shook with the synchronicity of it all. I had to go to this party.

Christopher Reeve stood just in front of me on the escalator up to the ninth floor. Although I had an admission ticket, I told the security guard, "My uncle, Lou Marx, everybody knows him, right? Well, he sent me the ticket."

I spent a few hours absorbing and engaging with the celebrities. There I was, a skinny Cinderfella type, perhaps provoking questions from guests, "Who the hell is that tall guy?" I waited until midnight to make my getaway. As I reached for the door, a woman stopped me. She owned Broadway theaters and had evidently paid for tonight's party. "I sent all the invitations out. Who are you?" she asked.

"Lou Marx's nephew," I told her. She smiled and I got away clean. This night was a personal benchmark that you can do things with will-power, a fictional uncle, and a sprinkling of synchronicity.

A JERSEY GUY IN MONTANA

Rules are made to be broken. When Martha Olney had graciously given me an account in Great Falls, Montana, as long as I serviced them in person once a year, the whole orchestration seemed far out, but there was serious commission to be made. She mentioned how much the account liked my Jersey swagger, honesty, and modesty. Indeed, we'd broken a major company rule about integrity of territories: you don't cross state lines to steal someone's account.

On a Wednesday in May 1990, I flew out to the great American West to service my account in Montana. I planned to spend Thursday with the account, then take the weekend to explore a veritable God's country and search the strange dreams I'd had about Montana.

In one recurring dream, I spent Christmas Eve in a small cabin near a mountain covered in evergreen trees. Just before midnight, I took a long walk in freshly fallen snow while I stared at bright stars. One in particular seemed to be moving across the sky. Walking through town, a couple asked if I'd like to join a block party and bring my wife.

"I'm not married," I told them.

They seemed thrilled. The party featured a dozen locals, locally slaughtered fresh beef, hard liquor, and singing. I was introduced to Audrey. By 4:00 a.m., I was in her ranch bedroom. But I'd always wake up at this point. Who the hell was Audrey?

Martha picked me up at the airport and dropped me off at a log cabin–style motel near the Missouri River. The old motel was replete with way too much ambiance. Everything was musty and dank: pillows, towels, carpet from the roaring twenties.

"Are you sure? Wouldn't you like to stay at my ranch?" Martha asked as she dropped me off. "It's a big ranch—horses in the barn, a dozen dogs running around. Real Western charm."

"You know what, maybe tomorrow. I need to get the lay of the land," I said.

The next day, my account bought 200 frames, almost $1,500 in commission—well worth the trip. Martha and I had dinner to celebrate, as she'd gotten the manager's override, but still it was a bit strange. *She* was strange, a mountain woman who could clearly sell the shit out of anything. Our dinner conversation drifted to her hunting four-legged animals, to which I injected that I did not eat four-legged anything.

"Then going hunting with me tomorrow is not a good idea," she laughed. "Why don't you come back to the cabin? Spend the night. See how the real American West lives along the Rio Bravo River, beyond John Wayne Westerns."

I trusted myself. This whole adventure was strictly business, pocketing thousands in commission out of Martha's generosity. Did she have other motives? She was ruggedly sexy, but she was business. I didn't check out of my damp motel, but after a few more drinks, I followed her back home.

She opened her front door without a key, as this was real America, and warned me not to be frightened when eight large dogs enthusi-astically greeted us, sniffing and jumping around my groin. I looked around to take in the scene. This Jersey boy was in a real log cabin. Lights illuminated a sparsity of furnishings. There was a small sofa capable of sitting just three humans, wooden floors, a coffee table, and a few scattered piles of dog droppings.

"I'm cool with everything, Martha. This is all a wonderful expe-rience." I didn't know what else to say. Somehow, I had to stifle my discomfort and prepare myself for the impending downhill journey.

In the kitchen, a pile of dishes smelled of rancid meat and alcohol. Martha offered me some cabernet. I passed, so she chugged from the bottle. The large bay window revealed several spider webs with one big, hairy residential spider—for all I knew it was a tarantula.

"Are you okay with that spider as big as a Ford living in your kitchen?" I asked with a fearful voice.

"Ford, as in car?"

"I borrowed that line. I might as well say 'lah-di-dah' now." Martha looked confused. "Not important. I just don't do well with spiders bigger than a thumbnail. Maybe it's time for this Jersey boy to close his eyes and drift off to wonderland."

I followed my leader into her bedroom, and so did the dogs. Before I could react, I saw two beds on opposite sides of the room. Martha explained, "The dogs sleep in the other bedroom. I figured you'd be more comfortable here—and no, we're not sleeping together. Just nearby. Are you okay?" she asked. I said yes.

After separate showers, we both appeared in pajamas. I said good-night with a muffled thank-you for her mountain hospitality. At three in the morning, the dogs invaded, barking, jumping into my bed, licking my face, and stepping on my unprotected crotch. What most annoyed me was that Martha was still solidly sleeping.

I got dressed and nudged her awake. "Mountain life is definitely not for me," I said, pardoning myself. "I'm better off back in my moist cabin by the river. I'll call you tomorrow for lunch."

Back in bed at the motel, I tossed and turned, digesting what the hell had happened. I'd been sleeping in the same bedroom with a beautiful woman 2,000 miles away from my jetty in Belmar, and the only thing I could think of was getting far away, fast.

A year later, I gave up the Great Falls account. The great commissions no longer felt worth the obligatory phone calls to Martha or trips to Montana.

Chapter 18

ON THE ROAD TO REVELATION

Noah turned six in February 1992. Our life together was a marvelous miracle, a work in progress, and a constant joy. Ten times a day, I kissed him and pronounced how much his daddy loved him. We spent endless hours together discovering the world through his eyes, reading books and comics, building a K'NEX roller coaster, and listening to music by Sharon, Lois & Bram. Our life as a family felt perfect and meant to be.

Our world proudly knew about our journey to adopting Noah, but he didn't—yet. There were two prevailing schools of thought regarding adoption. One said that when a child is still in the crib, begin whispering, "Mommy and Daddy love you, and you're adopted." Keep repeating, reinforcing. The other approach was not to burden a young developing mind with difficult abstract concepts like adoption. Give the child a chance to grow, feel love, adjust to the world, and once they're mature enough, then talk about birds, bees, and adoption lawyers.

Marjorie, an elementary teacher, subscribed to this second school of thought. I did too. We never verbalized it, but we feared we could lose a piece of him if he knew early on. If he didn't know, it wouldn't hurt.

When we picked up Noah at the hospital, the birth mother let us decide if we wanted to meet her in person, so we opted not to. We felt that not having the visual of her would help Noah become more ours. It was complex psychological stuff.

That year for spring vacation, I took a short road trip to Atlantic City to sell eyeglasses. Despite his age, I brought my boy along so he could get a sense of what I did. It was our first road trip together, setting the stage for a lifetime. When Noah called his mother from Atlantic City, he said, "Hi, Mommy. Daddy and I are going to party now."

In late June, Incanto and Vero had a national sales meeting in Scottsdale, Arizona. Something made me want to bring along Marjorie and Noah and trip up to spiritual Sedona, so we could explore the desert, mountains, and cacti in our downtime.

After the meeting, which recognized my region finishing third nationwide, we had two days to explore Arizona. I rented a white Cadillac. Back in Newark, if you had a Caddy, you had moved on up. Arizona Highway 17 reminded us we weren't in Jersey anymore: brown rolling hills and families of cacti everywhere majestically praying to the silent gods of pristine nature. Noah slept in the back seat, a great travel companion.

Our first stop was Montezuma Castle, a well-preserved cliff dwelling and perhaps one of the first North American high-rise apartment complexes, going back to the Sinagua peoples in 1100 to 1400. An exhibit in the visitor's center said *Sinagua* meant *without water*. The constructions were ingeniously haunting. We walked around in a deafening silence. Even Noah stared quietly. "Daddy, where are the people who lived here?" he asked.

"They disappeared a long time ago. No one knows why," I explained.

Following the trail around the dwellings, by a gently babbling stream, I could feel something. I was unnerved, saddened that the people had simply vanished. Something was here, making me feel reverent, curious. I spoke in a constant whisper to Noah and Marjorie.

"Why are you whispering, Cam?" Marjorie asked.

"Because I don't want to disturb them."

Suddenly, I was chilled. A pocket of cool mountain air slapped my face. My neck hairs stood erect. Something was with me. I held Noah's hand tightly. As we left, I turned to see the dwellings, abandoned, silent, and sad. For a moment, I wanted to crawl back in time through a wormhole to visit the Sinagua and get absorbed into their society. Marjorie yelled for me to catch up.

We got back on the road to Sedona, or so we thought. Arizona travel literature highlights Sedona's majestic red mountains, sometimes the set of old Western movies with John Wayne in a stagecoach. But there were no red mountains in sight.

"Are you sure you're on the right road, Cameron? Maybe we should stop and ask?" Marjorie suggested.

"Stop and ask who? There is nothing here."

But as if someone had waved a magic wand, all of a sudden, red mountains were everywhere. It was like they rose out of the soil at the push of a button, like movie props. Craggy, surreal, glowing mountains. I'd read that some mountains were dotted with vortexes, which contained special energies of the universe. Sedona's red soil and dust particulates were all special invocations of magic, well-being, and connectivity to something higher.

I gently veered the car to the side of the road. Marjorie yelled, but I was already out the door and jumping into the red soil, scooping it up and rubbing it over my arms and legs, caking it underneath my fingernails. If there was truly magic in the red soil, I wanted some. "What the fuck are you doing?" Marjorie mouthed at me. Noah just laughed.

Back in the car, I felt strange and red and dirty. In town, we signed up for a Pink Jeep Tour, which took us into the mountains toward the silence of the red rocks, the coolness of the forest, and sacred, godly feelings. The jeep literally drove straight down boulders, moving slowly, precariously. I thought I could live here, waking up in the morning and seeing the sun paint the red mountains in earthy colors. I envisioned myself writing about loneliness, hope, and growing up in Newark— this was the first time I ever expressed a serious interest in writing.

After the tour, we browsed a Western arts and crafts village, Tlaquepaque. We saw a magic carpet—it just lifted and moved—that made me aware of the beauty of Native American culture and history embedded with sadness. At one of the shops, I bought Coyote Oldman's *Tear of the Moon*, featuring Incan panpipes and Native American flutes. I would listen to that CD almost obsessively.

A few days after flying home, I played poker with some friends. I didn't feel any different since visiting Sedona. Then, late in the game, I hit a royal flush. A few days later, I randomly bought a Pick-6 lottery ticket and hit five out of six numbers, winning a few thousand. I never win anything. Some would say that was just luck and statistics. I was having an epiphany: *Something* had happened to me in Sedona, after I'd bathed in the red soil. I should've stripped naked, rubbing the red soil everywhere on my body to absorb as much energy as possible. Maybe that would've yielded enough energy to pick six correct numbers instead of five.

After that, I became more aware of my sense of déjà vu. It made me feel warm, safe, and familiar. Driving down a street far from home, I'd glance at a random Victorian house with a porch and weeping willow and know I'd been there before. Crossing the Raritan River on a train to Willoughby, I'd see an abandoned factory but I'd know I'd been there before too. It's like when/if I come back to another life, that's my house and factory, located in an atom on my left thumb that holds infinite universes. Sometimes the feelings were so strong, I wanted to get out of the car and walk around the building to see if I disappeared into a sparkling radioactive cloud. What the hell did it mean to see a shadow on the side of a building and believe I'd been there before? Thank you, Sedona.

Chapter 19

MORE ON THE ROAD STORIES

Vero Eyewear was a very desirable company to work for. When I hired new workers, I'd throw candidates' qualifications on a table, and when a White candidate and a minority candidate were equally qualified, I chose the latter. I wanted a diverse region. I spent lots of time with my reps, training them and learning just as much about their world in return.

As part of my job as a regional manager, I would visit my reps' accounts and evaluate their selling performance. My visits were planned ahead, affording my reps time to prepare Potemkin villages, making everything seem better than it really was. My region was spread geographically, so I had to fly to some locations—and I hated flying.

On one flight home from an evaluation, I was peacefully watching the sun set when I noticed a blip far away on the horizon. The blip was heading toward us perpendicularly, getting closer and closer. I froze, praying in disbelief, angry that this was how it ends. My stomach filled with a terminal pain and fear, but the rest of the plane went about their business as if nothing was happening. Was I the only one who'd seen that plane?

The plane passed beneath us. I took a few seconds to compose myself, then my anger festered at our near accident. Accosting the flight attendants, I screamed, "Am I the only one who just saw that? We were almost hit by another plane!"

"Shall I report this?" an attendant said, soothing me with rehearsed words. They called the pilot, explaining why a passenger was irate, then relayed a question from the pilot to me. "Could you see the face of the pilot in the other plane?"

"Of course not," I said. "It was too far away." The tortoise was making me feel like a schmuck now.

On an evaluation trip to Virginia, my rep, Joseph, took me to the southwest part of the state for two days. Our accents conflicted, as did our cultures, sensibilities, and views on race and the Civil War. The first morning, we had breakfast in a diner similar to the one in *My Cousin Vinny*, where they served grits at a lunch counter on swiveling seats. Against a backdrop of folks in Western hats with undecipherable drawls, I stood out in my tie and suit. Joseph knew some of the grit-eaters at the counter; he'd taken me there to expose me as a Northerner, freedom rider, and voter registration supporter.

My morning hunger vanished. I asked to leave. "Never take me here again," I told Joseph. "From now on, I'll only be with you when you work *Northern* Virginia—Alexandria and Richmond."

Over the years, favorite reps and territories, cities, towns, motels, eateries, and accounts were inscribed in my invisible who's who. Harrisburg, Pennsylvania, suited me perfectly. Tom Anderson, substantially mid-American, plain, was a friend and rep. He was folksy and honest. He made a good living and the price of white bread was cheaper in

Harrisburg than Philadelphia, he said, so after having a few good sales early in the day, he'd often head home to have sex with his wife. Money and commission were clearly not his motivator. Reps are supposed to work and write orders like machines.

Honesty is good, I told Tom. From my vantage point, it was more important to bond with reps and win their trust so that, subliminally, they'd want to work harder for me in the long run. Philosophically, there was a problem when the company never let long tenures develop if reps weren't producing. Then I had to get rid of them. I had a problem in pharmacy school when I couldn't pith the frog in bio lab. There was no way I could fire a human being with a family. I'd often put my ass on the line to try to save a rep—and it worked almost all the time. I did everything I could to make them succeed.

Inexplicably, Tom used to take me to the same account each time I came to visit, two or three times a year. Finally, I called him out on it.

"They're my best account," he said. "They like you and tell me to stop by for a big order whenever you're in town. I can't turn that down. Besides, the owner, Constance Nolan, is divorced, six feet tall, and attracted to you."

"Tom, I'm married, happily," I told him.

"Cam, it's strictly business, not personal."

"Please, no *Godfather* today."

October leaves were vacating the trees and Halloween's autumnal aromas were in the air when I had dinner with Constance Nolan. Tom somehow got called away to his sick father at the last minute, leaving the two of us alone. Constance was alluring, intelligent, and owned two successful stores. In another life, our abundant chemistry would've entangled us somehow. Our dinner conversation bounced around from Vince Foster's suicide to Rabin and Arafat shaking hands, and the loneliness of long-distance runners and divorced women. Directionally, I was not pleased with where the conversation was drifting. Politically, I needed to be correct and keep the account happy at the dinner table. I had to reach her with my personal inaccessibility, gently and creatively playing the precipice game. *How far could this evening go?* I wondered, remembering cliffs, mountains, and falling into oblivion.

"Doris Duke died the other day," I said, pivoting the conversation.

"Who is that?" she asked, clueless.

"The heir to a tobacco fortune. She inherited a billion or so, but she lived a very lonely life near me in New Jersey. "

"A billionaire? Why lonely?"

"She grew up in the twenties and thirties, was six feet tall, and in those days tall men were hard to find. I devised a plan, as she was aging, to offer myself to her in any way. I'd drive by her estate, pretend my car broke down, and ring the bell for help. She'd see me, so much taller than her with all the bells and whistles. Make no mistake, I drove by her estate several times."

"What happened?" Constance asked, intrigued.

"I'm a married guy, so I turned down the wild chances of tapping into serious money." I smiled. I'll be damned: she got the hint. We ended the night with a handshake.

A few months later, trouble was brewing in the Caribbean. My sales rep Carlos Lopez was in Puerto Rico with a large family to support, and his job was on the line.

VP Hayden Sommers called and told me, "Cameron, fire him immediately." Hayden was all business, focused on productivity. There are no emotions or human feelings in eyeglass sales. If you didn't produce and get increases, Hayden wanted you gone. I had to be a nice guy, disguised.

"Give me two weeks. I'll fly down and change Carlos," I promised.

I spent two weeks in San Juan (at my expense, because the company wanted him out) at the Caribe Hilton, excoriating, praising, and ripping into Carlos, building his confidence and finally pleading for him to change and succeed. One night, he brought me to meet his family at their lovely home on top of a mountain in Caguas. The reality of his dependent family had me turn up the burners. I had to save him.

And I did. He became a good rep for many years, even outlasting me. My philosophy of personalizing battles, winning hearts and loyalty, conflicted with the company's policy and procedures, but they made my soul feel full.

My last night in San Juan, I walked to the hotel area where they fed tropical fish, some small sharks, and other indigenous species. A woman there initiated small talk with me, which we continued at the bar. Suddenly, we were in the elevator to my room. It wasn't the alcohol, but something else deep within me, like playing chicken with a bus while I'm on a bike. Or I was Charles Bronson in *Death Wish*. My life was good in every way. But something was eating away at my stability, trying to fuck me up.

Back in my hotel room, I opened a bottle of wine from the minibar and we clinked our glasses and toasted the coqui, a small frog native to Puerto Rico. The woman dropped to her knees, reaching to undo my belt. Suddenly, inside my mind I was standing on a cliff, looking down at inhospitable rocks thousands of feet below. I almost fell off the edge—but I stopped before anything happened. I thanked her for inflating my ego and making my day, though I'm convinced she had no idea what I was talking about. In the hallway, I pushed D on the elevator and watched her disappear, wondering what the fuck almost happened. At least I was still as guilt-free and innocent as a coqui.

Chapter 20

WINDS OF CHANGE

On New Year's Eve in 1995, as the ball in Times Square descended on the TV, I kissed Marjorie longer and harder than ever, not wanting to let go.

"Cameron, we have a house full of company. Let me go. What the hell got into you?"

"I just realized that in addition to loving you," I explained, "I like you too."

"What a nice thing to say," she said, smiling.

I told her how great and precious our time together has been—almost two decades now. An uneasy feeling consumed me, like maybe an asteroid was heading to Earth or Charlton Heston was coming down the mountain with the Ten Commandments again, pissed off that we were reveling too much.

Whatever it was, it sure wasn't alcohol kicking my ass. I was a great amphetamine-taker, but never alcohol. Perhaps deeply buried in my subconscious was my revulsion with my father's drinking. Jack loved Scotch in particular; the smell had always sickened me.

One Friday night in college, when I was living in the fraternity house, I was sitting in the TV room, feeling sorry for myself. Everybody had gone to the dating moon—parties, movies—except me, who'd been rejected three times in a row by Emma, a Tri Delta, an all-blonde sorority.

My closest brother, Butch, had an idea to help me get my mind off Emma. "I've got a fifth of gin in my closet. Take a swig and relax," he said.

I took up his offer and chugged the bottle. My memories of what happened next were washed clean by the gin, but my brothers said I fell down a flight of stairs and hurt my back. The hours of heating pad use that followed gave me a volleyball-sized blister. This experience was like pure aversion therapy, like in Anthony Burgess's *A Clockwork Orange*, and I was never able to smell gin again.

TENNIS REPERCUSSIONS

A big part of my world, as I expanded my pursuits of health and exercise, was tennis. Two years after I lost a hundred pounds in two and a half months, I started playing obsessively. One summer, I played sixteen days in a row. I liked running, sweating, and competition, so I thought it best to play singles with guys I particularly disliked, turning on my engines and playing with a powerful desire to kick ass. But if I lost, it was a hard fall for my ego.

During a field visit to one of my reps in Baltimore, Lenny, we spent our nights playing tennis. Business is business, so we played intensely. Lenny hit several drop shots, taking advantage of my size and slowness. In one particular lunge, I reached too far. My knees gave out, went peculiarly airborne, and I landed on my chin, which exploded in blood, down to the bone. Hours elapsed at the hospital, sitting with a triage towel over my wound. It was a bad summer in the city night, with an abundance of shootings, which put me at the back of the line. The wait was so long, my chin eventually ran out of blood. Finally, near 2:00 a.m., they treated me with IV antibiotics to prevent infection because of how long I'd been waiting. After ruling out broken bones with an X-ray, an intern sewed my sutures, scarring my beautiful Kirk Douglas chin for life.

Two months later, a terrific, persistent pain set in my jaw. The pain so bad that I fell to the floor, writhing in pain, at a manager's meeting in Florida. Someone whipped out a Percodan, which did shit. While I was trying to find relief on the floor, the company owner, Vincenzo Gallo, had arrived from Italy and climbed over my spread-out body, clearly annoyed. Hours later, the pain of realizing the boss had climbed over me exceeded my jaw's physical pain.

Back home, days of tests and X-rays finally revealed I had two broken mandibles that had been healing the wrong way. A dental surgeon said I had two options: to painfully re-break the mandibles and set them the right way, or use wires to manipulate the bones and restore them to an earlier time.

"What does that mean?" I asked.

"We wire you shut for a few months," he explained. "No food, just liquid. You walk around with a pair of pliers, just in case. No talking, really, but grunting is good. And if it works, your bones are brought back in alignment."

"And pain?"

"Way less, if we wire you right."

I spent the next two months wired shut in hell, incarcerating my soul, spirit, and tuna-loving intestines. Solid food was gone. The spirit to choose what I tenderly, joyfully masticated was gone. Wired with metal, my world was lonely, without empathy or understanding. Who the fuck in my world ever got wired shut?

Family and friends visited to console me, bringing laughter

to my wretched body. Marjorie brought me food, including tuna salad, my epicurean orgasm. My dependence was so great that at night I'd sneak down to the kitchen and try to inhale small particulates of tuna through the spaces in my teeth, like a drug addict. The process was laborious, unfulfilling, and non-caloric.

When I was finally freed of my wires, I'd refer to those two months as the best of our marriage. I loved communicating with Marjorie through grunts alone. "Are you done yet?" she'd ask during sex, and I'd grunt affirmatively.

Despite this significant injury, I still loved tennis, though I started to wonder if it loved me back. I spent all those years pounding my knees, abusing my body parts with reckless abandon, with no palpable awareness of my mortality. I still had breath to blow out candles. I occasionally felt twinges in my knees, but because of my masculine persuasion not to ask directions or go to doctors, I ignored the warning signs.

One fine day, as I was about to open the front door, I collapsed. My right knee gave way and Humpty Dumpty fell in real life. A local orthopedic surgeon diagnosed me with a torn meniscus, requiring surgery and six weeks on crutches. I intellectualized that everything in my body worth having rested on my knees, including my genitals. At my tennis club, I asked a friend, a world traveler and horseback riding dilettante who had bad knees, for advice. He referred me to Dr. David Altair in New York City. Dr. Altair agreed I had a torn meniscus, but with his treatment plan, I could be shooting hoops two days post-op and forget about crutches altogether.

Two months after the operation, my other meniscus went. Dr. Altair was so good, he justified each trip across the Hudson River and each toll fee at the Lincoln Tunnel just to see him. Once again, I was back to full force in two days' time.

Following my second meniscus surgery, I became crucially aware of how the body's life is not infinite. Extending my body's life became an obsession, and I treasured every freaking body part I had, taking precious care of them.

NOAH AND CHANGE

Late in the 1995 school year, nine-year-old Noah was down the block. Our street was great for playing: the cul-de-sac was full of kids his age who actually liked each other. Near dinner, Marjorie attempted to call Noah inside with an old-fashioned yell—with her prominent accent, she sounded like someone screaming from a fire escape in a television commercial for Brooklyn.

We sat down to a diverse dinner spread, Noah with his omni-present macaroni and cheese, me with my obscenely big salads. In the middle of our meal, the phone rang. Marjorie answered, speaking to the person on the other end of the line with mostly one-word answers. After hanging up with a "Thank you for your thoughtfulness," she turned back to us, her face now an ashen gray color.

"Noah, Mommy and Daddy need to talk. Go up to your room and play," she told him. We watched as he went, then she turned to me. "That was a classmate's mother, Sylvia. Her son said all the kids were talking about Noah being adopted. She didn't care whether it was true or not, but figured we should know what's going on. We have to tell Noah now, before he hears anything in school tomorrow."

One of the most important times in our lives had jumped on us, years before we thought we'd have to confront it. We needed to find the exact right words and attitude for this moment in world history. This stuff could influence our son for a lifetime, and we were being thrown into it with no preparation or forethought. What a fucking revolting development.

We called Noah into the den, and I started a soliloquy about birds and bees, assuming Noah already had a vague understanding of them. I tiptoed around our medical attempts to fix me and Marjorie, and then explained our in vitro experience. "So that's why Mommy and Daddy adopted you," I said, "to complete our dream of being parents and a family."

The next five seconds were long, silent, and heart-wrenching. Then Noah spoke.

"I'm adopted?" he asked.

"Yes, but that doesn't change anything," Marjorie said softly.

Noah exploded into hysterical tears. Marjorie and I looked at each other. We felt each other's pain because our son was in pain. Helplessly we sat, Noah's cries drowning out any words we could offer. Eventually, his tears subdued into whimpers and sniffling. The sounds of silence. Noah was ready to listen again.

"Nothing has changed, Noah," I said. "We love you. We're a family. Adoption is such a gift. First of all, Mommy and I are not related to each other. We met in a bar in New York City. We're still strangers, almost like we adopted each other. We're not blood to each other. We never did that Native American ceremony, cutting our wrists and becoming blood brothers. All of us are strangers who make up a special family and love each other. That's what it's all about."

"Who knows I'm adopted? Do my cousins know?" Noah asked.

Marjorie, the quintessential mother and elementary school educator, took Noah by the hand to the mirrored wall in the front hall. I followed curiously. "Noah, look in the mirror at us. Is anything different than it was this morning?" she asked. "It's you, me, and Dad. We're all the same, no matter what. We're a special family and we love each other. Look in the mirror again. Nothing changed, except maybe Dad's hole in his sock."

The slightest yet most important Noah smile dashed on by. Marjorie explained that everyone important in our lives knew he was adopted, but we waited until the right time to tell him. "It's that time now, Noah."

When he'd finally processed all he could today, Noah asked to go to sleep. An hour later, I went into his room and deposited my ritual kiss to his warm forehead. "Daddy loves you, Noah."

The next day, I cut off selling early to come home and greet Noah as he got off the school bus. As he alighted the bus, I took a critical look at his face, hoping and praying he'd come to some terms of acceptance. But there he was, with a huge smile and an energy in his step, bopping up the steps to his parents, whose hearts were heavy with the unknown.

"Mommy, Daddy, I told everyone today that I am adopted," he said proudly.

And for the rest of our journey, a lifetime together, Noah has been that happy, adjusted, loved son. "Mom, Dad, you're my parents— and that's it," he'd always say.

Twenty-one years later, Noah and I did genetic testing and analysis with 23andMe. He needed that background of where he came from and which genes could mess with health issues. Noah's test revealed a healthy set of genes that came from a wide band of European countries.

My test results, on the other hand, haunted me with deep senses I'd long had but could never explain. My trips to Sedona, fixation with Native American culture and music, and that pulling sense of restlessness and curiosity. Between 1670 and 1780, I may have had a Native American ancestor. It was a major wow moment, explaining some of my leanings and spirituality.

GOING TO HOUSTON

In June, Incanto and Vero held the midyear national sales meeting. Four hundred salespeople descended to Houston's Inn on the Park. It was a trendy hotel, with kitschy food and a state-of-the-art gym. I began each day there on an exercise bike, listening to classics from the sixties era, drifting into my different worlds. Each song conjured an old girlfriend, encounter, party, and piece of history. I'd go on to spend small eternities on the exercise bike.

My second morning there, a young woman jumped onto the bike next to me. Twenty minutes into my solitude, sweating, listening to Peter, Paul and Mary's "The First Time Ever I Saw Your Face," the woman hand-signed for me to remove my headphones.

"Aren't you Cameron Simmons, the manager from Jersey?" she asked. I could barely distinguish her words through her heavy Southern accent. "Everybody knows you, the tallest rep in the company. I'm Mary O'Hara from Mississippi." I extended my moist hand in greeting.

At the end of the day, when I retreated back to the gym while the other employees checked out the Houston bar scene, Mary O'Hara was already on the bike. We talked eyeglasses for a bit, then the real discussion started when we walked outside. Mary shared she was recently divorced and outspoken about her ex and the institution of marriage. We continued talking at breakfast, and later at the company trip to the rodeo. At the rodeo, strangely, Mary and I smiled whenever we made eye contact. My smiles were friendly and perfunctory, protecting my values.

As a manager, I had my own room at the hotel. At 10:00 p.m., I was showered and sitting in a bathrobe, sipping wine from the minibar and taking in the view of Houston out my window. Suddenly, a knock on the door. Mary smiled at me through the peephole.

"If any of this doesn't work for you, it's all good," she said. "My being here is completely innocent. You fascinate me. I've never talked to a Jersey Yankee before. I sensed you'd be okay with a knock on the door."

"It is all good. Conversely, I've never talked to a Mississippi rebel before. May I call you a rebel?" I asked, offering her some red wine.

Your honor, it was all innocent, purely cultural fascination. This was my defense in court. Time blurs, and so does wine. Hours elapsed. Suddenly, Mary was sitting on my lap and kissing me, and I was returning in kind. Our want was powerful. But what hit me in that moment, like a thunderbolt, was the notion that I am in control of everything in my life—even if I only control my own feelings and emotions. If I ever give in to temptation, to whomever, then I am a slave to that person. The most precious commodity in the world is controlling your own destiny. Peace of mind before piece of ass, always.

All these thoughts raced through my mind while we kissed. I was so close to slipping my hands around her breasts. But I could see so clearly now. I could never trust anyone except myself.

When we separated ourselves, I thanked Mary profusely for understanding. She thanked me back.

"I meant to ask," I said as she left, "are you related to the O'Haras who owned Tara plantation?"

"Perhaps!" she said, throwing me the greatest smile.

The next day, the sales meeting finale was a cacophony of cryptic messages: Work hard. Sell like you never did before. Let's get the company to $50 million. And always have the mindset that change is good. Then they brought in a local high school marching band. The reps cheered, and I pretended to. I don't like change—but it was coming.

BACK TO SEDONA

I was always in the mood for exploration. Sedona was only one state away from the sales meeting in Houston, so I called Marjorie to ask if I might go there before coming home.

"Have fun, Cameron. I wish I understood you and what you're always looking for," she said.

I could never explain the source of all my energy, my yearning to find something in my head, my heart, or my soul. It had to be good—residual warmth with some déjà vu stirred in, a proximity to God, an embraceable universe. It was a long way to Tipperary, Newark, and the Beth Israel Hospital, the portal through which I came into this world in 1945.

The Phoenix airport was alive with Southwestern vibes. I wished I had my cowboy hat. During that 1980s TV show, *Dallas*, I bought one and wore it proudly, mostly when I went to local diners. When the writers of the show fucked up, wasted a year of story line with a character's dream, I threw away my hat and gave up watching all network TV soap operas.

The ride up Route 17 excited me, like I was six years old and sitting wide-eyed in the front of the bus again. Blue sky, sun, pure air. I stopped at Montezuma's Castle, sat on a bench, and stared at the caves in the mountain. The silence so deafening—ghosts of people long gone, letting me think, dream, and wonder. A family walked by with a boy Noah's age, and for a moment I wished my own family was there. But I was glad they weren't—the thought of being alone in the red mountains for a few days titillated me.

I love how the red mountains just arrive. Randomly, I picked out a motel called Kokopelli. Tired and hungry, I found the Heartline Café for dinner, where I sat on a large patio with an outdoor fireplace at a table for one. Nighttime in the desert is cold. I felt like driftwood on a Jersey beach, smooth and weathered. I pinched myself because of where I was. Fantasy caught up to me as I looked around to see if there was a single woman at a table drinking red wine. I imagined us putting our tables together and winding up in bed together. Instead, the waiter brought my check and I got a perfect night of sleep alone.

The next morning, I went to the Bell Rock Vortex. Walking around in the silent, chilly air with a dark blue sky overhead, I felt grateful to the universe for where I was and what I had waiting for me back home, Marjorie and Noah. At noon, I took a Pink Jeep Tour into the mountains again. The six tourists in the jeep came from a diverse geography: California, Montana, Illinois, Alabama, New Jersey (me). Our tour driver, Andy, was a junior at UCLA.

Every few minutes of the tour, I raved about the scenery, its beauty, mystery, and energy. Finally, Andy stopped the jeep and accosted me. "I've never, in my years doing this, seen anyone so enamored with Sedona scenery, and with so much knowledge about it. Why don't you just move here?"

The jeep fell silent while I contemplated this. "I can't move here," I joked. "I'm addicted to the smell of car exhaust in the morning back in Jersey."

Later, I sat motionless at the Chapel of the Holy Cross, built ethereally into the red rock. For two hours, I looked out at nature, wondering who I really was. I thought how cool it would be if I were single and a girl walked in with long blonde hair and sat down next to me. We talk, have dinner, sleep together, and get married in the chapel the next day. It's a simple gift to look at a person for the first time, hear a few spoken words, look into their eyes—always the eyes—and know everything you need to. I'd get better at it as years went by.

The vortex at Airport Road was my favorite place in all the red lands. It was a long climb up the hard rocks to a summit overlooking all that mattered in the world. At thirty feet or so to the summit, I removed my sneakers and socks and climbed to a view of heaven. When you are barefoot, you allegedly absorb more vortex energy through the soles (souls). I borrowed a small red rock from the summit to be returned whenever. It'd spend the next five years in every pocket I had; I took it with me every day I ventured out of the house. I liked feeling lightly weighed down with a piece of peace and vortex.

On my last day, I drove to Oak Creek Canyon with a paper map by my side. The road curved, snaked, and lifted precipitously higher and higher until I came to a plateau overlook where Native American women were selling trinkets, souvenirs, and jewelry. Their faces were so old, wrinkled, weathered, wise, and tender. I felt a powerful force of care and admiration for them, their history of sadness and struggles. If only I'd known that a very small percentage of me was Native American. It was a testament to the universe, that attachment inside my soul all these years—a continued reason to believe.

Life is funnily curious. Years later, I'd go back to Sedona with Noah, where he'd photograph me sitting barefoot on the Airport Road summit for the back cover of my first novel.

Hugs and kisses intense when I returned home after ten days away and opened the door to see Marjorie and Noah. There is no place like home. Before my shoes came off in the hall, I ceremoniously clicked my heels together.

Chapter 21

AND NOW, LADIES AND GENTLEMEN: THE CHANGE

When I was growing up on Goodwin Avenue, I loved Thanksgiving and Christmas. The holidays began on Mischief Night, the night before Halloween. Time tried to fly recklessly, after I threw toilet paper on trees, soaped up car windows, and broke windows in developing buildings—all on Mischief Night in New Jersey. The next night I blackmailed people into giving me candy. Nobody ever tricked me; all bullshit.

And in the blink of an eye, I was going to my grandmother's house in Plainfield for Thanksgiving. Another blink and I was scouring the neighborhood for a discarded Christmas tree just to have one, inhaling the aroma of the holidays and keeping it hidden from my mother in the basement. I stored it next to the coal bin.

As I aged, I became transfixed with Christmas music. Once in East Brunswick, in my forties, I taped Pavarotti singing "Adeste Fideles" and listened to it for three straight hours. The music transported me back to Newark, when all my relatives were alive, happy, and touchable. Every year after Halloween, I opened my eyes wide, made a list of my anticipations, and savored the journey to Christmas Eve.

On Wednesday, December 6, 1995, Hayden Summers called an emergency meeting in Edison. Forty managers and executives gathered in the company conference room. Some folks must've known what was going down; their faces were solemn, sullen. A sense of foreboding was in the air. My stomach was in knots, sensing a world about to come apart.

Hayden delivered a campaign speech, something about vertical integration. He and Antonio Gallo never cracked a smile in the meeting—this was serious shit. "So, that's why we decided to buy Strictly Eyes, a growing eyewear retail chain," he announced to a room of confused faces, as if we'd all just been slapped by Cher in *Moonstruck*.

To our credit as a group of managers, we sensed the world as we knew it was over. Simply, this bold move could help facilitate a change in the eyewear industry. Other companies were doing it, manufacturers vertically integrating into retail. This meant many retailers would not want to buy from companies that were now perceived as their competition. It was a brilliant strategy. In the year after the official announcement, I watched my income drop with fallout of anger, frustration, and fears that I would not be able to support my family. Much that I had worked for simply disappeared, like the Conestoga wagons that had once circled the American West with cowboys and cowgirls.

What a rough fucking future road. My new job description signaled a world of difficult components. I had no place else to go, no fallback, no savings. Confusion, self-pity, self-loathing in New Jersey. Every day I battled with my accounts, trying to convince them it was a good and positive change. When I came home to Marjorie and Noah, my incredible oasis of love and unconditional support, Mr. Hyde took over my deep insides like an invisible evil. I knew myself and my propensity to lean to depression and take out my shortcomings on the people I loved. Marjorie and Noah must never see my descent into job despair. I'd have to be the great actor I'd never been.

By March of 1996, the news of these changes in the optical world had officially impacted my sales. The shit storm hit. Marjorie decided, with little prompting, to start substitute teaching to augment our income. She was getting back to being an essential teacher after being an at-home mom. In September, she was teaching full-time. But my loss of income had firmly set the stage for my desperate mindset. I was needy, scared, unsure—and ripe for spiritual intervention.

My downhill journey began. But there was Noah: my light, energy, hope, and pure joy. I slipped, with my preoccupation, about telling Noah several times a day that Daddy loved him. On a hot Saturday in July, we went to Belmar on the Jersey Shore. We found the jetty at the Shark River, sat on a comfortable boulder, and stared at the horizon with the universe just behind it. It was a poignant moment—my lifelong dream of taking my own child here was finally realized. Maybe life wasn't that bad?

We held hands, walking underneath the Belmar Fishing Club pier, sinking our feet into the wet sand, and scaring a few seagulls. I helped Noah climb a boulder on the jetty. "Dear God," I quietly whispered, "I've been gifted. I was ten when I pondered this. Now my son is ten and here I am. Thank you."

We sat in silence for a while. Could Noah have sensed this profound moment? "This is where I've been coming since I was exactly your age," I told him. "I'd just sit here, like we are now, and stare across the ocean, dreaming of tomorrow and wondering about our relatives who came here a long time ago from Russia to find freedom in America."

"I've been dreaming too," Noah said, "about Superman and writing comics someday. And you know what? Someday I'll bring my child here too. But when they're ten."

Choking up, I ran my fingers through Noah's hair. I loved the universe for letting me do this. This was a day we'd both remember. Before we left for home, I took one more long, mechanical look skyward and directed another whisper of thanks way past the cirrus clouds.

MY SON THE NON-ATHLETE

Early Noah exhibited little signs of athleticism, instead preferring to build models, play video games, and read comics. Still, suburban life stressed joining the community kids' sports leagues. Noah showed he wasn't down for being kicked in the legs on a soccer field, so he drifted away from that sport. Little League was similar. In the last inning of one game, Noah made an appearance in the outfield. He looked like a future Yankee.

All that really mattered to me was that Noah was a happy, content child. So when sports didn't pan out for him, I sought alternative ways for us to bond. Noah liked movies, monsters, and being silly. When he was seven, we watched *Animal House*. Not wanting to incur scrutiny from the Division of Youth and Family Services, I coughed loudly so Noah couldn't hear the evil conscience standing on Larry Kroger's shoulder, telling him to fuck her. We watched that movie together for the next twenty-three years, part of our unique father-son bonding routines.

Once, on a whim, I asked Noah if he'd like to see a Rutgers football game, thinking it'd be good for bonding. Perhaps the rah-rah of college football—the marching bands, cheerleaders, pretzels with mustard, and the cheers of campus kids—might ignite him. I'd never been to Rutgers football, nor had I been back on campus since 1969, so I wasn't sure where this inspiration came from. A grand design of the universe? That innocent game would eventually bring me to campus 150 times a year.

Noah loved our first game together. "Dad, can we do this more next season?" he asked.

"Of course. Let's do it all. Basketball, football—everything."

So began our journey to employing the public university's vast resources to help us continually bond over sports, art, theater, music, and even travel. One of our best weekends was when Rutgers played Arizona State in the 2005 Insight Bowl in Phoenix. We stayed a week, climbed the red mountains in Sedona, talked about the world and his dreams of a comic book career, and I even snuck my underage son into a bar to hang with other alumni.

Noah and I have been on a journey. If there had been a Nicole, it would've been the same bonding, love and expressions. When Noah was eight, I told him one Sunday morning that *Wuthering Heights* was a ghost movie. "Let's watch it together." Every interlude, he asked where the ghost was. At the end, Cathy and Heathcliff, ghosts, stroll along a snowy mountain path. Next day at school, the teacher asked the class, what they did over the weekend. Noah watched *Wuthering Heights*. If only. That is our relationship; still about those bonding memories. Still saying I love you, through his beard. Still thank my dad Jack for the ultimate lesson of being a relevant father and my love for him grows. Noah will be the same and I'm comforted.

Chapter 22

A DECENT DESCENT

As the eyeglass industry came to terms with vertical integration and big-time retailing institutions, my daily battles with small business increased in frequency and intensity. Trying to stay alive, earn an income, hold tightly onto accounts I'd serviced for years—competition feasted on my vulnerability. The writing was all over the walls of my mind. Every day I felt anger and frustration. All the eyeglass people I'd been loyal to didn't give a shit about me now. Business is business. Michael Corleone had warned me it's not personal, but I took it personally anyway. It was only a matter of time until abandoning ship could be a course of choice.

At the end of every day selling in the trenches, I'd come home to Marjorie and Noah, who could never know the depth of my despair. I was so committed to never taking my frustrations out on these two people who were my only supportive world. I'd have to learn to dig so deep to pull this off.

Of course, I never sought professional help, but I did watch *The Grapes of Wrath* looking for something to help me. Henry Fonda's Tom Joad ripped my conscience. Joad talking about being everywhere and fighting so hungry people can eat.

Marjorie and I talked often about my eyeglass world. I knew she could never understand the big picture of my intestinal linings. So be it. She'd supportively implore everything would be all right. I hated that thinking. Life was ominous and sucky. Every headache was a brain tumor. Every stomach ache, colon cancer. Over the next few years, I'd try to escape, finally—without using drugs, food, or tobacco—and let *something* move me around, taking me to a new spiritual reality.

By 1997, all the realities and exigencies of a new life and escape mechanism were there, but with no way forward. Life was going through the motions. I couldn't think of a future because I was stuck in a place without resources, money, a real career, or anything to fall back on. My mother needed money to augment social security and to help with the terrific cost of prescriptions. She never asked me for money directly, but she sometimes cried on the phone about how hard it was to survive because they had no money. My father had never earned a living as a shoe salesman. Guilt beat the living hell out of me, highlighting all my wasted opportunities to be comfortable or even rich.

CELEBRITY ESCAPE

Whenever I had a chance to escape to a make-believe world, I was off to see the wizard—any wizard would do. One day, my sister Carol called about a gossip columnist's new perfume launch in New York. We had a practical way to crash this celebrity event at a prominent salon near Bloomingdales, filled with politicians, madams, actors, and TV personalities. Once we'd infiltrated the party, I learned I could talk to anyone—I jumped into a picture with Donald and Ivana Trump, asked Regis Philbin to mention me on his show, praised actor

Anthony Quinn, and struggled with politically correct dialogue for the Mayflower Madam.

Late in November, Carol called again, this time about a major film shoot in our hometown, Maplewood. *One True Thing*, directed by Carl Franklin, was having a six-month shoot in town. Meryl Streep, William Hurt, and Renée Zellweger were starring in it. As I readied to leave to watch the filming, Marjorie said, "Cameron, you're a schmuck, always running to these ridiculous things, thinking you're going to be in a movie."

In one scene near the film's end, Meryl Streep's character Kate Gulden was dying and being honored at the Christmas tree lighting. The town was transformed with fake storefronts. In the distance, a machine was making snow. Barricades blocked access to the street for us onlookers, but the police informed us we could walk onto the set before shooting, if needed, to get a container of milk or a slice of pizza.

Carol and I set a New Jersey pizza mastication record. It took us ninety minutes to share one slice as we watched all the activity on the set, readying for the shoot. We stood just underneath an old-fashioned theater marquis. Suddenly, I felt a presence next to me. Slowly I turned to see Meryl Streep, William Hurt, Renée Zellweger, and Carl Franklin emerge from the warmth of the theater. The best I could do was tell Meryl how much I admired her work. She thanked me.

A production assistant saw me talking to her and assumed I was part of the entourage. "We need to place you now on set," he said.

I elbowed Carol gently in the ribs. "Sure, let's go."

"Do you know everything you have to say and do?" the assistant asked.

I was quick to answer: "It's been a long day. Please go over it again."

Our directions were to sing "Silent Night" while the mayor turned on the tree lights. Carol and I stood in the back of the two hundred extra townspeople. We'd come so far, but I had an idea. I motioned for Carol to follow me, but she stayed put while I pushed people out of the way. Thanks to Simon and Garfunkel's song "7 O'clock News," I knew the words to "Silent Night." This did wonders for my fleeting sense of self. Years later, while I worked the red carpet at the New Jersey Hall of Fame Awards, I spoke to Anna Quindlen, author of the book *One True Thing*, which had inspired the movie. I recanted my story about crashing her film, eliciting a smile.

The next two years brought more frustration, anger, loss of income, and bad thoughts as I looked for any way out of my black hole of despair. By the springtime of 1998, I'd found no solution, no magic lottery ticket, no employer who saw promise in my ability, no parents to inherit a fortune from, and no mechanism for Incanto to really help its employees. I wasn't even a real employee, but an outside contractor—a fucked place to be in life while crossing over to being fifty-something.

I tried to keep it all within, sheltering Marjorie and Noah as best I could. Sometimes I'd indulge to escape, wiping out an entire chocolate layer cake or downing eight bagels over a four-hour period. My blood sugar was through the roof. I knew the voracious eating was all wrong, but like the Id monster from *Forbidden Planet*, I couldn't control myself. Driving through New Jersey, looking for business, I prayed to God for help like George Bailey did on a snowy bridge in Bedford Falls. Wouldn't it be beyond if Clarence, the angel, came to help me now?

In May, Frank Sinatra died of a heart attack. That bothered me. I was enamored with Frank's life, achievements, perfect voice, fame, and philanthropy; I had bucket-listed him as somebody I'd love to meet. I could've told him how many times I'd watched *From Here to Eternity*. "Why did you have to walk off guard duty and go AWOL, then the stockade?" I'd tell him about his character Maggio. All those tech-noir movies are replete with moody themes. Color fucks things up; black-and-white films stir my soul. I want to jump in the scene, selling newspapers on the corner with the headline "Lusitania Sunk."

An eerily favorite movie of mine is *Key Largo*, the last film Humphrey Bogart and Lauren Bacall ever did together. It's a gangster movie, with Edward G. Robinson as Johnny Rocco and Bogart as Frank

McCloud, an antihero. I'm not sure why I was attracted to the movie except that I loved Bogart. Maybe it was the period; he was around. The Second World War was over—no worries about nukes, China, climate change, or Incanto Eyewear. Everything about his life—his loves, lusts, drinking, and sailing—innervated me. *Something* had been bouncing around between my earlobes. In June, I went to Marjorie.

"Maybe I should call you Saint Marjorie for always being there for me," I said. "I know sometimes you feel my anguish, which I try to keep inside. Maybe it's the chocolate stains on my T-shirt that give my emotions away. I function, but sometimes it's hard. I guess I'm still searching for a perfect world and job."

"So, Cameron, where do you want to run off to reenergize yourself? Satisfy some lame need?" she said, always so incisively, filling me with a twinge of guilt. "I'm not too concerned where you go anymore. Have a good time."

"I just need some downtime," I said, "to think, ponder, dig into myself. I want to go to Key Largo and find the dock that Bogart and Bacall stood on in that movie, kick off my shoes and absorb their molecules."

"It's not the eating eight bagels, but you do need help," she said. "This is about as fucked up as you've ever been. But go. Noah and I are here. We're always here. Maybe you'll find something and come home with that endearing Cameron smile."

To lessen the madness, I came back to Marjorie with real intent for this trip: to visit my parents, who'd retired in Boca Raton. No loving wife could deny her husband a visit with his aging parents. Marjorie felt better about the whole thing—but I really wanted to go to the dock in Key Largo.

FLORIDA

When the plane landed in Fort Lauderdale, I pinched my left forearm. I was here for an extended stay, but I didn't really like South Florida. The air was redolent with human aging, cat food, Buick and

Chevrolet car exhaust, and prune juice consumed in slow motion. My parents lived in Century Village—a certain family member used to smugly tell me to get used to it; one day I'd be living there too, maybe even in my parents' two-bedroom apartment. That comment forged a life-long revulsion in me. But it also slowly ignited something deep within—a hissing, an escape, like gaseous explosions on the surface of the sun creating my new universal awareness of betterment and elevation.

In the schematic of best-laid plans, staying with my parents for three days was wonderful. Most of the time, we sat around the kitchen table talking, drifting back to Newark and Plainfield, those formative years filled with innocence, peace on earth through Eisenhower, no locks on the back door, and buying two sticks of Breakstone butter weekly from Kravitz's Grocery.

"We only use margarine now. It's much healthier, so I read somewhere," my mother said.

I slept on a pull-out sofa in the den, which was a second bedroom. The second night, around midnight, my munchies led me to the kitchen, passing by my parents' ajar bedroom door.

"Not now, Jack, especially with Cameron in the next room. Control yourself. Go back to sleep," I heard my mother say. It was a great revelation that my parents still messed around. Jack was eighty-three, still carrying his early sexual reputation around like a gray badge of courage.

Saying goodbye to my aging parents ripped my intestinal linings with the thought that this could be a final goodbye. Inevitability came closer every day.

Mom asked where I was off to. "Islamorada and Key Largo," I said. "I need to find the dock where Bogart and Bacall stood in the movie." I should've never laid that out.

"Cameron, you're running around like a teenager. You have responsibilities!" Amelia chided. "That's all I'm going to say."

I was really too old for guilt trips, but she was still so good at it.

The two women in my life were perfect instillers. I gave my mother an especially long hug before I left out the front door.

KEYS

My next stop was at the Chesapeake Beach Resort in Islamorada, next to Key Largo. I had a small room, furnished with tropical 1950s decor. I felt a particular presence, the emanating power of enduring literary achievement, that Hemingway was once close by in Key West. As I sat by the pool, I wondered about becoming a writer like him, the king of less is more. I was desperate to uncover what was inside me, but writing was never on any vocational list, so I never did it except for school papers. Who knew it was there inside me, waiting for a chance to be free at last? I needed a few more years before I could excavate my soul.

The heat of the day was intense. The pool barely cooled me off, so I went back and forth, immersing and drying myself out. Barely anyone else was around. A lone couple jumped into the pool and moistly humped each other. Pretending to read a local paper, I watched them as a basic voyeur, not noticing a woman arrive two lounge chairs away. An hour later, she got up and asked, "Can I get you a water? It's so freaking hot."

I said yes and thanked her when she handed me a bottled water. Sunglasses covered her face. "You don't realize the heat, then you get lazy and can't get off the lounge chair to hydrate yourself," I said appreciatively. We watched as the humping couple got out of the pool and walked away. "Now we're the only ones hanging here."

"They probably went to consummate," she said. She spoke with a slightly twangy accent. "I'm Georgia Burns. You'll never guess where I'm from."

"Not the Deep South. Of course, not New York," I guessed. "I give up."

"You give up easy."

"There are forty states that are viable guesses," I said. I knew intelligence was talking to me and I liked it.

She sat down on the lounge chair next to me and we faced each other. "Fair enough. I'm an Okie."

"That would've been my fortieth guess. What in the world—"

"Am I doing here on the Keys?" she giggled. She lifted her sunglasses on top of her jet-black short hair, revealing a beautiful face and large brown eyes. She was probably thirty-something and had perfect teeth. I found her raspy voice alluring. Who did she remind me of?

"A recent divorce. Bitter. Depressing," Georgia said. "I had to get as far away as geography would let me. It was either the West or East Coast, by a body of water, to soothe and help me forget and move on. I'm a writer back home."

"Funny, I've been sitting here, thinking about writing. Hemingway's molecules in the air help," I said. I told her about what had brought me there too. "In some convoluted way, I'm trying to divorce myself from what I'm doing in sales."

She leaned closer, a sign of captivating conversation. "I'll never guess. You pretty much signaled an absurdity. And I like the way you talk."

"You familiar with the noir movie *Key Largo*, with Bogart and Bacall?" I asked. "I'm here to find the dock where they stood in the movie and take my shoes off and absorb their molecules."

"And maybe you're searching for something else?"

"I think I am."

"Then we should have dinner tonight."

We made plans to meet up later, then she went back to her lounge chair and the book she was reading, *Portnoy's Complaint*. The Phillip Roth reading spooked me out. An Okie woman reading a Jewish man from Jersey.

I rested my hands behind my head, staring at ripples in the water. What the fuck was I doing? Then again, it was nothing but two people talking over dinner.

That night, Georgia drove us to a local restaurant on the beach. The tables were in the sand, and so were our bare feet. The setting sun dipped into the ocean, painting the sky in pretty pink pastels. Strands of cirrus clouds made a fine ambiance. Georgia and I bounced our life stories back and forth, discovering some parallels and commonality. When she rested her chin in her hands and leaned close, it was troublesome—meaning signs of affection or other motive.

After dinner, we walked on the beach. I stopped when she slipped her hand into mine. I whispered, "They make movies about what's happening. You've rocked my soul and my bosom. If I dare keep taking steps, which could lead to white, starchy sheets in someone's room—and make no mistake, would I ever love that—it could send me into bad places for a long time."

"It's all okay. I know what you're saying. There's some powerful chemistry here. I felt it the instant we met by the pool," she said. "I should've never offered to bring you water. Let's just hang out here and there for the next few days, but please take me to the dock from the movie. I must see you barefoot absorbing them."

The next night, we hung out at a beachfront bar. All local establishments had ocean water views; romantic scenes. We danced, fueled by her favorite drink, Jägermeister. I liked it because I sensed it was almost strong enough to get me into bed with her. I knew what these few days could've been, but I also knew the potential dangers ahead. For someone else, this could have been nirvana.

Two days later, my last full day, we explored the highway, looking for the bar that advertised the dock from the movie *Key Largo*. We got there early, before the bar opened. Around the back, we found the now long-corroded dock. It was just a few sheets of wood by itself, but it was good enough for me. Taking my shoes and socks off, I stepped cautiously onto the dock and smiled, eyes closed, dreaming, hoping to contact Humphrey Bogart and let him know I'd finally made it. Little did I know how much my love of Bogart would dramatically change my life forever a few years later.

Georgia and I had dinner at a local hamburger place that night. I had a Caesar salad. Her father owned a ranch, she told me, and I shared how I still don't eat meat.

"Cameron, these few days have been so special. I'll never forget you," Georgia said. "And I know we won't be in touch."

"Me too. Just one kiss goodnight for the both of us to hold on to," I said, quoting *Gone with the Wind*. We were just two level-headed adults in a messed-up world who did not jump into bed.

Back home, Marjorie asked about my head, if it was in a better place. I said yes—Florida would satiate me for a few more years before the nadir shit started again. I thanked Marjorie and Noah for being understanding and slept better in the weeks that followed.

Chapter 23

HITTING BOTTOM TAKES YEARS

The morning of September 11, 2001, I was showering and getting ready for a sales appointment in North Jersey. I'd reached the point in my career where I no longer wore a suit and tie. The morning television was on, when a news flash broke: a plane had hit the World Trade Center. I froze, dripping, nude, letting the overhead fan dry and chill me. Minutes later, another plane hit the towers. Disaster was slowly unfolding without comprehension.

Heading north on the Garden State Parkway, around Cranford, I saw smoke billowing in the distance. By the time I reached my appointment, the buildings were gone; humanity was lost. A relative's son was a teacher in downtown New York. I thought to drive into the city to bring him home until things settled down, but on Route 3 heading east, all the tunnels and bridges were shut. Life had halted.

By 4:00 a.m., I finally drifted to sleep after absorbing the news for twelve hours. The following morning—and I know not where this came from—I decided to resign being a manager. My overrides as a manager had been cut dramatically and my expenses had increased, so it was a losing proposition. My sixth sense, as Incanto and Vero continued to expand retail acquisitions, was that managership resembled a vestigial tail and I might as well get out now. A few years back, the company had reviewed its managers. I sat for two hours with Hayden Sommers, answering a barrage of questions that were perhaps taken from *Cosmopolitan* or *Psychology Today*: "Tell me, Cameron, about your ego," he asked.

My first thought was that Hayden must think I'm doing such a great job, so perhaps I could replace him someday. But I wanted to reassure him with a perfect response. "Hayden, I have one of the most convenient, sensible, practical egos. It spends most of the time in my back pocket, only stepping out when really needed," I said, "but not now."

Perhaps that response bought me more time. I was unhappy with the world, especially now after 9/11. I was suffocating in place without meaningful income and anywhere to go. For the first time in life, I cerebrally encountered the notion of aging, pushing sixty with fewer opportunities floating around for a graying eyeglass salesman.

In the months ahead, perhaps in a real clinical depression, I experienced fits of crying in the car. Once, after crying and beseeching God, I thought of the worst possibility, beyond reality, of ending my life. Right then, the strangest pain navigated along my waist and stomach. Obscenely, it felt good, and I felt even sorrier for myself. The pain was a banshee, leading me into temptation and eternal rest. The more I thought about ending things, the more intense the pain. Self-pity fed into it. At some point, I bounced back. Once again, I put on a happy face to sell sunglasses and eyeglasses.

2003

By early 2003, my mindset, part roller coaster, part grave digger at a local cemetery, meant I was emotionally up and down almost daily. My thoughts were often funereal, about death, the afterlife, and heaven—but no hell. Hopefully, I didn't fit the requirements for that. I cried in the car often, letting myself go. My income diminished as I stopped managing. With intestinal resolve, I packed up my ego in an eyeglass suitcase and continued working to sell to people who annoyed and disrespected me.

A week later, I read a small newspaper blip. Harold Russell had died—he had once won an Academy Award for his portrayal of Homer Parrish, a sailor who'd lost his hands during World War II, in the 1946 film *The Best Years of Our Lives*. I loved his movie. In 1992, struggling and needing money, he was the first actor to ever sell his Oscar. His battles with money and obscurity bothered me. It's a cold world.

That day, I was late for an appointment, being hard to motivate to get out of the house—I was incoherent, distant, not paying attention. Two blocks from the house, I flew into a car just in front of me. I'd been so immersed in my own problems; I had no clue the car was there. Failed brakes were my alibi to police. Whatever my self-war was, I was losing—and felt it.

Later that night, Noah slipped into his room of comics, rock music, graphic novels, and his model of the Millennium Falcon. Marjorie walked across the street. I sat at my desk, staring at the computer desktop and listening to "Catch the Wind," feeling clueless as to what the hell I was doing with my life. I pondered my options for ending the pain eternally, thinking there was only one way out.

Then something far away, at the end of the galaxy, landed in my occipital lobe. The image was distant, out of context, but powerful. I saw myself writing a novel. *Something*—a companion, unrecognizable spirit, angel—made me think of writing. Perhaps it would be a story about my fucked up, dysfunctional family. I scribbled an early outline on a legal pad. I called it *A Song for Rachel*.

Marjorie took my confession a few days later that I was writing a novel. She met me with no particular priceless look of surprise or spousal pride. "I don't know what to say," she said. "Yes, dream, because you're good at it. Maybe it helps you fight your problems with being an eyeglass salesman in a changing world. Remember how a few years ago you spent money we didn't have to design an environmental T-shirt about global warming, and a few hundred still sit in the guest bedroom? Just be careful—don't lose perspective."

"I don't know why I'm writing and I don't understand where it came from, but I'll do it as long as the energy is there," I bargained. "I'll do it on Saturdays and late at night."

"So, another excuse not to get a good night's sleep?"

"No, just to fulfill whatever is inside me, making me do this."

Marjorie became more supportive once my tenacity was more evident. A consumptive reader, she listened to me read my writing aloud after every few pages. I read to Noah too. Their early comments were sparse, generalized, and obligatory. Truth be told, that writing sucked. But something helped it change and become something more.

I stuck with writing—it innervated my mind, keeping me busy. I even stirred in a few dreams that maybe I could succeed as a writer, but I reread my pages often and concluded it was embarrassing to project beyond. My writing sucked. Finally, one cloudy day in December, I abandoned my saga about the Simmons clan.

An hour later, I saw a news blip that Soviet Premier Putin would not ratify the Kyoto Protocol, an international agreement to curb greenhouse gas emissions. Later, the news reported that 2003 had been the third-hottest year since modern recordkeeping. Coupled with the business of selling eyeglasses at year-end depressed—everyone had excuses not to buy—I felt lousy. The environmental movement is so undermined by billions of earthlings who don't give a shit.

A snowstorm hit on December 6. Those first few hours after a snow are nirvana. I love the pure white, silent world with no cars or pedestrians—just me in the driveway, shoveling, sweating, dreaming, remembering Goodwin Avenue after a snowstorm. I projected images of being on top of a cloud, waiting for my angel to escort me to the next stop. I thought about my grandparents Rachel and Colman, immigrating from cold, snowy Russia.

My tongue liked to capture renegade snowflakes. Endorphins to the rescue. I felt good. Something came over me as a cloud made room for the emerging sun above. Another novel flaked into my consciousness—a story about the evils of the oil business and how that black, sticky ooze fucks up the Earth. All the while, fossil fuel companies promote that oil does not contribute to global warming, and they pay for food and drinks at key environmental conferences. Their cousins at tobacco companies still deny cancer and cigarettes.

I had an idea of what needed to be said and I knew I had massive research to undertake. I was supremely clueless where this idea came from. A skinny guy from Monmouth County knew absolutely nothing about oil and we weren't even allowed to pump our own gas in Jersey.

I imagined the faces of the office staff at *Petroleum News* in Anchorage, Alaska, when a subscription request came from Cameron Simmons, from Marlboro, New Jersey. I spent my time voraciously researching oil, quiet companies, Texas, Alaska, Canada, and tar sands. My story would tell about the evils of money, oil, and secret societies, while still being filled with murder, intrigue, and hope.

Therapeutically, this story took my mind off my misery, not being able to support my family, knowing my job was poised to disappear, and having nowhere and no one to turn to. I had a small glimmer of fantasy: Could someone in my close world step up, feel my pain, and offer me something? Loyalty and remembering where you came from, how you got to a place in life, is a redeeming, everlasting quality. Regrettably, I knew you either get it or you don't. There are no familial moments of clairvoyance, understanding, or Ghosts of Christmas Yet to Come for people to get it if they don't. Blood is not thicker than water.

By the middle of the month, my writing was moving quickly, as was my mood. Christmastime is a notorious time to be depressed. I was languishing—crying in the car again, sleeping late because I went to bed late. I had no place to go. No money in the bank. Not a soul on Earth to turn to. Loathing was good business for me. I hated myself, my inadequate preparation for aging. I felt like George Bailey in *It's a Wonderful Life*, when Potter tells him he's worth more dead than alive.

The next morning, I collated insurance policies. But my love for Marjorie kept growing like a cactus on a desert hill without water. Looking back, I should've told her that more often.

I was finally at the lowest point in a life. Life had no meaning. My stomach hurt often with self-induced pain. I was ready in my heart, mind, and soul to finally go to Scarborough Fair, pick up a cambric shirt, and meet my maker. I was so done. Yet I still continued to write, so that meant something. Something in me was fighting back and waiting on a new year.

Chapter 24

THE SPIRIT ARRIVAL

In addition to the other difficulties I had with modern life, I suffered from horrific sleep patterns. In bed at midnight, watching anything—news, documentaries, old movies—I'd drift off to sleep by 2:00 a.m. Before nodding out, I'd turn off the TV. An hour later, I'd be downstairs, dipping salt-free pretzels in cream cheese and sitting in front of the computer. If the mood was there, I'd write. By 3:00 a.m., I'd be back in bed. Marjorie, a world-class sleeper, almost never knew I was gone. Falling back to sleep was difficult. Old sixties CDs soothed my soul, and seduced my brain waves into memories of a glorious past. Actually, it wasn't glorious. I latched onto anything perceptually better.

Sunday, December 28, was Amelia's birthday. At 2:00 a.m., like clockwork, I headed downstairs. This night, I'd stay on the computer for only a few minutes, tired of this routine and tired in general.

As the sun rose around seven o'clock, something tripped my wiring.

I was up early, mind firing away about New Year's, college football bowls, my novel, and my despair. I propped my pillow slightly higher and stared at my reflection in the mirror on the dresser.

Then, clearly, I heard a loud, discernable voice: "Trust."

It shook me, because it was so real. I turned to Marjorie, whose back was facing me. "Are you up?" I asked. I knew she wasn't.

I jumped out of bed and ran into Noah's room to see why he'd yelled "Trust." But he was soundly asleep.

When Marjorie officially woke up that morning, I recanted the story. "Are you sure, Cameron? Your imagination has been active lately," she said.

"I'm as sure as ever. I just don't understand."

This was a new experience. It was something spiritual, or not, but it was definitely not my imagination. The meaning of it was not evident, but it was something: a companion, curiosity. Nothing in the routin- ization of my life would change just yet. But I pondered what "trust" meant. My mind went away for a time.

Days later, it was all a distant memory. Thinking back, I had no clue as to the gender of the voice. It was just a voice, almost like a dream that fades into vague splinters once you're awake. But I knew it had happened.

THE NIGHT THAT CHANGED MY LIFE

One February day in 2004, my life would finally find meaning, spirit, warmth, and life hereafter. I wore blue jeans with a sweater and tie. Wearing jeans as a professional salesman means I didn't give a shit about the selling process anymore. Now I had a manager to answer to, but he didn't give a shit either; just get good numbers at the end of the week. I'd been with the company for two decades. My accounts knew me, mostly liked me—I made them laugh. Maybe longevity hinged on an entertainment factor. This day I banged out a hundred frames. My week was saved, so I cut off the day and rushed home to write. Every page brought me closer to a dream.

Marjorie hated my office, littered with piles of papers, boxes, makeshift files resting on carpet that hadn't been cleaned in a dozen years. Her speeches, imploring sensibility, bedtime habits, were always done standing at the doorway, never crossing the dusty, inhospitable threshold.

"Cameron, are you coming to bed at a decent hour? Your horrible sleeping habits will catch up to you one day," she chided.

I told her I'd be up soon—I was immersed in researching about the Inuit peoples in the Arctic regions of Canada and Alaska, an area lush with oil reserves.

"Cameron, read my lips: I don't care. Good night."

I finished writing after midnight, Tuesday, February 24. Tossing and turning, pounding the double pillows into the semblance of my cerebral contour, I drifted to sleep somewhere around 1:00 a.m. Repose didn't last long. An hour later, my mind, swimming in oil ideas and re-climbing red mountains in Sedona, nudged me out of bed. I went back to aimlessly staring at the computer monitor for several minutes. I had no idea why I was there. I was not in the mood to write or do anything. The bottom right-hand corner of the screen read 2:22 a.m.

Then something, as distant as another galaxy, startled my memory of an old Bee Gees song, "Lamplight," from 1969. I hadn't heard the song in decades, and all of a sudden, I needed to hear it. I searched for the song on Kazaa Lite, a wholesomely illegal file-sharing program. At 3:11, I found the song and began a slow, tedious download. I passed the time playing online backgammon with a stranger from Sweden. By 4:30, the download was complete. I pressed play. Words about lamplights burning and maybe my heart yearning. Immediately, I remembered why I loved this song. The sound was bittersweet, surreal, moody.

When I finished listening, I started for bed; my work alarm would go off in a few hours. But something quickly brought me back, convincing me to Google my mother's maiden name. Why the inexplicable hell would I do this? The sun was nearby over the western Atlantic. I typed "Crast" into the search bar. A millisecond later, twenty-five items came up. Strangely, the first twenty-four concerned my second cousin Holden, from Boston, and his testimony at an infamous trial in Massachusetts. An au pair from Paris had robbed a convenience store, killing the clerk. Holden had hired the au pair for his two children, but dismissed her months before the crime.

Then the last search result caught my eye. It was an entry on an old Newark trivia site about Crast Pharmacy in the 1960s, back when I had worked there. The writer's name was Bill Tyler. I had worked with a Bill Tyler, befriended him, went to midnight mass with him, but we'd lost ourselves in the space-time continuance of the sixties and Vietnam. Could this be the same Bill Tyler? It probably was. Confronted with thousands of entries on the trivia site, I had to sleep, so I randomly scrolled, closed my eyes, and landed exactly on Bill's entry. I had a 1-in-3,000 chance of landing in the right spot. This was all morphing into something strange, synchronistic, and curious. What a grand design. Had I lived this once before?

Bill's email address was there in the entry. I had to connect and see if he was that Bill Tyler. I wrote:

> Dear Bill:
> Well, it's 4:44 a.m., Tuesday. I've been surfing around for hours. Couldn't sleep. So, before I start going down the sentimental highway, let me ask, did you work at Crast Pharmacy in Newark in the early, mid-sixties? Was your brother Jim a priest? If the answer is yes, well, I'm Cameron Simmons. I was there too. Of course, you'll remember me. We'll have a lot to talk about. I live in Jersey. Never left, except for pharmacy school and a brief stint as a newlywed in Brooklyn. Please let me know. I love the internet and the Bee Gees song "Lamplight."
> Cameron (Simmons)

Then I went to bed. A few hours later, the alarm nudged me awake to sell eyeglasses. But first, I checked my email. Sent at 9:01 a.m., there was Bill—finally reunited after a piece of a lifetime bygone.

> Hi Cam:
> Absolutely, positively, un-effen-believable! Yes, yes, it is me! How wonderful to reconnect with you . . .

He went on to remind me how I'd taught him to sneak downstairs at Crast Pharmacy, push together a few large boxes of Kotex sanitary napkins, form a mattress, and take a nap. No one went into the cellar except us clerks. I'd taught him what a Herm count was; measuring a girl's breasts. Simple precious memories resurfaced, rekindled by twists of time and fate wrapped around an old Bee Gees song.

Bill and I continued catching up over email. I told him about my mundane life journey from pharmacy to selling eyeglasses. Bill had been to the Taj Mahal, dined at Mount Everest with the son of the Sherpa guide who'd taken Sir Edmund Hillary to the summit, graduated Purdue, served in the army, saw the world, and settled in the Ozarks on a large tract of land. Multi-page emails brought us together with indelible, heartfelt memories. I dreamed about a wormhole that could take me back in time—I'd go back to hang out with Bill in a heartbeat.

On our third night of emails, Bill wrote:

> I've got to tell you something, Cam. When you wrote your first note, it was at 4:44 a.m. That is a very special time for me. For years, I've awoken at precisely that time, 4:44, without a clock or alarm. That number appears often in my daily life. I open a book and it's on page 444. I draw a number at the Rotary Club and it's 444. I turn a corner and there is a license plate, 444, etc.

Dozens of these examples. So, although I was surprised
to see the time on your note, I was also delighted and
intrigued. There was a book written on the subject of
the 4:44 hour and there is a belief that it's spiritually
charged with angels, unexplained activities, etc.

As I read this, nothing moved me. I had no impressions of rela-
tivity, just some happenstance words that exited my cerebral cavity as
quickly as they'd entered. I quickly forgot it and my life went on.

THE PLOT, OR A THICK SHAKE FROM WHITE CASTLE

The cold, dreary, late winter days in Jersey suck, especially if
you've already been operating in a depressed state for several years. By
mid-March of 2004, we had a stretch of ice, snow, hail, and plagues.
Business was bad and people were not buying eyeglasses. I felt lower
than an amoeba's asshole, looking up at the insurmountable mountain
to climb just for survival. The flotilla that kept me afloat was writing.
This day, someone close called, castigated, and laced into me for my
ridiculous writing dreams. I should go back to being a dedicated
salesman, they said. It was someone impactful in my life. I'd spent years
trying to win their respect. Never happened.

The following day, I was feeling particularly low. As I drove around
locally, trying to sell a few frames, I thought about my growing up poor
while I had a millionaire writer uncle in Beverly Hills and a dysfunctional family everywhere.

Then I drove by a White Castle, an orgiastic, better-than-sex,
hamburger joint. They sell them by the sack. I hadn't had meat in my
life since 1975, but "fuck the world" was my new attitude. I could be
gone tomorrow. Not once had I ever cheated with meat, but maybe it
was time. I ordered six hamburgers, fries, and a thick chocolate shake
to take out. I pulled onto the highway and unwrapped a burger. I loved
this fast-food stuff, but I always denied myself.

Then the thought reverberated within me, thinking of the years I'd invested in not eating meat. Eating this food would leave me hating myself even more. Sanity prevailed. My quest had to be preserved. It was self-worth, respect. With no time to think, as I was passing a patch of green, I opened the window and threw the bag of burgers and fries away. The thick shake stayed. I'd littered, but I saved myself.

With that boost in self-respect, I went home early, not having sold anything. That night, after ten o'clock, I began to write. An Italian lawyer from Essex County, New Jersey, was being recruited for a secret project in the oil industry. First, he had to move to Washington, DC, and be transformed into a waspy, bland, invisible, nondescript attorney. Back in Essex County, he was demonstrably Italian, a Tony Soprano type. I needed a perfect Italian and WASP name derivative for when he moved to Washington. I spent an hour sitting at the screen, reverting to a game of solitaire, salt-free pretzels, and seltzer, but nothing came to mind. That freaking wall of non-productivity bumped into me. After eleven o'clock, I went to bed, mentally exhausted.

"Cameron, what brings you to bed before the witching hour?" Marjorie asked, shocked. "Are you feeling all right?"

I went to hug her for the warm bedtime greeting, but her hands were covered with thick, odorous white cream, so I backed away. "Thanks, honey, for rolling out the welcome mat."

The next morning was foggy and drizzly. I didn't feel like selling eyeglasses, as usual, but I pushed myself. On the TV, I heard a morning news anchor announce, "Scientists say Earth may be in the middle of the sixth big extinction. Update at five o'clock." That bothered me. *Extinction* is a nasty word. I always laugh absurdly at news teasers— what if a fleet of Russian ICBMs was heading toward us, due to strike in three minutes? The freaking update at 6:00 p.m. (Thanks to George Carlin for this inspiration.)

Suddenly, the sun came out. I had several appointments down the Jersey Shore, a forty-minute drive, and I was determined to pass the time thinking of a name for my fictional Italian lawyer. Possession was my passenger. After merging with Route 35 South, I was almost at my first appointment, car window open, stopped at a red light. And out of the cold, mysterious universe arrived a haunting inspiration for my character's name: Louis Del Priore. When he goes to Washington, becoming a WASP with a secret presence, his name would be Louis Delpy. From where it came, I know not, because I'd never heard that name. I worked for an Italian company and knew scores of Italians. This inspiration arrived like ragweed blowing in the wind, making my nose sneeze and my eyes tear up.

After writing three orders, I headed back home on Route 35. The car clock read 4:30 p.m. I was approaching one of my favorite accounts, Dr. Paul Manner, a mild-mannered optometrist who liked me and my product. It's an unwritten rule to never walk into an account past 4:30.

Sheepishly, I pulled off the highway into the strip mall with Dr. Manner's office and walked inside. I still had no clue why I was there. The receptionist, Eva, who was busy with a patient, yelled, "Hi, Cameron. Doctor will be right out." So far, all positive.

Dr. Manner emerged from the exam room. "Glad you're here," he said. "I could actually use forty designer frames, mostly women. Want to write up an order?"

"That's not why I stopped, but I'll do it," I said—a bullshit statement, because this was a great order, despite breaking all the rules of engagement.

While I sat at a small table to write the order, a patient walked to the front desk. "I'm here to pick up my contact lenses," he said in a distinct Brooklyn accent.

"Name please?" the receptionist asked.

"Louis Del Priore."

I heard it too clearly.

"Excuse me, sir. What did you say your name was?" I asked, my arms covered in goose bumps.

This man was average height with crew-cut hair, and ethnically Italian—a dead ringer for Tony Soprano. He turned toward me, fists semi-clenched as in altercation or defense. "Louis Del Priore," he repeated.

Eva and Dr. Manner stared me down, wondering what the hell was I doing with their patient. It was right there at 4:44 p.m. I stood up, apologized for being unprofessional, told Louis Del Priore the whole story of me envisioning his name for my novel, and congratulated him for being in a work of fiction. He dropped his hands to his side, unclenched his fists, and shook my hand, wishing me good luck.

"Just one quick question about the name Del Priore," I said. "Where are you from? Is it a common name? I work for an Italian company. My world is half Italian, but I've never heard it before."

"I'm from Brooklyn. Best to my knowledge, it's a very rare name. Maybe two families in all of Brooklyn, with their millions of Italians, have that name."

My life had magnificently, spiritually changed forever. Slowly, methodically, I'd been taken, opened, and exposed to spirit far beyond my comprehension. Now I knew something had really happened to me when Bill Tyler gifted me with words and expressions of 4:44. This day was beyond normal or scientific. Something had happened to me a few weeks ago with the knowledge of 444, and was now manifesting itself and directing me by stark example to open my soulful awareness in order to receive it.

Driving home, I tried to conjure a rational explanation for this, but I knew for certain I'd been gifted with something so beyond it. Now I needed to be aware of a kind of world different from the mundane, maddening world of selling eyeglasses. Something was out there, guiding and watching me. A unique warmth came over me. I opened the window and inhaled, whispering, "Thank you, God." Something (someone?) was in the passenger seat next to me.

Suddenly, I remembered that recent December morning when

a voice had said "Trust." Fragments of my spirituality were coming together, yet I was still a spiritual virgin. I sensed I had a long way to go before I could rest. I couldn't wait to tell Marjorie.

Chapter 25

CASABLANCA WATER

A new spiritual vibration had consumed my world. Signs were omni-present, frequent, haunting, and distanced from normal explanations like coincidence. My diary, which I kept for several years, became redundant with the often happenings. The more I opened myself to receive spirit signs, the more I got. I was like a great antenna to the unknown, centering around 444 and 111, and combinations of the two.

According to Bill Tyler and his priest, those numbers are signs of angelic intervention. Being conscious of those numbers is really about being aware of a mysterious presence. With time, I realized this spirit communicates by making me aware of their presence by noticing those numbers and realizing they were nearby, watching, making me feel warm all over. Finally, I felt secure not being alone in the cold, dark universe. Sometimes, strangely, I'd get choked up; these experiences were so powerful, beyond coincidence. A few times teary.

Coming to terms with what was going on took a long time; a tedious, gratifying learning process. Eventually, in a few years, I'd realize these experiences were gifts. I found the song "Simple Gifts" by Judy Collins and listened to it as if each time was the first time. What are my simple gifts? Health. Spirit. Love.

One morning, back in my early days of discovery, something came to me and I had to listen to "Who Knows Where the Time Goes" also sung by Judy Collins. The song was 4:44 long and the time was 11:11 p.m. The next day, while I was proofreading my manuscript on my exercise bike, I suddenly stopped and gazed down at the readout: 111 calories and 11:11 elapsed.

Once, I spent three awful days trying to sell in Atlantic City. I stayed in a motel for two nights, not earning commission, dining in my room with a turkey sub sandwich. Because I'm Pavlovian, I knew gambling is a waste. Instead, I played tennis with an optician who'd bought a pile of frames. Our court in Ventnor, near the ocean, had a great view. Smelling the salt air while we served yielded an olfactory high.

My last night of the trip, driving down Pacific Avenue after another depressing sales day, I caught a red light and a beautiful woman in a slinky white dress blowing in the wind like Marilyn Monroe in *The Seven Year Itch*. Maybe she was hitchhiking? I leaned forward. That innocent gesture of curiosity propelled her to my door handle. Next thing I knew, she was sitting shotgun.

"Hurry up, pull around the corner and go down the street," she said. She was idyllic and I was filled with naiveté.

"Huh? I thought you were hitchhiking. Why all this evasion down the street?"

"Just in case cops saw you pick me up. You do know what I do?" she asked.

"I think I do now. But I'm filled with more disbelief than when

Lyndon Johnson said he wasn't running for president. You're too beautiful to be that."

"You lost me. What about Johnson?"

"Not important. My name is Alan," I lied. "Nice to meet you."

"I'm Sylvia. What did you have in mind?"

"I've never done this before, if you can believe me. What about spending the night?" I asked, mostly out of curiosity. I hadn't a fragment of intent to carry this out.

When she told me her rate was $1,000 for the night, I balked. That was a little out of my budget.

"How much is your budget?"

"$25. I'm just a poor salesman," I said, blushing. "I'm so sorry I wasted your time."

"You seem like a nice, honest guy. Drop me off by 7-Eleven."

I chalked it up to a lousy three days of selling. Driving home the next day, I realized I was poor, I'd never finish writing, and the future was fucked. I had no way out, but the only good thing was a spirit in my life, delivering a four-letter word, hope, wrapped around special numbers.

Somewhere around Ocean County, I talked out loud in the car, beseeching my spirit, if they were around. "I need you," I said. "I'd love to know you're here, maybe riding shotgun. And who are you? Perhaps give me a sign you're close."

I was driving in the middle lane. Suddenly, a car passed on the left. Something made me look at the license plate—it had the number forty-four. A moment later, another car—forty-four again.

I smiled broadly. "Thank you."

It didn't stop. The next car—another forty-four. My head was swimming, my eyes were teary. This was beyond probability—it had to be a force in the universe, a wonderful presence, an angel, guardian, and friend.

Throughout these revelations, I battled internally. Was it real? Why me? It was beyond basic human grasp. I'd come to accept it all as a simple, wondrous gift. I'd look forward to new appearances each day. Through it all, I sensed the need to be a better human being, to be worthy of these simple gifts.

CASABLANCA

How I want to say that with all these spiritual interactions, I was settling into a renewed life. But I was still unhappy with work, struggling to earn a living, worrying about Noah's college, and dwelling on the concept of retirement. I was difficult to live with. Marjorie deserved medals for putting up with me.

Even with my head not in the right place, I loved playing tennis. It was a great venue for my frustration. My dream was to serve hard and accurate, hitting an opponent (I didn't like) in the crotch. My doubles team stayed together for a decade, partly because all four of us guys disliked each other. Enmity is that powerful.

"So, what did you guys talk about?" Marjorie often asked when I got home from a game.

"Nothing," I'd say. "We play, grunt, spit, curse, and yell 'See you next week' as we all rush to our cars. This isn't mah-jongg. It's serious tennis."

One early Sunday morning in April 2004, my doubles team was set to play. I hate early weekend mornings, but for tennis and dreams of a perfect passing shot, I got dressed; grabbed some juice, a bagel, vitamins and carried a can of balls out the door only to be greeted by an unpredicted quiet rain. No tennis today—and no going back to sleep.

Sitting at the edge of the bed half nude, pissed because a sliver of sun had just sliced through the verticals, the local Jersey news bored me to extinction. I stared at the muted TV, then something came to mind. I suddenly had to watch *Casablanca*, my favorite movie. It's perhaps the greatest love story. The ending rips my guts. When Rick and Louis talk about a beautiful friendship walking in a foggy drizzle.

I put *Casablanca* into the machine. My unhappy life was ninety minutes away from a powerful directional change. Something out there in space, time, heaven was directing me.

Why was I so glued, still sitting at the edge of the bed, watching in my underwear? Something paralyzed me. *Casablanca* made me feel the pain of people trying to get to freedom. Maybe my pain needed company.

Near the end, Bogart's character, Rick Blaine, shoots Major Strasser, a German bad guy. Claude Rains as Captain Louis Renault instructs the police to get the usual suspects. Bogart delivers a faint smile of gratitude. Louis picks up a bottle of Vichy Water, French mineral water, for a celebratory drink after the Nazi's death. Vichy Water—I'd seen that label so many times before in this film, but it never registered until now. Louis turns the bottle and realizes anything with the word "Vichy" in the 1940s generally meant conspiring with the Germans. He dropped the bottle into a metal garbage can. A second elapsed until it hit bottom. Leaning closer to the television, I watched intently.

"Oh, my God!" I yelled.

Marjorie ran to the landing steps. "Are you all right, Cam?"

I came downstairs and hugged Marjorie. "There's a new novel in my head. It's all there, this novel called *Casablanca Water*. The whole story is stuck in my head. I have no idea how it got there. I know what I have to do now."

How strange the day had been. The rain, once I started watching the movie, gave way to warm sunshine. Now at my desk, I was outlining a complete novel with a beginning, middle, and end, all neatly, cerebrally compacted. This mystery of life would continue to unfold. In effect, it was *Casablanca Water* that ultimately launched this memoir.

THE OUTLINING PROCESS

Three weeks later, I'd birthed a complete outline. All throughout the process, I marveled from whence, whom, and why it all came. It took a millisecond for a bottle of mineral water to hit the bottom of a garbage can and an entire novel lodged in my head. Of course, with spiritual interventions irrefutable proof, now I know exactly how it got there.

Casablanca Water is the story of two boys meeting for the first time in a vacant lot in Newark in 1960. The boys are of vastly different backgrounds—one Jewish, the other Muslim and Coptic Christian. They were culturally miles apart, but developed a most beautiful human friendship of lifelong loyalty and understanding.

I was content doing this writing—I often heard Claude Rains as Mr. Jordan, saying, "Cameron, you are home, you're a champion, where you're supposed to be, so finish this and your life will never be the same." I believed I'd finish this book, get published, and embark on a journey that began when I heard that voice say "Trust."

In my earlier efforts at being a novelist, I began to feel a curious something. My words were part of a world where I presided—my game board, my rules, and my willpower. I could say and do anything, with no one to answer to. Yet, I wasn't totally free. I fought an internal battle over saying what was really on my mind—to tell the whole world that I want to get off, and the people who I cared nothing for to go fuck themselves. I couldn't be that free. I reasoned that if and when I became successful, I could finally say what I wanted. If not, then I had to behave and maybe find clever, vague ways to say what I really felt.

In *Casablanca Water*, I'd go further than intended. When I finished the outline, I was proud this novel would give me a chance to speak about racism, feminism, tolerance, the human species, environmentalism, friendship, loyalty, infidelity, existentialism, and a few American corporations. I disliked greed, what some American companies were all about. It may do us in as a species in thirty years, according to a couple scientists. I tried to express this in my novel.

Somewhere in time, I read Ayn Rand's *The Virtue of Selfishness*. My interpretation, weaved into *Casablanca Water*, is that it's a virtue to be selfish. My main character, Ellis, subscribes to that premise. He believes the purpose of marriage is to make the other person happy, but you can't do that and be virtuous unless you are happy first. And what would make him happy? If he had an affair and was fulfilled. The affair is virtuous. Marjorie and the rest of my family would knee-jerk to that.

Selfishness was one aspect of Ellis. I dreamed that Ellis would circumnavigate all my bucket list places: Montana on Christmas Eve, Guadalcanal circa World War II, Sedona, Key Largo.

Writing was a powerful energizer. I was a wind-up toy, running downstairs on weekend mornings to write. My head was in gear, constantly thinking where I was and what I had to say. Sometimes I'd get an idea while driving in the car and I'd pull over to scribble a few notes. The more I wrote, the more I jumped on the exercise bike to proofread, drifting into this world I was creating. I'd pedal every night, endlessly rereading, correcting, changing. In the midst of it all, often I'd stop reading and look at the read-out on the bike—444 calories, 111 calories, 11:11 minutes—and I knew a spirit was in the room with me.

Chapter 26

THE BUSINESS OF 2004

I was a man of consumption, obsession, devotion. I plunged my molecular constitution, my daily bread and dreams, into the story of *Casablanca Water*. Marjorie woke up on a Saturday spring morning suggesting, with a heavy dose of guilt, that we take a ride to New Hope or the Jersey Shore and suck fresh air into our winter weary lungs.

"Marjorie, I've been selling for twenty-three years, driving endlessly around the state, five long days a week, and how many Saturday mornings do I have to tell you the same thing: the last place I want to be is in a car on my weekend," I said. "You're the only woman in America who leaves the house at 8:00 a.m. and gets to work at 8:00 a.m. You have a three-block commute to teach."

In a classic pose of obstinacy—arms folded, eyes fixed—she fired back, "Cam, learn to live, explore, and get your ass out of the house.

We're still a family. Noah hardly sees you. I hardly see you. And this writing obsession—you are not Stephen King."

It's a hard rain to admit she was always kind of right. I still couldn't give complete submission, so I walked away internalizing a make-believe state of mind that she wasn't. Writing is a hard undertaking, lonely and devoid of instant gratification. No matter how many years *Casablanca Water* took to write, in the back and front of my thinking lobes was this notion: What if I never get published? Where do I go? What do I do?

Strangely, spiritually, I kept renewing my conviction that this was the right road. Every day was filled with self-doubt until I saw signs of spirit with me, 111 and 444 all over my life. Sometimes it was inexplicable. Over Noah's high school spring break, we went down to Atlantic City for a few days to a sunglass-selling exhibition. He worked the Vero booth with me. Noah had grown tall, with long hair and hazel eyes—if you squinted, he looked like me on a cloudy day. His mannerisms, shtick, and temperament were all me. Marjorie claimed his intellectual curiosity and determination were her contributions. Screw heredity. We'd raised him in a loving environment.

In the Vero booth, Noah was born to sell. He was smooth, poised, eloquent, and mystically sincere. People loved him. I felt pride all over, like a radioactive cloud, making me feel ten feet tall.

Later, back in our eighth-floor hotel room, with a view of the ocean and boardwalk, I flicked on lights and stopped short, dramatically staring at a cheap oil painting over the double beds. The painting depicted a beach scene with a broken wooden fence that was almost lying down in the sand. Two seagulls flew above toward the ocean. "Holy shit," I said. "I described that exact scene last Saturday in my novel."

"How can that be?" Noah asked.

"I think I know. This spirit I keep telling you and Mom about, it's all around me, everywhere, planting things in my gray cerebral matter."

"Oh, come on, Dad. That's a little far out."

THERE'S A TORTOISE IN MY HAIR

"After sixty years, me suddenly writing a novel? That's far out. It's the same spirit, Noah."

By the end of our trip, having sold a pile of sunglasses, Noah and I treated ourselves to an Italian dinner with calamari, a large plate of baked chicken parts, potatoes, onions, and peppers, and a Caesar salad. I basked in the white light of our loving father-son relationship, sending gratitude vibes all the way up the chain of command.

By nine o'clock, we were heading home on the Atlantic City Expressway, a trip I'd done a hundred times. Noah had fallen asleep a few minutes after we'd hit the road. Exit 7 to the Garden State Parkway was cemented in my consciousness. But somehow, inexplicably, I missed it, and we were now heading west toward the City of Brotherly Love.

"Son of a bitch. How did I do this?" I grumbled, stirring Noah awake.

There was no GPS yet, so I was moderately screwed. I didn't know where I was.

A few exits later, I got off the expressway and tried to turn around. But there was no exit back to the highway. I was driving blindly in dark surroundings, no streetlights or signs, but I could make out fields of weeds and corn on both sides of us, a farmhouse and silo silhouetted in the distance.

"I think we're in Kansas, somehow!" I said.

"I'd like to get home before I graduate in June," Noah laughed, but he was pissed.

I drove around for twenty minutes, never asking directions. "Relax, Son, there is no way we can get lost in Jersey. Head west, the Delaware. Due east, Atlantic."

Finally, we found a streetlight illuminating the iconic green and yellow Garden State Parkway sign. An arrow told us to proceed straight. Strangely, as soon as we merged onto the parkway, something made me look at the mileage signpost to see where we were in relation to home. Milepost 44.4. It was as if all of this had been directed by a powerful spirit intervention, like a Spielberg or Scorsese film. I felt a warm, elevating feeling of being watched over—another reason for me to believe in the word "trust."

JUST A SALES CALL

A few weeks later, I was selling in North Jersey, cold-calling on accounts, which I hated doing. Accounts also hate when you walk in, smiling, tail wagging, looking for an order. After five accounts in a row had bounced me out with excuses not to buy, I was in Ridgewood, Bergen County, visiting an essence of eyeglass pomposity and conservatism, listening to yet more reasons why he wasn't buying my eyeglasses anymore. Mostly, he said, because people were going to malls and chain stores. I'd been selling long enough to know when to abandon ship and get the hell home, so this seemed like a good time to call it a wrap. Tired of his bullshit, I said goodbye, good luck, and have a nice life. Fuck him.

Heading south, something led me toward Belleville to see a favorite optician, Anthony. He was old-world, a craftsman, a Calabrese Italian, and stubborn in matters of modernization (he wouldn't give up smoking). It had been six months since I last saw him.

I was always in a quandary over where friendship ends and business dwells. Obsessive about loyalty, I never presumed friendship. Friendship precludes the presumption of business. Anthony and I occasionally got dinner, but only at small, almost invisible neighborhood Italian restaurants. North Jersey had dozens buried into the framework of the history of immigration. Each one had a unique red sauce ("gravy"), handmade pasta, and knew Anthony going back to when he sang doo-wop on the street corners in West Newark in the late fifties and sixties.

Walking inside his shop, I was clobbered with a stale nicotine smell of death.

THERE'S A TORTOISE IN MY HAIR

"Cameron, this is the strangest thing," he said, greeting me with a genuine hug. "I've been thinking of you all day, hoping you'd come visit. You scare me with your sixth sense."

Anthony's world was withering too, just like the schmuck I'd just visited in Ridgewood. Business was down; he apologized for not buying from me. I admonished that I only wanted to see him, and left after another human, endearing hug.

Back in the car, I had another inexplicable thought. For some time, I followed whereabouts of my ex-wife, Valerie. My searches for her were a vehicle for me to apologize, but mostly to show that I'd righted my ship, made something of myself, and became a father. There was something else too, deeply contorted: the fantasy of a last fuck. No lingering torches; decades wiped it out. I pondered the morality of sleeping with her. It was probably legal with an asterisk in the original Ten Commandments, because she'd been my first wife.

Passing Clara Maass Hospital, something made me head to an outpatient building. Valerie supposedly worked there as an occupational therapist. It was near 4:00 p.m., when people punched time clocks. I sat in the parking lot with a view of the front door and waited. No Valerie. Maybe so much time had elapsed, I might not recognize her. My powers of salesmanship were fine-tuned, so I could talk my way back into her life, her bed, and her forgiveness—but I didn't expect anything. Four times, my hands went to the ignition to get away. After fifteen minutes, my prodigious, ballsy guts had me walk in and ask about Valerie.

"Sorry, there is no Valerie Scott here," the receptionist said.

"I know she worked here. I guess years ago. How long have you been here?" I asked.

"Six years."

I thanked them and left. This was my last active pursuit of this fixation. Like the last scene in *Marjorie Morningstar*, with Natalie Wood on the bus, when she realizes you can't go home again.

ANOTHER KIND OF SPIRIT

I disliked early selling appointments, always discouraging accounts from bringing me there at 9:00 a.m., which meant a seven o'clock shower, startling my sensibilities. Three million Jersey neighbors drove on the early morning road. This morning, I left at 7:30 for an appointment in Somerville, just down Route 202/206 from towns like Bedminster, where Jackie Kennedy rode horses, and Peapack and Gladstone, with resident descendants from the Mayflower.

In a strip mall around the Somerville Circle, a few miles from the estate of Doris Duke, the tobacco heiress, was Diamond Vision Eyeglasses. Procedurally, I got to the door at nine o'clock and schlepped my bags inside; the store opened at ten, leaving me an hour to sell.

Connie, the buyer, reminded me of a young Shirley Temple with her blonde curly hair and large eyes. I followed her to the lens lab. One side of the long and narrow space was lined with machines and a small mirror painted with artsy designs. The other side had shelving for supplies. The empty store was eerily dark, lit only by a single overhead florescent bulb. Faces close, we talked about her new motorcycle and our sons.

A few minutes into talking, I felt a strange sensation, like a breath on my neck. I turned around, but nothing was there. Then it happened again. And again. After several glances behind me, Connie asked with a giggle, "What's the matter? We're the only ones here."

I told her what I'd been feeling. My neck hairs were standing erect.

"Congratulations, you've just met George. I think he likes you," she said. When I looked confused, she explained, "Our resident ghost. For years, many strange things happen. Machines turn off by themselves—and it takes a tremendous push to turn them on and off. Lights go on and off. Sometimes, I see a vague form by the mirror. I get a strange feeling being here, especially when I'm alone."

"Oh, come on, Connie. A ghost?" I said.

Her smile was gone. Her penetrating eyes were serious. "A few years

THERE'S A TORTOISE IN MY HAIR

ago, I went to the library and researched the land where this mall was built. Back in the 1800s, it was a farm owned by a poor farmer, George Miller. He had a rich girlfriend whose parents tried to discourage her from dating a poor farmer, to no avail. One day, George Miller was found murdered in his house. George is still here—he never moved on. He hangs out, and I think he watches over me."

The best I could do was shake my head incredulously. "No comment, Connie," I said, "but I did feel something."

Three months later, on another sales visit to Diamond Vision, my cell phone kept turning off. It screeched when I was talking, then turned off. I never touched it. The power button was hard even for me to operate. The only thing on my mind was that George had taken up residence inside my phone, an unacceptable scenario. I drove to a Verizon store for a repair. "I don't know how to explain this properly, but I think there's a ghost inside my phone," I told them.

Later that year, close to Halloween, I'd have another spooky encounter— this one more certain. I was working on my novel when the ceiling light above my computer flickered. It was hot to the touch, so I got a cool, moist towel and placed it on the bulb. The bulb exploded into thousands of pieces. I'd been looking directly into the light, so my eyes should have been doomed with injurious glass, yet somehow not a piece touched my eyes, dispersing instead all over the desk, floor, and my shoulders and hair. Something beyond, something spiritual, was always comforting and confounding me. I knew to continue the journey to finishing my novel, which was meant to be; part of a designed destiny.

Somebody up there likes me, pulling the strings and keeping shattered glass out of my eyes. I wasn't alone in a dark, cold universe. How I wished knowing the identity of who had been hanging around me since I was born. I now understood something had steered my car between that tree and pole when it was rolling over at 50 miles an hour—and not a scratch on me.

SEE YOU IN SEPTEMBER

Noah graduated high school. Watching the processional, Marjorie and I choked up with tears of joy and wonderment. We're not perfect together—we have differing philosophies about the origins of the universe, how to run a house—but we're special partners in life's emotionality. That's our glue.

A week later, something propelled me to visit Amelia and Jack in Boca Raton. Intestinal energies stirred up by my spirit, a nameless something, guiding me there. For weeks, I'd felt an empty feeling about the fragility of life, mortality, inevitability, and death. I was angry at the universe. How dare it take away my parents, who'd given me life? The universe is big enough to keep them around. All my relatives, who'd come to America for freedom, were gone. I never asked any of them how hard it was to come to America. I could've learned so much, like how it felt to be hated by their neighbors and strangers.

When my parents greeted me at the front door, I marveled at how great they looked. My parents were like cheese, aged and sharp. I hoped to be like that when I'm an octogenarian.

That night we went out to dinner, and my parents ordered sodium- and nitrite-enhanced hot dogs with baked potatoes. I was cool, keeping my nutritional lectures to myself. We talked about Noah, Marjorie, and my sister Carol. Whatever existed was mendacity, right out of *Cat on a Hot Tin Roof*. While parents were alive, I lived the harmony game.

While I was there, I'd decided to take three mornings of tennis lessons at a famous academy nearby. Playing tennis in Florida outside in late June was miserably hot. Another student was a woman named Rebecca. She was forty-something, tall, heavily accented, and beautiful. Chatting around the water cooler, she told me she was from Israel, divorced, the CEO of her own company, and passionate about tennis. Somehow—words, eyebrows, smiles, flirtations—Rebecca and I met for an oceanside dinner the next night. I don't know why it happened. An anti-aging mechanism, or an intestinal lining of restlessness?

The last day of class, I was filmed by the academy head, a former pro who'd once ranked 100 in the world. The purist asshole suggested I give up the game of tennis altogether. I had too much to fix, he said, between my footwork, serve, ground strokes, positioning, and my grasp of the game. I was too classy to say "fuck you" as my response.

That made for adequate dinner conversation with Rebecca. A few times, we leaned close to each other, the kind of body language that lands people in bed together. But it was just too much trouble for both of us. I kicked guilt in the ass again. We parted with a handshake in the moonlit night.

Near the end of my trip, my parents and I sat around the kitchen table. It was a simple gift to spend precious time together. Then Amelia blurted out how I'd been conceived in the attic of the old Buena Vista Hotel in Belmar. They wanted to celebrate Franklin Roosevelt being elected to a fourth term. My conception was based on their love of FDR. I had my doubts about him. In *Casablanca Water*, I wrote a supposition that he knew about the Japanese invasion of Pearl Harbor, but needed to get us into the war quickly as England was weakening. Amelia frowned at my blasphemy, so I let it be.

"The weekend after Thanksgiving, in 1944, your father and I went away for three days, walked on the beach late one night. It was so romantic—" Amelia started explaining.

"Mom, I don't need details."

"You're a big boy. We went back to the room, had a glass of wine. It was so cold. We were under the covers. Then in August, you arrived, right after Hiroshima and Nagasaki. My special son was born into a world of peace. I prayed for the world and you. We lost so much family in Europe."

My eyes teared up. I exited to the bathroom. I didn't want Amelia to see me like that.

A few weeks later, Amelia sent me some old family pictures, because as the oldest child, I was the family historian. That box of sent pictures would illuminate my life.

By August, Amelia rushed to the hospital with a severe stomach ache. I flew down to give the doctor permission for exploratory surgery. Complications from a stomach aortic aneurism took her two days later.

In the middle of mourning, Marjorie and I took Noah to Rider University, helped set up his room, and delivered a final lecture on girls, protection, and pot. We hung up a poster of John Belushi in a "College" sweatshirt, and cried in the parking lot when we said goodbye.

The empty nest had arrived; it freaking sucked. It was lonely, filled with new sounds of silence. But our sadness was really for ourselves, approaching life's autumn, no longer being in charge of a life, watching it fly away.

Chapter 27

SAINT ANTHONY

Early one morning, flirting with REM sleep, I lapsed into an intense, graphically real dream about going back to the University of Toledo. Back in Ohio, as a sixty-something adult, registering for classes, living in a dorm, pulling a drawer out from under my bunk, and finding an open container of strawberry jelly. I was invisible to my roommate because I was old. When I awoke at nine o'clock, I wanted more, so I forced myself back to sleep. I kept awaking and going back, like Christopher Reeve in *Somewhere in Time*. The third time I woke up, it was 1:11 p.m. That kicked the hell out of me the rest of the day. I couldn't write, so I watched the Jets lose to Miami.

College football was born on the Rutgers campus in 1869. Rutgers football also brought Noah and I closer than I could've ever dreamed, tailgating, talking about everything, cheering, hugging after touchdowns, and being a part of something bigger. I love when Noah said, "Dad, I'm going to take my children to Rutgers games, just like we do."

After Christmas in 2005, Noah and I flew to Phoenix for the Insight Bowl, Rutgers versus Arizona State. The stadium was filled with energy and an effusive sense of belonging and pride. Two days after, Noah and I went to Sedona. Climbing near the Airport Road summit, he took a picture of me, barefoot (absorbing the energy through my soles), hands folded, pondering the gift of parenthood. That picture was destined for the back cover of *Casablanca Water*. When we turned on the car to go back to Phoenix, at that exact second, the clock read 4:44 p.m.

After our trip, the year 2006 blurred by. Selling eyeglasses was like sitting on a freshly painted white picket fence—no matter how I positioned my job, company, manager, or family, it hurt, leaving indentations on my pink gluteus skin. I hated everything about selling. Marjorie was still amazingly supportive, even when I slipped out fleeting traces of my insensitive prickishness. At least Noah was safely ensconced in college.

My novel was moving along. I loved Saturday mornings, just after sunrise, when my mind raced with plot ideas and fantasy appearances on late-night television, where I'd finally be able to whip out my fuck-you list. It was fun jockeying positions, seeing who had moved into first and second place. Inside my constitution was the notion of a perfect world, where people really cared about each other—especially people of all shades—the planet, and a secure tomorrow. Maybe that's why I'm frequented by a special spirit.

Whenever the Vietnam War was in a movie, the news, a documentary, or a veteran obituary, I thought about how I'd evaded it. Would I have been a better man if I'd served my country? I knew I'd done a smart thing, but moments of guilt still festered within me. Marjorie reassured me that I'm alive with no debilitating PTSD. I just don't know what's right or how to feel.

One night while surfing the internet, I strangely arrived at Shakespeare, whom I detested, because I had no clue what the hell he meant. I'd found *Henry V's* act 4, scene 3. It was about a band of brothers, camaraderie, fighting, and sharing. I'd been a loner for so long. I'd let good friends disappear from my life, like my Toledo roommate Tank, whom I'd never called after my marriage to Valerie. I had a wasteland of lost friends. Sometimes I'd say, "They have phones too." But maybe it was also my place to initiate. I'd almost wasted my life by not knowing my place in it.

Here's what I found in *Henry V*, which rested my Vietnam guilty soul:

Go by, from this day to the end of time, without our being remembered: we few, we happy few, we band of brothers—for whoever sheds his blood with me today shall be my brother. However, humble his birth, this day shall grant him nobility. And men back in English now safe in their beds will curse themselves for not having been here, and think less of their own manhood when they listen to the stories of those who fought with us here on St. Crispin's Day.

I did curse myself for not being there with them in Vietnam. I watched the Ken Burns documentary *The Vietnam War* for a third time—thirty hours of binge-viewing to understand where I was in my mind. It's all right, I know now. I did the right thing.

THE APPRENTICE

In early March, I heard *The Apprentice* was having a special casting call at Rutgers. The previous winner had been a graduate there. Something told me to apply. I downloaded the application, which required an essay. One in particular tickled me: "What is your most impressive business work or academic achievement?"

In the real world, I'd never impressed anyone. When I considered my greatest achievement, Noah came to mind. A few weeks back, he'd called me with an invite to his frat house to come hang out with the guys. So I did. We played beer pong, spurring memories from my

Toledo frat. Bright light bulb: Noah was comfortable enough with me to introduce me to his frat brothers.

I didn't write about business or academics for the essay, but about the tremendous responsibility of raising a child. Teach your child well and prioritize life—that was my essay. I'm sure no one at the TV show got me. I auditioned with 124 other people. Then I learned the losing teams had to sleep in a tent in Los Angeles. I don't do tents. I soured on the gig.

RUTGERS FOOTBALL 2006

In October 2006, Rutgers football was undefeated. It's a good feeling to realize your team has gained national recognition. On Thursday, November 9, Rutgers was playing Louisville, the also undefeated number-three team. A week before, I'd received a strange medal in the mail from St. Anthony of Padua. I didn't know who St. Anthony was or why I, a Jewish guy, was on their mailing list. But I couldn't throw the medal away. Something intrigued me about it. I wrote a check to Saint Anthony's Order, scribbling in the check register so that Marjorie wouldn't question me about it—I had no answers myself. Little did I know, spirit was about to raise the stakes.

Winning and losing meant too much to me. In all my years with Marjorie and her unwavering support, she never understood the role winning and losing played in my world. Losing was banging the drum slowly. Back at Weequahic High, losing in football meant accepting my place of destiny. Some people always win and some always lose. My long-evolved motto: "I just want to be fourth." Could winning at football be a sign from above?

Right before Noah and I left for the game, something took me back to my office for Saint Anthony's medal, which I'd wrapped in a handkerchief. I slipped it into my pocket, along with a red rock from a Sedona vortex. Spiritual ammunition. Why Saint Anthony?

The Empire State Building was lit up in red for Rutgers. The stadium was filled with electric energy, deafening sound, and so much red. Noah and I (and most of New Jersey) knew it was a basic improbability for Rutgers to win.

At halftime, Rutgers was losing 25–14. Throughout the first half, I'd squeeze the medal, but acknowledged there are more important things in life than winning. Eventually, Rutgers caught up, now 25–22. A dream was so close. The big screen flashed the game's attendance, the largest crowd ever to see a Rutgers football game. When I saw that number, I immediately assured Noah of our victory.

"Why, Dad?"

"The attendance," I said. Brightly posted on the big screen, defying numerical odds, was: 44,111. I squeezed St. Anthony until Rutgers won. Spirit is a precious, simple gift.

The numbers 444, 111, and their permutations are all over my life. It's the energy force to stop what I'm doing and take notice. No matter what, how, and why, those numbers are around: on the side of a truck; a license plate; the readout on my exercise bike; the time remaining in a basketball game, 1:11; my car's odometer, 11,111 miles; waking up randomly at 4:44 a.m.; the $4.44 price on a supermarket tuna salad container; the blood pressure machine quickly stopping at 111; the latitude where I was born, 040N44; the winter temperature, 11.1 degrees; 1,111 views on a YouTube show.

The frequency of these appearances increases with awareness. I had a profound need to know who, why, and what it was all about. So, I started talking to this spirit when I was alone in the house or car, starting by simply expressing my gratitude for changing my life and my passionate curiosity. "Hi, spirit," I'd say. "How will I ever know who you are? How can I discover you? One small favor: please never materialize. I couldn't handle a basic apparition. I'm cool leaving things as they are. Keep raising my awareness of your presence. I love anticipating you, knowing you're around."

Once, while driving on Route 18, I had an idea. "Spirit, suddenly I see a truck with a phone number 444-4444 or similar. The name on the truck could be Leon's Furniture. I'll know you are Leon, and figure out why you're with me."

This was a borderline infantile approach, and one-sided conversation. A view of a very complex dilemma. A spirit needed identity. I was convinced I was gifted with a spirit. But who, and why?

Chapter 28

A MARBLE ROLLS UP A HILL

The big O. On March 10, 2008, I finished my novel. It was indeed orgasmic, like nothing I've felt before, lasting all day, not minutes. For the first time, I'd finished something to be proud of. Universal spirituality held my intestines together through dreams of inevitability—now that the writing was done, I needed to find a publisher.

I spent the next month refining and editing my manuscript (Marjorie also helped with grammar), and searching for a means to publish it, except I didn't know what the fuck I was doing. For the past few months, I taught myself about agents, query letters, and publishers. Forget the accounts I'd sold eyeglasses to for decades. In this world, no one knew about me. I was a hangnail on the fickle finger of fate.

Sending query letters was an exercise in self-loathing. I emailed hundreds of letters. After each, I tweaked my philosophy from meek to bold and a bit absurd, then back to meek. Philosophically, I knew

I wasn't Steven King and no agent in any ivory tower would let down their Rapunzel hair or throw me a sliver of a compliment or shred of hope. The fucking power they wield. I once emailed my book pitch to an agent at 2:44 p.m., and three minutes later, at 2:47, their rejection arrived: "This subject matter is not for us. Good luck." I wanted to respond, "Go fuck yourself," but determination and revenge spilled over. Someday, if only I could deliver a massive fuck you. I knew it was not personal, strictly business. Michael Corleone was always around to rectify reality.

A few hours later, the rejection pain had abetted. Marjorie called me down for dinner—one of my favorites, turkey meat loaf. Dinner was sparsely conversational. I preferred reading the *Star-Ledger*. To further down my day was an article about how an array of drugs, including antibiotics, anticonvulsants, mood influencers, and sex hormones, had been found in the drinking water of over forty million Americans. Next, I felt myself up to see if I had breasts engorged from hormones in the water.

The next day, after selling, I had dinner with Maggie, who owned three stores in Northwest Jersey. My friend for over ten years, Maggie was always loyal to me. Her story: a terrible divorce, no kids, and seductive Cheshire smile whenever I was around. My friend Elvin said Maggie used to tell people in the business she'd jump into bed with me without giving it a thought. Dinner with her had been on the planning table for years, like dangling fruit.

Sometimes I don't know what I'm capable of. Sitting across the table from each other, I absorbed Maggie as we clinked our cabernet glasses. She was beautiful, alluring, seductive, and successful. And she was a $15,000 account. For a fleeting moment I thought that if she played me right, perhaps I'd sleep with her, reasoning it might ameliorate my frustrations with the query letter campaign. I'd do her for hours with visions of that San Francisco agent at every thrust.

"Cameron, the wine you keep pouring is wobbling my knees,"

Maggie laughed. "Can I be brutally honest? I suspect you feel vibes at this table."

"I love brutal, especially when it's stirred into honesty," I said. "Go right ahead. I'm a big boy with shoulders."

"That's what this is about. You're big, broad . . . and I wonder if life is proportional." Her speech slurred. I hate playing on an uneven field.

"Heavy stuff. Life is proportional. An interesting concept, and I think you're referencing anatomy," I said, supporting my face with two palms, leaning in close to her.

"You know what I'm thinking? After dinner, coffee at my house. Anatomy. You've fascinated me for years. Is that direct enough?" she said, big smile shining.

"I would almost do this. I'm so ready. I'm needy, confused, and frustrated with the universe. Notwithstanding that, you haunt me. The thing is, if we did, the whole state would know in the morning. Elvin is probably waiting under your bed to take notes and measure mattress movements," I explained. "What I mean is, the only thing I have left in this fucked-up world is my innocence, sense of self, and freedom of conscience. But I'm beyond words right now how much your flattery means to me."

Naturally, she hugged me next. Then she kissed my cheek moistly. "Cameron, remember this: A marble rolls up a hill, pushed by something invisible, defying gravity, logic. You never know in life. You're a special guy. Maybe someday."

"You leave me in an unreal state. I'll be thinking about marbles and hills for a long time. Like what Scarlett said after Rhett Butler left, 'There's always tomorrow.' Or as you just said, maybe someday—I like that ending for you."

My pride swelled in delivering that perfect bullshit. My head needed this ego boost. Always aware of business, preserving the account with her three stores, I headed home down Route 280. Marjorie was sure to ask what we'd talked about.

GETTING PUBLISHED

In all the months I'd been sending manuscript query letters to agents, I'd received not a particulate of positivity in response. One August day, I was listening to "Ode to Joy," trying to elevate myself—if I couldn't get high from "Ode to Joy," then nothing was left. Suddenly, I got an email from an agent. The den TV echoed Michael Phelps swimming into history as the winningest Olympic athlete. The agent was asking to read the first three chapters of *Casablanca Water*. The next day, another agent emailed me, saying they liked my plot and wanted to read a chapter.

A week later, ode to reality. My novel was confronting a changing industry. Best of luck. I'd try self-publishing next. But I'd need an artsy cover, so I called Maggie. She'd mentioned how her friend's husband was a starving artist.

A few nights later, tossing and turning, mind racing, I kicked my legs to a sitting position. The cable box read 4:44 a.m. "Holy shit," I whispered.

I got up to doodle at my desk, bringing along a few salt-free pretzels and seltzer. I put on *Parsley, Sage, Rosemary & Thyme* for auditory ambiance. In my mind, I was on an island in the Caribbean with palm trees, a full moon, smells of sweaty sex and cruciferous plants in the air. Then, from somewhere out there in the vast universe, the design for my book's cover arrived by slipping right through the verticals. The design would be a bottle of Casablanca mineral water. Inside the bottle, the two main characters sit on a train station bench in Maplewood, New Jersey, waiting for a train that may never come. The bottle's image was so strong in my vision—how did it get there? But I did sense the image was somehow deposited in me, because I'd gotten out of bed at the right time.

The artist rendered this image beautifully in brooding brown and gray colors. A lamplight shines on their countenance, while a lonely maple leaf, still green, is on the track bound for New York. Next, I found an old-fashioned book printer in Maryland. In the year I spent editing on the exercise bike, I could've ridden it to Willoughby. My mother never lived to see me publish a novel, but her picture hung near my computer all throughout this process. She never stopped smiling at me.

SOCIAL MEDIA

Noah—my best friend, and a comic book aficionado and gamer who'd gotten me hooked on Mario and King Koopa—advised it was time for me to experiment with Facebook. "Dad, one day you'll be a published author. People need to know you. As you always say, it's a brave new world. It may also be a world without tuna fish," he said, referencing the disappearing Atlantic bluefin tuna.

So, wearing jeans and a red Rutgers sweatshirt, I joined Facebook in October 2008. My mission was obsessive: build a portfolio of friends. Occasionally, I'd friend a celebrity like David (a political consultant). Then the plot gets thicker. From David's list of friends, someone found me and sent me a friend request. Her name was Brenda Wright. Her profile indicated she was a part-time poet in Minnesota.

Brenda was meant to be in my life. We messaged back and forth, and she shared some of her work—it was intense, delightful, visual, and poignant. She told me her original relatives had arrived in America on a slave ship in the 1600s. Today, they have over 400 descendants.

Then, the epiphany light bulb. "Let's graduate to a cell phone. I think we're ready," I messaged her. On the phone, we were comfortable and genuine as if we'd spent years together. Perhaps it's one of my simple gifts to grow a relationship where people feel warmth. We talked semi-seriously about a new addition to my bucket list: to drive out to Chicago and spend a day at the Burr Oak Cemetery, where Emmett Till and his mother, Mamie, are buried. From there, I'd follow the winding roads to Minnesota to meet her in person.

In my search for spirit, I went to Dr. Martin Luther King Jr. for part of my meditation. I'd always regretted that I could've heard him speak six blocks from my house in February 1963. That regret influences my life to this day. Never let life pass you by; learn, push, climb, and do as much as you can to survive, and don't forget to take it all in. Social media would one day bring me close to one of Dr. King's relatives. Full circles can reside in social media. A positive particulate.

Next comes one of the most important elements of my relationship with the tortoise, my existence and destiny, and the cosmos. I'd spent years trying to identify the spirit/angel in my life who'd gotten me out of that Volkswagen that rolled over at high speed. Who'd brought me the numbers 111 and 444. Who'd kept me from overdosing on enough sleeping pills to kill an elephant. Who'd put the Bee Gees song "Lamplight" and the concept for *Casablanca Water* into my head. Who'd whispered, "Trust."

On Wednesday, November 11, 2009, I came home early from the trenches of selling. Around three o'clock, I logged onto Facebook and randomly stumbled onto a notice for a poetry contest. Brenda came into my consciousness. During our last conversation, she'd mentioned a box of her poems, long buried and forgotten in her basement. A light bulb of loyalty—this contest was the perfect opportunity to rekindle her writing. I messaged her the link to the contest information with an encouraging note.

In those early days, when sending links, Facebook sent two security words to verify your humanity, words like *light, car, tree,* and *glove.* My two words were *chair* and *summer.* I clicked send. A few minutes later, something hit me with insecurity. What if I didn't send it? Better do it again.

So, I sent the same note with an addendum, "Just in case you didn't get my message from a few minutes ago, I'm sending this again. Cameron." Two new security words appeared: *door* and *Colman.*

I froze in disbelief. Goose bumps crept up and down my arms. Colman is not a word, but my grandfather—my mother's father, after whom I was named. He'd died suddenly in 1937.

The impact didn't arrive with full force. For a long time I sat there and stared at my mother's picture. The universe had orchestrated the spiritual identification I'd been seeking for years, and it hit me like a slap in the face. Not necessarily mathematically, I computed the odds. There were five hundred million people on Facebook, and hundreds of millions of security word combinations. The odds were one in half a billion, or maybe more.

This was the beginning of a beautiful friendship. "Grandfather," I said out loud to him, "now I know it's been you in my life from the day I was born, watching over me, protecting me, perhaps stepping over the line, breaking a few rules, saving my life. I'm your namesake. And so proud. I love you, Colman Crast. I have a lot to learn and be grateful for."

Then I started to panic. My guardian angel had been revealed, but did I have a picture of him? I remembered my mother mailing me family pictures. Racing at a warp speed, I tried to remember where I'd put them. My office had accumulated twenty years' worth of boxes, piles of papers, and magazines. Something steered me toward my metal file cabinet. In the bottom drawer, buried under old newspapers, one from the *St. Louis Post-Dispatch* with the headline "D-Day Invasion," was the box of pictures. Amelia had categorized them meticulously. I rifled through them, my cardiac chamber pounding away. Then, an aura of discovery. Picture in hand: three men posing, two sitting at a table, Colman on the right. I knew it was him. He was handsome, mustached, serious, with not even a faint smile.

Then my eyes caught something I couldn't immediately process. In the middle of the small wooden table was an empty bottle of water in a familiar shape. The best "holy shit" moment of my life—it was the bottle from *Casablanca Water's* cover. The picture had been taken in 1902 in Newark. Who poses for a picture with an empty bottle of water? That image was obviously implanted in my mind a long time ago. Months ago, I'd thought the cover design had just come into my consciousness. But now I understood everything had been planted into my subconscious by grandfather Colman and he'd also orchestrated my novel, the vehicle of life's change.

I told Marjorie everything, but she wasn't really sure what had gone down. "Cameron, I just got goose bumps," she said. "Your life has been strange this last year, I grant you that. Your preoccupation with 111 and 444 and how they appear all over your life. Sometimes I want to say to just keep this between us. People might think—"

"No, this needs to be shared," I said. "I need to open up. Maybe I can help people. Maybe the more you open, the more you receive from up there."

A new chapter of my life was literally built around this picture of Colman, like a performance stage. Now, every day, I talk to Colman, thanking him for his loyalty, promising to make him proud of what I'll become.

Soon, I'd also be thanking Saint Anthony, the patron saint of lost things, for being in my life too. Time would clarify why and how.

Chapter 29

PUBLISHED

On a cold day two weeks into 2010, the front doorbell rang. "Where do you want the thirty-five cases?" asked a delivery man. His eighteen-wheeler was parked at the curb behind him—perhaps the first trailer to visit my cul-de-sac. I wonder what the neighbors thought; the verticals across the street seemed to move.

"How about the garage?" I said.

Pallets to stack a thousand copies of *Casablanca Water* were a gift from my printer and publisher in Baltimore. They housed a mountain of boxes, almost hermetically sealed.

When Noah got home from his job at a New York comic book company, I gathered him and Marjorie to help me open the first box. "I'm sharing this journey of a lifetime, a feat beyond my imagination, only achievable with the love and support of the only two people in my life. Marjorie and Noah, this is for you," I said in a shaky voice, "with love."

The box cutter slid with precision down the middle vein, and then I was holding two books in my hands. Marjorie and Noah each got a signed copy by America's newest unknown author. Signing my novel was strange—I was a million miles away from counting pills.

"I finally did it," I said, sounding like Charlton Heston as George Taylor in *Planet of the Apes* when he realizes mankind finally blew themselves up. The road ahead would be daunting and debt-ridden, between Noah's college tuition and my books destined to hang around. My Uncle James had left me some money when he died. Of his six nieces and nephews, I got the least, despite being his caretaker for everything. Maybe he was under the illusion that we didn't need money. What a great fucking illusionist I was. Lah-di-dah.

I wished the Ghost of Christmas Yet to Come would visit in a dream and tell me things would be fine. One day after the box opening, while I was on the exercise bike, reading Phillip Roth's *Goodbye Columbus*, something made me stop. The monitor read 44:44 elapsed time, and I knew Colman was with me, signaling everything will be fine. Still new to this intervention, I'd have to trust his spirit.

Perhaps the pedaling, the 444, and the solitude make me so thoughtful when I produce endorphins on the bike. This was my latest big thought: Maybe it was finally time to leave Incanto and Vero after twenty-five years. Something inside me was so strong. Where would I go? More importantly, how would Marjorie react? I knew I had to sell Marjorie. And I'm a great salesman.

THE END

When I deposited the notion on Marjorie, she rifled through a dozen emotions. "You can't just plunge into being an author," she said. "It's a pipe dream. It can't buy white bread and chunky peanut butter at Shop Rite."

"On the other hand, I'm knocking on social security's door," I reasoned. "As you've said, things always work out. I'll look for part-time selling and capitalize on my reputation."

She seemed relieved, but when we hugged, it felt strange, half-assed. It was missing something, as if she was unsure, not of love or caring, but of our familial stability as we headed into murky, unchartered waters. Later, as I was shaving in front of the mirror and dabbing hyaluronic acid on my neck, which was beginning to wrinkle with age, I whispered, "Do you really know what the fuck you're doing? Do you really believe in Grandfather Colman?" I was so unsure.

Two weeks later, at a diner on Route 22 in Bridgewater, I met with Bob Post, the East Coast manager at Incanto and Vero. "This is painful for me," I began. "Just yesterday, I was all right, but then I got stuck at an excessively long red light. I just can't do selling and driving anymore. I'm spent. I love the company. Love you. It's just my time."

He stared blankly at me in disbelief. "Are you sure about this? You're a legend in this company. We're growing. More designer lines to sell, more money. I know things have been hard the last few years."

You motherfucker, I thought. *It was you who chopped my territory after I resigned being a manager.* "No, my time is done," I said. "It's as big a shock to me as you. I'll miss you and the company."

Such pure bullshit, but Dale Carnegie was entrenched in my head. I was going out as a gentleman. A symphony of tinnitus rang in my ears as I recalled Dr. King's speech: "Free at last. Free at last. Thank God Almighty, I'm free at last."

News of my shocking departure spread. Within a week, I was selling multiple lines for different eyewear companies. Marjorie was relieved how fast it evolved, and we both were reassured by how well I was liked and respected.

A few months later, an optical acquaintance called. Larry French (I used to call him "the kiss" behind his back) thought we should partner and develop a product line, importing eyewear from China. At our new Pass Go Eyewear, I was the dedicated sales rep and the recruiter for our new salesforce. Shortly into the gig, I pulled out all the stops because deep in my soul I knew this probably would never work, but still contacted people I knew I could count on for orders. I called up Maggie, who'd wanted to sleep with me in the worst way. Over another dinner, she gave me a $10,000 order.

"Maggie, you really are special. A bright light bulb just went off. Pastel pink light. I'm kind of fucked up now," I said, my head spinning from the wine. "One day I'll call you, if you'll have me. Am I making sense?"

She leaned across the table, pushed the small candle between us to the side, grabbed my right hand, and squeezed it tight. "I am crazy about you. Something real, warm, caring, and so fucking sexy. Good, you're hopefully telling me one day."

"I think I am."

Afterward, at the car, we shared a great kiss. She shoved her tongue into my mouth and swished it around. "I love you, Cameron, as a good friend. And ship those orders right away."

When I got home, Marjorie asked whether I'd gotten a worthwhile order from the lady with three stores. I shook my head, disappeared into my office, and tried to picture Maggie nude. I let out a sigh of relief at my innocence and purity. I felt like Jimmy Carter, because I'd only lusted in my heart; I didn't actually pull down my pants.

In the end, Pass Go Eyewear was another pipe dream, but we almost made it. At the end of the first year, I took the few hundred extra eyeglass frames they'd given me, shook hands with Larry, and never saw or talked to him again.

GROUP HELP

Sales of *Casablanca Water* were nonexistent. I gently played relatives, friends, my best accounts. A particular family member ordered two books. "I won't read it," sister Carol said, fearing it would stir up unpleasant memories of poverty growing up in Newark. "I don't need that in my life. I try to bury those memories."

The notion of what I'd accomplished—writing a novel, when so few people do—didn't hit me over the head right away. It was a slow realization. Prestige-wise, I was a notch below a doctor. One day on the jetty in Belmar, it hit me. Never once had my father expressed being proud of me. That notion sat inside me, growing and poisoning until an eventual reckoning.

I heard about a writing group of small-time authors, dreamers, and wordsmiths who met once a month at the library in Manalapan. At the first meeting I went to, there were perhaps a dozen pretenders there (I labeled them—and myself—that). Introspectively, I was looking for a community of other writers, in a similar rowboat, who'd appreciate my journey.

Next to me sat Dolores Ryan, an effervescent woman. She artfully told me her life story in two sentences: Growing up Black in the South was hard, so Dolores's family moved to Jersey, where she'd gotten a master's degree in nursing. Writing was her hobby.

"College is better here in Jersey to get an advanced degree," she explained. Then she noticed my Rutgers sweatshirt and hat. "Do you like college football, Cameron?"

We clicked instantly, building a bond of friendship tinged with a quirky awareness of social absurdity and life on Earth. Little did I know she would go on to dramatically, irrevocably change my life.

A CHANGE IN MY HEART

One Sunday morning in April of 2010, something happened at doubles tennis. While running down a passing shot, I made a jerky move, twisted, and felt my heart pounding. There was always a dentist around the tennis court, so I called someone over to superficially check on me. My heart rate was approaching 150—fast and too hard to process. I continued playing, but I was scared straight.

A few years back, I'd seen a cardiologist because of mitral valve prolapse (a congenital heart murmur—which couldn't keep me out of Vietnam). A joke of a physician attended to me. Over two years, he never ran a stress test or took bloodwork to check my cholesterol levels.

I had a medical epiphany about how inept he was, so I was off to find a new wizard cardiologist.

Dr. Greg Nardone came into my life. He was meticulous, caring, thorough, and a fellow Rutgers graduate. I never told him about the episode on the tennis court, figuring it was an aberration. But a few months later, I had another episode—my heart pounded and raced for two days. Another few months, same thing. Finally, I Googled my symptoms. After Greg hooked me to a heart monitor, he diagnosed me with atrial fibrillation. Atrial fibrillation can kill you fast. The heart suddenly races, and when you go back into normal rhythm, blood hanging around heart valves could form a clot and mosey up to your brain—and you're done. Motherfucking scary. For a first time, mortality beat the hell out of me. My neck hairs stood erect; I wondered who'd be at my funeral. Does the afterlife allow you to go to your own funeral to see how many cars are in the procession?

I wasn't at a high risk for a stroke or death, but Greg directed me to take a baby aspirin and heart rhythm medication. And so I began a new way of life with an end perhaps lurking around any corner.

A few months after, Jack Thomasek, a Weequahic friend and historian of old Newark in the 1950s and '60s, called me. We'd never said a word to each other back in school, but became friends at our thirty-fifth reunion. Jack told me our classmate Steven Sunder had died suddenly on vacation. It had taken a week to return his body to New Jersey.

There are deaths, but this was the first classmate I'd been close to, so it beat me up. If only I could go back through a rabbit hole to cherish growing up, hold my memories tight, and tell people I loved how much I needed them. If there was a safe way back—a heaven in my own mind, a sure thing, a guarantee I could get there—I'd be gone. I wanted out.

Chapter 30

A SPIRIT GANG

What inspired this chapter title? For several days, I stared at a blank page, lost for words, worried this condition could linger. I'd been chugging along like a locomotive in Montana without a roadblock. After spending a few hours roaming on the internet, watching a World War II concentration camp documentary, suddenly I knew to stop putzing around. In my life, I'd assembled a group of spirits I could relate to and rely on.

Something in my persona lent itself to being a frequent recipient of religious artifacts. My neighbor Milad, a Coptic Christian, somehow picked up on that. We often sat on his porch, talking about the old and new country, as well as spiritual aspects of our lives. One day, Milad knocked on my door and gifted me a replica of Michelangelo's Pietà, the famous statue depicting Jesus wrapped in his mother's embrace after his crucifixion. The Pietà brought an awareness of Jesus I'd never had because I was Jewish. As I've come to learn, things that mattered to Jesus mattered to me too, like homelessness, hunger, and poverty.

There are energies in the universe we don't understand. The following year, just before Christmas, we were slammed with a blizzard. I opened the garage to reveal a foot of snow and a bleak, inhospitable landscape. With a shovel, I tested my body and mind and pushed a snow drift away. My chest hurt, a classic heart attack scenario. It was hard to grasp the reality that I was now decades past shoveling capability.

I felt sorry for my helpless self. I couldn't do it, and no one was around to help shovel or plow—so I prepared for a long winter night's sleep, thinking we could be snowbound for days. I thought I heard something echoing outside as I pulled the covers under my chin and drifted off to sleep.

The next morning soon became afternoon. Marjorie informed me she'd shovel the front steps. "Do you think that's smart?" I asked. I was feeling inadequate, and I was never in the mood to lose her.

"I'm a woman. We've got some built-in heart attack protection via hormonal advantages. I'll be fine," she said as she walked out the door. But a moment later she came back. "Cam, you better see this."

Our entire property, sidewalk, and driveway was plowed.

"Who did this?" she asked.

I had an idea. I went over to Milad's house and rang his bell.

"How strange," he explained, "I felt you last night. You needed help and watching over. Perhaps the Pietà brought us closer."

I smiled and hugged him. "Perhaps."

PERSONALITIES

One windy morning, tree branches scratching the bedroom window in a scene out of *Poltergeist*, I propped myself up in bed and threw my hands behind my head. Something was there. I felt the need to ponder my life with meditation. Saint Michael the Archangel was on my mind. I knew nothing about him—was he partly responsible for my spirituality?

I liked being retired—getting up whenever, watching morning TV news. A retired regime is hard to process. No longer did I have to drive the state, endure nasty traffic, circle the block twelve times for parking, and cower for orders. Could I get used to the fact that this stuff was not in my life anymore? Now I was mostly concerned with getting people to buy my book and solemnly riding the exercise bike.

Shortly after Archangel Michael arrived, so did Albert Einstein. I had a strange supplication with Einstein—for years, I'd had a picture of him hanging on my wall, his eyes haunting and piercing. Every few years, the picture disappeared, then resurfaced. Lately I had it taped behind my computer. Walter Isaacson's biography, *Einstein*, suggested he was an all-around guy. I needed to tell Einstein how much of a hero he was to me, how his mind grasped so much of the universe without Google or the internet. I didn't know what I was doing, but it felt right. Afterward, I swear my writing improved, like Albert had turned on a switch inside me. Now he's part of my spirit gang.

Next, I needed to reach out to Dr. King. Then, of course, came my mother. I thanked her for her nurturing, loving, and instilling life lessons into me.

I never talked to either of my grandmothers about what they endured in Russia and Poland, seeing the Statue of Liberty for the first time, how they liked America, and how they met my grandfathers. My father-in-law was also part of this group—in life, I'd never engaged him either. He'd immigrated to America, escaped Nazis, joined the US Army, fought in North Africa and Italy, and lost most of his family in concentration camps. Everyone loved and respected his humanity, warmth, caring, and intelligence. I have all their pictures hanging on the wall facing me while I hit the keyboard. Part of my spiritual assemblage. An alpha wave of reaching out to them. They're around—my senses tell me.

When my father, Jack, died, I was called to fill out his death certificate. At ninety-three, he hadn't died of anything related to old age—diabetes, cancer, heart disease, dementia, hypertension. He'd donated half of my genetic composition, which was mostly healthy, despite a few fucked-up genes like vertigo, spinal stenosis, and flat feet. No, the reason for his death was debility. With my mom gone, he'd gotten tired of living. Time had gently aged my thinking that it was my responsibility to have engaged my father, draw him out and understand where he came from: six brothers growing up with parents who slept in separate bedrooms; there was no love anywhere. So, Jack was now part of my spiritual gang too. I do love him and will always be grateful for his sperm's genetics.

The everyday gang: Grandfather Colman, Dr. King, Albert Einstein, the universe, Mother, Father, father-in-law, Archangel Michael, Saint Anthony, Jesus. They are there with me when I'm riding the exercise bike, driving, sitting at the edge of the bed, and walking outside after midnight. Gratitude, human species, peace, climate, healing. Hard to verbalize the comfort of reaching out to them with their infinite knowledge and compassion. They make me feel that I'm not alone in a very hostile world. I'm digging deep to express their place in my life. A daily working responsive bread.

Never did I ask them to help me win the lottery, because that's not a real world. It's not my earthly place to possess money. If I did, I'd be hanging upside down from a banyan tree on a remote Pacific Island, harboring sexually transmitted diseases. Lah-di-dah.

Chapter 31

EVOLUTION REVOLUTION RESOLUTION

Ushering in 2011, we spent New Year's Eve with our friends Meryl and Keith, sharing takeout Chinese and sweet Moscato wine. Marjorie was pissed we didn't go out, so I set the table with red plastic plates and utensils. Before the ball drop, I suggested watching *Sideways*, because the main character was sort of like me. Miles Raymond (Paul Giamatti) submitted his novel to an agent and waited, hoped, and dreamed of being published. His pain and anger were mine too.

When the ball came down, it opened an influential year in my life. I whispered to Marjorie, "I love you and I'll never be able to adequately thank you for constantly supporting me in my endless changes of life."

She said, "I know."

That February, five weeks into the new year, it snowed deeply. When the world is white, no cars or people outside, just a few birds sitting on the power lines, I love going for a walk and contemplating who I am and what I could be when I grow up. I watched a deer run into a vacant lot. *How do animals endure cold?* I wondered. *What if, instead of going to hell, bad souls were reincarnated into animals who roam harsh winters?* I imagined lost souls lying in a grave, feeling cold, nowhere to go. Awareness of death, spirit, goodness, and evil was with me these days.

Later that month, I went to a lunchtime meetup writer's group at the Algonquin Hotel. It was the same spot where the Algonquin Round Table, a group of New York City writers, critics, actors, and smart people—like Dorothy Parker, George S. Kaufman, and Tallulah Bankhead—met from 1919 to 1929. Some of the people with me thought we could absorb the vapors and particulates of those who'd been here a long time ago. For me, just breathing intellectual air where those brilliant minds had once presided felt like magic. But the best I could do was a two-time experience with this group—there were just too many narcissistic assholes sitting around the lunch table, pretending relevance, interfering with my mindful absorption.

One night, Noah came home to do laundry and restock his supply of Cinnamon Toast Crunch, gummy bears, and bottled water. It was a surprise visit; the house alarm tripped and I knew we had a visitor from Rider University. We opened a cheap bottle of cabernet and chatted about college basketball.

"Dad, I know you don't drink fucking merlot," Noah said, referencing *Sideways*.

"Smart guy. Part of the reason I love you, Son."

"'Son'—that's a good segue to ask something I've been thinking about. Are you down?"

"I'm down and ready," I said. I put my arm behind his neck and led him into the den, where we sank into the worn sofa. I slid close enough to feel his breath. Proximity felt necessary; his look was serious and needy. I couldn't imagine he was having girl trouble.

"This is hard, Dad. Maybe the hardest thing I've ever asked, but I often wonder . . . I need to know how you feel. Yet it's not important. Am I making sense?"

"No sense at all," I said, "but you're a good boy, a sensitive boy. You are me in so many ways."

"That's just it, Dad. I'm not you in the genetic department."

"But you are me and mom in so many ways. Love environment. Fuck heredity."

He chuckled, flashing a small, bright smile. "My life has been perfect, magical, filled with so much love and caring. You and mom are the best. I'm a lucky guy."

The air was heavy. I'm adept at interjecting humor to lighten the mood. "Yes, a lucky guy. We rescued you. At this exact moment, you could've been barefoot with a long blade of grass hanging out of your mouth and suspenders holding up ripped, tattered jeans in a foreign backyard, maybe the Great Smoky Mountains, dancing to 'Dueling Banjos.'"

"You talk like a writer," Noah laughed.

"I think I'm ready to be called a writer."

Now Noah was ready to be serious. After a deep, dramatic breath, he began, "Do you ever wonder about creating your own biological child to carry your genes and name? Do you feel like you're missing a part of life? Are there any regrets or longings in your life?"

"Kick off your shoes. It's going to be a long night." Now it was my turn for a deep breath signaling no more funnies. "Noah, you're a special gift. A sweet, loving, sensitive, caring son. I've never had one day of regret. You're a perfect son in every way. Well, except that one day when you punched a hole in the cellar door during a temper tantrum and ran out of the house," We laughed. "Makes no difference, blood or water—you've fulfilled our dreams and completed our lives. You are me. There is no other collection of genes or chromosomes that could ever come close to you. Spiritually, and you know how spiritual I am, I was given this awesome gift and responsibility to be your father. I wear that badge of honor with so much pride. Therefore, you have obviated any malingering thoughts of biology and procreation. Anyway, we're all related here on Earth. We don't know any better. I'll say it again, Noah: You are me."

"Obviated?" he asked.

"Made unnecessary. You were completely meant to be. This is our road together. I love you, Son."

His eyes teary with emotions, Noah jumped up to hug me, and he knew to reach down to help me up. "This fucking sofa ages people twenty years," I grumbled.

As we embraced, Marjorie came home from shopping and walked into the den. "What did I miss?" she asked.

"Nothing but Rutgers and Rider basketball comparative analysis," I told her. Noah and I looked at each other and shared one of the best smiles of our lives.

ANOTHER TRIP TO PRECIPICE

Going to the precipice means playing brinkmanship with your-self. Holding a Bible in one hand, wearing a blindfold, and walking to the edge of a cliff above craggy boulders battered by ocean waves. Do you keep walking, then tumble to infinity, smelling salt air on the way down? Precipice is irrational, self-loathing behavior that could irrevo-cably get you into trouble. You can't fix it—even if you pass precipice and advance to GO, you collect nothing.

Part of my life has been precipice in spite of times of clarity and a closeness to the universe and spirit. I should've died a few times—the Volkswagen car accident, a few overdoses, and a precipice suicide—but I'm human, so I self-doubt at times, wondering if I was saved by spirit or something else. Maybe precipice is a possession, a cocktail of circumstances conspiring to lead me to the cliff. I am a fragile soul.

One day, I stumbled into an online chat room. I called myself Alan Magnon, a play on the caveman species Cro-Magnon, which I'd always resented for creating the framework for modern misogyny. After a few weeks, I started bonding with the regulars, making my own assumptions of their gender and honesty. Then one user named Margaret pulled me into a private chat. As we chatted about the Tōhoku tsunami wreaking havoc on Japan, I had a strange feeling of being imaginatively seduced.

"It's kind of special we both share the same empathy for the people killed and injured by the tsunami," I typed to Margaret. "It says something about you and me. I'm glad I met you."

"Alan, there is a bonding with us. We've been chatting here for a few weeks. We know glittering generalities about each other. Maybe now is a good time?"

"Good time for what?" I asked.

"You're a guy, I assume, and I'm a gal. I'm married but brutally unhappily," she wrote. "He's a drunk."

She told me about her daughter, who was married and lived in Alabama. I told her about my writing, my son, and my un-brutal marriage to my supportive wife.

"You're a real writer? I've never met one. I like heady, smart-thinking people," she wrote. "Do you ever think about the adventure of meeting someone from a chat room live? "

"No, but you're the first one." I was aroused. Something was happening. I felt like I was in my early thirties, which was probably bullshit. I had too much time on my hands.

I told her where I lived—but I specified South Jersey, just in case I had to escape. She was from Woodbridge in Central Jersey.

"Near the Raritan River and Rutgers alma mater?" I asked.

"Rutgers alma mater?"

"Not important. I'm tall. Long hair. And a nice guy."

"I haven't been with a man with any kind of hair in a long time. I love tall men. A fantasy."

I suggested we get together for coffee. "I'd come to Woodbridge," I wrote. "I think this is so cool. Two strangers in the night."

"'Strangers in the Night,' a Sinatra song."

I smiled. "Now I know I like you."

"Really like?"

"As best as I can staring into a screen," I wrote. "We're just friends exploring the world. Keeping secrets between us and trusting each other. I know it's only coffee. I'm meeting you for research purposes. Someday I'll write about this. But I can't unless I lived it first."

"I'm liking you more and more. Keep typing away."

One morning three weeks later, I drove to the Wonderland Diner in Woodbridge. I wore sunglasses, a hat depicting an Alaskan Kodiak bear, a scarf, a black sweater, and a black leather coat in an attempt to blend in with the diner's demographics. I even hunched over to lose a few inches. I felt hugely guilty. What if someone recognizes me? But I also really believed this was research for my next novel.

Margaret had described herself as tall and full-bodied with blondish hair and glasses. When I'd jokingly asked if any teeth were missing, she'd typed LOL. When I saw her drive up in a black Buick Regal, I had a ridiculous thought of taking her to a motel.

"I knew it was you," I said when she found me waiting inside the vestibule, with cracked tile flooring.

"Do you like what you see?" she asked.

"I do. And you?"

"You're tall and handsome," she marveled. "I love your hair sticking out. I can't believe this is happening."

We sat in the most remote table in the back. Two hours. Three cups of coffee. Two English muffins with different toppings. Our conversation tiptoed carefully around sexual innuendos. Her intelligence, without a college education, caught me off guard. She was worldly, sad, abused, and sexy. She touched my arm and I reciprocated—a bridge over troubled water.

"Would you like the next round in a motel, if I'm reading things right," she suddenly blurted out, "or maybe we could just sit together in a car somewhere?"

Her remarks clobbered me. "A car somewhere is perfect. Quiet time away from clattering plates, smell of overdone home fries, and an obnoxious waitress."

"You talk like a writer," she laughed. "Follow me, Alan."

That world was rather close with fields of dreams and wild weeds. I followed her car to a nearby dead-end street with no civilization in sight. Margaret pulled over, jumped into my car, and threw her arms around me for a kiss. My mouth tried to stop her exploratory tongue. She tasted like muffins, home fries, and a distant cigarette, which was a prodigious turnoff. Swirling inside me were sexual situations, suppositions, and sadness. I could have a fantasy and disappear into the sunset.

She leaned in close, resting a hand near my ear, then caressed my earlobe. "Alan, you held the door open for me. One look and I wanted you. I just knew."

"Slow down, Margaret. You don't know me. We need time."

"I do know things. I've been around. I don't know how to say this. It'll come out wrong. I know you are way out of my league." Tears were welling in her eyes. "Here's my thinking. Being with you in any way would be such a breath of fresh air. An escape from a brutal man. Rescue me, Alan."

"Rescue you?"

"Yes. Just be with me when you can. Talk to me in our chat room. Anything for me to escape. I know you've got instincts. You can have me any way you want. You can do whatever you want to me. Fulfill any fantasy you've ever had. I am all yours."

I didn't know what to say, and I always know what to say. I thought of things happening suddenly in the car. How much time would it take for a cop to get there from the top of the hill? Would I allow my innocence to be lost? I realized it was enough of this precipice self-destructive shit. She unzipped me and started to lower her head. I couldn't allow that.

"Don't worry," she said, "my husband is a cop in town."

That was it. I knew this whole Margaret thing was fucked up.

"Let's do this right next time. Not in a vacant lot. I'll talk to you later in the chat room."

She closed the door, blew me a kiss, and was gone forever. I'd never see or contact her again. I had so much self-loathing for playing these chicken games with life. I didn't know who I was, but I was still searching for something. I never went into a chat room again.

ME AND MY BOY

I was situationally depressed. Noah was moving out, spreading his wings, leaving the nest, kicking his aging parents into the next part of life. I hated aging, mortality, arthritis, reading obituaries, and waiting for my prostate to enlarge so I couldn't piss like I did in college. Noah and two friends were sharing an apartment in Williamsburg, Brooklyn, a trendy, under-forty place to live.

We helped pack Noah's comics, pots and pans, video games, Monopoly board, vinyl '60s albums, Cinnamon Toast Crunch, bottled water, virginal guitar, and a dozen boxes of macaroni and cheese, then drove them to his new third-floor apartment in a remodeled factory building. My stomach hurt with a strange opiate-like pain—seductive, unpleasant, scary—because I was missing him already. But as his father, I was so happy for him.

In the lobby were vestiges of the building's former factory history, including several old wooden support pillars. As I rubbed my hand over the wood, which had worn smooth with time, my eyes caught some graffiti, hand-carved and overwritten with black ink: *Noah and Cam.* I asked Noah why he'd done that. He was clueless. Upon closer examination, those names had been there a long time. I felt better knowing something was watching my son.

Every day we talked. His voice seemed older, wiser, more capable and less in need of me. I started getting the feeling that I'd need to come up with another purpose, something else to occupy soul and mind.

But in mid-June, Noah called me, distressed. Clarence Clemons, the sax player from Bruce Springsteen's E-Street Band, had died. Noah made me promise we'd finally go to a concert in Asbury Park, where Springsteen and Clemons had begun their journey. "No excuses. This is a must for us," he said.

I explained I'd never been to a rock concert. Growing up in the sixties for me was folk music—words of civil rights, environment, peace, love, and a dragon smoking pot.

But I'd have to go. On July 3, rock legend Southside Johnny performed at the Stone Pony outdoor stage in Asbury Park. Five thousand people were there, standing up. Noah put his arm around me. We had good ambiance for my first time at a rock show: setting sun, pastel pink clouds, salt air, and Jersey folk in beach attire. I didn't want to disappoint Noah, but I couldn't do this again. I needed the sounds of silence for my restless soul. I needed Benjamin and Elaine on a bus bound to Santa Barbara. But yet to be seen, something terrifically special would come from this night.

A HARBINGER OF CHANGE

July brought intermittent thunderstorms, native deer foraging outside my kitchen window, and mental images of Scarborough Fair, where I'd like to go one day. Having run out of friends and family to buy my book, I turned my promotional efforts to the Rutgers alumni office, because the university backdropped several scenes in *Casablanca Water*. Two alumni people listened, but I sensed they didn't really care because I was a nothing. Walking down three flights of wooden stairs on my way out, "Remember the Alamo" came to mind. Next time, they'd know me.

I was still going to my writer's group meetings because Dolores Ryan was swimming right there with me in a round pool of accomplished nothingness. She knew about my yearnings, no earnings, dreams, and abundance of spare time. We liked each other in the midst of the group's bullshit and other authors' unrealized dreams. But I was a dreamer too. Who the fuck was I to put them down?

Then, a week after the Southside Johnny show, Dolores emailed about an opportunity that might be "right up my unfulfilled alley." A local magazine, *Monmouth, Our County*, needed a journalist. Whenever journalism as a profession rang, there was Woodward, Bernstein, and Ben Bradlee. I knew nothing about journalism except who, what, where, when, and why. But I was a Rutgers pharmacy graduate, therefore I thought, could do anything.

I pondered the opportunity while "Kathy's Song" and "Scarborough Fair" played in a loop. My whole life catalog flashed back and forth. Do I apply for a journalism job? Is it FUBAR? It was certainly not the *New York Times* or *Star-Ledger*, but it was still journalism. I think I wanted this.

"Cameron, isn't this a little far out?" Marjorie said when I told her. "After all . . ."

"Do you want me out of the house, making a few bucks, feeling productive and good about myself?"

"It pays?" she asked. I nodded. "Then try. You have no experience, so you won't get it anyway."

That remark kicked me hard. I wondered if she'd carefully chosen her words to motivate me. Marjorie was brilliant.

So, I emailed Tammy-Jo Vento, the assistant editor. She quickly set up an interview with her and Steven Degnan, the publisher. We met in a conference room in the basement of a recreation center. For the first time in my life, I had no resume to share. Instead, I slid my novel across the table like a shuffleboard.

"No resume, no journalism experience, just a recently published novel, a lot of energy, time to explore Monmouth, and a passion for people, places, and words."

"Tell us about yourself," Tammy-Jo interrogated. She was ebullient and focused, and I instantly liked her.

I told her about my career in pharmacy and eyeglasses, sharing some lighter moments and non-political, non-religious proclivities.

She looked at Steven, then back at me. "May I keep the novel? You are now a writer for *Monmouth, Our County*. Congratulations."

After we discussed salary, she asked me to autograph my novel. "Call me TJ," she said.

That day, my life found a special meaning, direction, and understanding of the voice that had spoken to me that one December morning: "Trust." Yes, Mr. Jordan, I'd finally found a place, destiny, and the elusive reason to believe.

THE SETUP

What a great mental state, to think as a journalist. It didn't matter that I wasn't on assignment in the Middle East, Guam, Moscow, Africa, or Washington. Just Monmouth County.

Marjorie made eggs for breakfast twice a week—the same number of times she said, "Cameron, don't think for one moment you're ever going to be writing for a real paper. I can see what's in your eyes."

Her practicality and sensibility gently pissed me off—these qualities she'd inherited from her mother, who'd come from the shtetls of Eastern Europe.

I'd reply, "Maybe I'll surprise you. You never know the forks in the roads."

"Yes, I do. If you come to a fork, take it."

NOAH BET

One midsummer weekend, Noah came home.

"Who was Betty Ford?" he asked. "She died recently. There is some kind of addiction clinic in her name."

I told him about President Ford's wife. "Had addiction problems in the White House. Brave lady. Beat her problems."

"President Ford?"

"No shit. You don't know?" I asked. Noah shook his head. "While he was running for reelection, New York City was in bad financial times. The mayor needed help, but Ford told the city to drop dead, so he lost the election."

"Dad, tell me more about your journalism. Are you covering music?"

"I detect sarcasm in your voice. Now that I'm a writer free spirit, soon I'll get involved in the Asbury Park music scene," I joked, then turned serious. "Let's say we do a little father-son bet that I get completely involved in the whole Jersey Shore music scene."

"Yeah, right."

"The challenge is herewith witnessed by Marjorie Simmons," I said.

It was the beginnings of a journey. Looking in the mirror, I said, "I don't know who I am, what I'm going to be, and what's really inside me. This is a discovery and an adventure. I know Colman's leading the change."

During those pharmacy and eyeglass years, something had always been inside me, wanting to come out into creativity. This journalism gig pierced a small hole in me, like gas shooting out of a pipe, hissing. I was a leaf blowing in the wind. It didn't take much blow to change direction, just a gentle nudge by a loving spiritual grandfather.

My byline was "Cameron's County." In my first few months, I covered a historic Revolutionary War house, an antique car show, and Olde Freehold Day by a stagnant lake. I hit social media with my adventures—the beginnings of serious networking. Always floating around was the music challenge with Noah, a powerful motivator.

AN APPLE A DAY

My sixties were a portent of things to come. I'd begun sliding into middle age on my thirtieth birthday, getting an early glimpse of what it was all about. Each decade since, I'd rationalized that turning forty was better than fifty, fifty was better than sixty . . . and when sixty slapped my senses, it was still better than seventy.

But sixty had brought bodily changes. Atrial fibrillation was kicking the shit out of me. When I'd go into A-fib, sometimes for a week, I'd swallow aspirin, worried about throwing a clot and dying.

Once, after five days of a racing heart and brutal fatigue, I couldn't take it anymore—I lost my temper, angry at the world, waiting to die. "Fuck you, A-fib, I'm done." I ran into the kitchen for a long, sharp meat knife, held it over my heart, and began pushing it into my skin. I gritted my teeth, then I stopped.

Motherfucking awful how close I'd come to the end. Pain from the knife puncture scared me off. I wasn't thinking of Marjorie's or Noah's pain, but my own. I was a selfish prick. I called my cardiologist, Dr. Greg Nardone, who set up an electric cardioversion to help treat my A-fib.

The night before the procedure, I thought about what would happen if I dropped dead. Dr. Greg would come out to console Marjorie. His last words would confirm I was a nice guy. After my funeral, people would come back to the house for bagels and tuna fish. Clearing my thoughts in the dark of the den, I prayed to Colman and Jesus. Something worked. By morning, I was out of A-fucking-fib.

But still my body was failing and it pissed me off. My left shoulder lost mobility, accompanied by terrific pain. Same with my knees, which creaked with achy, breaky foreboding. What if I couldn't play anymore tennis and I had to get titanium joints?

But my mind was magically sharper and more productive than ever. I felt cerebrally limitless to create, express myself, and write. During my meditations, I wished for health, youth, spirit, old age, and a purpose to journey. I was fixated on youth. Mirror, mirror, on the wall, I wasn't aging cerebrally like my contemporaries. Maybe my prayers were working.

Chapter 32

AND ALONG CAME OCTOBER

October 10 was a chilly autumn Jersey day. The leaves were slightly tinged with change. I took a rare walk down the cul-de-sac, loading up my lungs for a difficult decision. I played on Facebook. At 1:11 p.m., the phone rang. I saw the time on the computer. It was an apparition from what I deemed my past life. A ghostly form of negativity and unhappiness. The conversation was short as I reached into my duodenum and decided to excise "that" permanently from my life. A very hard thing to do. We said goodbye to each other. (It occurs to me that I never used the word "douchebag" in this memoir. So be it.)

The phone banged down softly.

Suddenly, I felt a rising exhilaration, a high of freedom. I really did it. I wiped out something not meant to be in my life. I was never sure where this came from. If only I'd sensed how positive this would be, it could've helped reasoning to my family and lessening their outrage with me. It would take a few years to realize I was so incisive in people relations via spiritual deliverances.

The day after parting with the ghost of Cameron past was October 11, 2011—the elevens. I sensed Colman was close. How a life can change direction innocently without symphonies and fanfares? Despite the euphoria of getting rid of something I hadn't been sure about in my life just the day before, I felt lingering abdominal pains. How do you tell someone with personal history a harsh goodbye? It was a new day in my limited time here on Earth. How and why the hell did I do this?

OCTOBER 11

My writing for *Monmouth, Our County* had pleased TJ and Degnan. They liked me like a morning cereal. TJ praised my writing as inventive, embracing, and captivating. By September, I was writing three columns a month, securing $300 and moving into a new tax bracket. I marveled at the universe for orchestrating this, and for Dolores nudging me to a brave new world via email.

On October 11, TJ had set up a meeting between me and Chris Cadora, a videographer at Jersey Glimpses, a production company involved in Central Jersey life. TJ had called me about the meeting at 4:44 p.m.

The staircase to Chris's basement TV studio was precipitously steep, covered with decaying leaves from years ago. The railing was heavily rusted. Heavy winds added mysterious ambiance.

"Fuck this," I said. I wanted to turn around, but something kept me moving.

The metal studio door was ajar. Inside was a control room leading to a small blue and green studio where Chris was filming a group of exceptional high school students. TJ motioned me to a swivel chair. On my first glimpse of Chris, he looked something close to Tony Soprano: stocky, short, pure black hair, and an engaging, warm smile that put me at ease. Instant chemistry; I liked Chris. My X-ray vision into the soul is almost never wrong.

When we started chatting, I learned how abrupt, rapid-fire, and strictly business he was. His voice was much softer than his persona.

"I'm a writer, you're in production, and I have a lot of time," I told him. "I don't watch soap operas in the afternoon or any television. I love social media, so if you need someone to write and post on Facebook, I've got an imagination and a style. It would be my pleasure."

I hoped he took "my pleasure" as an offer to do things out of passion without borders or money. He did. He immediately handed over the passwords to his social media accounts.

"Post what you want—pictures, captions, all decent, and all Jersey. Never politics or religion," he said, packing his cameras and gear.

"Never a winner with those topics," I agreed. "I always want people to like me. No one gets into my soul or head."

"Perfect, Cameron. We're mirror images." I loved that description.

I thanked TJ walking up the stairs, slapping the rust off my hands. "I knew you'd like Chris," she said, smiling.

This next chapter began so blissfully and innocently—no road maps, no business plans, just a crystal ball wrapped in a cluelessness.

BEGINNINGS OF A BRAVE NEW WORLD

Jersey Glimpses was strictly a production company with resources to produce quality content. Early on, I loaded Chris's social media world with positive content relevant to Central Jersey, nothing overdone, just tasteful and journalistic.

One afternoon, I went to the Zombie Walk at the Asbury Park boardwalk. Twenty thousand zombies attended, dressed to kill in pursuit of Guinness World Records recognition of the most zombies in one place on Earth.

Suddenly, I felt a tap on my shoulder. It was Chris Cadora.

"Funny meeting you here," he said to me amidst the sea of tens of thousands of people. He told me he was doing a video for local cable television. "Would you like to interview zombies on camera?" he asked.

The next thing I know, I'm holding a microphone in a petrified state. But I felt a sense of cloudy destiny, power, and dizzying opportunity. My stomach muscles clenched. My head ached. I had no one to advise or support me. For a second, I worried about busting a blood vessel and having a hemorrhagic stroke on the boardwalk. But I had to do this and make it good.

I was under enormous pressure with no time for thought. Chris gave me a twenty-second tutorial about holding a microphone in someone's face while they're talking. I got it right the first time. Chris praised my technique. Briefly, I thought about the tortoise in my hair. What a way to kick the shit and excel at something difficult but valuable.

I spent hours watching my zombie interviews on repeat. It felt good to say I was a journalist. I called TJ, thanking her profusely for orchestrating the opportunity, and suggested we approach Chris to see if we could turn Jersey Glimpses into a specialized journalism, covering obsessively New Jersey things most media cannot devote time to. TJ was down. Chris liked the idea too and offered a revised website, cameras, and editing with Final Cut.

By November, I was a journalist of purpose. Chris reminded there is no money involved.

"It's all right, I'm on social security," I said. Perhaps this was all meant to be. Marjorie even supported it.

One chilly November morning, we grabbed a camera and randomly drove to Asbury Park's Cookman Avenue. TJ was exuberant. "Let's go into that antique store, Beyond Memory. Grab the camera," she said.

Our collaborative journey began with an older woman selling antiques. Grace Fine was a pioneer: one of Jersey's early female pilots, who'd taught other young women how to fly. Occasionally, she flew Senator Barry Goldwater while he ran for president. We nailed our first random interview.

Later that November was the Garden State Annual Comedy Festival at the Paramount Theater in Asbury Park. It was a charity gig to raise money for battered or addicted women. The headliner was Monty Martino, a pure Jersey ethnic Italian comedian. Later that night, he and I took a comical picture together and born was my special enduring friendship with one of the funniest humans, who also wants to run for president (part of his act).

The festival's after-party was at the Wonder Bar. A cold, pre-winter wind blew in off the nearby Atlantic. Marjorie was pissed off. She wanted to go to bed. "Just five minutes?" I asked. "So I can experience the Wonder Bar."

A few weeks earlier, I'd had an epiphany: I needed a brand. The vision was there: I'd wear a Rutgers hat everywhere to distinguish myself. This behavior became obsessive and compulsive. A few years later, I'd teach students to find a brand for themselves. The hat became transformative for me. Marjorie hated it, warning that my hair would thin and fall out.

Three minutes elapsed at the Wonder Bar; Marjorie was counting. Then I noticed someone seated at the bar also wearing a Rutgers hat. I walked over to say hello. His name was Tony—he turned out to be the son of Teddy Custer, one of the best drummers in America. Music royalty was just sitting there with a beer. Tony was a producer of the comedy show.

I introduced myself: "Cameron Simmons. Journalist, writer, and huge fan of your father. So sorry about his passing."

"Nice to meet you," he said perfunctorily.

I handed him my business card, which mentioned that I was a writer. His hand barely lifted to receive it.

Marjorie got her bed.

A BOOK DEAL

In early December, late in the morning, the phone rang.

"This is Tony Custer," said the voice on the other end of the line. "A few weeks ago, you gave me your business card. You're a writer?"

It took me three seconds to process. "Yes, I'm a writer. Somewhat new to the business—just being honest."

"I like honest. You know who my father was?"

"The whole world knows your father."

"I want to write a tell-all book. Teddy Custer, drums, sex, rock 'n' roll, being on the world stage, and being an absent father. A big bicoastal agency is interested. Are you?"

Tony Custer lived close—geographical synchronicity. He could move and shake my life. What was key to the book were the contacts given to me. Me, an unknown journalist, talking to American music royalty. All I had to do was remember lessons from Incanto and prepare well before talking to anyone. They'd think I was a real journalist. I was getting close.

The side effect of all this was my swelled ego kicking the shit out of the tortoise. Writing was therapeutic. I was growing up, reaching for the stars, and pinching my arm. Was this really happening?

Tony and I became friends. But there were road blocks with the book project. People didn't know me, so they weren't sharing with me the salient shit I needed to sell books. I'd get obligatory, banal, perfumed comments from interviewees. Nothing to help sell a book. One day I just stopped writing. Tony lost his energy as well. Another dream faded but confidence in defeating tortoise elevated.

THANKING MY WINDS OF CHANGE

While others spent Christmastime talking about Santa Claus and Jesus, I spent the season sending my gratitude to Saint Anthony for all his spiritual gifts. New Year's Eve 2012, however, was far more traditional: Chinese dinner with friends, including Meryl and Keith, then watching the ball drop. After tiramisu at 12:30 a.m., they went home.

"No one fucking makes it to 1:00 a.m. anymore. Are we really getting older?"

"Happy New Year, Cam," Marjorie said. "Yes, almost there."

"Almost where?"

"In the land of new AARP cards every August, chilled prune juice, complaining about our knees and backs, and stool softeners. Remember, it's all about the sun on your face."

"It sucks," I grumbled.

After Marjorie went to bed, I stayed up watching a *Honeymooners* marathon on mute. Silence captured me in the den. I considered the winds of change in my brave new world. This journalism thing was coming together. I talked to my spirit gang: "Thank you all. My life is evolving, changing, becoming fulfilling and secure. I'm learning about spirit in a life, becoming a better human. I need to get into the Kingdom. I'm different than Scrooge. I know I can change. When I heard that voice, 'Trust,' I could've never known its meaning. Happy New Year."

Chapter 33

WHO AM I?

On April 22, 1970, I participated in the first Earth Day even though I was married to Valerie, who was possessive, obsessive, and jealous. Valerie and I were different cellularly. Environmentalism made sense to me but not to her. I never pushed it. Just enjoyed her tuna noodle casseroles.

When I wanted to go to Woodstock, she threatened to leave. I stayed home, but I shouldn't have. My modern life is composed of synchronicity strings. At the fiftieth anniversary of Woodstock, I met Elliott Landy, the festival's official photographer. When I saw a photo of the 500,000 people, a light bulb beamed in my mind that I didn't really belong there. The tortoise was still stuck in my hair.

Earth Day made me environmentally aware. The bulb was dim back then, just a tinge aware of the changing climate and planet. But it's a bright bulb now, aware that no power on Earth, human or otherwise, can arrest behavior, dependence, greed, or ignorance. Our magical species won't be able to stop destiny, not even if Clark Kent spun the Earth backwards to a gentler time. The environment is always on my mind. Sometimes I think it could precipitate my early exit. I could post a video of me wearing a toga and setting myself on fire on Facebook, but no one would give a shit. At least I stopped eating everything with four legs in 1975, infinitesimally slowing down the release of methane into the atmosphere.

I'M NOT CNN OR NBC

Jersey Glimpses was a good place to be. Chris Cadora gave me complete freedom of expression—just no politics, sex, or religion. Jersey Glimpses was designed to elevate people and places. I learned nothing could move people to different political persuasions. Nobody peeks into my soul. Keep your friends close and your enemies closer.

One day, I got a Facebook friend request from someone named Sam Galant. His wife, Myra, was an accomplished Jersey Shore singer-songwriter. Would I like to see Myra perform and perhaps teach her blogging? I joked to Noah that I might now become part of the Jersey music scene. I already dabbled with the son of the late rock drummer Teddy Custer, so I had chances of winning our bet early. There was no money to exchange, just father-son pride.

I went to meet Sam and Myra Galant at a small Asbury Park bar with seven stools and a stage with a purple backdrop. Outside it was freezing with snow flurries, but I was possessed to push myself and go to everything musical. Myra was on stage at the bar with a few dozen patrons—captivating, alluring, grainy, earthy. She belted out her own words, some funny, introspective, and socially aware. Sam recognized me by my Rutgers hat. We shook hands. After her set, Sam introduced us.

"Maybe over some rainbow, you could interview me," Myra added. When spring set in, Myra called. My first musical interview was on. It was pretty cool for Cameron to be sitting with a local celebrity, drinking unsweetened hot tea with Tastykake Krimpets, taking in a view of the Navesink River while clutching my yellow legal pad. Now I had a newfound kinship and advanced degree with real-life divas. I knew so little about needy singers in this new world. I felt like a six-foot student in first grade, significantly out of place. Myra would teach me a plethora of lessons about the music business. A special friend and mentor from that first time near the river.

CENTURY-OLD PEOPLE AND GHOSTS

When you least expect it, something strange arrives from deep space. I was at a local hospital, covering a news conference on maternity. The hospital administrator was yammering on about the competitive business of family health—self-serving stuff. Not what I liked to write about, especially if I'm not getting paid by anyone.

In the parking lot, another journalist approached me with a tip. "You might find a human-interest angle in a birthday party next week at Oak Shores Residences for Eva Castle, turning 101. Call her."

When I met with Eva, it was my first close encounter with a centenarian. Stereotypes couldn't be helped—Eva was mobile, opiniated, and cerebrally sharp. She lived in a senior residence, not a nursing home. Herbert Hoover was her favorite president. She had no children.

Our friendship birthed. Once she was on camera, she invited me back to her room—jokingly, but perhaps seriously. "Just because I'm over a hundred doesn't mean I don't think about those things," Eva said, smiling.

Later, I'd go on to interview a collection of centenarians, invisible people who are very much alive in Jersey. One of them was William, who'd been on a ship that pounded German installations on D-Day at Omaha Beach. I was the first person he opened up to about it.

On the way home from Eva's birthday party, TJ and I took back roads. We passed a sign that read, "Historical Presbyterian Burial Ground."

"Stop the car!" I shouted, like Natalie Wood at the end of *Miracle on 34th Street*. "We have to go in."

"It's freezing cold," TJ said.

"We must. I don't know why."

When I got out of the car, a strange, cold wind slapped me around. All the grave markers were flat and faded, barely discernible etchings. "Everybody here died before America was born."

"How haunting," I said.

TJ went silent, introspective.

"We'll come back when it's warm."

The next day, I posted pictures online from the cemetery. A new friend, Georgia, a college professor and ghost hunter, messaged that she'd like to come along if we ever went back.

So, on an early Saturday morning in late June, TJ, Professor Georgia, and I went to the cemetery. It was nearly 80 degrees already and the sky was perfect, without a cloud.

Georgia held a special microphone over the grave of a twelve-year-old girl who'd died in the mid-1700s. "Were you a little girl?" Georgia repeated several times, holding the microphone close to the grave.

We gathered in a circle as Georgia replayed the tape. Faintly, a voice said, "Yes, I'm a little girl." Georgia and TJ heard it clearly; not so much for me.

"I really heard the girl's voice," TJ said, struggling with her words. She had goose bumps. Her face, always smiley, was now pale and distressed. "How can that be, to hear a voice?"

"No explanation. I can't know why she hasn't moved on," Georgia said calmly.

We stood in disturbed silence. Then it started to rain on us—just the three of us. I rubbed my arms, feeling moisture and disbelief. The sky above was still sunny and cloudless. "How can this be happening?" I asked Georgia.

Georgia was approaching sixty and wore her quintessential gray hair in a bun. She spoke with a twinge of regal Southern accent, unfazed, with no emotion. "Sometimes these things happen and there is no earthly explanation. At least we didn't get soaked," she said.

I took the rain as a happy notion that we were not alone. The universe is beyond human understanding. This new journalism gig was all right.

APRIL, SHE TAUGHT ME WELL

As my world gently expanded into journalistic pursuits, I marveled at how this was happening. I'd been an unhappy pharmacist, taking excessive naps and pills to escape, and now I was morphing into a semblance of a journalist and creative dilettante. From where it all came, I was beginning to understand. Colman had orchestrated me.

April 2012 began in spirituality. One day on the exercise bike, reading, pedaling, CNN muted on the TV, something made me look at the cable box: 1:11 p.m. Elapsed time on the bike: 44:44. Teary, I thanked Colman for that awareness energy. If only I could bridge our two worlds. What's the big deal contacting another world? Is something keeping me here to fulfill a destiny?

Social media alerted me to a concert for Tent City on Easter Sunday. Tent City was where up to 112 people lived in tents without heat, electricity, food, or running water—just twenty miles south from where my son had grown up middle-class, comfortable, and far from the realities of human neglect. For him, homelessness was a thirty-second spot on the evening news or a glimpse of legs protruding from a cardboard box on a side street in Manhattan.

I gently persuaded Noah to accompany me. "It's good for your development as a young man to see a real side of life."

"You could've asked me," Noah responded. "I still would've gone. Don't lay guilt on me. I hate that routine."

At the event, a few dozen people gathered in a plaza to listen to the singers and bands. The day was cool, breezy, and sunny; spring was arriving stubbornly. Noah filmed while I interviewed. Eventually, a mistreated bus arrived, unloading homeless people stuck in Ocean County. Strangely, I kept a distance from the residents, and it bothered me.

One of the residents offered, "Why don't you get a hot dog?"

"Thanks, but I don't eat meat," I said, keeping my purified distance.

The following January, 2013, in the dirty snow and bitter cold, TJ and I would spend several days covering Tent City for Jersey Glimpses. Half the humans were victims of the Recession; the other half, drugs, alcohol, and physical abuses. A man named Anthony proudly took us into his tent to show us his new wood-burning stove and floral bedspread. Just down the dirt road, he said, they had a community portable toilet fixture. He was eloquent, documenting society's failures and his own. The top eighty-eight richest people in the world have accumulated more wealth than the poorest three and a half billion. And there was Anthony, thirty-something, stuck, and homeless, yet he possessed a strange element of prideful contentment.

TJ and I gently argued on the way home. She thought the people we'd met were actually happy. A sense of belonging and hope filled their wooded encampment.

Angrily, I said, "You are so wrong. No human wants to live like that. They don't even know where their next meal comes from or if they'll get stabbed over a bottle of beer or can of food. You are so insensitive."

The car was quiet for a while as we drove on Route 9, then we laughed at our unresolved differences.

My next assignment was to learn about hunger at the food bank. In 1980, there were forty-five food pantries in America; these days, 45,000. Food insecurity has become rampant—your next-door neighbor could be food insecure, embarrassed to ask for help.

I dwell here because this was all life-altering, clobbering me with despair and questions for my spirit gang. Our species' problems are overwhelming. I'll never make a sizeable difference, but I'm aware now. How can people let others be homeless in America, or anywhere?

One night that April, in 2012, I went for a walk down the cul-de-sac. The brisk spring night was rejuvenating. Under the full moon—like the one Valerie and I made out beneath on July 20, 1969—my journalistic vision became clearer. Journalistically, I'd focus on New Jersey, uplifting, elevating its people and places. Maybe I'd make a difference in a life. He or she who saves a life saves the world.

Chapter 34

STORIES ABOUT STORIES

Marjorie raised her teacher's voice, watching *Shark Tank*. "Cameron, make sure you don't bore readers with too many details. You'll lose me and all of them."

I'd never tell her, but she was always right.

I jumped into Asbury Music. Inundated with free CDs to review, I'd never denigrate or dislike anyone's work. I always wrote positive reviews, and if something was beyond my taste, I'd find reasons not to write anything at all. For years, I got away with elusiveness until a disc jockey friend, Don Korsky, said I was masturbating my credibility by not being critical and that I was hanging out too often at music venues, sometimes four times a week.

"Masturbating? Don."

"Yes, Cam. You need to be real," Don said. "Don't mess with

credibility. If you don't like something, say it and why. And you've got to be selective. Show up at gigs once in a blue moon, so when you do show up, it's an occasion."

The music flowed on. For example, I should've been more open to hip-hop when Jay-Z released his album *4:44*, but I kept listening to Peter, Paul and Mary, Donovan, Simon and Garfunkel, and Joan Baez. One night, looking for sixties music on YouTube, sleet tapping on the window, memories flitting and floating, I landed on Mimi Fariña, Joan Baez's sister, singing "Pack Up Your Sorrows" with her husband, Richard Fariña. Mesmerized, I plunged into Mimi Fariña. There was something there. Mimi had founded Bread & Roses, a nonprofit that brought free music and entertainment to institutions such as jails. Mimi was now in my consciousness. Why the fuck did I have my head up my ass back in the day, never going to Greenwich Village when I could've met Mimi, Bob Dylan and Peter, Paul and Mary?

I went to BookExpo America in New York, a large publishing industry trade show. In a quiet aisle away from the maddening crowds, I saw a guy in front of a display for a memoir titled *Blood, Sweat, and My Rock 'n' Roll Years: Is Steve Katz a Rock Star?* The man was Steve Katz himself, from Blood, Sweat & Tears and American Flyer.

"I'm a huge fan and here you are. You made my day," I said, swooning over the synchronicities of life. I asked him for an autographed copy.

That summer, while Marjorie and I took a cruise, I dove into Steve Katz's world from a lounge chair by a three-foot pool. I learned that he knew Mimi Fariña well.

The following year, I met him again when he did an acoustic show in South Jersey. We met, hugged, and he posted my positive book review next to Judy Collins's.

GHOSTS FOR MY KINGDOM

Journalism was taking form. I was reporting on meaningful causes, Jersey people doing the living and dying, caring and sacrificing, things going unnoticed. In the back of my mind were two unexplainable occurrences: the one with George Miller, the poor farmer who lived in a mirror in an eyeglass store in Somerville and messed around with my cell phone, and the twelve-year-old girl from the mid-1700s whose voice Georgia, TJ, and I had recorded coming from her grave.

Once, my friend Davey Callman, the quintessential music journalist, a supporter of New Jersey independent music and radio show host, invited me on his show. Afterward, I told him and the group about my ghost stories. A month later, Davey's nephew Tommy called. He told me he was opening a pizza restaurant in South Jersey in an abandoned building from the 1800s. During the certificate of occupancy inspection, he'd escorted firemen and cops through the building and down a wooden staircase into the basement, where several boxes blocked their passage. Tommy moved them. Then, with flashlights, he guided them to the electrical box on the far end of the basement. Ten minutes elapsed. When they returned to the staircase, the boxes were back blocking the stairs. A cop, obviously chilled, said, "Don't ever call us again to come here."

Tommy asked me about doing a story for Jersey Glimpses. I was immediately down; this is journalism many people preferred to avoid.

"The cops were really spooked out?" I asked.

Tommy laughed. "It got strangely cold. The cop meant it; he'd never come back. Someone leaked the story to the Women's Club, and now everyone in town knows."

In February 2013, I went to that cold building with Tommy, TJ, Georgia, and Noah, who still loved *Ghostbusters*. Tommy's fiancée took a cell phone picture of the empty gray basement. On the screen, the picture showed a large white orb. Something tugged at Noah's coat when no one was around. I always hoped I'd never see a full torso apparition.

Summer 2013, Jersey Glimpses got permission to film inside an abandoned psychiatric hospital. Thirty years of mold, asbestos, legend, decay, and mystery lay ahead. It was a dangerous place; police insisted on accompanying us because of looters, animals, and the unknown. I stayed with Noah and TJ on the main floor while others ascended the decrepit stairs. A few minutes later, the group screamed. They came back quickly.

"We heard children crying," Chris Cadora said.

At Halloween time, I went to the Proprietary House in Perth Amboy. Ben Franklin's illegitimate son, William, as royal governor of New Jersey, had moved into the house in 1764. Many ghost stories had surfaced since. A psychic friend, Judy Dove, conducted our tour. While we waited to begin, I needed to piss. The bathrooms had no urinals, just toilets. I was in a stall aiming at the perfect center of the bowl when I heard bells clanging and banging. I looked over the stall: nothing. I tried to finish, but there was more noise.

Then I realized why I was there. Did I ever think I was special? Just that I was as open as an antenna. I'm a regular guy; I can't walk on water. I moved closer to being a good human being, closer to Jesus's thinking, which I knew so little about because it wasn't in my regular world. Something was warmly taking me there.

Across the street from the hospital was a cemetery for the 924 patients who had died over the life of the hospital. They had no grave markers, just numbers. The cemetery was administered by the county park commission because it was a real park. I thought about how women had been treated as patients: raped, abused, beaten, murdered, and buried here. I really wanted to do meaningful journalism confronting the harsh reality that their truths were probably hidden in a basement in Trenton.

On Sunday mornings, I'd visit grave 444. It belonged to someone named Peter. The county finally erected a plaque which listed the cemetery numbers, names and dates died. I set up a small chair and talked to Peter, recording our conversation on a special microphone. There's a potent picture for a police cruiser: a guy wearing tennis shorts, a red Rutgers hat, sitting by a grave with a dangling microphone. I never heard anything from Peter, and I was all right with that. I didn't fancy a voice coming from a grave.

On one of our trips to the abandoned psychiatric hospital, I invited real ghostbusters along. It was an unbearably hot, buggy, unforgiving day. That day's building had originally housed violent criminals. To get us inside, our police escort pulled out an industrial crowbar and ripped the plywood from the door. "There's something wrong with this picture," I whispered. "A cop is breaking into a building."

On another day with Sandy from the ghostbusters team, we went right to grave 444. I started talking to the Peter and recording. "Peter, it's Cameron Simmons. I've been coming here often. You're the only one I talk to. I don't know what to say. Perhaps if I heard something from you, I'd be induced to come back. I have just one question. How did you die, Peter? I won't bother you anymore." Playing back the recording later at home, I heard nothing, as I expected.

A few months later, Sandy's team was premiering a documentary at a haunted restaurant where people had been murdered back during the Revolutionary War.

Sylvia, one of Sandy's researchers, walked up to me. "By the way," she said, that night, after we recorded you at grave 444, I listened to the playback."

"And?"

"We heard something. I forgot to call you," she said. I was annoyed. "When you asked the grave how he died, the voice said, 'It doesn't matter.'"

For whatever eternal reason, Peter had never moved on. It scared me beyond. For months, I pondered life, death, punishment, goodness, godliness, Jesus, humankind, and our earthly existence. What could be the worst punishment for being a bad human? To be conscious of thought, confined to a dark, cold, and lonely grave, only to think for eternity about what you did wrong. Forget burning in abundant heat—that's a real hell.

ROCK SYNCHRONICITY

My ongoing bet with Noah about the Jersey music world was always on my mind. Slowly, I was becoming a fan of the rocker world, but I still needed the sounds of silence.

When my publisher at a new gig, *Jersey Shore Thing* magazine, secured me an interview with one of the best friends of a world-famous rocker who lived nearby, I asked Noah if this interview won our bet. "Not yet, Dad, but I'm impressed," he said.

The rocker friend lived in a modest apartment building. We shook hands warmly. I took a long, slow walk down his green hallway looking at all the music memorabilia on the walls. In the kitchen, we sat at a 1950s vintage Formica table with metal legs and green plastic seat cushions. A cuckoo clock on the wall chimed with two loud bursts. When he excused himself, I elbowed my publisher, Stuart. "We're really here. This is great."

Stuart said, "This is going on the cover." He beckoned me over to look at something on the wall. It was a note written to the rocker's agent. I had no time to look, so I took a picture of it.

Later, in the car, I examined the note. The rocker had given his agent a list of movies he wanted to watch to help him write songs: *The Philadelphia Story, East of Eden, To Kill a Mockingbird, The Searchers, The Last Picture Show, Used Cars, How Green Was My Valley, Diner, Raging Bull, North by Northwest, The Hustler, Dr. Strangelove,* and so forth.

"I'll bet that note's worth a quarter million!" Stuart yelled.

But the list was priceless to me. A few years before, I began ordering movies to help me escape exercise bike boredom—my list had been virtually identical to the rockers. How Strangelove the world. The wind blew east. I heard the roar. Lah-di-dah.

HURRICANE SANDY

Hurricane Carol had hit New Jersey hard in August 1954. Amelia was in the hospital recovering from giving birth to my sister Carol.

Subliminally, I think my parents named my sister after the storm. When the wind slowed, I got my bike and pedaled around the block. I've always been fascinated by hurricanes—even as a nine-year-old, I appreciated the power of nature. As I got older, when hurricanes approached, I wanted to see first hand the coming of a storm. Used to fantasize going to Galveston to watch a hurricane do its thing.

Once, I took Noah with me to the Jersey Shore to see the foamy white waves. Marjorie yelled, "If anything happens to him . . ."

In late October of 2012, Hurricane Sandy clobbered New Jersey as a perfect storm. For ten days, we had no power. And it sucked. "Nature and God are smart, getting me born in an age of power, video, headphones, pills. I could never exist on permanent candlelight," I said.

Fourteen days post-Sandy, we covered the Shore for Jersey Glimpses. Union Beach had been horrifically damaged. Martial law protected the remains from poachers and thieves; the state had called in Michigan State Police for help.

When TJ and I went into the ruins to take pictures, I didn't notice a trooper approaching on foot. TJ yelled—his hand was on his holster.

If I made a wrong move.

MURRAY

At a Rutgers tailgate (with a roasted pig, eyes open), my friend Debbie came in for a hug. As a Rutgers professor, she quested that I teach there someday, despite it being an extremely high mountain to climb—it was virtually inaccessible. Then Debbie introduced me as a journalist to some nearby people masticating pork.

One of them, a pleasant, forty-something woman, gave a look that locked me in place. "My father, Murray Gordon, is a Holocaust survivor," she said. "He's ninety-four but still sharp. He lectures at schools and has quite a story to tell."

I'd never met a Holocaust survivor in person before. "I'd love to interview him," I said.

It took us months to set up a time. Finally, Murray, Marjorie, and I sat down by his coffee table with homemade Polish pierogi between us. With tears in his eyes, he told us about being a young teen in Poland when the Nazis invaded, rounded up Jews, including Murray's whole family. He never saw them again.

"I was blondish, big, and strong," he said. "I didn't necessarily look Jewish, so I survived going from one work camp to another. I was in one camp, working in a coal mine, and my shovel broke. A Nazi officer thought I did it on purpose, so he decided to kill me right there. He took his gun out, aimed at my head, but his arm shook and the bullet went through my shoulder, not my head. So, they took me to the hospital. Jews got no anesthetics. The Polish doctor took a liking to me because I looked German, not Jewish. The next morning, he gave me anesthesia and operated. He saved my life. After that, Dr. Josef Mengele, the Angel of Death, one of the worst human beings to ever live, came in every day to look in on me."

Murray also told us about being in a camp with Amon Göth, the German commander who loved shooting Jews for target practice. "He used to drive by me and wave."

Murray had also survived one of the infamous death marches. Somewhere along the road, someone threw him a piece of meat. It sustained him.

Listening to Murray speak, I realized I loved this human being—his strength, courage, warmth, emotion, gentility, passion, and mission. Part of his energy was to make sure people remembered, so it never happens again. But it is always happening somewhere again.

I suggested doing our Jersey Glimpses TV show on location at his home, but as I fumbled around for the right time, Murray died. I sat in the last row during his funeral with tears in my eyes. I was so tired of still learning lessons about seizing time.

MOVIES AND FILM FESTIVALS

One day in the early 2000s, while I was still selling eyeglasses, I got a tip about casting for Steven Spielberg's *War of the Worlds* in Newark.

What the fuck? When I went there, they took my picture and eventually called me to be an extra. But at my job, I couldn't take eight days off.

"If anything else comes up . . ." I said.

Casting called back. Maybe they needed my height, so I got cocky and wanted a guarantee of screen time, to which they said, "We don't even do that for Tom Cruise." So, I declined. I'd fucked up. My role could've had ample screen time in the movie's long opening scene.

Years later, the notion of being in a film still swirling in my head beneath the tortoise, I used my Jersey Glimpses press pass to get into the Garden State Film Festival. I walked around the cocktail party in my Rutgers red hat, blazer, and jeans. Loved being a journalist. I chatted with three filmmakers—each in a different genre: social commentary, horror, and childhood cancer documentaries—who soon became new friends sitting around my kitchen table, and eventually guests on my TV show.

One woman at the party saw my hat and asked if I was a Rutgers professor. I'd recently dreamed about teaching, but the thought of mentoring students and running back and forth full-time wore me down. The woman introduced herself as Gale Bartholomew, MD, OB-GYN, and we would go on to become great friends. Somebody up there likes me. Gale was in charge of the Women's Research Project at the medical school. By summer's end, I was on the project's advisory committee serving as a social media and content promulgator. I'd come a long way from Wendy Paul asking me if I knew how to use a Tampax.

Chapter 35

A THICKENING PLOT

Mickey Mantle once said, "If I knew I was going to live this long, I'd have taken better care of myself." My health consciousness wasn't raised by any specific event or brush with death, just brief interludes of bright light. While studying pharmacology at Rutgers, I began taking supplements daily—just in case I'd live long, I'd try for longer.

In 1989, I weighed 350 pounds—I was smoking, dying, unable to walk up a flight of stairs without gasping for breath. One night, I had a Tralfamadorian dream—or I was visited by an angelic spirit implanting critical timeliness. I woke up Marjorie to share the notion of fixing my life, losing weight, stopping smoking, exercising, and getting healthy. No one diets, stops smoking, and loses a hundred pounds in two and a half months. I loved smoking after a tuna sub sandwich, turkey burger, fries, bagels—anything, really. But I had a mysterious instant energy to change. How did I do it? Somebody was pulling my marionette strings.

Early in life, I had a heart murmur. Amelia thought I'd die young. My pediatrician told her murmurs are common and often disappear. So, I worked in a grocery store, shoveled snow, painted picket fences, swept the driveway, dusted, and washed and dried dishes, all before I was thirteen. The pediatrician was right—my murmur eventually disappeared.

Heart stuff couldn't keep me out of Vietnam. Palpitations, chest pains, imagined heart attacks, and a string of cardiologists followed during my eyeglass-selling days. One Sunday in my forties, I ran to the hospital (while Marjorie stayed home knitting) with heart attack symptoms. After misreading my isoenzyme test, the cardiologist suggested I get a pacemaker.

I tiptoed through cardiologists after that. Nothing was really wrong with my pump, but I always worried every pain was a tumor—I'd inherited that mentality from Amelia.

Then, in 2012, I developed a pain in my left shoulder that was so bad, I lost mobility. I tried fixing it by leaning against a doorway, pushing hard, trying to realign it, but I didn't know what the fuck I was doing. I was so pissed off at my failing body, I'd punch my bad shoulder. I didn't respect my body. So what? I couldn't lift my left arm. At least I was a righty.

But by early 2014, my poor quality of life had beaten me up. I went to a local orthopedist, Dr. Steve West, who told me there was nothing left of my shoulder's ball joint, so it was bone on bone. Months later, I had a titanium shoulder replacement. Successful surgery, but I couldn't piss to get released from the hospital afterward. My aging prostate had gotten too big. A huge lah-di-dah.

Five weeks after getting my new shoulder, I (and 400,000 others) went to the People's Climate March. On the train ride there, I was somewhat worried, as I was handicapped (in an arm sling) with one functioning arm. But I'd never gone to Woodstock or the March on Washington, nor did I ever hang out in Greenwich Village. I'd resolved not to miss any more human expressions of solidarity over Earthly causes and species survival.

At the march, I met my younger friend Mary Gianni at a church across from Central Park West. We sat on the church's concrete steps for three hours as the march organized. I pondered being thirty years younger.

Then a random man with disorganized white hair and a plain blue button-down shirt passed us, making a right on the side street. "Mary, help me up. Let's follow that man," I said.

"Who is he?"

"Maybe a presidential candidate. Bernie Sanders."

I moved fast, but not menacingly so, with the one arm. Bernie was with an aide. When we caught up to them, we introduced ourselves. I told him I was an apolitical reporter with Jersey Glimpses. "Senator, can we pull up a brick here on the steps and chat?" I asked.

And we did. Bernie was delightful. "Are you running for president?" I asked. "Because you should."

He thanked me. "Probably."

After we parted ways, Mary said, "Cameron, you are the second coming of Forrest Gump."

Just before Christmas, I had severe chest pains, flutters, and fibrillations. A blood pressure cuff said my heart rate was 42, so I was almost dead. My A-fib meds had slowed my heart. This was bad shit.

The next day, I sat with my friend and cardiologist Dr. Greg Nardone and an electro-physiologist cardiologist, Dr. Jain. "We're in a pickle, Cameron," Dr. Jain said. "Ease up your A-fib meds and your heart rate goes up, but you may go into A-fib. Increase meds, and you'll have no heart rate. There's only one thing left: ablation."

A-fib is fucking miserable. Ablation petrified me. Dr. Jain would go into my heart with a catheter, poke around for hours, and maybe find the cells causing the A-fib. Maybe not. If there was even a minor earthquake, the operating room would shake and the catheter would puncture my heart, leading to my hopefully nicely attended funeral.

Dr. Jain laughed. "I understand your concern, but we've run out of options."

I needed to think on it. But there was no other way out. A few months later, I scheduled the procedure. In the days leading up to it, I anguished, writing my last will, divulging my passwords, cleaning up my affairs, paying bills, and avoiding social media, as if this was my final fade into a Jersey sunset. Would people remember me as being a nice guy?

The night before was hell. Pacing in my bedroom, stomach muscles tight, heart fluttering, head aching, I felt caged. I was convinced my time was unfulfilled. I had so much living to do. But I felt a strange kind of acceptance. Death is a great equalizer—I saw flashes of homeless, hungry, old, and sick people.

Then, on the beige carpet, out of nowhere, I saw a copper penny. Marjorie often said she found pennies as messages from her mother, as if dropped out of the air.

An inspiration came from somewhere: I knew I needed to talk to Jesus.

"Dear Jesus," I said, sitting on the edge of my bed, "I'm lost, beside myself. Desperate and scared. I love life. I have so much to do. I've been gifted with a certain spirituality, angelic intervention. There are so many people with problems beyond me, but tomorrow this A-fib procedure. If there was a way for you to look in on me, briefly . . . I've said my prayer. I'll always understand and thank you."

The next day I was prepped for surgery and wheeled to operating room on a gurney. The lights in the cold hallway overhead were faded and blurry. The paint was peeling around one light. I didn't want a paint chip to become a Junior Mint. In the operating room, two aides slid me onto the slab. I rested my head on an unsubstantial pillow. Something pricked my arm. "This could be hours, so have a nice dream," someone explained.

I think I said, "Let Rutgers go to the Rose Bowl." I was gone.

When I awoke, a few nurses were around. Most importantly, I was alive.

Dr. Jain came in. "Cameron, you're fine," he said, smiling. "I've been doing this a long time. This has never happened to me. The milli-second that we went into your heart to search for those renegade cells, you went into A-fib. We saw the cells right away, ablated them, and you went right out of A-fib."

I smiled. Something special had happened. Someone was in there with me for that brief moment.

NOAH, MARRIAGE AND MY HEAVENLY KNEE

After Noah had moved out, he called every night to touch base. He ended every call saying, "Love you, Dad." An amazing feeling. One night, he subtly mentioned he was dating Diana, a girl he'd met at kickball. Marjorie had visuals of a caterer. A month later he asked us, "Can I bring Diana home?" We picked them up from the train, and within three minutes of talking in the front hall, we knew they were meant for each other. A perfect universe.

The kids wanted to get married in October 2015. When they told us at Sunday brunch, I ran into my office to check the Rutgers football schedule. I couldn't miss the first game against Ohio State.

An hour before the wedding, I helped Noah adjust the bowtie on his tuxedo. I savored the moment. It had been a long journey from when the nurse wheeled him in to see us for the first time, his face slightly wrinkled from being pushed out. Now my handsome son was getting married.

During the first dance, I slipped on Diana's bridal train, painfully twisting my right knee. But no one could know, so I kept dancing and smiling. I didn't want to bring down the evening.

Out of this joyful innocence, I quickly began a yearlong medical odyssey, but I had no visions of ever getting a new knee. My menu for the year: completely legal cortisone, PRP (blood platelets), and hyaluronic acid injections; slightly illegal DMSO injections (Europeans use the drug to help horses run faster); anti-inflammatory meds; acupuncture; biomagnets; ozone (yes, the stuff from the atmosphere). Nothing worked. I felt like a downhill skier who couldn't stop, heading for a snow-covered tree—or in my case, a new knee. My pain and immobility increased, though I never took opioids.

In the summer of 2016, after twenty years of planning, I traveled to Israel with Marjorie, her sister Lisa, my sister Carol, and my cousin Abby. Israel was a serious place of mind for me. I realized who I was becoming: an ecumenical, open-minded, caring human. The only important things to take care of, I thought, are the Earth, the homeless, the hungry, the sick, and the old—Jesus's things.

The conflict: I was in pain, walking with a cane. Would I ruin the trip for everyone? Could I even walk? I decided to get a new knee when we got back; I'd put up a valiant fight.

My quid pro quo for not backing out of the trip in pain was planning our itinerary for two of the ten days we were there. I planned for us to see the Church of the Holy Sepulchre, Christ's tomb, where he was buried and resurrected. The following day, we'd go to Nazareth.

When we finally got to Israel, with its thousands of years of history, I was in awe. On the second day, our guide got permission for me to climb to the roof of a Muslim school to get close to the Temple Mount (Haram esh-Sharif). Up there, I marveled at its beauty and solemnity. What if a heavenly stairway suddenly dropped down? *We're losing the planet*, I thought, *and all we really have is each other*. Cerebral thoughts when you're 5,600 miles away from Route 9 in New Jersey.

One day, I had a rough stomach after several rounds of falafel, and I was feeling severely weak and dehydrated. Our guide urged me to head back to the hotel, but I needed to see the Church of the Holy Sepulchre.

"It's much more than a church to me," I tried to explain. "I must gather all my strength to go there. I'll never have this chance again. Something is driving me."

"Follow me," the guide said, leading me and just Carol to a large courtyard. Once inside the church, the guide pointed to a second floor. "That's where Christ was crucified. It was that hillside now on our right." I felt a chill of awe.

I took off my Rutgers hat when we entered the church. My mind was firing away, being close to Jesus, history, and my own humanity. I remembered to give thanks for my successful ablation. A thought came to mind: Could my relatives understand my spirituality?

Because of ongoing renovations, only two people at a time were allowed to enter Christ's tomb towards the rear of the church. We'd have to go through a tunnel. "Cameron, you will have to crawl because you're tall," our guide explained. "No pictures. Stay a few minutes."

"Do you want to do this, Cameron?" Carol asked.

I twirled my cane nervously. My knees were secured with braces, exposing my boniness and arthritis through the little holes. I knew I had to do this.

Inside the tunnel, my braces cushioned my knees from the hard floor. The tomb's small room was warm and the air smelled of antiquity. Carol stood next to me, but she was thousands of miles away. I touched the crypt, rubbed my right hand a few inches along the surface, closed my eyes, and whispered quietly, "Thank you."

I can't remember how we got out of the room. But there was the guide with my cane. My knee hurt terrifically. I was so overcome by the experience, I'd forgotten to say a special prayer for my knee.

The next day, we went to Nazareth. In the square near the two churches, a man cavorted with a lot of pigeons. One of the churches, St. Joseph's, was built over Joseph's carpenter workshop. I went inside the church by myself.

Instantly, I fell into a state of queasiness. I had rapid-fire shots of déjà vu: I was at the Weequahic Park gazebo. Walking home from Crast Pharmacy, chain-smoking menthol cigarettes. Standing on a window sill, looking into the morgue at Beth Israel Hospital with a stench of ether and formaldehyde. I shook my head to snap out of it.

Outside, my group had disappeared. So, I went next door to the Church of the Annunciation, where Gabriel had told Mary about a child to be born. Below the main floor was a shrine to Mary. Slowly, cane in hand, I walked downstairs, feeling like I was ninety. I fixated on a plaque that said, "Here the world was made flesh." I sent a few thoughts through the metal grating to the shrine of Mary.

Suddenly, without provocation, a tremendous jolt of pain ran from my right knee down to my ankle. I gasped, sucking in a lot of air. Steadying myself on the railing, I started up the stairs. All the tourists had disappeared. On the side of the chapel was a small open door. I stepped outside, trembling in disbelief. I stopped after my left foot touched concrete. Something had happened. My life had changed again.

"Oh, my God!" I yelled.

Marjorie and our group had been waiting outside. "What happened?" she asked.

"I don't know," I said, "but my knee is healed. The pain is gone. I don't need a cane. I don't understand. You're all witnesses. This Jew was just healed walking out of Mary's church."

And my knee stayed healed. I couldn't play tennis anymore, but I'd healed enough to avoid another replacement surgery.

When we got back to Jersey, I went to see Dr. Steve West, my orthopedist friend, who kept me put together. I asked him what happened.

He flashed a bodacious, almost comically sinister smile. "I don't know."

Chapter 36

A TIME FOR ALMA MATER

It was an intricate, multi-decade process for me to become aware of the influence Rutgers had over my life. I'd never planned any of this, but one day it was there, rolling down a hill, gathering speed. First I was a student. Then I was taking Noah to our first Rutgers football game. The following year, we were season ticket holders, and our father-son bond was sealed forever.

Somewhere around 2015, I attended a Rutgers alumni-student speed networking event as a journalist and broadcaster. I was always careful to remind people I was not with CNN, ABC, or NBC. For two minutes, two students sat across from me, so close that my arthritic knees touched theirs. Then a bell went off and the next pair of students filed in to touch knees. This memoir is hundreds of pages long. How could I ever deliver a message about my journey in two minutes?

In the car on the way the back home, I thought, *Who the fuck are you, Cameron, mentoring college students?* But I related with the students; I bonded with them. I could chat on any subject—except bitcoin.

One LinkedIn student, nicknamed Colorado, messaged me, and then we morphed to phone chats. After four weeks, I exclaimed, "Oh, my God!"

"Are you all right?" Colorado asked.

"I just realized I'm a half century older than you." He understood me immediately.

At my peak, I hit campus 150 times a year for everything, including mentoring fourteen students a semester. I'd never say no to a student.

In the spring of 2019, I was on campus for career night, manning the communications and media table. Every ten minutes another group passed by to receive my animated, passionate inculcation. A young woman named Professor Clancy asked for my business card. In August, she called and asked: Would I like to teach a course called Journeys to Careers?

This was one of the most impactful, poignant opportunities. Life's journeys these past few years had tiptoed around a dream to teach students how to navigate life.

I met with Professor Clancy to discuss the syllabus and arranged to sit in on her class to get a feel for teaching. It would be hard work: reading assignments, grading, meeting before or after class with students when they needed me. "Why me?" I asked.

"Your magnetic, genuine effect on students," she explained.

I still had no clue who I really was. The tortoise in my hair was still whispering reasons not to do this. Marjorie and Noah lobbied hard for me to teach. I'd regret not doing it, Noah said, like how I regretted not going to Woodstock or not being in *War of the Worlds*. That was the final nail.

In mid-October, I began teaching the mini course. The course load was intense. Guiding my twenty-five students to make right career decisions using tools, testing, psychology and endless articles to dissect.

And my social media expertise was actually two lectures. I was there twice a week. No tie just a sport coat with patches on the elbow.

Walking down College Avenue to my classroom, I was filled with more pride than I'd ever felt before. It was a major life highlight, an accomplishment beyond my dreams. My students were obliged to call me "Professor." These past nine years I'd been a novelist, a journalist, a broadcaster—and now a teacher at Rutgers at seventy-four years old. Who does this?

At the end of the semester, my students gave me As and Bs. I mattered. I also turned down teaching spring semester. Just as well. The COVID-19 pandemic was coming. The deciding epiphany to not teach second semester was realizing how difficult and intense teaching was. Shaping the minds of Gen Z. I took it seriously—I had to be on top of the game twice a week. To get the energy and stay at that level. And the lengthy time I had to spend reading and watching all the assignments. Satisfied, I'd been to the mountain top and notched my belt of life.

One day the following January, something told me to connect with mostly Rutgers people on social media. A light bulb nova. Four hours a day, seven days a week for two years. I had organically collected 14,000 Rutgers and other people into my network. Later that would become transformative. An endless array of people could contact me. Some would impact my life's journey.

MY SPIRIT GANG GOES TO RUTGERS

Part of my spiritual attachment was to Dr. Martin Luther King Jr. I despise racism and strongly believed in everything he fought for in the Civil Rights Movement. I'd also looked up to Mamie Till, who helped ignite the movement when she insisted on an open casket after her son Emmett Till was brutally murdered by the Klan in 1955 in Mississippi. In *Casablanca Water*, my main character goes to Chicago to visit Emmett and Mamie's graves. A spiritual journey to feel their souls.

In February 2020, I met a professor from Rutgers who taught about Emmett Till's meaningful life. The next night, through her orchestration, I presented a copy of my novel to Emmett's cousin, Reverend Wheeler Parker on Rutgers campus, who had been in the next room the night the Klan pulled Emmett from his bed. Again, a full circle in my life.

When John Lewis visited Rutgers, I waited behind hundreds of people in line for his autograph. I was last in line. I told him about my rabbi marching with him and Dr. King at the March on Washington in 1963. When we spoke, he clutched my hands and held them tight, long enough for his touch to be indelible. What does this all mean? A connectivity fills my soul and destiny. And another haunting full circle in my life.

I was giving so much back to Rutgers. A force leading me beside a stillness of purpose. Nothing was ever planned or devised. From teaching, mentoring, advising, cheering, supporting—it all just happened. I was a spiritual marionette; a grand Cameron design. Never stopped to think about things. It was there on the night table when I woke up. Indeed, it was Colman. His son, my uncle Harry Crast went to Rutgers too. It's my spiritual circular destiny. I can't answer why.

Crossing into my seventies, I often felt chest pains, arrhythmias, strange twinges in my head and groin, dizziness, vertigo, and other signs of age. Each time, I'd talk to my spiritual gang, asking for intervention, imploring how much I loved the gift of life. I knew they're all busy. I tried to conceptualize how they could hear me out of seven billion voices. We're not supposed to know, but it works. Colman was still teaching me, guiding me to spirituality. Perhaps the more you open, the more you get—the antenna theory.

I feel disbelief when I process where I was a few years ago—on the brink of questioning life—to where I was today, feeling relevant and accomplished. My internal battles with money and providing for my family were gone. Feeling more secure, Marjorie and I began traveling. I was in a good place. Amelia was still smiling at me from her picture—I made sure to tell her I was happy and grateful for the life she'd given me.

And it *was* a wonderful life, especially in retirement. And strangely, I often spent these days alone in my office watching black-and-white DVDs: *Casablanca*, *From Here to Eternity* (I wished Maggio never hit Fatso with a stool), *Gentlemen's Agreement*. Inevitably, something in those films would kick up a memory, usually of someone gone, and I'd be on the verge of tears. I'd cry almost every time I saw the last scene in *Eternity*—wreaths floating onto shore, Hawaiian music, a new war, a black and white horizon.

When I cried, I'd never let Marjorie see. Was this depression, stress, or dementia knocking on my door? If I ever knew it was dementia, would I give dementia the ultimate "fuck you" before it was too late, like Robin Williams did? Was this part of turning seventy?

I never knew what this all meant. Something inside me was not right. How often did I see something floating by? Was it a vaporous apparition, or just a floater in my eyes? *Something* was deeply buried, like a herpes virus waiting to come back to life. I wanted to overlook those thoughts. Sitting in my office was a nice place to be. When Marjorie walked by, I'd turn to say hello, thinking how much she meant to me. My gratitude for all she is grows daily. How could I ever be without her?

Chapter 37

AN OLD-FASHIONED "THE END"

By February 2020, pandemic prognostications were all over the news. Life went on for everyone here in Jersey; most people thought it'd never come up the Turnpike or across the Hudson. On a Sunday in mid-March, Marjorie and I hosted an investment breakfast for a former NFL star receiver we'd become friends with. There were eight potential investors—including a renowned North Jersey gastroenterologist—two dozen bagels, a few photo ops, and hugs goodbye. Two out of eight guests invested. That was the last time we'd be with real humans for a long time.

The next day, the world slowly began to shut down. By April, a hard reality hit that this was an end of a comfortable world; no one on Earth could comprehend it. Every night the news listed cases and deaths from around the world. I cared about all the people in every country.

Marjorie made dinner every night for months. After eighty-seven days, we ordered takeout vegetable pizza. By June 2020, three months into the pandemic, Marjorie and I were so paranoid that we never left the house except to go to the bank and post office. When Marjorie braved a trip to Shop Rite for groceries, she often lamented the scarcity of toilet paper, almost like we were in Moscow in the sixties. On Father's Day, Noah and Diana came to visit. We never took off our masks—we couldn't even trust our children. But caution and prudence worked. Marjorie and I were both alive, with no loss of taste or smell.

I spent the early days and nights of the pandemic with documentaries: *Eyes on the Prize*, Ken Burns's *The Vietnam War*. I watched them repeatedly. I didn't give a shit; I was stuck in the house. Buried in that obsession was my lingering guilt over getting orthodontic braces to get out of serving in Vietnam. I also watched Ken Burns's *The Roosevelts: An Intimate History*, but only the parts about Franklin and Eleanor, not Theodore. I always tried to like Franklin Roosevelt, maybe the greatest pure politician ever, but it was a hard rain. His anti-Semitism and racism got in the way.

When I wasn't watching documentaries, I was sitting at the computer, writing and missing being on campus. I was still mentoring Rutgers students and recent grads, chatting with them on the phone for hours a day. My early takeaway was that this generation of college students and new alums was going to need more support (beyond financial) than any other. I worried what was beginning to happen to the craniums of the entire global population.

I collected endless messages on social media from people who wanted to connect on video calls. One Sunday in August, while Noah and Diana were visiting, I yelled from my office, "What is this thing called Zoom?" Diana downloaded it for me, and I mock-recorded myself. The recording file was an mp4. I knew enough about technology to know I could stick this anywhere.

The next morning, I connected with Candace, a Rutgers track star in the 100-yard dash. Our call morphed into a Zoom. Minutes later,

Colman waved a lightbulb in my eyes. Why don't I begin recording my conversations with people and create a YouTube channel? I asked Candace if she'd like to be first. That night I trademarked "A Chat with Cameron and the Tortoise." You never know when something could become winds of change, except for an occasional dried brown, crunchy leaf underfoot when no others are around.

This YouTube channel became my life during the pandemic. It rescued me from the prison of my faraway dreams. I was scared of how fragile our world was and how fast the cataclysmic, irreversible environmental end was approaching. It bothered me that my grave-yard plot would be underwater. I wanted the sun on my face. So many interesting, diverse, accomplished people were eager to be interviewed by me and the tortoise. People asked, but I never introduced the tortoise—who was still around, just less often these days.

A lot of work went into preparing for an interview. I never left my office. I interviewed everyone while wearing my Rutgers cap, often still in my pajamas because the recording captured only my top half. The channel began in September 2020. By June 2021, I had a magical 1,000 subscribers. I'd yell to Marjorie in the kitchen, playing computer mah-jongg, that I reached another YouTube subscriber plateau. "Who would've ever imagined how this is freaking growing, ay, Marge?" Engrossed in game, she grunted approval.

THE BEGINNING OF THE BEGINNING

One random morning, October 9, things just felt different. Some-times I liked staying in bed until noon's local news. Marjorie called me a sleepyhead as I slipped on by to the kitchen sink to hydrate. A secret kept from Marjorie; some of the sleep aids I used, including melatonin, kicked me into the strangest, deepest, most fascinating dreams. Every so often, the dream was so good (no sex stuff), I tried to get back. Like a tortoise going down a rabbit hole.

I always started the day by promoting my YouTube channel and answering messages. My new LinkedIn friend, Gennaro Labriola, texted me this morning about hosting a cannabis panel with researchers, foodies, physicians and lawyers on my podcast channel. It had only been six weeks since we met and I felt like I'd known him forever. We'd spent hours Zooming together each week. Gennaro had significant roots in the Jersey cannabis space and was a potent advocate for legalizing it in the upcoming November 6 ballot. His family had come to Newark from Italy a century back. I'd sold eyeglasses for an Italian company and was born in Newark. Therefore, we were paisans. I wore that word with deep pride. Don Corleone, Michael, Sonny, and even Carlo had taught me life lessons (always be loyal). A few weeks back, I'd texted him, "Much too good friends now. Someday a pasta dinner in Newark."

At 11:50 that morning, I responded to Gennaro's cannabis panel text, saying, "YUP." Then I placed the phone to my left on a ledge. Fifteen minutes later, I randomly reached out to feel that cell phone in my hand, knowing it was more powerful than the computers that had put a man on the moon in August 1969. But when I looked at the screen, I saw my message hasn't sent. Instead, in the text box was the word "Mom." I hadn't typed that. How the fuck did it get there? Goose bumps ran down my arms.

I looked up at the picture of my mother near my computer, smiling down at me. I thought back to four years ago, one eerily cloudy September morning, when *something* had possessed me. I needed to listen to Mario Lanza sing "Only a Rose." I don't know why. My mother loved him and that song. With a bandana in her hair, she vacuumed, dusted, and washed dishes while it played endlessly on the Victrola. Now the song was a perfect way for me to connect with her. For three days, I listened to "Only a Rose" and told her how much I missed her. Marjorie yelled every few hours, like a cuckoo clock, "Stop playing that fucking song all day long." Whenever the f-word appeared, I knew she was pissed off.

Looking at the word "Mom" on my phone, I was in denial. Then I had a realization. I called Noah to ask how this could've happened. I took a screenshot to show Marjorie. She couldn't fully grasp it. No one could. It was only real to me. My mother had come out of the picture to tell me she was there, conscious, real, and somewhere beyond. Which means there is a place beyond our comprehension. Never before, with such conviction, had I believed in eternity and the hereafter. Now I knew I had something to look forward to. Would I ever want to accelerate my reunion with her? That was a scary thought, but I liked it.

Nine days later, October 18, at 10:26 p.m., I was texting with Candace from Rutgers when the same thing happened. But this time the word "Dad" appeared by itself in my outgoing message. I was on my way to a whole new understanding, comfort, anticipation, and acceptance of death. The bravest new world. For weeks, I thought intensely about how my mother and father had stepped back into my dimension and told me everything is all right. They're good and alive—whatever that meant. Somehow, they'd had permission to step into my consciousness with a simple depression of three cell phone letters. Simple, but so profound. I'd never be quite the same.

Each passing week, I found it harder and harder to accept what had happened. I needed comedic relief from the whole thing. So, I got a haircut sooner than I needed because I knew my mother was watching me. I tried to tell my sister Carol about it, but she didn't understand. I really couldn't tell anyone; my world was full of daydream disbelievers.

A month later, during my annual physical, I asked my doctor for help calming myself down. I'd never before had a Valium in my world. I'd only ever wanted uppers, not downers.

"A tricyclic antidepressant or Xanax?" my doctor asked, knowing I had a pharma background.

"No, I'm not depressed, really," I said. "I mean, if I ever thought of suicide, it wouldn't be because I was depressed, only because I couldn't wait to see my relatives."

The doctor smiled, appreciating my humor. I walked out with Xanax.

* * *

They'll be writing about the pandemic for the next fifty years. For me, every day was the same thing, pandemic or not. My world was still normal. I wore the same five old Rutgers T-shirts, alternating them each day. I putzed around my office all day, acting my septuagenarian age: my temper often flailing, passionately cursing my desktop computer or the cellophane package I couldn't open because of my veneers—so I'd pop a Xanax. In one scene in *Starting Over*, Burt Reynolds's character is hyperventilating in a department store. Charles Durning's character asks the thirty spectators, "Does anyone have a Valium?" Each person produced a pill. If only I could channel that.

Three weeks before Christmas, I'd begun playing my *Time-Life Treasury of Christmas* CD. Pavarotti singing "Adeste Fideles" lifted me for hours at a time. On this quiet Sunday in the throes of the pandemic, a new president freshly elected, the front doorbell rang—a rare sound. Noah and Diana had come for a surprise visit.

We filled ten minutes with obligatory chat. Then Noah stood up. "Mom, Dad, we want to show you this piece of paper."

It was a two-month sonogram. Our granddaughter was coming in June. We hugged and kissed. Marjorie teared up. For weeks, I thought about becoming a grandfather every day. What was I to be called? When the kid was thirteen, I'd be pushing ninety. This thinking meshed with the visits from my mom and dad—if I ever wanted to rush our reunion, there'd be no guilt. The kid would never know me.

The conflict was that I liked my life. I was gifted, being relatively healthy, busy with my YouTube channel, mentoring students at Rutgers, and eating a home-cooked meal every night as if these were the days of the original thirteen colonies, like in *Drums Along the Mohawk*. How often I thought about something inside, restless, yearning, angry, happy, uneasy, and ruthlessly insecure? I thought I was dying several times a week of almost every kind of cancer, even breast. But I also knew somebody up there liked me, watching over and keeping me healthy.

* * *

By April 2021, the pandemic was a year old, by my record-keeping here in Central Jersey. I continued numbing myself with self-imposed pandemic incarceration, mourning all the deaths, cases, and the way of life we'd lost. When would we be able to go to the diner? One man in California had bragged on social media about all the reasons why he would never get vaccinated. He died from COVID three weeks later. I suspect the last person left on Earth, after climate change ends it all with a last tidal wave, would still deny it ever happened.

My YouTube channel kept growing, shifting its leanings to global environmental topics. Each video got a few hundred views. It bothered me that a fifteen-second TikTok dance video could get hundreds of thousands of views. I dreamed of young people waking up, because it's their world and wind to inherit. I wrestled with notions of people finally giving a shit. A dream someday?

I never really felt downtrodden, just overwhelmed. I just didn't feel right. Good things happened, spiritually, with Colman. My ailments quickly disappeared—even a headache lasted only a few minutes. The pandemic meant no eating out, rarely seeing the kids, and only watching Diana's stomach grow via Zoom. Being a grandfather was the only thing I had on the horizon. I was approaching seventy-six, and death was all around. It's built into our DNA to ignore it, or else you'd never go to high school. I had five friends on Goodwin Avenue growing up, and they were all gone. I used to hate the concept of death. People say "rest in peace," but I'd never want to rest. I'd have to move on and see my parents—and Colman, especially. I counted on my fingers how many years to get to my mid-nineties. I'd be so grateful for that. I think.

Grandfather and spirits were around all day, showing me signs of 444 and 111. It was so powerful, I teared up and thanked Colman out loud when Marjorie wasn't around to observe my eccentricity. But still, I didn't feel right. Maybe I needed a jolt, a major reinforcement, like the cavalry riding down from a red clay hill to flank my Conestoga wagon.

THE FIRST JOLT: THAT DAY AT BELMAR

So I decided to enjoy what was left of life, perhaps by getting laid as if I was in college (which had never happened). I knew a few women who would jump into bed with me if I showed up. Guilt would drive me hard, but I'd have to deal with it this time. I planned the day that led off the first chapter of this memoir, right down to watching "my ashes" blow in the wind off the jetty at Shark River.

This day at Belmar had been in my consciousness for a long time. I knew Marjorie, my pillar of love and support, must never sense anything. I wrestled with this for a long time. I could never leave Marjorie unless she was protected and guarded. I'd never been over the precipice of infidelity. The notion of a last sexual encounter to take with me titillated. At this stage of my life, Belmar was all good and guilt free and where I was conceived back in 1944. The ultimate full circle to take with me to meet my spirits.

Spreading my ashes to that wonderful microplastic-filled Atlantic Ocean seemed like the right thing to do. Sand from my basement could simulate my ashes, so I could see where I was headed to. Europe? New York Harbor? Delaware?

And finally, I'd break my non-meat-eating status since 1975 by eating earthy hotdogs and hamburgers a first and last time. I covered everything this practice day at Belmar. Those two women I was certain would jump into bed with me. One has been waiting a few decades.

I'm not quite sure where all this was coming from. Why, Cameron, do this? It seemed like a good thing for an aging septuagenarian to do. And also, I just didn't understand what was deep inside doing the driving.

What I didn't say in the first chapter was how perfect that day was, fucking (and that's all it was) two uniquely different women, one for brunch and the other (Maggie, with the three eyeglass stores) in the afternoon over black and white cookies in Livingston, the town where I'd touched my first naked breast. Both women had bottles of merlot waiting for me. "What the fuck," like Miles Raymond, my alter ego from *Sideways*.

I'm not sure why I had that day of two distinct orgasms when they are so hard to come by. They were part of a jolt, meant to prepare and satisfy me before my ashes could be blowing in the Jersey Shore wind. These jolts are accelerants, moving this story to an end. Jolts are spiritual for me. They're here and telling me something, helping me rationalize, plan, and justify my life choices. Powerful stuff. I think Colman, as stern as he looks in the picture behind my computer, is smiling now, satisfied by how much he changed my life.

THE SECOND JOLT

A few weeks before Memorial Day, I still didn't feel right—reflecting on my strange emotions, staring at my desktop. Suddenly, something made me need to watch *Bang the Drum Slowly*. I hadn't seen it in thirty years, but I knew the story: De Niro playing a dying young baseball player. Not the kind of movie you'd watch again, but I was haunted by the title song, a sad, bittersweet song I needed to hear.

What does "haunting" mean? Someone was in this surreal room with me. Colman was staring at me differently from his picture. Was it a faint smile? Strange thoughts started generating in my deep gray matter: my mother buying me a sugary egg salad sandwich in downtown Newark when I was seven; a boxer dog biting me in the head when I was eight. Was something nearby shooting off these energies? It was like mind control, which I didn't mind. It was a gift to be possessed nicely.

When I finished the movie, I had to listen to "Bang the Drum Slowly" again. An obsession was looming. The first video I found on YouTube was Emmylou Harris's version, set to photos of Arlington National Cemetery in honor of Memorial Day 2017. Something made me look at the number of likes on the video: 4.44k. Holy shit—there was Colman, pulling the strings on my marionette, like on the cover of *The Godfather*. You never know when your strings are being pulled.

I was mesmerized by Harris's voice and the sad photos of military funerals. For nearly three hours, I watched the video—like I was directed from beyond. One scene in particular resonated with me: a soldier kneeling by a grave of an obvious fallen comrade. I didn't pay attention to the name on the grave at first, but eventually I saw it. The name hit me in disbelief: Stephen Rodriguez. Eight years previous, I'd done a story on Mary Rodriquez, a Gold Star mother whose young son Stephen had died in Iraq. I stopped the video and incredulously realized this grave belonged to Mary's son. I emailed Mary at 3:30 a.m., asking if she knew Stephen was in this county singer's video. She emailed back—at 11:11 a.m. Mary believed Stephen was using me to tell her all was okay.

This episode was a badge of courage for me. Something was out there. My entourage of spirits were well connected.

LIFE IS GOOD

With a jolt, I came to an epiphany one early summer morning in 2021: orthopedically, I was my age. My knees hurt, but they'd been so much better ever since I walked out of the Church of the Annunciation in Nazareth. I never needed a new knee, but I got juiced with injections of viscous hyaluronic acid (which is also good for neck wrinkles), synthetic meniscus cushioning shit. With those things you never know if it works; you're just afraid not to do it. My back also had severe spinal stenosis and bulging discs, so I stretched several times a day. That did work—I was asymptomatic and in no pain. I could pick up a paper clip, but I was a little shaky in the shower. Now I know why my generation always falls and can't get up.

I'd been asking my spirit world for two decades to keep me young and healthy. They came through. I was still sharp cerebrally. I wasn't close to my age in the thing supported by my shoulders. I interviewed legions of people all over the world, and I interviewed like the best of them, even the anchors on *The Today Show*. I was that accomplished.

What a great feeling to be able to talk to anyone on the planet about almost anything. When my interviewees found out I was approaching seventy-six, it was a ceremonious "holy shit" moment. I was proud. When I looked at my image on Zoom, I saw a youngish, good-looking, gray-haired guy. No way was I seventy-five. I fantasized about all kinds of stuff, and buried in that was some sex.

One morning, it was raining hard and thundering. I hate thunder—when I was ten, it scared me right into a windowless closet in the cellar. In addition to my morning routine of checking on my channel and reading emails, sometimes I took a quick peek at an old girlfriend's pictures, hidden away on my computer for no particular reason. Marjorie knew I looked. She even liked when I came running to hug her after I found another girl I once knew—now an old woman—on Facebook who hadn't aged gracefully.

"Why do you men look so good when you age?" Marjorie once asked.

"Because you did for so many years. Our turn," I said.

This morning, I had an email notice from Facebook. A Valerie Scott had started following me. I froze in the headlights of a strange disbelief. I'd been searching for Valerie on Google and Facebook for years, to no avail. It was a strange compulsion; I wanted to see what she looked like today. I needed a musical accompaniment for my obsession with staring at Valerie. After our first few years of marriage, I started listening to the Seekers—"Georgy Girl," "I'll Never Find Another You," "Colors of My Life"—songs that defined my early years with Valerie.

Once, my Googling led me to find our engagement notice in a Maplewood paper from early 1969. Valerie was twenty-two, a baby—strangely or not, she looked beautiful. My seventy-five-year-old thinking was that I'd fucked a twenty-two-year-old girl a half century ago. I didn't remember what it felt like being with her, just my first time ascending at Tuffy's beach house at the Jersey Shore.

I stared at her photos for hours, listening to the Seekers, trying to remember what it felt like to have sex with her. I thought of the time I went under the covers with a flashlight and a medical book, trying to find her clitoris.

"Why are you looking down there? It's so ugly," she said, her voice irritatingly penetrating.

"Because I have to learn someday," I said.

I'd never found Valerie, nor her clitoris, anywhere—just her parents' obituaries. Now she'd surfaced almost on top of me. She never liked that position, but I did. Another reason for our marriage's failure.

Her page was blank. No pictures, no contacts, and no listed friends. I didn't know what to do with this. Second only to my guilt about not serving in Vietnam was what I'd done to this young, innocent girl. I called myself pretty fucked up, with demons of trapped creativity, misguided paternal letdowns, and a tortoise in my hair for the long run. It all reared itself into me not loving Valerie properly and respect-fully as a young man. Valerie had gotten my very worst. I didn't know a flying fuck about nurturing a relationship back then. I was nothing like I am now with Marjorie.

A few years back, I found a box of Valerie's diaries, pictures, diplomas, and love letters from before me. I asked Marjorie if she thought I should try to find Valerie to mail them to her. She was angry at my thought, telling me a resounding, "No."

Still, my fantasies of Valerie abounded. The door was open too wide. It took me three days to compose the right letter to send her on Facebook. I confessed that I'd been looking for her online. I told her I was sorry about her parents. Her father had saved my life by instrumenting the orthodontics that had kept me out of the army. I was always grateful to her and her family. I mentioned the box of her things I'd found, and I sent the link to our engagement announcement as proof I still thought about her.

Three days later, Valerie responded. The timestamp on her message was 4:44 p.m.—that meant my spiritual world was okay with anything that went down in my especially raw, extreme, guilt-laden fantasies. Snap out of it, Cameron.

I read her message a few times: "If you're ever in the vicinity of Summit, where I live, I think it's all right if you drop it off or mail it if you think I'm too forward or inappropriate."

I wondered whether to respond right away or wait a few days. Who am I fooling? I sent her an immediate response. "I'd think that would be very special if I dropped it off. A half century is a long time. And I'm double-vaccinated," I wrote.

Valerie and I set a date a week away. I'd lost twenty-two pounds since the middle of the pandemic, down to the weight I'd been when she knew me. I reckoned if our meeting ever warmly materialized, kind of like the reverse-melting of Margaret Hamilton's Wicked Witch of the West, I'd fuck Valerie and it'd be legal and moral because she was my first.

My next conundrum was what to say to Marjorie if I disappeared for a few hours when I basically hadn't left the house in eighteen months. I told her I needed to get out and resemble a journalist again by doing a photo essay. The morning of the fantasized assignation with Valerie, I performatively charged up my two cameras. I felt discomfort spinning that lie to Marjorie, but no one could understand my need to attempt to apologize to Valerie. And if there was any kind of sex, I'd be a hero to the tortoise, my nemesis. Such a dreamer I was. A strange desperation had consumed me. I was searching for linkage to my spiritual world. The 4:44 timestamp on Valerie's message was the clincher that I was doing the right thing.

Heading north on the Parkway, I oscillated every few mile posts. This was insane, maybe dangerous. Who knew what lurked in the mind and heart of a woman I'd so deeply hurt? On the other hand, what an opportunity for me to strut my stuff. I'd become a creative, successful, normal, happy guy. Did I want to make her feel bad? Valerie's father should've never tried to have me committed for drug abuse. I was just trying to find myself, fighting demons deep inside me that wanted to come out.

This whole day was fucked up. I yelled in the car, "Cameron, you're an insensitive asshole. Give it up." By the time I got to the Cranford bridge on the Parkway—the same bridge where I was on September 11 where I saw smoke coming out of the World Trade Center—I knew I was calling Valerie and mailing her belongings.

I left the door ajar with Valerie, telling her an emergency came up. I felt an indescribable relief. I knew I'd done the right thing. On the way home, I pulled off the road and took ridiculously random pictures to show Marjorie.

LET'S MAKE A DEAL: THE COCKTAIL

The cocktail of ingredients swirling around my cerebral process could lift me up or knock me down. It's the bottom of the ninth. I take a deep breath, exhale, and will I finally be depressed? It's been a great run, never being clinically depressed—maybe because I ate a lot of iceberg lettuce. Distant random thoughts were shooting my mind. I never know where/why they come from. I'm manning a machine gun turret on an island with no comrades left alive, surrounded by the enemy closing in all around. I smell a hint of salt air. I love the ocean. I keep turning around and firing. The enemy keeps coming. Strangely, I don't run out of ammunition. But I'm tired of shooting. And I miss my buddies and parents.

Cameron's world has been full of marvelous fulfilled dreams and promises. My YouTube channel is as diverse as the real world. I've interviewed people in the Cameroon, France, Ecuador, India, and Lebanon. I'm able to cross divides and oceans and champion my promises to my spirits to recognize we are really all one species.

My five-month-old granddaughter, Rory, has filled me with so much love and awe. I recently sat with her on my lap, learning the words to "Five Little Monkeys Jumping on the Bed" on YouTube, when she reached up to gently touch my nose. I kissed her head a few times, avoiding her lips and rosy cheeks because of COVID. "It's too bad Rory will never remember any of this," Marjorie said. Yes, Rory will never remember or know me.

For thirty years, I've been a news junkie. This is the information cocktail I consume every day: My favorite city, New York, is full of murders, rapes, beatings, hit-and-runs, people pushed onto subways, and innocent children shot. This bothers me so much. Then there was the January 6 Capitol riot. No force on Earth can ever bring people together, not even climate change or Greta Thunberg saying, "Blah, blah, blah," to UN delegates. No earthly power will stop us from heating the globe another 1.5 degrees. Do I want to see 250 million humans, climate refugees, moving away from underwater coastlines? Forty percent of humans get their drinking water from glaciers, which are disappearing. For the last time: Lah-di-dah—or, what I really mean, "What the fuck?"

I made a deal with myself to enjoy one last Thanksgiving and Christmas. Fuck New Years—I've never been inclined to go to Times Square and not be able to piss for twelve hours. It would be my luck, with the tortoise around, to wet my pants in front of half a million revelers.

Once September flipped, I started thinking about Thanksgiving morning and watching *March of the Wooden Soldiers* on channel eleven, all because my father made me watch it when I was eight. Anything my father suggested, I was down—I needed him. I've seen that movie sixty-eight times in my life. Even got Noah into it with me—we watched it together well into his twenties.

Christmas Eve was my last viewing of Alastair Sim as Scrooge in *A Christmas Carol*. Dickens was a genius, writing that in 1843. The Ghost of Christmas Present tells Scrooge the two children underneath his robe are Man's. The boy is Ignorance and the girl is Want. Beware them both, but most of all, beware this boy, the ghost says. Nothing has changed since 1843. Did you know 95 percent of people in Afghanistan are food insecure?

It was a nice Christmas, albeit ravaged a bit by inflation. Gas was up 50 percent from a year ago. So was lettuce. Three days after, I told Marjorie we needed a new plunger and I was off to Home Depot, where the owner had gone to Rutgers pharmacy school, just like me. What I really needed was tubing to hook up my SUV's exhaust pipe through the window. I'd thought of taking an overdose of Eliquis and bursting into a total hemorrhage, or taking heart rhythm meds that would shut me off right away—those options were untenable. It had to be gentle and painless, just like the movie *M*A*S*H*. Somehow, I wanted and needed that last-ditch option to rescue myself. So, I chose carbon monoxide.

Marjorie left for two days to visit her sister, Lisa. I bought a pound of tuna fish salad, potato salad, and coleslaw, remindful that I'd once done that a day before the Cuban Missile crisis ended. I burned thirty minutes of only Simon and Garfunkel's "Scarborough Fair" onto my SanDisk; my Dome Audio headphones would transmit the sound through the bones of my ears. I had no real final wishes, except that infinite jetty windy disposition. I typed out instructions to Noah on how to finish this memoir, and asked that he please find a way to get it published. I was thinking of everything. I'd bring my cassette recorder with me to collect my last thoughts.

I wore jeans and a bright red Rutgers sweatshirt. It was dark outside. I tried to time it perfectly. It was 4:27 p.m.; I was shooting for a 4:44 departure. I hoped to wind up at Scarborough Fair or bump into Humphrey Bogart. Would he know how much I loved *Casablanca*? The last thing on my mind, as the car engine purred, was turning on the cassette recorder and telling Noah and Marjorie how much I desperately loved them and that there was no explanation for this. Maybe they should read this book for more insight.

I felt nothing. I guess you never do. I yelled into the recorder, "Finally, fuck you, tortoise, and whatever you rode in on back in 1945. I'm leaving you with a full head of thinning white hair."

The garage was cold with my comprehension of finality, loss, and what-ifs. What the fuck was I doing? I felt my eyes get heavy. I saw my mother. She was not smiling. I shut off "Scarborough Fair" and my recorder and reached for the door handle. I smiled, shook my head, and opened the door.

About Calvin Barry Schwartz

Calvin graduated from Rutgers University with two bachelor's degrees and spent twenty-five years in sales and as a regional sales manager. In later life, he became a journalist for NJDiscover, a novelist (*Vichy Water*, 2007), and a broadcaster, producing and co-hosting a local cable TV talk show in central Jersey. He serves on the advisory committee of the Women's Health Institute at Rutgers Robert Wood Johnson Medical School, ONE HEALTH (Human, Plant, Animal) NJ steering committee. He taught Career Explorations at Rutgers University, New Brunswick (2019). And in September 2020, he started a series of YouTube global podcast interviews: "Conversations with Calvin: We the SpecIEs" focusing on the diversity of content, people, and careers. Recently he helped form a global group of environmentalists, Climate Optimists (Everything NOT Fine). He thrives on reinvention after sixty.